I0641006

Her Forever Cowboys

.

Cowboys Online, Volume 6

Jan Springer

Published by Spunky Girl Publishing, 2021.

Published by Spunky Girl Publishing
Copyright 2021 by Jan Springer
Cover art by Talina Perkins ~ Bookin' It Designs

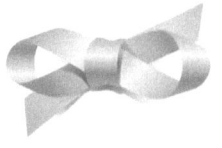

License Notes

This book is licensed for your personal use only.

Author Note

This is a work of fiction. Characters, places, settings, and events presented in this book are purely of the author's imagination and bear no resemblance to any actual person, living or dead or to any actual events, places, and/or settings.

Dedication

During the writing of this book, both my parents passed away.

I would like to dedicate this book to my mom and to my dad and to all the readers who have waited patiently through all the delays for me to finish the story. I truly appreciate you all.

I hope you like Her Forever Cowboys as much as I enjoyed writing it and I have plans for more Snowy Creek Ranch (and Moose Ranch) stories in the future.

Hugs!

Jan Springer

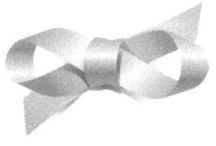

Chapter One

S askadia Women's Federal Prison
Saskatchewan, Canada

"You probably have no idea how lucky you are to get accepted into the Freedom Run program, do you?" Milena Allen's parole officer asked as she leaned back in her chair and smiled smugly at Milena.

Blah. Blah. Blah. Tell me something new, or please let me get back to my dishwashing duties.

She'd heard this lecture many times over the past few months. It happened every time the two of them got together to discuss how Milena would integrate back into society through the Freedom Run program...when the time came.

If the time came.

She tensed as Officer Brown prattled on with all the conditions.

Milena's prison release would be dependent on several factors. She needed to stay out of trouble. No fighting with the other inmates. She had to stay physically and mentally healthy. Stay off drugs and no alcohol and keep taking all those prison courses and stay busy with her chores.

Milena sighed inwardly. It appeared as though this meeting would be the same as all the others. She didn't know why she always anticipated good news when she came to this office. She should know by now nothing ever good happened to her. No one on the outside wanted to take a chance on her.

No one wants me.

Milena forced herself to quell her disappointment and focused on a ladybug that crawled across the parole officer's desk.

Huh, ladybugs were said to bring good luck. Too bad she was still incarcerated. She wished she could reach out, pick up the little bug, open a window, and set it free. But she'd learned not to make any sudden moves within the prison system. Unexpected movements got inmates shot dead.

Besides, how could she set it free? All the windows were locked tight. The only way out was the same way it had come in, whatever way that had been.

"Okay, I went out on a limb for you on this one," Officer Brown's voice snapped through Milena's thoughts.

Milena had tuned her out, so she had no idea what the woman was suddenly talking about. She was staring at her, and if Milena didn't know any better, there was a tinge of a genuine smile lifting the woman's thin lips. But then it was gone, leaving Milena with the impression she must have imagined it.

The officer suddenly stood and walked to a nearby closet. She opened the door and dragged out a large dark blue knapsack, and a moment later, she plopped it onto her desk.

Dropped it right on top of the ladybug!

Oh no! Sorry, little bug. Hopefully, you didn't feel any pain.

Milena pushed down the sadness that welled inside her for the fate of the small creature.

"I was able to get this knapsack with the meager funds in the budget for miscellaneous expenses. You'll need it where you're going," the officer said in a condescending tone.

Where am I going? What is happening?

Milena's gaze snapped to the woman's face. If she didn't always have a weird smirk curling her lips, she would have been a nice-looking woman. She had shoulder-length hair the color of strawberries, a dusting of rust-colored freckles across her cheeks, and pretty green eyes.

But that smile she had now...it was a direct contrast to the genuine smile of happiness she'd thought she'd seen moments earlier.

Despite the officer's vulgar expression, a flare of excitement began to uncurl inside Milena.

She was about Milena's age of thirty-two. She had replaced her previous parole officer, Sadie, an older woman that Milena had liked, but Sadie had taken a sudden leave of absence to care for her husband after he'd had a devastating stroke.

Sadie had made it a point to be very personal with the inmates, had truly cared. She'd been the one who'd gotten Milena into the Freedom Run program, and last year, she'd been given a temporary job through Cowboys Online, a program for convicts under the Freedom Run umbrella.

Sadie had always given Milena glimmers of hope that good things would come her way, but she would have to be patient. Most of that hope had died when Sadie left.

This officer wasn't nice. Or reassuring. And she was probably playing a sick twisted game with Milena right now because she still had no idea what the woman was talking about.

"As you know, it would be a conditional parole. Many strings attached. You won't be released into the public like a regular parolee. You might even say you're trading one prison for another. Except this new place has no bars," she said with a chuckle.

Milena's mind whirled. What was she saying?

"Just plenty of trees, very few people. There is a railroad, but it's rarely used. You could try to escape by following it, but it would take you weeks to get out, and by then, the cops would be swarming all over the area, and you wouldn't have a chance. Or the wildlife would kill you before you starved to death in the desolation. You'd either be killed or captured and sent back to a prison somewhere for the rest of your sentence with another ten years tacked on for trying to flee," she paused and stared at Milena with a cold, stern look as if daring her to try an escape.

Milena couldn't stop the shiver of dread rippling down her back. What kind of place where they sending her? It didn't sound pleasant at all.

"The only way in and out of your new home will be a float plane. That's where this knapsack comes in. Suitcases won't get you far in pioneer ranch living. They don't even have electricity or indoor plumbing out there. Talk about off the grid. So yeah, some inconveniences, but hey, you should be used to that after being incarcerated, right? How many years have you been on the inside?" she asked as she drew her attention to her computer screen. The woman knew exactly how many years. She just wanted to rub it in.

Milena stuffed down a flinch and remained quiet.

"Fourteen years plus. You came in at seventeen years old. Young and stupid," the parole officer said. Then she made an odd grunt.

"Some might decide to stay here and forgo the lions, tigers and man-eating bears of the wilderness. But I'm obligated to ask you if you want to go. If so, then sign here and go back to your cell and grab your shit. You could be out of here by nightfall. But think hard before putting pen to paper, Miss Allen. I will give you five minutes to consider what you want to do. Prison is a posh hotel compared to this place. Life on a real working ranch is pretty rough, especially in this case, with this ranch just starting. Only a year old it is. The pay isn't great, but hey, you'll have nowhere to go to spend your money anyways. No stores. No internet access. No nothing. It's a place called Snowy Creek Ranch and located in the Northern Ontario wilderness."

Snowy Creek. Why did that name sound familiar? She'd heard that name before somewhere, hadn't she?

The officer left the knapsack on her desk and then started toward the door.

"I'll be back in a few minutes so you can think. Don't go anywhere," she said with a sarcastic chuckle, and then she left.

Don't go anywhere? Milena shook her head and frowned.

She'd never gotten used to the so-called humorous incarceration remarks that were flung so smoothly around here by the prison personnel and the inmates. She had never liked the authority the guards held over her. The power they used every chance they got in telling her what to do, where to go, and what and when to eat.

Don't go anywhere? Seriously?

Milena rarely swore. Her mother had taught her it was improper for a lady to swear. Inside the prison system, many women did, but she'd always refrained.

Today she'd make an exception.

"Fuck you, bitch," Milena muttered in a low voice.

It felt good to swear. Felt even better to flick her middle finger at the door the parole officer had closed only moments earlier.

And it felt awesome to pick up the pen and sign her name to her release papers.

. . ⚶ . .

NORTHERN ONTARIO, CANADA

Ex-convict Milena Allen stared out the passenger window of the floatplane. She studied the scraggly spruce trees, the towering white pines and other coniferous trees that embraced the rocky shorelines of the shimmering blue lakes down below. She still couldn't believe that after fourteen years of being locked up in prison, she was now free.

Well, kind of.

Everything had happened so quickly, just like the parole officer had said.

Only yesterday morning she'd had to make a rash decision. Take the chance at freedom or stay in prison for the rest of her sentence. It was a no-brainer.

She'd accepted the job, packed her meager belongings into the supplied knapsack, and said her goodbyes to the several inmates whom she considered friends. They'd all cried and hugged her, wishing her luck.

There had been many brief moments during her goodbyes when she'd wanted to change her mind and stay with the familiar, but she'd stuffed her fear of leaving prison deep down inside herself and took this chance of a lifetime. Within the hour, she'd been handcuffed and ushered into a prison transfer van.

Twenty-four hours later, she was here.

It was all surreal.

She wished she'd been able to enjoy the scenes of green forests, rock-filled meadows, shimmering lakes, and the late evening, mid-May golden sunshine streaming through the cockpit windows, but uneasiness clambered through her.

Had she made the right decision coming here?

As the sun began to set, it was turning the puffy white clouds into gold, purple, and pink billows and everything below the plane was falling into darkness.

"Touchdown in two minutes. Buckle your seat belt," the lone female pilot said from beside Milena.

Her nervousness increased as she spied a lake looming in the distance.

She nodded jerkily, and the tinge of plane fuel and oil that hung around inside the cockpit suddenly made her stomach tighten with queasiness. She struggled to buckle her seat belt and winced at the clinking sound of foot-long chains on the handcuffs that held her wrists captive to the armrests of the seat.

To be in shackles like this and to be thought of as a troublemaker humiliated her.

The guard who had accompanied her overnight at the hotel and then to the airport had outlined the necessity of shackles on the small floatplane. It was for the safety of the pilot; the guard had explained. Sometimes convicts had the overwhelming urge to try to take over the flight and if something terrible happened like that it wouldn't look good for the programs that helped convicts get early conditional parole.

"That's their dock," the pilot, who was around Milena's age, nodded to the lake.

If she thought Milena could see a dock, she was sorely mistaken. The lake was big, maybe a mile across and two miles long. Everything else looked miniature. The shoreline was rock-lined, and a gloomy black wilderness surrounded the lake.

Goodness, with the sun setting over the land, everything was looking so creepy.

She tensed as doubts dangled over her head like a hangman's noose. This was freaking crazy. She should be happy to be out of prison. She was free. Yet, she was terrified.

As the lake loomed bigger, it appeared midnight black in color and daunting.

Her heart pounded with insane speed as she began to experience visions of the plane crashing into the water and here she was with her hands bound by handcuffs, and she didn't even know how to swim!

Milena closed her eyes and struggled to calm her breaths. She wished Cowboys Online had given her a normal job in a city or a town. Somewhere far away from water. She did not like water. Never had.

She cried out as the plane's pontoons splashed onto the lake, gently rocking the plane. She jerked and cursed beneath her breath as water thumped against the hollow metal floats.

The thunderous roar of the engine had her wanting to plug her ears. Thankfully, the roar quickly turned into a purr and Milena was finally able to relax. A little.

Whew! Safe landing. Everything was good.

Thank you, God! She prayed silently.

A few minutes went by as the plane continued to move.

She kept her eyes closed. The bit of queasiness still clung to her stomach, and she knew without a doubt, she would be sick if she didn't get out into the fresh air and soon.

"We're almost there," the pilot said. There was an underlying tone of amusement to her voice. What had been her name when they'd been introduced back in Thunder Bay? Kay something. Kayley, that was her name.

"I thought you said you weren't afraid of flying?" the pilot suddenly asked.

"I'm not," Milena answered.

She didn't feel like expanding on any details about her fear of water and she was grateful the woman merely grunted.

The plane moved smoothly over the water now and Milena sensed they were slowing.

"I don't see a welcoming committee. Are you sure they know you're coming?" the pilot asked.

She'd said barely five sentences to Milena during the two-hour ride and now she was asking questions?

Milena frowned and opened her eyes. She wished she hadn't.

The dock they were heading toward was too small and too damned close to the creepy water. There were little silver things shooting out of and then splashing back into the water leaving behind rings that rippled outward.

"Fish are jumping tonight. You know what that means?" Kayley asked.

Milena shook her head.

"Fish are hungry and they're looking for mosquitoes for supper. A delicious meal." The pilot laughed. Her eyes were bright and cheerful as she steered the float plane toward the dock.

Milena remembered seeing a similar happiness in her friend, Jennifer Jane Watson, or JJ as everyone called her, when she made a safe landing with her own float plane.

Just thinking of JJ made Milena wish she'd been able to reach out to her friend and let her know she was somewhere in the deep Northern Ontario wilderness just like JJ.

Her old prison friend now had three cowboys to keep her safe, a little baby to love and a rustic ranch house to tend and there had been many a night that Milena had sent up prayers for God to keep her friend and her new family safe.

She'd also dared to say a prayer or two for herself. An appeal asking God if He could see fit that she could be half as lucky as JJ, and He could find a place for her to call home.

A wilderness pioneer existence hadn't been what she'd envisioned but her mother had always told her God works in mysterious ways and she needed to have faith.

"Not sure what to do with you with no one here. Can't bring you back and I'm really running late for my next job."

Kayley was frowning and Milena realized that Kayley could decide to turn the plane around and bring her back to the city.

Heck! There was no way she was going back to prison. She'd prefer starving to death out here if need be.

"I was told by my parole officer that all the information had been sent to them. Maybe he's just running late?"

"He? Which one? There are three of them," the pilot said with a frown as she maneuvered her plane closer to the dock.

Milena's tummy hollowed out.

Three? Why had she had assumed the place was owned by a couple? A man and a woman. Why had she not asked more questions?

"Come to think of it, I wasn't told who would be here. Everything happened so fast," Milena admitted.

The pilot said nothing, and Milena swallowed tightly as the dock drew closer. It was just a few planks of wood for heaven's sake.

Thankfully the sickness in her belly didn't get worse and a moment later the plane nudged against the dock. Luckily it didn't fall apart.

The engine sputtered and then died.

The pilot rushed out of her seat and using the key she'd placed on her keychain, rammed it into the keyhole of Milena's handcuffs. They popped open and fell away. Milena quickly rubbed her sore wrists.

"Sorry, protocol. I would lose my job if I'd let you loose and you hijacked the plane."

"But I don't even know how to fly," Milena burst out with a sudden bout of irritation.

"You'd be surprised how many prisoners learn how to fly using flight simulation programs while in prison."

Darn. Why hadn't she thought of that?

"I could jump you right now and take your plane to Tim buck Two," Milena teased as the pilot placed the cuffs onto a nearby console.

"Hell, girl. You're already here." The pilot winked.

Ouch.

"Listen, they wouldn't send me out here for nothing. So, I am sure your bosses are just running behind. I'm running late myself. And it's getting dark. I can give you my flashlight. Just follow the all-terrain trail that starts at the end of the dock. It'll take you directly to their cabin. It's about a fifteen-minute walk and is near a creek all the way.

The trail opens into a huge meadow and that's where you'll find their cabin."

A creek? More water? Shit!

Suddenly Milena had the urge to ask the pilot to get her out of here and bring her back to prison. She was not cut out to work on a horse ranch in the middle of nowhere.

"Here, put some of this on. It's homemade bug spray. Citronella oil, some apple cider vinegar, some witch hazel and some lemon oil. It's your best friend out here during the evening and early morning when the mosquitoes are at their worst," the pilot said as she produced a plastic bottle containing some yellow liquid. Milena watched the pilot spray her own bare arms and dabbed some onto her face. The smell of it was nice. A scent similar to lemon.

"Your turn," she handed the bottle to Milena.

Milena just stared at it, not knowing what to do with it. Crazily she'd never had a spray bottle before.

Kayley must have noticed her hesitation and began showing her parts of the bottle.

"Just press the top button but make sure the spray isn't aimed at your eyes. Here's the hole where the liquid comes out. Keep it away from your face and then just spray any exposed skin. Keep the bottle. Consider it a housewarming gift."

Oh, dear Lord, what kind of a place is this when a bottle of bug spray is considered a housewarming gift?

"Here, take this too. A present from me. I can pick up another one at the airport."

The woman handed Milena a large red plastic flashlight. Then she left the small cockpit and moved quickly down the aisle stopping midway.

A moment later Milena heard the plane door slide open. She twisted in her seat and watched Kayley slip out the open doorway. She'd disappeared so fast, Milena didn't know what to do, so she did nothing.

In prison she'd learned not to make a move until she was told to do so. So, she sat and awaited instructions. She watched the pilot appear on the dock, tie a rope attached to the plane to a metal hitch on a plank.

Through the impending twilight, the pilot suddenly gazed up at Milena, smiled and did motions with her hand signaling Milena to spray herself with the bottle.

Milena nodded. She pointed the hole away from her as she'd been directed and sprayed her arms, back of her hands and her neck. She liked the scent. She just hoped the mosquitoes didn't like it.

When she was finished, she noticed the pilot was now waving at her to come out.

Nervousness zapped through her as she left her seat and on trembling legs headed toward the doorway.

Halfway down the aisle she grabbed her knapsack, lifted the flap, stuffed the spray bottle inside, then slung the knapsack onto her back. With flashlight in hand, she stopped at the entrance of the plane. There was a metal ladder just outside. Below it, she spied the black water moving creepily against the dock, ready to strike, grab and drag her under if she made one wrong move.

Oh my gosh. She did not want to go down this very steep ladder.

"Hey! Are you coming? Daylight is burning!" The pilot's shout made her jump back to reality.

She called this daylight?

Such a good idea coming here, Milena. Real stupid.

She did not dare look around as she descended the ladder and stepped onto the slightly moving pontoon.

Thankfully Kayley was right there. She thrust her hand out and Milena eagerly grabbed it. The pilot must have sensed her uneasiness and awkwardness because she was gentle and slow as she helped Milena onto the dock. Thankfully the planks were solid beneath her feet and a moment later she stepped onto hard ground.

"Come on, I'm not as late as I thought. How about I walk you up a few minutes," the pilot said.

She waved for Milena to follow her. Milena thought it odd that all this protocol of having her restrained and now she was set free. Weird.

Well maybe not so weird. The parole officer had warned her about the wildlife killing her out here.

Milena shivered and quickly followed Kayley. She could barely see as they entered the forest and followed a well-worn path with fresh tread marks. She stumbled several times, but quickly learned to stifle her curses and lift her feet.

"The creek is to your right, past the line of trees about thirty feet away" Kayley said. "Don't wander off this atv trail. If you do, make sure you always go to the right because you'll meet the creek, and it goes right through the meadow where their cabin is located. If you go to your left, you'll get lost in thousands and thousands of desolate acres of forest and meadows."

Lovely.

Now that the lake was out of sight, Milena was noticing shrieking sounds coming from their right side in the woods.

"What are those noises?" she asked in a loud voice so she could be heard above the shrills.

"Frogs. It's mating season in the creek and the mates are calling out to each other."

"My God, how many of them are there? It sounds like a symphony gone out of control."

"Probably thousands. But they're harmless. They do like to eat the mosquitoes, just like the fish do. Do you see the mosquitoes?"

"Yes," Milena answered.

She'd have to be blind not to see them. There were bugs flying right in front of her eyes and she could hear the buzzing as they flew close to her ears. They weren't biting her, but their small bodies were bouncing off her face. It was rather annoying.

"There will be hardly any mosquitoes when you get into the meadow. Oh, and you can turn your flashlight on now. It will help you see," Kayley suggested.

Milena had forgotten about the light held tight in her grip, and she quickly flicked it on. She shone it upon the ground and found it easier to walk. A few minutes later, Kayley stopped.

"Well, this is where I go back. There's still enough light for me so I won't get lost. Just stick to the trail and maybe do a bit of singing. In case."

Milena swallowed as her throat went dry with fear.

"In case?" she croaked.

Kayley shook her head, which sent her straight shoulder length blond hair bouncing around.

"Oh, nothing serious. Just so the animals know you're around. That way they will steer clear of you. Okay, so like it was nice meeting you and I'm sure we'll see each other again sometime."

"Thanks for the bug spray and for the flashlight and for walking in with me for a bit. I really appreciate it. I owe you big time. If there is anything you need, you know where to find me."

That is if she made it to the cabin alive.

"No problem. And don't worry about the guys. They wouldn't hurt a flea."

Guys? Like no other woman was here at this ranch?

Oh great. Just freaking great.

With a wave, Kayley disappeared back down the path they had just come from, and uneasiness wrapped tighter around Milena as she forced herself to keep walking ahead, alone. The strong yellow beam of light gave her just a bit of comfort and she dared not look into the darkness on both sides of her or behind her. The shrieking of frogs grew louder as Milena strolled forward. Man, what a noisy bunch of animals.

To her surprise, the trail was easy to follow with the light. Ankle high ferns hugged the sides of the path and

Milena tensed as she spotted little creatures jumping across the trail.

Frogs. Dozens of them. They were hopping this way and that way, and she struggled not to step on one. Other creepy sounds began to sift through the darkening damp air.

Icy shivers scrambled up her spine as a branch snapped somewhere to her left. Fear snapped through her when an owl hooted from almost directly above her.

Oh, God please help me get to safety.

She picked up the pace and pleaded harder.

A few minutes later, the rumble of the plane pierced through the shrieking frogs. The roar of its engines grew louder, and Milena could picture Kayley's floatplane rushing along the surface of the lake in order to gain speed for liftoff.

Gosh, this place was noisier than prison. Who would've thought?

Soon the drone of the plane grew quieter and then it was gone. Kayley had left her here.

Milena's heart sank. She was alone. Totally on her own for the first time in fourteen years.

Is this really happening?

Unwanted emotions overwhelmed her. Tears bubbled up and blinded her. Oh, man, she had not expected to break down the instant she was alone.

Frustration at her sudden lack of control made her sob. She wiped her eyes with the back of her right hand and forced herself forward.

She was crazy. She had to be to come out here to live with strangers. What had she been thinking? What kind of insane person ran Cowboys Online? To allow a woman fresh out of prison to fend for herself in the middle of thousands and thousands of acres of forest and lakes?

What if she ran into a bear?

She remembered encountering a bear last summer during her short work stay at Moose Ranch. Not a pleasant experience at all. Thankfully a stranger had come along and saved her. But it appeared there was no stranger coming to her rescue now.

She swore she heard a growl in the woods to her left.

No!

A second later she was running and then the path suddenly ended, and she burst into a mist enshrouded meadow. She stopped abruptly when she realized there was no more path to follow.

Seriously?

Stay to the right if you get lost, Kayley had said. Or had she said left?

Milena's heart began to thump way too fast. She forced her breathing to slow down. She'd had a panic attack or two over the years and she felt as if she might have one now.

Kind of hard not to have one with the situation she'd been stuck in. Prison did that. Crushed your confidence. Screwed with your head until you felt like a nobody.

Well, she *was* a somebody and she *was* free. Kind of. She just had to make the best of this situation.

She shone the flashlight to her right. In the ankle high wet grass, she noticed a trail. She would follow it.

She stepped forward into the swirling cold mist and stuck to the rutted trail that veered to the right. A few minutes of walking and she stopped short when she spied a log cabin right in front of her.

Milena frowned. No lights splashed out of the windows. Either the owners went to bed really early or nobody was home.

Oh boy, she hoped someone was home. If not, it was going to be one long cold night out here. Aside from being so scared that her teeth were now clattering, she realized the air had turned colder, and damp and she didn't have a jacket or a sweater!

Shyly she walked up the steps to a very long and very wide porch which consisted of a roughhewn picnic table. At the far end of the veranda, she spied three white wicker chairs. A sturdy handmade pine railing accented the porch.

It looked nice. Homey. Welcoming.

On shaky legs, she opened the creaky screen door and knocked on the wood-plank door. Her knocks snapped through the frog-shrieking air like explosions and anxiety clawed through her as she awaited any movement from inside.

Silence.

No!

Her fingers were really shaking now as she reached up and knocked again. The white mist was curling in all around her like a ghost trying to suck her up. She waited impatiently. No one answered.

She jumped as the owl hooted from the woods where she'd just come from. The sound was ominous and encouraged her to try the doorknob. She was surprised when the door easily opened.

She shone her flashlight inside. Mild air breathed against her, and she whispered a prayer of thanks. She stepped inside, closing the door and shutting out the singing frogs.

It was mild and comfortable in here.

Pioneer was Milena's first thought. Rustic, her second thought.

Set in the middle of the room, stood a black cast iron wood stove. A blue tin coffee pot had been set on top. Beyond the stove, against the far wall, was a kitchen area with a wood-plank counter with a sink and single silver colored faucet. Hanging from long nails on each side of the single kitchen window were several blackened cast iron frying pans and pots.

"Hello? Is anybody home?" But she knew she wouldn't get an answer. No one had come to the door when she had knocked.

She angled the beam of light to the back of the room.

Beds. She counted three. They were primitive with no headboards. Just a mattress placed on a metal frame set up on cut logs. Blankets were tucked in tightly under the mattress and each bed had two pillows. Simple but cozy.

Milena yawned.

Where were the owners? She thought about grabbing a couple of pots off the wall, heading outside and banging them together to create some noise so someone might come to inspect, but she liked the silence in here.

Milena removed her knapsack and carried it to the bed furthest from the front door. She was so tired. She hadn't slept a wink last night at the hotel and it was catching up to her now. Drowsiness was hitting her like a ton of bricks. She hoped the owners didn't mind if she took a quick power nap. Feeling dopey, she lay on the bed, placed the flashlight on a nearby night table, and stretched her arms up over head.

Suddenly she noted the night darkened windows and a creepy feeling hit the pit of her belly.

No curtains? Seriously?

Anyone could be out there looking in at her.

She cursed softly as she leaned over and grabbed the flashlight. She shone a beam of light toward the door and easily made out there wasn't even a lock on the doorknob or anywhere near the door for that matter.

Oh great.

She should get up and place something against the door. Something that would fall over if someone came in. But that idea was fleeting as an inner voice told her animals didn't know how to open doors. Only people. And there didn't appear to be people here at the moment.

Besides, they were expecting her...

She placed the flashlight upon the night table again, flipped it off and realized she didn't even care about the gloomy darkness. Her eyelids became so heavy she could no longer keep them open.

. . ⚓ . .

"HEY GIRL, YOU'RE GONNA be just fine. I'll take good care of you," Paul said softly to the young gyrfalcon cradled in his hands.

Mitch grinned as he watched Paul gingerly place the white bird about the size of a large crow back into one of several screened wood cages that lined a barn office wall. Paul was a veterinarian, and he was always finding some injured, weak or abandoned animal to tend to.

"You're talking to it like she's your wife," Mitch joked.

Paul smiled as he watched the wobbly bird immediately pounce upon the field mouse Paul had put into the cage moments earlier.

"She's rare like a wife too. Do you know how rare a gyrfalcon is this far south?"

"Yeah, you've told me about a thousand times since you found her," he replied.

"Whoever shot her is a complete idiot," Paul complained.

Mitch grimaced as the mouse shrieked in pain when the snowy white gyrfalcon's claws gripped it. One peck of its beak to the head of the mouse and it was dead. The mouse was devoured within seconds.

"She's hungry like a wife too," Mitch chuckled.

"You're just jealous," Paul replied with a wink.

"Nah, she's too feathery for me. I prefer my wife to be nice and bare, if you know what I mean," Mitch said.

Paul cursed softly.

"Come on man, don't get me visualizing about a woman or I will be forced to go to the city looking for female companionship."

Mitch didn't reply.

They both knew that hunting for women companions was totally out of the question. No lady in her right mind would want to come out here into the wilds of Northern Ontario and experience pioneer life for a prolonged period of time.

It would take a strong woman like the one his older brother Brady had gotten through their sister's Cowboys Online convict program. And Mitch had already extracted a promise out of Jenna that she wouldn't be sending a female to Snowy Creek Ranch like she had done to their brother. She had assured him she'd send them a strong man who would be able to do the extra manual labor and who enjoyed solitude.

Mitch hung the bridle he'd been working on upon a hook and then headed toward the office door.

"May as well get back to the cabin, grab a snack and get some sleep. It's getting late," he said as he lifted the lone gas lantern hanging on a hook.

"Are you coming?" he asked when he realized Paul was still sitting on the stool in front of the cage. He watched the gyrfalcon who was now nestled in the generous amount of hay that Paul had placed in the cage corner.

"Yep. The wife is all settled in for the night. With a nice full belly, she'll sleep well," Paul said as he finally stood and strolled to Mitch

Mitch shook his head, and they both walked outside. It was pretty dark out here and the lantern would come in handy illuminating the trail on their way back. Usually, they took the all-terrain vehicles to the barns, but since it had been such an unusually warm evening, they'd decided on a walk to the closest barn to feed the gyrfalcon that Paul had found injured a few days ago.

Tonight, it had grown cool. But this weather was a hell of a lot better than the icy nights and freezing days they'd been through during their first winter here. Thankfully from here on out every day would get warmer and Mitch couldn't wait until he wouldn't have to wear a jacket anymore in the evenings.

He held up the gas lantern so Paul could get enough light to latch the barn door and a moment later they were walking along the path that went down the slope.

The lantern cast an eerie glow against the cold white mist that had settled over the pasture, and they picked up a brisk pace, stopping only to open and close the gate to the meadow, then following the trail until they finally reached the cabin half an hour later.

They remained silent as they ascended the steps and a moment later entered the building.

To Mitch's surprise, Paul stopped abruptly, and Mitch crashed into him almost dropping the gas lantern.

He was about to give Paul a punch to his arm and tell him to smarten up with his stopping so suddenly, when Mitch sniffed the air. It smelled faintly of lemons. It was a nice odor.

Mitch tensed.

Female?

"Do you smell that?" Paul questioned in a quiet yet alert voice.

"Yes," Mitch whispered.

"Do you think Daeg is already back from the city?" Paul asked.

He had lowered his voice to barely a whisper which made Mitch figure that Paul was thinking the same thing he was thinking.

Daegen had brought back a woman from the city. That's the only thing Mitch could come up with regarding the fresh lemony scent.

The perfume wasn't overpowering or anything. It was just gentle enough to hold his attention. Mitch lifted the lantern and the light splashed further into the one room cabin. The beds immediately came into view.

There were three of them lined against the west wall of the cabin. The first one, Daegen's bed, was empty. The middle one, Paul's bed, was also empty.

His breath caught as he spied *his* bed, tucked near the far corner.

He swallowed as his mouth suddenly went dry. He could easily make out the slender outline of curves beneath his blankets.

And there was long light brown hair splashed across his pillow. And a face that was slightly turned toward them. A very pretty face.

"What the hell? Looks like someone's sleeping in your bed," Paul whispered from beside him. Shock laced his voice.

Mitch couldn't answer. He could only stare at perfection.

She was lying on her back. Long black eyelashes framed her closed eyes. She had a flawless shaped nose, high cheekbones and a generous shaped mouth that pouted in her sleep.

"This would account for the plane we heard earlier. Daegen must have brought her back." Paul whispered.

"Yeah, well why is she sleeping in *my* bed and not in *his*. And where the hell is he?" Mitch whispered back.

Irritation was beginning to saw through him. Daegen had some nerve bringing a woman back, especially after the three of them had agreed there would be no women until the ranch was flourishing.

"Should we wake her up?" Paul asked.

Mitch could barely hear him now as his anger began to soar, and his ears began to buzz. He was tired and now some woman was in *his* bed.

"I swear when I see him, I am going to hang him from his balls on the clothesline. We agreed no women until we were established."

Paul shrugged. "Maybe he's out in the shower after they..."

"Well, I certainly hope they didn't do the nasty in my bed!" Mitch growled.

"It's not his style to pick up a strange woman and I don't see any evidence of him being here. His duffel bag is not here. And he always has a meal or snack waiting for us when he gets back. I could see why not in this case...but I don't think he came back. He's not due yet. Maybe she's a trespasser? Break and enter?" Paul suggested.

"No locks on the doors. No breaking in," Mitch mumbled and tensed as the body beneath the blankets moved.

Mitch took a step back.

Shit! What should they do?

"Well, if Daegen brought her back or not, it looks like we have a female on our hands," Paul whispered.

Mitch nodded. Nervousness rattled him. He could only watch the woman and wait and hope she didn't wake up.

Chapter Two

Milena blinked her eyes open, and confusion rocked her. Where was she? She didn't recognize the ceiling. It was wood, not white stucco. Why wasn't she in her cell? What was going on?

Ok. Calm yourself. Piece this together.

She blew out a slow breath, stifled her panic and struggled to grab hold of her racing thoughts.

What happened? Where am I?

Ok. A meeting at the prison. Cowboys Online. Bush plane. A creepy lake. A misty meadow. Frogs. A growl. Owl. Cabin.

Yes, cabin. Now she remembered. No one was home.

She'd been exhausted. She'd plopped down on a bed and gone to sleep. Then she'd awoken cold and had removed her damp shoes and socks and slipped under the blankets. But now there was a light on in the room.

Had she left the flashlight on? She blinked. No, she'd put it on the night table beside her.

"Excuse me miss, but what are you doing sleeping in my bed?"

A man's gravelly, irritated voice echoed from the other side of the room.

Oh, no. Oh, no.

His bed. The owner?

This was not the best way to make a first impression to the boss. She should have remained outdoors and taken refuge on one of those white wicker chairs on the porch. Oh, why had she come inside?

She couldn't help but cower as a tall figure appeared beside her bed. Correct that. His bed.

She blinked up at him. Felt unexpected heat zing through her.

Cute, was her first impression of him. Sexy cute. He had wide shoulders and a sturdy jaw shadowed with dark hair. His medium length hair was dark brown and wavy, and windblown. He could use a haircut, but she liked the way he looked just the way he was.

Casual, western and rugged.

Not to mention dreamy blue eyes...And so tall. Well over six feet. Goodness. He kind of looked familiar. Had she seen him before? But where?

She simply could not place where, but she knew if she had ever met him before, she would have remembered.

"Hi. I'm Milena. Cowboys Online sent me? And—" Was pretty much all she could manage to say when the man cursed. Violently.

"Shit! She screwed me over. I am going to kill her!"

Oh, dear Lord! The man was crazy! And she had no weapons to protect herself!

Instinctively she cringed further into the bed and clutched the blankets tight around her neck.

"Easy, Mitch. you're scaring her."

Another man suddenly appeared beside the crazy one. He was just as tall, just as wide in the shoulders, but a thinner torso. He had shorter brown hair and gentle brown eyes. Just as good looking as the first guy.

Thankfully, this one didn't have a scary scowl. But he did have a wobbly, warm smile.

She tensed as he suddenly held out his hand. He wanted to shake hands with her?

"Howdy. I'm Paul. This here is Mitch. He's not usually so unmannerly." Paul shot the other guy a frown and a shake of his head. It appeared as if he was warning him off.

Good. Because crazy people scared her.

"We live here. Jenna must have sent you. She owns Cowboys Online."

Oh, thank God. This guy knew Cowboys Online.

"Yes. yes. That's right." She had to be in the right place.

Another curse came from that Mitch fellow. Or maybe she wasn't in the right place?

"Reign it in, Mitch," Paul growled.

He was still holding out his hand to her.

She wasn't sure if she should shake hands with him. She had a feeling she should leave. She was not welcome here.

Sadness clutched at her.

Nobody wants me.

Defiance crashed through her as it usually did when she experienced the familiar sense of abandonment. She'd been sent here. She was in the right place. There was no way she was going back to prison.

Milena grabbed the man's hand and shook. His grip was solid and warm, and she made sure her handshake was just as strong.

"Pleased to meet you, sir. No one was here to meet me, so I made myself at home. I hope you don't mind."

The angry one was about to say something, but a quick jab to his side from Paul kept him silent.

Milena stifled a smile. Grouchy was easily persuaded. Maybe this might work out after all.

She sat up. Despite feeling insecure and foolish, she forced her voice to be strong and confident.

"If you could show me to my quarters, I can freshen up and put my stuff away. Then you can fill me in on my duties."

She frowned as the man named Mitch closed his eyes, took a deep breath and shook his head. Clearly, he was trying to gain some form of self-control. She almost asked what was his problem but stopped herself.

These two men appeared to be her bosses. She had already gotten off on the wrong foot but whatever was going on, it was not her concern. She had fulfilled her end of the deal. She was here. The rest was up to them.

"Um, yeah, freshen up. Well, um," Paul threw her a weird smile.

"What Paul is trying to say is the outhouse is out back," Mitch replied. Amusement was quite evident in his blue eyes.

"And there's a bar of soap on the shelf just over there. Towels are there too. You can freshen up in the creek, if you need to freshen up."

No! Creek? No shower? Shit. Not good for a person who was afraid of water, especially swimming pools, lakes and yeah, creeks. No way was she going to wash up in the dark either.

It appeared her parole officer had not been kidding about the rusticity of this place.

Man, she was in big trouble.

• • ◦‰ • •

PAUL WATCHED THE WOMAN'S face twist from fear to defiance and then to a grimace which made him believe she might not have been told about how rugged it actually would be out here.

Well, she may as well know the truth.

"The fact is, we were not expecting you," he said.

Her crestfallen expression made Paul change his mind. No need to tell her they were not expecting a woman.

"Today. I mean we weren't expecting you today," he added quickly. Who was he to devastate this lady? If she was from Cowboys Online, she was fresh out of prison, expecting a job.

Thankfully Mitch remained silent as he continued to stare at her with a nasty pissed off glare. Paul swore he had never seen Mitch behave so badly. Usually, he was such an easy-going guy and always behaved like a gentleman around women.

Sure, it appeared Jenna had duped them, but their beef was with Mitch's sister. No reason to scare this lady.

"We can string up a line. Hang some blankets for privacy for tonight," Mitch suddenly said. His frown had suddenly disappeared, and Paul relaxed a little.

Okay, the civil side of Mitch was starting to shine through.

"I'll get everything set up in here. Give me a second to start up the lights. Paul, you show her where the John is."

Me? Why not you? Paul wanted to ask. It had been Mitch's idea to go to his sister for help around the ranch in the first place. *He* should be taking charge of this situation in a professional manner, not expecting Paul to do the dirty work.

Suddenly he felt nervous as the girl pulled back her blankets and elegantly swung her long legs and shapely body out of the bed.

Naughty sensations sizzled through Paul. Heat whipped into his cheeks and his lower belly tightened. To his horror, his shaft began a familiar throb of need.

Oh man. Why was he reacting to *this* woman?

Because you've been without one for over a year, that's why, my man, an inner voice teased.

Suddenly the room was ablaze with light as Mitch lit the indoor propane lamps in their kitchen area.

Seated at the edge of the bed, the woman smiled up at them. Hope flared so evident in her eyes.

His gut clenched.

Oh man, she did have a *very* nice smile. He swore even her dark brown eyes twinkled with happiness, despite her appearing afraid only minutes ago.

He noticed Mitch had fallen silent and was watching her with interest as she grabbed a pair of white socks and white running shoes from where she'd stuffed them under the bed. He noted her nice long legs. Thin ankles. Attractive feet. Delicate seashell-like toenails.

Oh, yeah. She was all lady. A pretty one at that.

"Um. Okay. I'm ready," she said after she finished tying her shoelaces and then stood.

Cute. Sexy. Sweetly scented. All rolled into one. He wasn't sure if he should tell Mitch to kill his sister or to thank her for sending this cute doll to them.

Paul cleared his suddenly dry throat.

"Follow me. I'll give you the grand tour."

From the defiant look on Mitch's face and the firm set to his jaw as he began to tie a rope to a hook beside the bed she'd been sleeping in, Paul doubted that she would be here long enough to get her sparkling white running shoes dirty.

· · ♈ · ·

DAMN YOU, JENNA! What in hell was his sister thinking sending them a woman after he had extracted a promise that she wouldn't do the same to him as she had done to his brother!

And he had believed her! What an idiot he was to have trusted her. She had betrayed him. But he would not let this betrayal stand.

The instant he had access to a working phone, he would get Jenna to send this woman back to wherever she came from. Then when she was gone, he would make sure he did not speak to Jenna for the rest of her life. It would teach her a bloody good lesson.

He was so stupid! He should have known better!

Mitch yanked the utility rope across the room in an almost straight line into the kitchen. From beside the kitchen window, he whipped a pan off the wall and tied the rope to the long nail there. He grabbed a sheet and strung it over the rope using several clothes pegs to secure it. Then he draped another sheet beside the first one, securing it too.

He stood back and admired his work.

There. She would have some privacy.

Since she'd had the gall to claim his bed, he would use Daegen's bed tonight. Thankfully it was the furthest away from her. He hadn't liked his intimate reaction when she'd climbed out of bed with her hair all sleep-tousled and her body full of womanly curves. Not only did she smell nice, she looked too damned nice too.

The faster she was out of here, the better.

He walked back over to the kitchen window, cupped his hands to the glass pane and peered out.

He caught Paul's silhouette where he stood in front of the outhouse about a hundred feet away tucked in between a thatch of saplings. She stood there too. In the lamplight the two were chatting as if they didn't have a care in the world. He heard her laugh. It was a hearty sound, straight from her chest.

Mitch frowned as renewed anger burst through him.

Leave it to Paul to make it romantic showing off an outhouse to a woman.

He had to admit he did feel embarrassed by his bad behavior. But he'd been caught off guard.

He felt uncomfortable too that they hadn't put up a fancier cabin. Something like the one his brother and his partners had put up over at Moose Ranch.

Now *that* place was big. Two stories. A fireplace in almost every room. A bedroom for everyone. All the modern conveniences. A woman like this chick should have a beautiful accommodation like Moose Ranch's ranch house.

Mitch cursed softly beneath his breath. How could Jenna do this to him? Why would she do this?

This was no place for a female. The three of them spent most of their time caring for the many horses here on the ranch. People paid good money to have their prized animals flown in here. Some owners wanted their horses to relax during downtime between races. Others wanted their horses to retire here amidst the pristine natural surroundings.

Everyone loved their horses and Mitch took pride in making sure every single horse was well cared for. Working here was a full-time job for the three of them.

All he'd wanted was to hire just a little help so they could have a shorter workday and truth be told, it was because of Daegen too.

He had lingering issues from his time spent in the military and from what had happened in his personal life. Once a month he flew out of here for a few days to touch up on some visits with renowned PTSD doctors across the border or with his shrink in Thunder Bay.

When he was away, they felt the loss. It was why he'd gone to Jenna for the cheap labor aspect of having help.

Just thinking about his sister set him to cursing her beneath his breath.

Despite it getting late, he would get started on some food for the newcomer. His mother had always taught him to be polite and offer food to guests. If he couldn't be polite then at least he could offer her food. Maybe eating something would put him into a better mood too.

But he doubted it.

. . ⚓ . .

"SO, WHAT'S YOUR NAME again?" The man asked as he walked beside her across the foggy meadow.

"Milena Allen," she answered.

He nodded and threw her a watery smile. Why did he look so...confused?

"Right. Okay. And you said Jenna sent you through the Cowboys Online program?"

"That's right."

"That would mean you're fresh out of prison."

Did he disapprove?

"Yes. Did Jenna not send all the details?"

In the lamplight, she saw him grimace and her tummy hollowed out.

"Unfortunately, no."

No?

But she had been told by her parole officer that they knew about her. If they didn't know why she'd been sent to prison in the first place, they would send her away for sure when they found out. Nobody in their right mind wanted a convicted murderer near them. Unless, of course, if one was ordered through the Cowboys Online program, right?

She bit her bottom lip to keep from crying out in disappointment.

"But you said earlier that you were expecting me."

"Just not today. We were expecting someone. Just later on in the season."

Exactly what does that mean?

He fell silent and they kept walking toward the area where all the frogs were shrieking. The mating sounds of the frogs grew louder the closer they got to the creek, and then suddenly all the frogs fell silent.

"Blessed peace," Paul chuckled. "They know we're here and figure there is danger, so they go quiet."

Wow, how all the animals could go noiseless at the same time was interesting.

He stopped suddenly and began talking again.

"When it's warm enough we use the shower. We get our water from the creek. This creek is upstream from the horses, and it is spring fed, so it is crystal clean. You can drink right out of most of the rivers and creeks around here. Even the lakes are spring fed. So, no worries about drinking water."

He lifted the lantern and pointed a few feet ahead. Past the curls of white mist, she saw the dark water behind a flourish of ferns. Anxiety pummeled her. No way was she going to bathe in that water.

"We are still very primitive out here. We lug water to a large bucket nearby and do our laundry there. I can show you when the time comes."

Lovely. Outdoor bathroom, bathing, and even outdoor laundry. Man, this was going to be so much fun. Not.

Milena brightened as she remembered something he'd just said.

"You mentioned a shower? Where is this shower?" She would use it until it froze solid. Then she would melt snow in the winter and take sponge baths. She could be handy if need be. Anything was better than prison.

He nodded toward a thicket of trees about ten feet away. When he swung the gas lantern around, she spied a narrow rocky path into the trees and noted a six-foot tall by six-foot wide wood-planked building. A large plastic barrel had been placed on top of the flat roof. A silver faucet and a shower hose were visible.

But no door.

Oh great. So much for privacy.

"Okay, it looks nice enough," Milena praised. She would take showers when the men were working or something. She was resilient. She would figure something out. She could survive here.

She saw a flash of white teeth as he smiled.

"Actually, the shower is nice when the weather is warm. We plan on getting a pump this summer and have the water propelled up, until then it's all done manually. But we already have water at the house during the spring, summer and fall seasons. Just one faucet and the water temperature depends on how cold it is outside, but it does the job."

She wasn't going to go into asking about the mechanics of how all this getting water into the house and shower was done without electricity, but she was sure she would learn along the way.

"Rustic and practical. I like that," she said truthfully.

"You do?"

Milena laughed. "You sound surprised?"

Paul shrugged his shoulders. "Well, I thought maybe because you're a woman you'd rather have the conveniences."

"After prison, I can handle anything." Except water, she added silently.

"Oh, that's good to hear." He sounded happy, almost relieved.

They fell into an awkward silence, and she gazed around. She'd walked to the cabin through this inky darkness? Man, she had to be braver than she'd ever imagined.

"It sure gets dark out here," she whispered.

"You'll get used to it. Come on, let's head back to the cabin."

"Do we have to?" Milena blurted.

To her surprise, Paul laughed. She liked the sound. Liked it a lot. He had a sense of humor. That's good. But she wasn't kidding. She did not want to go back to that grouchy guy.

"Don't worry. Mitch's bark is worse than his bite."

"That's what I'm afraid of," Milena muttered.

Paul laughed again. He turned and since she didn't want to be left here standing in the dark, she followed.

"You'll get used to him," he said.

Sadness descended upon her again. Yeah, sure she would get used to him, but only if they kept her.

A few minutes later, as they came closer to the cabin, Milena's heart began to pound like crazy.

She did not want to go back in there. Not with Mr. Grumpy.

Paul must have noticed her slowing pace, because he stopped and turned around. Due to the soft glow of lamp lights splashing out of the nearest window, she was able to see the curiosity shadowing Paul's face.

"Seriously, he won't bite. You'll be fine. Come on inside. I can smell food. He must be making leftover roast beef. We get the beef from our closest neighbor."

Oh glory! there was hope yet. Other people.

"You have neighbors?"

"Well, it's a fifteen-minute walk to the lake you came in on and a three-hour paddle by canoe with portages along a river into another lake and then half hour or so paddling to get to their place. With a plane it would be almost fifteen minutes. We don't get many visitors here. Just twice a month via North Country Air when they bring in mail and supplies. We order through cell phone, but the signal is sporadic, or we call our neighbor, and they place an order as they have Internet. But we have visitors less often in winter when mail and supplies is once a month, weather permitting."

Milena hadn't even realized she had entered the cabin until she felt the warmth from the woodstove caress her cool skin. She spied the nasty man standing by that stove.

He was hunkered over a huge cast iron frying pan stirring the contents with a long wooden spoon.

God. Please help me. Not even an electric oven to cook on?

Mr. Grump actually grinned when he spied them standing in the doorway.

Her tummy did a sweet little twist at his smile. He looked quite handsome. He should smile more often, Milena thought as she sighed with relief.

"Food is almost ready. Ice cold spring water on the table. Hunker down and I will serve in a minute."

It appeared the man had turned nice.

"You heard the man, let's eat!" Paul said.

Something weird and exciting fluttered within her lower belly as Paul pulled out a chair for her.

Wow. No guy had ever pulled out a chair for her. She'd only seen it done in the movies she watched on the television in the common room.

Who knew chivalry existed deep in the woods? Maybe this wasn't going to be such a bad place after all.

The food literally melted in her mouth and the cold water tasted exceptional as a few minutes later she was eating as if there was no tomorrow. She hadn't realized she was so hungry.

"I have never eaten this late before," Milena confessed between bites of the most mouthwatering roast beef, potato and carrot combo she had ever had.

"What time did they feed you at the prison?" Paul asked in an astounded voice. His green eyes twinkled with amusement as he awaited her answer.

"Every prison has a different routine. In the one I was last in supper was served in my cell at six o'clock sharp. Every evening. Everything was always on a strict schedule. In the morning, up at six thirty sharp. Do your bed. Exercise in your room. Personal hygiene.

Breakfast in my room at seven thirty. Roll call at eight. At nine the guards would accompany me to my job washing dishes in the kitchen. Then I would help prepare the food for the inmates' lunch. Then I was accompanied back to my cell for twelve o'clock lunch. One o'clock I was escorted to my class. I was taking advanced sewing. Then when the course was finished a couple hours later, I'm allowed to go to the common room to mingle with others or watch some tv or go outside for an hour to exercise. Then back to my cell for supper at six. Then I could leave and hang out again in the common room. But I had to be back in my cell for eight. Cell lights out at eight thirty sharp. Although the hall lights were always on, so there was never complete darkness, like you have out there."

"That must have been annoying not to have darkness to sleep," Mitch commented in that gruff voice of his as he heaped a second helping of the stew into her plate without even asking. Not that she would have told him no. The food was so good.

Huh, she hadn't even realized she was so hungry, she thought again.

"When did you have your last meal today anyways?" Mitch asked after he deposited the almost empty pan onto a wood cutting board set in the middle of the table.

"Oh, um," She wasn't sure. "Um, oh yes, we had fries and a pop at eleven this morning while we waited for the pilot."

"Lunch, wow. And only fries? No wonder you're eating like a horse," Paul said with a chuckle from beside her.

Horror at her bad table manners made Milena drop her fork. Both Mitch and Paul laughed.

"Come on, I'm just teasing you," Paul joked. "Eat. Drink. You're nothing but skin and bones, girl."

"Yeah, and skinny scarecrows don't do much work on a ranch. So, eat up, Miss Scarecrow," Mitch added as he suddenly scooped the rest of the food out of the pan for himself.

Milena felt her cheeks grow hot. Scarecrow was not a becoming nickname. She should scold Mitch about that, but she caught him wink at Paul and realized he was joking, and she was taking things too seriously. Besides, they were her bosses. Kind of like jail guards. She needed to keep her mouth shut and follow orders.

She forced herself to relax and stared at the food.

Despite feeling full, her mouth watered. Yeah, she wanted more. She picked up her fork.

"There you go. Good girl," Paul said and grinned with approval as she began to eat again.

"Only because it's so good," Milena admitted between swallows.

"Hear that, Mitch? She likes your cooking. You'll have to give her your recipe."

Milena noticed Mitch frown and shake his head. Suddenly she wasn't sure if that gesture meant he wouldn't share his recipe because she wouldn't be here long enough.

Damn! For a few wonderful minutes she'd allowed herself to hope that she might be accepted here.

Well, she would just have to make sure she would become indispensable, then they would be forced to keep her. First though, she needed to become more confident and professional. Just like an employee.

"What time does work start in the morning?" she asked.

"We roll out of bed just before the sun comes up," Mitch answered, between bites.

Oh.

"What time is that?" In prison she never saw the sun rise or set. That's one of the things she'd missed most being on the inside and last night at the hotel she'd enjoyed her first sunset and then first sunrise this morning. It had been so wonderful seeing the play of colors in the sky as the sun had set last night and then rose this morning.

"This time of year, it being spring, we are up at six a.m. and in the summer it's much earlier because that's our high season as we'll be growing our own hay, doing gardening and other chores. Autumn and winter, it's a bit later as it gets lighter later and a little less work," Paul explained.

"Okay, great, you can give me my chore list in the morning," Milena stated.

She tried to ignore the odd look that passed between the two men. She knew what they were thinking that she shouldn't expect to stay.

Well, she was here, and she would show them she could work.

"I'll have a list for you first thing," Paul replied with a nod.

Milena smiled and gave herself a mental high five at her newfound confidence. It felt good to be in control, and she had to make sure they wouldn't send her back to prison. If they tried, it would be over her dead body.

Now that she had a full belly, she was getting awfully sleepy again. She stifled a yawn, but the men noticed.

"Okay, let's get you ready for bed. You just sit there and relax. I'll call you when everything is ready," Mitch suddenly said as he stood. Paul was also up on his feet, a curious grin on his face.

Milena nodded sleepily and waited. Suddenly all her newfound confidence had disappeared. They were the jail guards, er...her bosses and she was used to getting bossed around, so no use in protesting and asking how they were going to get her ready for bed.

This time she covered her mouth and yawned like she'd never yawned before.

Mercy! She was going to sleep good tonight!

• • ᴏᴇᴏ • •

MILENA OPENED HER EYES and saw both Paul and Mitch watching her. They stood at the foot of the bed she slept in and gazed upon her nude body. She must have tossed the sheets and blankets aside while she'd slept. Their gazes were dark as they stared between her widespread thighs. She should be scared, shouldn't she? She'd just met them and now they were seeing her naked. But she wasn't frightened at all.

She was...aroused.

And she wanted them to watch her masturbate.

She reached down and touched her ultra-sensitive clitoris.

Sensually, she massaged herself with firm strokes. Her breaths coming faster, and her thighs tightened.

Mmm, that feels so wonderful.

Suddenly, she realized they were also naked. Their erections were thick and long as they stroked themselves.

Her eyelids grew heavy, and she watched Mitch crawl up the bed. She breathed even faster as Paul climbed onto the bed beside her.

Mitch was moving over her, and she slid her hand away from her clit as his smooth, hot cockhead massaged her bud.

Paul angled his torso over her head and aimed his large shaft toward her face. Neither of the men spoke as they both suddenly penetrated her.

She gasped at the intensity of their fullness. Moaned as nerve endings sparkled and sizzled. Her pussy clenched around Mitch's cock like a vice and her mouth clamped around Paul's shaft like a woman possessed.

Both men were groaning.

She arched against Mitch as he began to thrust into her. She licked and sucked Paul's flexing shaft. Felt their flesh thicken and pulse inside her.

Heat and pleasure exploded through her like sizzling jolts of electricity, and she rocked into the ecstasy. Whimpered as they pistoned harder and faster sending her deeper into blissful rapture.

Her mind splintered into a kaleidoscope of colors as she rode the carnal spasms.

Oh yes! Beautiful! Perfect!

· · ❧ · ·

MILENA CAME AWAKE ON a gasp, her body wrapped in heat and pleasure and her fingers damp, as she eagerly massaged her clit, unleashing wonderful pleasures. She went with the climax, convulsing and gyrating and enjoying the shudders and erotic sensations slamming into her.

Only after the erotic spasms ebbed did she realize she was staring at a wood-planked wall.

For a second, she didn't know where she was, and then everything came crashing over her.

She had slept in the same room as her bosses. She had just had an erotic dream about them. They were good looking men...but yeah, hello, they were complete strangers. What was up with fantasizing about them like that?

Lord! Had she made any noises in her sleep?

She was mortified just remembering the heat pummeling through her as Mitch and Paul had stood naked in front of her. Then Mitch climbing over her, entering her. Paul's cock thrusting into her mouth.

Milena blew out a tense breath.

Have mercy! What in the world was wrong with her? She'd rarely had sexual dreams in prison.

She knew everything was monitored on cameras in the pen, so over the years she had just learned to suppress the occasional craving for sex.

But this dream...she bit her bottom lip to prevent herself from moaning out loud as her pussy quivered and clenched with remembrance and need. This dream had been awesome.

She lay still and forced herself to calm down. She'd just orgasmed.

Had they heard?

Quietly she turned onto her side and gazed at the sheets strung up on the rope.

She remained quiet for what seemed like forever as thoughts about last night's brief time with Paul and Mitch floated through her mind.

She had enjoyed eating with them. The food had tasted great and despite their teasing, they seemed nice.

After supper, while she'd sat at the table and waited, as instructed, the men had emptied a narrow five-drawer dresser where they'd kept odds and ends and then they'd pushed the dresser against a wall just beside the curtainless window, designating the rustic furniture would be hers to use for now. While they washed the dishes and chatted about the horses, she'd quietly unpacked behind the privacy of the strewn sheets.

She did not miss that this so-called bedroom with the makeshift privacy wall was not much bigger than her prison cell. However, this place was quaint, and she had already fallen in love with the rustic single bed with burgundy sheets and several black and red square patterned blankets, two fluffy pillows, the dresser, and a night table. Everything was more than she could ever have hoped for.

She didn't have much to unpack. Just several pairs of underwear, an extra bra, two pairs of light grey track pants, a pair of grey shorts, and several grey t-shirts and bland blouses. Her entire wardrobe minus the bra, underwear and socks, had been donated to her by the prison at the same time she'd turned in her jail uniforms.

The drab clothing barely fit her and were not her taste, but beggars could not be choosy. She'd tucked her hygiene products in the top drawer and smiled as she set the bug spray and flashlight, the bush pilot had given, her onto her night table.

That woman's gifts had been so sweet, and Milena hoped she could pay the lady back somehow if she ever met up with her again.

Then she lifted out her most prized possession. A framed photograph of Moose Ranch, a place she had house sat last summer. A wonderful wilderness ranch where her friend JJ lived. Milena smiled as she remembered her short stay there. She hoped and prayed one day they would be able to get together again. She slid the picture into one of the drawers for safekeeping.

After she'd finished unpacking, she'd lain on the bed listening to the two men as they finished up the dishes. She'd almost drifted off when then they'd called out to her informing her that they were going outside to freshen up in the creek and she could have about fifteen or so minutes of privacy before they returned and went to bed.

While they'd been gone, she'd brushed her teeth, washed her face, quickly donned her nightie and hopped into the bed and fallen asleep pretty much the instant her head had hit her pillow. She hadn't even heard them return. Which made her wonder...*had* they returned last night?

Shouldn't they be snoring? Shouldn't she be hearing them breathing? But she heard nothing. Nothing except some birds chirping from the slightly opened nearby window.

Milena tensed. That window had been closed last night when she had climbed under the sheets. That meant someone had opened it, which meant they *had* come back.

Milena chuckled softly.

This was the first time since she was a kid that she had slept all night without waking at least once.

In prison, she'd been a very light sleeper. Every little sound would rouse her. It wasn't unusual for her to awaken four or five times, but last night she'd slumbered in a pleasant, stress free oblivion until that heated sex dream had begun...

Milena closed her eyes and inhaled slowly, forcing thoughts of sex out of her mind.

The air smelled nice. Cool and crisp with a tinge of pine.

As she gazed at the nearest window, she realized it was quite bright outside.

They *had* said they got up before sunrise. This brilliance felt more than just sunrise. It was daylight!

Alarm had her bolting upright. She suddenly sensed the men had already left.

No! Had she slept in on her first day on the job?

Milena reached out and flung aside the nearest sheet that separated her from the rest of the cabin.

She swore beneath her breath when she spied the other two beds were neatly made. No one was in the cabin!

Oh, come on! Had they skipped out on her? Was her sleeping in grounds for firing her? She needed to get dressed and get to work.

She practically jumped out of bed, opened the top drawer, grabbed her prison issue toiletry bag and headed toward the kitchen area. She needed to brush her hair, brush her teeth, wash her face...

She stopped when she spied the note propped up against a jar of instant coffee set on the table.

Good morning, sleeping scarecrow,

We didn't have the heart to wake you. Take the day off and explore the cabin and don't leave the meadow and never lose sight of the cabin. You'll find plenty of food in the cupboards. We will be back by nightfall.

P. S. Your work list is on the back. Don't do anything until we show you. You can start tomorrow.

Mitch and Paul.

Milena blinked as an awesome shock wave tumbled over her.

You can start tomorrow?

Oh my God. She was staying? They were keeping her?

She turned over the sheet of paper and was stunned at all the chores they had written down.

Oh geez. She was in serious trouble if they expected her to know how to do all these things. Clean out the stalls.

Assist in feeding the horses. Tack, groom and take horses on trail rides. Help chop firewood and pick up supplies from lake on atv when required.

Milena stopped reading and shivered as the familiar doom flooded her.

The lake. How was she going to handle the lake and the creek?

Maybe it was a good thing they had given her the day off. She would need to rest up to do all these things. There was more on the list, but she'd commit all to memory over some coffee.

She eyed the instant coffee jar. And then gazed over at the white propane stove in the kitchen area.

Last night, while she'd been half asleep, Mitch had shown her how to start a fire on the propane stove element. She spied another note there with instructions, in case she'd forgotten, the note said. It was signed by Mitch.

Huh. The guy had been such a scary mean man when she'd first arrived, but by bedtime he'd been a nice enough fellow. But now they were gone.

Shoot! What did they expect her to do here all day long?

A few minutes later, she had a pot of water boiling on the stove, she was dressed, and she was ready to tackle the day.

But first, coffee.

· · ❧ · ·

MITCH STOOD HIGH UP on the top of the tallest, steepest hill in the area and clenched his free hand with frustration as he held the cell phone to his ear and listened to Jenna's phone ring and ring. He rarely came up here, unless it was to catch a cell signal when they needed to call someone. And right now, Jenna was in his crosshairs.

He'd already left her several nasty messages while standing here for the last half an hour phoning every two minutes to try and get her. Unfortunately, he couldn't hang around up here much longer. There was too much work to be done today. When it went to voicemail, again, he cursed her up and down once more and disconnected.

Mitch frowned.

She was probably home and laughing at his curses. He should never have trusted his sister, and he never would again. Not after this fiasco.

He blew out a tense breath and looked down at the scenery below.

Normally the beauty of their property would calm him, and this time was no different. A ribbon of sparkling blue river meandered through the lush green meadows and a burst of happiness pushed aside his anger.

This scene was spectacular and so peaceful. The baby blue sky was filled with puffy white clouds; the clapboard grey barn tucked on a hillside about a half-mile away had lush green ivy beginning to climb up the outside walls. The rickety cedar wood fences that straddled the meadows glistened in the sunshine and a handful of horses of different coloring; brown, white, black and intermixed, were dispersed here and there. Some frolicked while others quietly grazed, their tails sashaying away the flies.

To the east, a strip of green meadow meandered through the forest and would lead to yet another large meadow where there was another barn and then further along would be their cabin and Snowy Lake.

To the north, west and south he could see the endless green forests and lakes beyond the valley. A cheerful chattering of chipmunks chasing each other nearby and the cries of blue jays and chickadees permeated the warm air.

This place was a far cry from the city life of downtown Toronto where he'd had a thriving accounting business. After getting burned by his ex-girlfriend, and then suffering a subsequent health scare, he had sold his business and he hadn't looked back.

This was where he wanted to be. He'd traded the noisy traffic for the whispering winds. He had left the towering skyscraper for a rustic cabin and left the airconditioned offices for warm barns surrounded by nature and horses.

Had someone told him a couple of years ago that he would be here in the middle of nowhere with no roads, no fancy restaurants and no women, he would have called them nuts.

Yet here he was and suddenly stuck with one pretty woman who made him very aware that he was a man.

Mitch frowned.

How in the hell was he going to get out of this pickle? Did he even want to? He cursed himself for even thinking of keeping *her.*

He pocketed his cell phone and walked toward the edge of a nearby cliff. He should just throw himself over and get it over with. Then he wouldn't have to go back and deal with the problem Jenna had created for him.

Mitch chuckled and shook his head. Jumping off a cliff sure wouldn't solve anything.

But he would need to be careful heading back down. The pathway he used was nothing more than an animal trail and there were plenty of loose rocks to make the footing tricky. The first few times that he'd climbed up or down he'd fallen flat on his belly or ass. Luckily, he had just gotten bruises and a sore butt.

As he descended the steep incline, he thought about the newcomer. She was pretty, and he liked the way she smelled. Liked the way her eyes sparkled too when she'd looked at him and how her cheeks grew pink when she'd gotten embarrassed when Paul and himself had teased her at the dinner table last night.

She had a vulnerable look about her. Yet he also caught glimpses of defiance.

He wondered what she had done to end up in prison and how long she'd been there. He could already tell she was the total opposite of his old girlfriends.

Mitch cursed beneath his breath when thoughts of Everly, his most recent, crowded his mind.

He had recognized right away that she was a spoiled rich girl. He should have stuck to that opinion and not allowed her beauty and her manipulations to wrap his heart around her little finger. He grimaced and remembered how badly it had ended between them. He hoped he never saw her again but knew he would. She housed several of her racehorses here at Snowy Creek.

Thankfully Paul had looked after her when she'd come to visit them last autumn.

He pushed Everly out of his mind and kept moving downward.

Once he safely reached the bottom, he grabbed the canteen from his four-wheeler and strolled over to the nearby creek. It was a different creek than the one they allowed the horses to use, and they'd had the water tested several times. Every time it had come up clean. It was drinkable and they hadn't had any problems with it.

Mitch perched himself on his hands and knees, set the canteen down, removed his black cowboy hat, a gift from his brother Brady, cupped his hands and dipped them into the cold, clear water. He brought them up and greedily drank. He did it several times and then splashed water on his warm face and tossed some on his hair. He plopped his hat back onto his head, grabbed the canteen, moved up the creek a bit, crouched and filled the canteen.

He liked the taste of this water. It was simply cold. Not an ounce of the chlorine that he had always tasted in city water.

He closed the lid on his canteen, stood and as he turned away from the creek, a weird growl erupted from nearby. The hairs on the back of his neck shot up a warning to him to run.

But he didn't dare move. He knew that sound.

Bear.

And he hadn't brought his rifle with him. Idiot move. He had stupidly left it in the scabbard on the back seat of the all-terrain vehicle, which was thirty feet away.

Another growl, this time closer. Mitch held his breath and waited.

Shit! He was so screwed.

. . ⚜ . .

PAUL STROKED THE RECUPERATING gyrfalcon's head and smiled as it closed its eyes. He had just tossed a live mouse into her cage and the bird had quickly pounced on its prey, ripped it apart and devoured it. Afterwards, he had managed to grab the gyrfalcon, checked the injured wing and was pleased with the healing progress.

The antibiotics had worked. The infection was gone. He could set the bird free in a day or two.

From what he could tell, someone had taken a shot at her and the bullet had nicked her. The wound had become infected.

Who had shot at a young bird? And why? Some idiots target practicing?

Since they leased this land for the nearest hundreds of acres and the cattle ranch closest to them also had hundreds of acres and a nearby sheep ranch was owned by an elderly lady, he knew they wouldn't shoot a gyrfalcon, that meant someone else was around on the nearby crown land to their south border or on their property.

Whatever the reason for shooting the bird, it was an uneasy feeling to think there may be an armed intruder lurking about.

Paul became alert when the falcon suddenly opened its eyes wide and tilted its head. It had heard something. Its heart began to pound a frantic beat against Paul's palm. A few seconds later, he heard the far-off drone of a plane.

"So, that's what you heard?" he spoke softly to the bird, who now gazed up at him.

"It could be anyone. A plane flying over the area, or maybe someone checking out the nearby lakes during a sightseeing trip. No need to be afraid."

The bird closed its eyes and Paul placed it back into the cage as the drone of the plane sounded louder.

Daegen wasn't due for another day and the mail, and their groceries was coming in with him, so he doubted it was him. No one was scheduled to visit over the next few weeks, so Paul relaxed, and his thoughts turned to Milena.

She had been dead to the world last night when they had returned from their dip in the creek. They'd peeked past the hung sheets and watched her sleep for a few minutes, Paul had held his breath the entire time expecting her to open her eyes. But she didn't. So, they had quietly gone to bed.

He'd smelled her lemony scent all night long. It had kept him awake for a long time and her unique feminine smell had caressed his senses while he'd slept. He hadn't dreamt about her, but he'd known she was there in the room a mere few feet away from him.

This morning when they'd peeked in on her, her hands had been tucked beneath her cheeks and her brown hair was splashed like a fan across her pillow.

They hadn't had the heart to wake her.

And man, he didn't want to send her away. But Mitch did.

Paul frowned. He hoped Jenna didn't answer Mitch's calls because having this pretty lady around this ranch just seemed to make everything feel like home. It was a welcome feeling and he liked it.

A lot.

Chapter Three

Milena enjoyed the refreshing way the cool water kissed her skin as she rubbed the soapy cloth across her tender breasts. After a delicious cup of black coffee, she'd taken down the rope with the strung up sheets and put them away. She'd made the bed, stuffed her empty knapsack behind the night table, grabbed a face cloth and towel from a shelf in the cabin and headed outdoors to find the outhouse and then the makeshift shower Paul had shown her last night via lamplight.

She'd found both and was now standing in the shower thoroughly relishing the spray of cold water embracing her.

Last night, Paul had shown her the rope to pull when she needed water. He'd also warned her to use the water sparingly because every bucket placed into the overhead tank had to be carried up from the creek, brought up a ladder and dumped into the above tank.

At the moment she paid no heed to his warning as she continued to pull the rope and lavish in the cool water shooting from the shower head and cascading over her.

She loved this privacy. There were no guards. No rush to meet the ten minutes allocated for a shower. Nor were there any inmates looking into her stall while she washed herself.

This freedom was pure heaven.

Eagerly she washed and soaked herself, experiencing an almost uncontrollable happiness.

Instead of black prison bars in front of her face, there was an open doorway and she caught glimpses of a large green meadow past the saplings that shrouded the stall. In the distance, there were rocky hills, and all kinds of trees. From silver aspen to white birch, and towering old red maple trees. There were scraggly green tamaracks and giant pine trees that had trunks that looked so wide she was sure her arms could never go halfway around if she were to hug a tree.

Everything looked so fresh and new. It was as if she'd been dropped into a fairy fantasy land.

She frowned. Or maybe she was dreaming?

Had she somehow slipped on a bar of soap in the prison showers, fallen and hit her head knocking herself unconscious? Maybe she *was* in a coma dreaming about these two sexy cowboy bosses who lived on a horse ranch in the desolate Canadian wilderness.

Oh man, if that's what had happened, then she did not want to wake up. She resisted the urge to slip her fingers between her thighs and relieve the ache of need throbbing there. She didn't dare. Especially when there was no door on this shower.

Oh, why was she feeling so sexually adventurous? She really should have a room of her own.

And she'd better get out of the shower too before she used up all the water. She wanted to make a good impression on her bosses, and she could see there was much work to be done around that cabin. The windows had no curtains, so she'd like to find some material to make curtains.

She'd had the forethought of packing her small sewing box. It would come in handy here.

She'd also noticed there were no pictures hanging on the walls. The pots in the kitchen area were all black from being on the wood stove or their gas stove and should be shined.

Cleanliness is next to godliness her mother used to say, and just because Milena had been dealt a rotten blow in life, she'd always tried to make lemonade from the lemons. Her side of the prison cell she shared with other inmates had always been tidy. Now it was time to order up this ranch too. But she would do it once she got firmly settled here.

Milena smiled as she stepped out of the stall and grabbed the towel she'd left hanging on the hook. As she began to dry herself, she caught movement at the mouth of the path.

Bear?

Fear shot through her and she scrambled back into the cubicle.

Oh great! No door! The bear could just walk right in and eat her! Man! What was up with this place. No locks. No curtains. No doors.

Talk about her going from one extreme to the other.

She cursed beneath her breath as she wrapped a towel around herself. She'd just have to sneak out before she got cornered.

Terror made her heart crash as she moved to the opening and froze.

A man stood right there on the trail about ten feet away from her. His face and chin were shielded behind a scruffy beard and moustache. He wore a towel slung low over his hips and the rest of him was...naked.

Oh my! A mountain man?

"What are you doing here?" His angry voice made her flinch and he stared at her with a scowl of disbelief on his face. She stared back at him and suddenly realized he looked familiar.

She'd met him before.

It was Daegen. The man who'd saved her from a bear last summer over at Moose Ranch!

The plane she'd heard earlier must have dropped him off on that lake and she instantly realized why she thought she must have heard the name Snowy Creek Ranch before. Her friend, JJ, who worked at Moose Ranch, where Milena had stayed briefly last summer must have mentioned this place. Yet back then Milena hadn't been paying much attention to anything but her newfound short-lived freedom.

And no wonder Mitch looked familiar when she'd first met him yesterday. He looked a lot like his older brother Brady, a part-owner of Moose Ranch and whom she'd met while she'd been there.

She'd forgotten how tall Daegen was, at least a head taller than her and he looked different with that beard and moustache.

Dangerous. Sexy. Very hot.

Oh boy. Oh boy. Oh boy.

She swore she could feel the heat wafting off his body despite him being so far away from her.

"Daegen?" she whispered. This was simply unbelievable.

"Milena? What are you doing here?" he asked again.

His angry voice dragged her gaze back to his face.

Oh gosh, he was still so handsome despite his scruffy look. Last year he'd been clean cut. Now his light brown hair was quite a bit longer and laced with golden highlights. That beard and mustache he toted made it appear as if he'd turned wild out here.

She couldn't even think straight when she gazed at him. Or remember how to speak. She was just so shocked to see a man she'd thought she would never see again.

"Did you escape prison? Are you hiding out here?" he growled.

It hurt that he would think she was on the run and that he would not want to help her.

She finally remembered how to speak as anger shot through her.

"No, no. Nothing like that. I'm here with the Cowboys Online program. They sent me here," she explained.

His scowl deepened and her heart ached. Another one who did not want her here.

"I hope you didn't use up all the water," he suddenly said.

Milena blinked. He was concerned about her water usage? How annoying.

He chuckled as she stepped out of the stall. She held her towel tight against her breasts and struggled to grab her clothing from the hook with her free hand. Quickly she stuck her feet into her snug running shoes.

"Just make sure you make some noise on the way back to the cabin. I saw a bear nearby when I came up the trail from the lake."

Adrenalin roared through her as she stared down the path.

"A bear?" she gasped.

"Yep. Seriously. I am sure she's harmless but whistle nice and loud and she'll go on her way."

He began to whistle as he placed his towel onto the hook, she'd just had her clothing on.

Goodness! A bear!

And a bare ass!

She got a good glimpse of his butt as he stepped into the shower, but it did nothing for her as she spun around and looked down the path again, fear ripping into her.

Was he kidding? He had to be kidding about the bear? Right?

She swallowed against her dry mouth.

Suddenly this peaceful, beautiful fairy land was anything but peaceful or beautiful. Stiffly, she tiptoed down the path and gazed out into the meadow.

Nothing there.

Her heart began to hammer as she took a long time to survey for any movement between here and the cabin.

She saw nothing but silver dew sparkling on the meadow grass and a black crow soaring in the bright blue sky.

She blew out a tense breath as Daegen's whistling grew louder. She swore she could hear amusement in that whistle.

He *had* to have been joking about the bear. Hadn't he?

She clutched her bundle of clothing closer to her and on trembling legs, Milena hurried to the cabin.

• • ⚬⟋⚬ • •

DAEGEN COULDN'T STOP his heart from pounding as he pulled on the cord. Water splashed over his head, and he cursed the coldness. Why in hell hadn't he stayed in the city a bit longer and enjoyed another hot hotel shower? Because he had wanted to come home, that's why.

His heart smiled at the word, home.

He'd been forging a newfound peace out here in the wilderness among the horses and nature. But that peace was now shattered.

Milena was here. How in hell had that happened? He'd pretty well figured he'd never see her again.

For almost a year, she'd haunted his dreams.

Spying on her while she stood in the shower, her hands soaping curvy areas of her body, he'd thought he might be having one very raunchy daytime fantasy. Seeing her completely naked, her luscious curves, her pert breasts, wide hips and long legs...

Man, what had Mitch been thinking bringing a woman here?

Especially Milena! He'd never told them about meeting her. But maybe Mitch's brother, Brady, had?

Had Brady set him up?

No, not possible. Mitch was adamant about no women here. At least not until they were established. He knew Mitch had asked for some cheap manual labor through his sister's convict company and Jenna had promised no stunts like the one she'd pulled on Brady.

Well, it appeared Jenna was a damn good liar.

He cracked a grin when he thought about how Mitch and Paul must have reacted when Milena had shown up. He assumed they knew she was here.

He cursed softly, let go of the rope and grabbed the bar of soap.

Of all the women he knew, she was the last one he would expect to ever see, in his shower.

Daegen closed his eyes as his cock painfully pulsed. His eyes had literally almost rolled out of his eye sockets when he'd spied her in the shower.

He wanted to stay here and masturbate this wicked sexual tension she had created. But he knew better than to indulge. He needed to hurry before the water died. Who knew how much she'd been using?

Daegen pulled on the cord and frowned. Nothing but a few drops.

Shit! So much for having a freaking cold shower to douse the flames Milena had created. He'd have to take a fast bath in the nearby creek.

Oh man, why in hell was Milena *here*?

· · ✿ · ·

MILENA TREMBLED AS she stared down at the pile of letters fanned out across the kitchen table. Daegen must have brought them in. One envelope in particular had caught her eye.

It came from the penitentiary. Her prison.

She did not want these men to learn the truth of her past. But surely, they knew already? Or maybe they didn't? Maybe this letter would tell them all about her and then they would surely send her back to prison.

Milena stared at the envelope and tried to still her pounding heart.

She should take it and hide it. But it was addressed to Mitch. The man already didn't like her and if he found out she had stolen his mail, he would have what he needed to send her back to prison. Stealing mail was an offense, wasn't it?

Milena swallowed.

A trip back to the pen might be sealed in that envelope. She glared at the enemy.

Take it! Take it! Hide it! Then get rid of it!

Milena's breath grew shallow as her nervousness soared.

Do it! Just grab it!

She reached out and cringed with fear as the screen door suddenly squeaked open and Daegen walked in. She settled her arms to her sides.

Thankfully she'd had the foresight to get dressed before inspecting the mail, because Daegen was practically naked and the last thing she wanted was for both of them to be semi-nude. It just wouldn't be...professional.

He wore that towel way too low around his hips and nothing else. His hair was wet and scraggly, and her breath caught at the luscious muscles rippling across his chest. Lots of muscles. Lots of hard flesh.

He cleared his throat, breaking her from her thoughts. Her gaze flew to his face and her tummy hollowed out as she spied the scowl burrowed between his eyebrows.

Oh, he was pissed.

"I ran out of water," he said tersely.

Oh dear.

"I am so sorry," Milena whispered.

Guilt wrapped around her. She had been selfish and hogged the water. He must have noticed her guilty look and to her surprise, his voice softened, and his scowl vanished.

"Not your fault. The guys should have warned you."

She wanted to tell him that she had been warned and to explain how luxurious the water had felt splashing over her body and that she hadn't been able to resist but her breath caught at how low that towel hugged his hips. Unexpected fever heat beat her into submission, and she watched him stroll over to a dresser and open the top drawer.

Plenty of sinewy muscles rippled across his back and along his shoulders as he pulled out a pair of black underwear, black jeans and a brown top. When he grabbed the knot on his towel, he hesitated and looked over at her.

Heat seared into her cheeks for him catching her watching him.

Goodness!

She quickly turned around to give him privacy.

"Gotta grab the ATV and head back over to the dock for supplies. Want to help? Do you know how to operate one of those machines?"

"Never been on one before," Milena replied as she stared out the nearest window, still not believing she had somehow been dropped into a fairyland of luscious green trees, a serene meadow and three sexy men.

"You're about to get a crash course on how those machines work. We'll take two of them with trailers. One trip. Follow me."

He'd already fully dressed himself, and he stopped at the front door where he slid his socked feet into a pair of worn looking work boots.

My, he dressed fast!

Milena followed him out the door. Because her hair was still damp, it made it seem like the air was cold. She shivered against the early morning wind and wished for a jacket. She didn't dare ask Daegen if he had extra one lying around.

No. She would wait until her first paycheck and then go and buy one.

But where? An inner voice whispered. *The store down the path?*

She laughed to herself.

Lack of modern conveniences might take some time getting used to.

They walked a few minutes in silence and Milena wondered where he kept those vehicles he had mentioned. All she could see was the meadow, the cabin behind them and the clump of trees that concealed the shower and the outhouse and the forest beyond.

He led her toward the edge of the meadow where an abundance of green ferns lashed the tree line. The closer they drew to the forest, the more she was able to make out a silhouette of a building behind the towering pine trees.

"This is where we keep our vehicles," Daegen said.

Moments later, they stopped in front of a very large building made out of logs. It consisted of a green shingled steep roof, three log walls and no doors. There was an exceptionally long overhang which probably kept out most of the elements. The floor was dirt.

There were many machines housed inside. Several atv's, a bright red tractor, three snow mobiles, trailers with skis, trailers with wheels, riding snow blowers, two large green riding lawn mowers, and other vehicles and machinery.

Daegen stopped in front of the three black all-terrain vehicles. Their wheels were dirt encased and helmets had been perched on each seat.

"Don't look so scared. I'll give you a crash course and you'll be running around the place like it's second nature to you"

"I wish I had your confidence," Milena said as uneasiness almost overwhelmed her.

She had never been on any type of machine like these things in this shed.

As Daegen began giving her instructions and then showing her what most of the buttons were for, confusion wracked her, and she wanted to run away.

Thankfully he had patience and went over the instructions several times, outlining that the key was jammed into this part and that button was the ignition and the weird grips on the handlebars were the brakes, and this other thing here was for different speeds. When she thought she was understanding things, he showed her again. And again.

What? Did he think she was a doofus or something?

Finally, irritation snapped through her.

"Okay! Okay! I think I got it," she complained.

He stopped talking and gently rubbed his scruffy beard and his eyes twinkled cheerfully, making her tummy feel as if she were on a rollercoaster.

Wow, he sure looked cute.

"Alright. your turn. Let's see if you can get this baby started and moving," he said softly.

There was no anger in his voice because of her outburst. Just patience.

Oh geez. She hoped she didn't screw up. She'd look like an idiot after her outburst.

Anticipation and defiance replaced her uneasiness. She strapped on her safety helmet like he'd instructed and straddled the machine.

She held her breath and within seconds she had the all-terrain vehicle rumbling and then she was angling it out of the shed.

Daegen jogged beside her as she followed the rugged trail he had indicated. A trail she hadn't even known existed until now.

"Okay, I want you to keep it going slow. Up ahead you'll see a turnaround spot. Come on back to the shed and we'll hook up the trailers."

Milena nodded and Daegen disappeared behind her. Ahead of her loomed the forest and beside her monarch butterflies fluttered amongst the tall blades of grass and dragonflies zipped back and forth in a frenzied dance. Cool wind whipped against her making her shiver, but she didn't care. Being outside in fresh air and sunshine was so freeing she swore she was on a high.

Just like the old days when you dabbled in drugs with Dwayne, an inner voice whispered.

No, not like that time in her life. This high was so much better and healthier. It was sweeter and best of all, no Dwayne.

• • ⚓ • •

DAEGEN STOOD IN FRONT of the shed, his hands on his hips as he watched Milena slow and then turn the vehicle nice and easy just like a pro.

Man, he just could not believe she was here. He'd never expected to see her again. He had forced her out of his mind during the days, but at night, while he slept, she was there in his sexual fantasies. The mystery woman from prison.

Tenseness ripped through him as she roared to a stop.

The sexy way she straddled the seat of that machine with her strong, powerful looking thighs made his heart pump fast as he envisioned those legs wrapped around his waist as he fiercely plunged his cock into her.

"Piece of cake!" she shouted above the roar of the engine.

Then she threw him a thumbs up sign. Daegen had already hitched a trailer to his machine, and as she waited, he quickly hooked up one onto the back of her vehicle.

He noticed she was watching his every move and he smiled.

Curious one, wasn't she? That was a good sign. It meant she was interested in learning.

Then his smile turned upside down as a thought bit into him. But would they be able to keep her?

. . ⁓ . .

THE RIDE TO THE LAKE along the rutted trail was both hard on her ass due to the bumps and dips, and pleasant because of the scenery. White and purple flowers, which she remembered seeing in magazines, were trilliums. They grew in abundance, covering the nearby forest floor. Pine trees towered so high she swore they could touch the sky and the air smelled fresh and clean with brief bursts of gasoline scents from Daegen's atv in front of her, but that was okay, because she was free!

Cool wind caressed her face and kissed her lips, and the sensations made her happy.

Deliriously happy.

Up ahead, past Daegen, she suddenly caught glimpses of the bright blue lake and her excitement deflated. She slowed the vehicle and by the time she burst out of the dark forest into the open, her heart was racing.

Darn.

Why did there have to be a lake involved in all this beauty? She knew her fear of lakes, rivers and almost all things water was irrational, but she just couldn't stop these feelings of anxiety.

In prison, she'd managed perfectly with her fear, but now being on the outside, her past fears were resurfacing.

Daegen had already hopped off his vehicle and was strolling casually up the rickety dock toward several large cardboard boxes piled at the end.

In the daylight, the lake didn't look as daunting as it had last night. But still, there was a darkness about it and feelings of impending doom overwhelmed her. She just needed to get away from here.

"Hey, you, ok?" Daegen's question snapped through Milena as he placed a couple of boxes into her trailer.

Shit! She needed to get out of here and away from the water.

"I, I need to," she stopped.

She should tell him about her crazy fear. But she couldn't let him know she had issues. They'd send her back to prison!

"I need to go to the bathroom," she lied.

"Okay sure, take what I've put into your trailer to the first barn. Do you know where it is?"

She shook her head jerkily.

The tension crept up a notch and impatience raged. She kept staring at the lake expecting something bad to happen. What? She had no idea.

"Up on a hill, end of the meadow where the cabin is. Just drive to the shelter and turn left along the tree line and follow the trail. It'll take you to a fence with a gate. Make sure you lock it after you go through and then straight ahead. Watch for the horses."

Please, let me go. Please!

"I'll find it," she said tightly.

"Good. Just put the boxes inside the barn door, then we can meet back here. Are you sure you're okay?" he said as he eyed her with concern.

How in the world did he notice she was uptight?

Oh, who cared. she couldn't get away fast enough. She switched on the ignition and took off without looking back.

The further away she got from the lake, the better she felt.

Man, that reaction was so freaking unwanted, and she sure was not in a hurry to repeat it.

. . ⚜ . .

OKAY, THAT WAS WEIRD. Daegen thought as he watched Milena disappear into the forest. She was driving as if the hounds of hell were nipping at her heels. It was a good thing there wasn't much traffic out in these parts.

Huh, when he'd returned with the boxes she'd been all pale and shaky looking. Maybe the atv ride had made her sick? He sure hoped not. The last thing they needed was a helper who got travel sick on moving vehicles. Not that she was staying here for long.

Jenna must have made some sort of mistake sending them a woman, especially after Mitch had been adamant not to do to them what she had done to Brady.

Daegen frowned as his stomach hollowed out in a weird kind of sadness. Jenna wouldn't have sent Milena here on purpose. No way.

He'd met Jenna several times since meeting Paul and Mitch and if she'd promised Mitch that she would not do to Snowy Creek Ranch what she'd done to Moose Ranch, then he believed her.

Shit, he had a feeling Milena's days were truly numbered here.

• • ❧ • •

PAUL WAS JUST LEADING the near-to-bursting pregnant mare back into her stall, when he thought he heard the far-off rumble of an all-terrain vehicle.

He frowned. Had Mitch run into some sort of trouble at their other barn, and he was already returning?

Their morning routine was pretty involved and lengthy. Getting the many horses out into the pastures, and then cleaning out each stall, exercising the horses, grooming them and many other things, which made him wonder why Mitch was returning so soon.

He smiled at Brownie Belle as she grunted in protest after he closed her stall door behind her. She was a bit ticked off being cooped up in here, but because of her age, her bad heart and her imminent pregnancy, he wanted to keep her as quiet as possible.

As he hurried toward the barn door, he hoped Mitch hadn't been able to contact Jenna. He was pretty pissed at his sister in betraying them, but Paul knew Mitch would mellow out about it if Milena was allowed to stay.

He strolled out of the darkness of the barn and into the bright sunshine which blinded him. From the corner of his right eye, he detected movement and then without warning, a flash of searing pain cracked across his forehead and before Paul knew what was happening, he was flat on his back. As he looked up at the blue sky, it was spinning!

What the hell? Before he could orient himself as to what might have just happened, everything went black.

. . ◦⊱⊰◦ . .

WHERE IS THAT BARN? Milena pondered as she slowly rolled the machine along the grassy trail that meandered along the forest edge. Suddenly the towering trees to her right side vanished, replaced by a lush green rolling meadow that stretched out for what seemed for miles.

Had she gone the wrong way or something?

Oh! There up ahead was the fence. She sped up and within moments she was on the other side of the gate, making sure to close it. Toward her left she spied several horses leisurely grazing. They looked healthy and their coats gleamed beneath the sunshine. There were white horses, brown horses and black horses.

She blew out a sigh of relief when she also spied a hill and perched proudly on top of that hill was a large grey planked barn. There was a black opening near the top of the barn where she spied rolls of hay.

Okay! Found it!

Overgrown dead foliage clung to the sides and most of the front wall of the old structure. At first, she thought maybe it was abandoned, but then she spied an atv parked outside.

This must be the first barn! She let out a happy whoop, shifted into a faster gear and headed for the barn.

Her happiness turned into confusion as she drove closer. Something was lying on the ground right in front of the open door. Her breath hitched with fear.

Was it a bear?

She almost turned around but realized the large bump wasn't black. It was human!

Fear turned to concern as she made out the figure of a man struggling to sit up.

Oh my God! It was Paul! What was he doing on the ground? Had he had some sort of an accident?

She couldn't get off the machine fast enough. By the time she reached him he was sitting cross-legged and holding his forehead with his hands.

Blood trickled down his left cheek.

"What happened? Are you alright?" She asked as she hunkered over him.

"Careful. Someone's around here. They clobbered me," Paul mumbled.

Milena tensed and surveyed their surroundings.

She thought she heard a crack from a branch breaking somewhere in the nearby forest, but she saw nothing except a couple of blue jays flying out of the woods.

She assessed the steep hillside and the meadow. The horses were grazing calmly. She looked upward at the old barn thinking maybe a board had fallen and hit him, but nothing looked amiss.

Nothing moved. Everything was quiet.

On the ground near Paul lay a long piece of two by four. Had that been the weapon used on him?

"Let me take a look," she said and gently pried his trembling hands off his forehead.

She grimaced at the large angry-red goose egg smack in the middle of his forehead. Blood oozed from a gash there.

"Did you pass out?"

"Yeah, not sure for how long," Paul said.

His voice was laced with pain, and he kept grimacing.

"You've got a two-inch long cut. Looks deep. Stitches would be good."

Oh man, that injury looked bad, but she had tended worse in prison. It was a good thing she had a strong stomach when it came to blood.

"Is there a first aid kit around? Clean towels to put pressure on the wound?"

"Yeah, clean towels would be back at the cabin. Did laundry the other day but haven't brought out any towels here. But the kit is just inside the office door. First room to your left. Be careful. I don't know why someone did this. He might be watching us. Might do something worse.

Might be in the barn. We should get out of here. Get my gun. I shouldn't have left it back at the cabin."

Paul made an attempt to stand, but Milena placed a hand on his shoulder, indicating he stay put. Reluctantly he digressed.

She bet he had a bitch of a headache and probably some dizziness too. She needed to move fast to get into the first aid kit and see what was available.

Caution came naturally to her. While inside the prison system, she'd learned to be alert and to be prepared for an attack from fellow inmates at any time. What was happening here and now didn't freak her out. Not much, anyway.

However, she was concerned about Paul and quite troubled as to why someone would attack him.

She moved quickly and immediately spied a pitchfork leaning up against a wall. She grabbed it and slipped inside the dark cool interior of the barn.

Once inside, she melted against the wall, holding the fork outward in case someone were to attack. She waited until her eyes adjusted to the semi darkness and then surveyed the interior.

The barn creaked as wind breathed against the grey planked walls and there were all kinds of scents in here. Pine, hay and leather were the most prominent.

She didn't see anyone, so she moved fast toward the first door to her left. It was open, and using caution, she peered inside. There was a large wood desk laden with papers, a couple of filing cabinets, several metal shelves and empty cages against a far wall.

Right inside the doorway, on a shelf, was a large shoe-boxed size red plastic box with the words FIRST AID. She grabbed it and almost dropped it due to its heaviness.

With a tight hold on the pitchfork and kit, she slid out of the office and found Paul in the barn doorway wavering on his feet.

"Let's get over to the atv, before you fall," she instructed.

When he didn't move, she reluctantly dropped the weapon and grabbed his upper arm.

Strong muscles flexed beneath her fingers, and she went breathless and hot as she steered him to the machine ten feet away. She positioned him right beside the atv seat and helped him to sit.

"We should get out of here. Get you to safety. I really don't know what we're dealing with," Paul said between clenched teeth.

He was keeping his eyes closed. Yeah, he was dizzy.

"Let's get you fixed up first. You're bleeding like a stuck pig. Stitches are in order."

He surprised her when he chuckled. She liked his laugh. It made some nice things happen in the pit of her lower belly.

"You know how to stitch?" he asked.

"You sound surprised?" She popped open the first aid kit and let out a slow whistle.

"Impressive," she whispered.

There was an arrangement of everything she would need. Latex gloves, gauze, sterilized threads and needles in packages, antiseptic, small scissors, antibiotics and so much more.

Throwing quick glances around to make sure they were alone; she spied an old fashioned hand water pump nearby.

"Does that pump work? Is the water drinkable?" she asked.

"Yeah. Cup is there. I used it this morning."

"Hold on while I get you some water. Pain killers here in the kit are not expired."

A moment later she was pumping the handle, trying to figure out how in the world she knew how to use it when she'd never seen a real one before.

She grinned. Probably from all the western movies she'd watched over the years in prison.

She gasped as ice-cold water splashed out of the spout onto her hand. She filled the tin cup and brought it back to Paul. She popped two painkillers out into the palm of her hand.

"Open your mouth," she instructed.

He did as she asked, and she placed one pill on his tongue. She allowed him to sip some water and watched him swallow. Then she gave him the second pill and waited until he drank all the water.

"To what do I deserve such babying treatment?" he grumbled.

But Milena detected the amusement lacing his voice.

She ignored the question. There was work to do.

"Did they hit you somewhere else?" she prodded.

"No, nothing else hurts. Just my head."

"Are you allergic to latex?" she asked.

"No."

"Good. This is going to hurt. A lot."

"Kind of figured," he said and followed up with a grimace.

She placed the sealed items she would need on a small tray that was inside the kit and then slipped on the latex gloves. Then she opened all the packages and laid out her paraphernalia.

She surveyed the surroundings again. Nothing unusual.

If they'd had a towel, she could have delayed the suturing until the cabin, but he would keep bleeding if the wound wasn't stitched.

"Okay, here goes."

He inhaled sharply as she started cleaning the injury with the sterile wipes, making sure to remove any traces of dirt.

"Tell me about this place," she instructed, trying to give him something else to think about while she hurt him.

"The water pump came with the barn. There is a cabin nearby, but it's not the greatest shape. Wild strawberries, raspberries and blueberry bushes have taken over all around there. Lots of fruit. We had a feast last year eating straight off the bushes and this year we're hoping to make pies. Lots of pies."

"I hope you don't think just cause I'm a woman, I know how to cook?" she queried.

She wasn't into cooking or baking.

He grinned.

"The thought did cross my mind. Do you?" He opened and then squinted his eyes as peered up at her.

Goodness he had such intense eyes.

A tinge of heat flared through her cheeks at that thought.

She swallowed at her suddenly dry throat.

"Not much. Maybe enough to keep you alive."

He chuckled and grimaced at the same time as she appeared to hit a particularly sore spot.

"Sorry," she whispered.

But she continued her cleansing attack on his wound.

"I realize an infection out here in the middle of nowhere should be avoided at all costs. I would assume that is why you have this awesome first aid kit which seemingly contains everything a doctor or nurse might need."

"That's cause I'm a veterinarian. I know what we need and yes you are right about infection prevention out here."

She smiled at his praise. She hoped she sounded smart enough for them to keep her and it was kind of cool that there was a veterinarian out here in the middle of nowhere.

"Okay finished cleaning. Now for the stitching," she said as she quickly ripped open a sterile package containing needle and thread.

"Do you know how to stitch? I mean aside from your sewing courses," he asked. She didn't miss the worry frown emanating around his injury.

"I've had non-professional experience in prison. Taken first aid courses too. Now hold real still," she warned.

"There's numbing gel in there somewhere," he said.

"Oh? That would be good." She'd never heard of numbing gel. She rummaged around and found a few packets in a zip lock bag. Not expired.

"How many can I use?" she asked.

"All of them might put a dent into the pain, but just one should suffice. I'm tough. Just give me a branch and I can bite down, like they do in the western movies.""

Milena laughed. Yes, she certainly liked his sense of humor.

A moment later she'd read the instructions and placed the gel over the area that would need to be stitched. While they waited for a couple of minutes, she wiped away the blood with more gauze and kept looking around, expecting trouble.

"You smell nice," he suddenly said.

His compliment stunned her.

"I do? Thank you. It's probably Kayley's lemon citronella bug spray. She gave me some last night when we got here. I sprayed some on this morning to keep the mosquitoes away."

Paul smiled.

"Bug spray, who would have thought that I liked the smell of bug spray."

"Okay, keep your head still, tough guy. Here goes," she warned.

He moaned as she slid the curved needle into his flesh.

She was grateful that he didn't so much as flinch.

"How bad is the damage?" he asked in a guttural pain-filled voice.

"It'll leave a sexy scar."

"Do you find scars sexy?" he asked.

She wasn't sure if it was a flirty question or if he was inquiring if women in general found scars sexy.

She laughed. He was an interesting man. He'd just had his head bashed and he was wondering about a scar.

"What's not to like about them. Shows you've experienced an adventure."

Paul laughed and then gasped as she continued with her stitching.

"An adventure. Geez, woman. The women I have known would have panicked at the sight of blood and called 911 for help."

"I'm not like most women. Besides no such thing as 911 out here," Milena stated.

Hmm, he spoke of women in the past tense. Did that mean there was no city girl or country girl in his life?

Milena's heart melted at that thought. Was Paul a bachelor?

For a second, she stared at him. He was a good-looking man. Well-built and he seemed kind. Any woman would be lucky to catch him. She shook her head and focused on the task.

She must have hit another sensitive spot for he hissed and sucked in a sharp breath.

"Shit, sorry," she muttered.

"She knows how to stitch and she's not afraid to swear. A woman after my own heart. Make sure you keep an eye out. I don't want you getting hurt."

"I'm tough and he cares. A man after my own heart," she joked.

He smiled and a really cool fluttering of butterflies in her tummy kind of feeling dipped through her lower belly. She swallowed against the heat that sifted through her.

She really liked his smile. It was a tad crooked with teasing lines that tugged at the sides of his seductive shaped lips.

Oh boy. She seriously needed to keep her mind on the task at hand. She forced herself to focus and within minutes, the wound was stitched.

"Is there any way I can contact Mitch or Daegen now that he is back, via cell phone?" Milena asked as she tore open another sterilized packet containing gauze.

"We're in a dead zone because of the cliffs nearby. You'd have to go up to the top of the surrounding hills and that would be too treacherous if you don't know the way up. I think I can survive. So Daegen came back a day early."

"Yes," she replied. She didn't elaborate about her experience in the shower or by the lake.

"Talk about good timing."

"Ok, brace yourself. I'm taping on the gauze," Milena said.

She grit her teeth as he groaned. But she had the patch on in no time flat.

"It actually looks pretty good. Probably won't even leave that sexy scar," she teased.

"Too bad. I was looking forward to growing my bangs longer to hide it."

"I've always liked long hair on a guy," Milena blurted. Horror at what she had just said had her quickly putting the unopened supplies into the kit. The rest of the items she'd used, she placed into a small plastic receptacle which had the words medical waste written on it.

She snapped the first aid kit closed and tossed it and the medical waste receptacle into the trailer with the supplies she was supposed to unload.

She decided not to leave the items behind until they knew what they were dealing with.

"Ok, let's get you back to the cabin so you can rest."

"I'm not sure that's such a good idea at the moment," Paul muttered.

"Why not?"

He grimaced, then reluctantly spoke.

"The slightest movement makes me sick to my stomach."

Oh crap. He must have a more serious head wound than she'd anticipated.

"Well, we can't stay here. Your gun is at the cabin, so we need to get it. Unless Mitch is around? Does he have a gun? Is he far?"

Concern for Mitch rushed through her. Was he in danger too?

"He has a rifle with him, but he could be anywhere. Usually, he exercises the horses on the trails every morning. I hate saying it, but I agree, best bet is the cabin."

"Okay, you'll just have to hold on to me tight and I'll drive slow. If you need to be sick, give me a heads up and I'll stop."

"You're a pretty tough nurse," he said.

"Keep your eyes closed. I'm going to help you to straddle the seat, okay?"

He grunted affirmation.

She reached down and grabbed his calf, noting the strong muscles flex beneath her fingertips as she moved his leg up and then over the seat.

A moment later, she had him settled.

"So how many people have you stitched up?"

"A few. In prison."

It felt nauseating to use that harsh word prison in this pristine place. She didn't elaborate why she'd cared for inmates. Sometimes they got into fights with each other, and they refused to go to the infirmary and there were times a guard got rough with them and they didn't want to report it. She forced thoughts of prison away and stepped to the back of the trailer where she had tossed the helmet after she'd arrived. She retrieved it and suddenly she had the creepy feeling they were being watched.

She gazed around studying her surroundings once again.

A breeze moved the branches of a clump of close by spruce trees. A couple of red squirrels scampered down the nearby slope and a blue dragonfly whizzed past.

Beyond the meadow, she watched for any movement. Despite the strong sunshine, the trees of the forest looked dark and spooky.

She stifled a shiver.

"Is everything okay?" Paul asked.

"Just checking around. Are the horses okay here? Do I need to do anything before we leave?"

"Daegen can come out. He knows the drill."

"Oh, okay." Good. Thank goodness for Daegen.

"What about Mitch? What if something happens to him too?" Concern for the man enveloped her. Irritation quickly followed. She shouldn't be overly worried for Mitch. He was a big boy. But still...

"Daegen can find him and tell him."

Relief whispered through her. She nodded and then gazed at the helmet and opted not to let Paul wear it due to his head injury.

She straddled the seat in front of him and once pulled on her safety helmet.

"Hold around my waist," she instructed.

She inhaled as he slid his arms around her waist. His hot body heat seeped through her belly where he held her, and she bit back a moan as she envisioned Paul moving his hands upward and cupping her breasts or better yet dipping one of his hands beneath her pants and panties to touch and massage her clit.

Oh dear.

Inappropriate thoughts during an extremely worrisome ordeal was not normal. She should have her head examined for reacting so physically to this man. But she was reacting.

This was not good. But it sure did feel good.

Milena swallowed, twisted the key in the ignition and a moment later she was driving slowly down the trail, back toward the cabin.

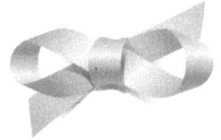

Chapter Four

A nasty headache had tightened like a steel band around Paul's head and nausea clutched at his stomach. He struggled to bite back vomit. Being sick in front of a woman was not his thing. It would turn her off. He was sure of it.

He. Could. Not. Puke.

Difficult as it was, he forced his thoughts to where he'd placed his hands. Right over her warm belly.

If he raised his hands, he could easily cup her breasts. He sensed her breasts would fit perfectly into his hands. Soft yet firm mounds.

If he lowered his hands, he could slip them beneath her pants. His fingers would find her clitoris and he'd rub her tenderly until she moaned and bucked and then he'd sink a couple of his fingers into her vagina. He wondered how tight she would be.

At those thoughts, his cock jerked against his pants, and he inhaled sharply at his arousal.

Oh man. The last thing he wanted was for her to feel his hard-on. He tried to wiggle backward a bit, but he inadvertently rubbed against her behind.

Holy! He hoped she didn't feel his erection!

He bit back at the hammering headache as he moved some more and finally managed to put a little space between their bodies.

He inhaled several deep breaths in an effort to calm the nausea and he could smell her.

She smelled nice and clean. He recognized the scent of the soap. She must have taken a shower. And he really liked that lemony citronella bug spray she said that Kayley had given her. He wouldn't mind spraying it *all* over her body and massaging the scented liquid over her soft curvy flesh.

Oh, Paul, don't go there.

Too late. He could imagine himself rubbing her curves, listening to her sultry moans as he massaged her soft breasts.

The exquisite vision was smashed to smithereens as she hit a bump on the trail and pain snapped through his head. Instinctively he groaned.

"Sorry! We're almost there!" she shouted.

A question suddenly jumped into his mind. It was something he should have noticed right away but because of his blurred vision and dizziness and pain, it hadn't registered.

She was driving the all-terrain machine. Did she know how?

"What happened?" came a man's shout from about twenty feet ahead.

Daegen. Thank you, God.

"Someone jumped him," Milena said the instant she shut off the engine.

"Seriously? Who? Why?" Daegen asked.

He was beside Paul now and had a hand across his shoulders holding him steady.

"Okay let go of Milena. We'll help you off."

He hadn't even realized he'd been holding onto her for dear life. When he uncurled his arms from her belly, he immediately felt tipsy.

Woah, he had really taken a bad hit.

"Who the hell is going around clobbering you?" Daegen asked as he and Milena helped Paul off the machine.

He moved gingerly so as not to start up the dizziness and he was grateful to both of them for holding onto him real tight as they ascended the stairs and then into the cabin.

"Don't have a clue. I was blinded by the sunlight and then someone hit me," Paul confessed.

"Where's Mitch? Did you warn him?" Daegen asked.

Paul recognized the worry in his voice.

"He's at the other barn. Probably on the trails around this time."

"Should I go look for him?" he heard Milena ask.

"No. We stay put until we know what we're dealing with," Daegen replied.

Frustration ravaged Paul.

"Brownie Belle is about to foal and the gyrfalcon needs to be fed. The horses in the meadows? They need to be taken inside for the night.

"They'll be fine for now. We've got plenty of time. Let's get you settled first. I will check on everything later."

Paul knew in the brisk tone in Daegen's voice, there would be no arguing with him.

And at the moment, he wasn't in the mood for arguing either. He just wanted to lie down to get pressure off this killer headache.

"It's going to be dark soon," Milena whispered as she stood on the porch and gazed out over the lush meadow that stretched far and wide in front of her.

Mitch still hadn't returned and fear for his safety was growing inside her by the minute.

"Sometimes he comes in later than this," Daegen explained.

But she heard the worry in Daegen's voice. Saw the frown creasing his forehead as he also kept his gaze glued to the meadow where he said Mitch would be coming from.

Daegen had gone out late this afternoon to bring over the supplies to the barn, leaving her alone with Paul, a rifle and a knife. Thankfully Paul was feeling better and had made her feel safe when he'd settled on the front porch with the rifle and had shown her how to use it.

She'd learned quickly and felt more at ease knowing she would be able to shoot one if necessary.

As per Paul's instructions, she could only allow him brief episodes of sleep, waking him every so often to make sure he was okay. They'd waited for Daegen to return and when he did, he'd come back without Mitch telling them he hadn't been able to find him, but he'd left notes at both barns for him. He'd figured Mitch must have gone to make a phone call or maybe was riding the trails to clear something.

Paul had been glad to learn that a pregnant horse seemed to be doing okay but saddened to learn the cage to the injured gyrfalcon he'd been tending had been open and the bird was gone. He insisted he'd closed the cage door properly the last time he'd been with the bird.

"I'm really worried for Mitch," Milena suddenly blurted.

She hadn't meant to voice her apprehension for Mitch's safety, but it had just come out. She didn't know why she was concerned. She barely knew him. She shouldn't be feeling this way. Truly she shouldn't. She shouldn't be feeling attracted to Paul, or to Daegen either. This was all weird.

To her surprise, Daegen curled an arm around her waist and held her tight to his side.

Feelings of safety and protection poured through her. The raw, unused emotions were so beautiful that tears stung her eyes.

She'd been in prison, living on the edge, always fearing for her safety. She'd refused to join any of the girl gangs, and she'd had no flesh-to-flesh contact other than innocent hugs to her trusted inmate friends. She wished she could hug Daegen right now. But it would be so inappropriate.

He was her boss, and he was simply consoling her. She dare not lean against him, no matter how much she wanted to for fear he would let go of her. So, she remained beside him standing stiff and simply enjoyed this rare contact from a man.

The mouthwatering scent of canned pork simmering in a couple of frying pans on the propane stove inside the cabin gave Milena a sense of civilization.

Earlier, while she'd been wringing her hands with nervousness about Mitch, Daegen had been busy bringing out several cans of food from a nearby pantry closet, then he'd taken the atv over to the cave for some potatoes and steak stored in there. Then he'd set her to peeling potatoes while he'd taken on the rest of the cooking duties, which she was grateful for, because she wasn't much for cooking.

"Is Mitch back yet?" Paul called from inside.

"The pest is awake," Daegen muttered.

"I heard that," Paul shouted.

Daegen looked down at her and winked. He appeared happy and he made her feel happy too despite her worrying for Mitch.

"Pest?" Milena asked, feeling confused.

"My off and on-again nickname for him. Paul's a veterinarian. He's always bringing home sick animals and expecting me and Mitch to help babysit them. He can become quite the pest in order to get his way. A million bucks says that Mitch will come home while we're eating. He is never one to pass up a ready-made meal. Come on, let's go inside and eat."

She was more than ready for another meal. For lunch they'd had sandwiches made from canned ham and some homemade vegetable soup. Now she was famished again. In prison she hadn't cared much for the food, but out here surrounded by fresh air and freedom, she was hungry.

Guilt pummeled her through the entire meal. The food was good, and she ate heartily, and she excused herself several times to grab a glass of water from the bucket Daegen had left on the counter so she could peek out the window for any signs of Mitch.

Something must had happened to him, or he would be back by now. Thankfully she only had one man to worry about because Paul was feeling better, and he'd joined them at the table for supper. He admitted his head still hurt like a bitch, in his words, but his vision had cleared, and the nausea was gone.

"Now that you're awake, I'll take a machine out and start a search for him," Daegen said as he finished.

"Yeah, you're clearing out, so you don't have to do the dishes," Paul said. But she could clearly see Paul was also concerned.

"Damn right," Daegen chuckled.

Daegen had strolled halfway to the door, when he suddenly stopped

"He's back. You can't get out of dish duty," Paul laughed.

She hadn't heard a thing, but just then she could hear an engine. It sounded far away.

"How do you know it's him?"

"When you're out here long enough you learn to tell the difference between sounds. It's Mitch." Paul reassured.

"Thank God," Milena whispered.

She couldn't get to the door quick enough and joined Daegen as he stepped out onto the veranda into the darkness.

The air was cool, and damp and a white mist curled over the meadow, but she could easily see two beams of bright yellow light slicing through the mist as someone on an all-terrain vehicle raced toward the cabin. As the machine neared, she recognized Mitch's form and without waiting she ran down the steps and waved to him as he drove into the yard.

He waved back and she was so glad to see that he appeared to be okay.

A moment later he'd shut off the engine and then removed his helmet. His dark brown eyes sizzled with some sort of agitated excitement, and the severe frown on his face had her stepping back.

Instantly she knew something was wrong.

"Had some trouble," Mitch said as he got off the vehicle and set his helmet upon the seat. Before he continued, he nodded to Paul, who had remained on the porch, leaning against the railing. The white patch on his forehead was clearly illuminated in the darkness. Milena noted that concern for his friend pushed away Mitch's frown.

"What the hell happened to you?" he asked Paul.

"Had trouble here too," Daegen interjected as he crowded in around Mitch, visually inspecting him for any injuries.

Mitch's entire body tensed. It was as if he now appeared on full alert.

"What kind of trouble?"

"You didn't read the notes I left?" Daegen asked.

"No, I saw that the horses were out of the meadows and figured Paul took care of them. Didn't go near the barns."

"Where were you? We got worried. I took a look out your way and couldn't find you," Daegen asked.

"Got cornered by a freaking bear. Didn't have my gun nearby. Thought my life was over. I played dead. Let's just say I never want to feel the wet nose of a bear sniffing my face again."

Horror raced through Milena. A bear had gotten *that* close to Mitch? And he'd lived to tell about it? Oh my God! Talk about lucky!

"You're shitting us?" Paul laughed.

"It was wounded," Mitch replied solemnly.

"What happened to it?" Daegen asked.

"Someone shot it. Had it not been injured; I might not be here. It was bleeding all over me as it sniffed me, but then it just walked away. I changed into my spare clothes that I carry in my pack. Had to bury the bloody clothing and washed myself in the creek before I followed its blood trail. He went pretty far before he dropped. I could tell he was beyond help, so I put him down."

Milena gasped.

"The poor thing," she whispered. She was afraid of bears, but she didn't want one to get hurt.

Mitch shrugged at her reaction.

"It would have died eventually. He was suffering big time."

Mitch nodded to Paul.

"He was shot, like your gyrfalcon. Bullet was lodged in his lung after going through his other lung. I was surprised it had so much strength to go as far as he did."

Paul cursed violently beneath his breath.

"Someone's shooting animals way out here?" Milena couldn't believe it.

"Maybe someone just target practicing? There are a lot of idiots around who shoot animals just for fun. But that doesn't excuse what happened to Paul," Daegen said.

"What happened? Someone shoot you too?" Mitch growled.

"Attacked him at the hill barn," Daegen said.

Mitch frowned.

"A good thing Milena showed up when she did, too. I think she might have scared them away before they could finish me off. Then she played nurse. Stitched me up really good. She's an asset already. She took a lot of first aid courses in prison," Paul said from the porch as he pointed to the white patch on his forehead.

Mitch turned to look at Milena. There was a slight nod to his head as if to say he appreciated what she had done. Maybe there was even a glimpse of respect in his gaze? The idea that Mitch might think she'd been of some help, warmed her.

"We're going to have to report all of this," Daegen said.

"Agreed," Mitch replied.

Daegen nodded to the trailer hitched to Mitch's vehicle. A tarp covered something large.

Milena swallowed. Was that black fur she saw peeking out one side of the covering?

"Did you skin the bear? Those hides are warm, especially in winter," Daegen asked as he reached for the tarp.

Milena turned away. She did not want to see a deceased bear.

"Come on, let's go inside," Paul called out to her.

She nodded to him, grateful that she had an excuse to leave. She tried to slip by the two men, but realized they'd moved directly in front of her, blocking her way of escape. It would be rude to just push on past, wouldn't it?

"Yes, I did. It's why I'm late. I cut him up too. Still had a bunch of wrapping paper in my trailer from that moose we got last year. Figured we could smoke him in the smokehouse over the next few days. The bear steaks will come in handy," she heard Mitch say.

Bear steaks?

Daegen passed by her and reached into the trailer. She heard the rustle of the tarp being moved.

Dear Lord. She started toward Paul.

"Milena can stay and help me with the meat. You go on in and eat, Mitch," Daegen said.

Milena froze.

Oh great. The last thing she wanted was to be around a freshly killed animal, especially a bear. But she supposed if she wanted to give the men a good impression of her, she would have to hide her revulsion and just get used to this primitive way of life.

Beats being in prison, an inner voice chimed.

"Hop on, Milena," Daegen called out.

Did she detect humor in Daegen's voice? Maybe they were playing with her and didn't really expect her to help him with the bear meat? She turned around and caught Mitch's weary expression. Guilt rammed through her. He was tired after today's brush with death, and she was being a wimp in trying to get out of going with Daegen.

They were serious.

Reluctantly she waved goodbye to Paul who shrugged his shoulders.

"Thanks, much appreciated," Mitch mumbled as he passed her toward the cabin.

"Come on. Hop on behind me and we'll head on over to the cave," Daegen said.

He was already wearing a helmet and straddled the seat of the machine as he held out Mitch's helmet to her.

"Don't we need a light?" It really was pretty dark now.

"The moon is our light. The atv has headlights and we have lanterns at the cave."

Oh. Okay. And a dead body in the back of the trailer. So not fun.

She was sure there was amusement tugging at the corners of his mouth as she accepted the helmet.

"Welcome to Snowy Creek Ranch, princess," he said with a chuckle.

Princess. If that nickname was meant to inflict pain, he'd succeeded. But it was better than scarecrow. She resisted the urge to punch him in the arm. That would be utterly childish.

Instead, she grabbed the helmet and strapped it on and tried like hell not to gaze at the trailer containing the corpse as she straddled the seat immediately behind Daegen. The available room he'd left for her on the seat was barely enough and his hard ass pressed against her lower belly. She tried not to inhale at this intimate pose.

"Hold on to my waist. Tight. Don't want you falling off. It's a rough ride over there," he instructed.

She had barely wrapped her arms around his waist when the machine roared to life, and he took off. He moved fast and Milena realized she was a slow driver in comparison, and she'd thought she was fast!

She flew a few inches up off her seat when he hit a bump on the trail, and she instinctively curled his arms around his waist and hugged him tight for fear of falling off as he'd hinted might happen. She enjoyed his hard tummy muscles flex beneath her hands, and she thought she heard him exhale.

But she couldn't be having an effect on him. She was just Milena, an ex-convict fresh out of prison. No man would be attracted to her.

The cool night air whipped against her body as he drove faster. She caught his man scent. Pine and outdoor clean. Strong. She suddenly felt safe, and she smiled.

Wow. She could get used to this intimate feeling of having his hard body pressed against her. She cried out as Daegen drove the vehicle down a steep incline. Dampness clung to her. There was a rattle of what she perceived to be wood. She gazed down and saw a boardwalk. Musty, earthy scents filled her nostrils and dark water glistened beneath the moon glow.

Oh no! The creek!

She scrunched her eyes closed and held Daegen tighter as fear sawed through her pushing away her momentary feelings of safety. The rattle of boards grew as he slowed. She pushed her face into his back, not wanting to feel this fear of something coming out of the water and grabbing her.

A moment later, the vehicle tilted as they ascended a sharp incline. She breathed easier as the ground grew smoother.

"Look to your left!" he shouted.

She dared to open her eyes.

Beneath the silvery moonlight, about thirty feet away in the meadow, she spied four large black silhouettes.

Her gut clenched in fear.

She noticed their long legs. They also had huge antlers that had an open palm look and she swore the antlers spread to six feet wide.

"Young male moose! Heading for the creek! They like aquatic plants, and they taste good in lasagna too!" he called out.

Oh, dear Lord! Bear steaks and moose lasagna. How pioneerish.

She held her breath, kept her gaze on the large animals as they continued to pass them. She prayed they didn't follow and attack. Thankfully the large beasts just stood there and watched them.

Finally, the moose were out of view and Milena turned to stare ahead. Her breath caught at the spooky black silhouette of towering pine trees directly in front of them.

She tensed.

Mercy! Did he not see the trees? He was heading straight for the forest!

She grimaced as she imagined them crashing into solid wood.

Suddenly Daegen slowed at the tree line and finally stopped. The lights were turned off and everything fell into darkness.

It was quiet here. It was so still she could hear herself breathing and the wind whispering through the pine boughs not even three feet away.

Whew! That was fun. Not.

Daegen was off the vehicle in no time flat and already at the trailer behind her. He was right about the moon being their light because she could now see quite clearly as he untied the tarp. She did a double take at the nicely wrapped packages in a pile instead of the corpse of a black bear that she had expected. The packages appeared similar to the one's her mother used to purchase in the local butcher shop where she would sometimes order steak, pork or lamb chops. Normal food.

There was no sign of the bear hide, but she sensed it was further back, beneath the tarp that was still covering a mound.

"Hold out your hands," he instructed. She grimaced but she did as she was told.

Milena swallowed as he began to place the cold packages filled with dead bear onto her outstretched arms.

This animal had been alive just earlier today. Alive and enjoying a leisurely stroll through the forest or meadow, maybe eating some berries or plants or whatever bears ate and then suddenly some horrid person shot him. And in his injured state he could have killed Mitch.

She would not be surprised if the same person who had shot the bear was the same person who'd attacked Paul and shot that gyrfalcon Paul had been nursing.

But why?

Man, what would have happened to Paul had she not been here? What would have happened to Mitch had the bear not been so injured? She shivered at the unpleasant scenarios of what could have happened to Mitch. It was all so surreal. And they were going to put this animal in a smokehouse so they could eat it later?

She grimaced at the idea of consuming bear and watched and waited as he placed a pile of packages into his arms. She could hear the frogs start to their chatter down by the creek. An owl hooted from nearby in the forest startling her.

"It's okay, just an owl. They don't cause you no harm. It's the man-eating bears and head stomping moose you need to steer clear of," he said with amusement quite clear in his voice.

"Ha, ha," she retorted.

In the moonlight, she noticed he winked at her and she relaxed. She needed to lighten up and get a sense of humor.

"Come on, follow me. Stay close and watch your step. Are you cold?" he asked as she followed him into the woods.

She wondered how in the world he could see in this dark forest. She was practically bumping into trees before she even saw them. Everything was pitch black.

"I'm fine," she lied. She was chilled from that ride through the damp meadow, but she dare not let him think she was a wimp.

Daegen remained quiet as he walked slowly around big tree trunks. A minute later she gasped as a wall of rock suddenly appeared right in front of them.

He'd stopped and placed his parcels onto something.

"Gas lantern should be right here," he whispered. She saw nothing but a bit of movement.

"Good, exactly where we left it." Then he was bending over, and she heard weird sounds.

Hiss. Hiss. Hiss.

Snake? Oh my gosh.

"What is that?" she asked wondering why he wasn't freaking out having a snake hissing at them.

"Pumping the lantern so it will start easily," he replied.

Then a flare of yellow light flickered as he struck a match, and the scent of sulphur blew along the wind directly into her nostrils.

Ugh. Stinky.

Suddenly their surroundings were aglow as the sack inside the lantern glass caught and then Daegen was thrusting a key into a padlock on a black windowless metal door propped into a stone wall.

"Bear proof cave. We found the cave shortly after we got here, made the door from some scrap metal we found at one of the abandoned barns on the property. Keeps all our stuff cold in the summer and frozen in the winter. I tell you there's nothing better than having ice-cold watermelon on a hell of a hot summer day."

Milena smiled. She hadn't had watermelon since before she'd gone to prison.

Daegen swung open the door. It creaked on the heavy hinges, and he held up the lantern for her to see.

Wetness glistened on the black rocky walls and frigid cold air blew from inside up against her. She shivered.

"Here, give me the packages. Hold up the lantern so I can see, and I'll be right out for the other packages."

He handed her the lantern. She held it up like he'd just done and absolutely loved the heat that wafted onto her face from it.

He took the packets from her and then went inside leaving her feeling so alone and spooked. Milena tensed as an idea struck her. What if the deranged person who'd shot the bear and attacked Paul was out here watching them?

She shivered as the owl began hooting again. Wind blew against the treetops making the branches creak. She gazed around wide-eyed and tried not to scream as she caught sight of the owl perched on a branch not more than ten feet away.

It stared back at her, bright yellow eyes blinking slowly as if he didn't have a care in the world.

Thankfully Daegen returned, but all too quickly he was back inside the cave with the rest of the packages.

The owl hooted again. The eerie sound sent spooky chills down her back, prompting her to creep a few feet into the cave. What she saw, impressed her.

It was *really* cold in here and there was plenty of food. On shelves were packages of what she assumed was smoked or salted meats because the packaging was similar to the wrapped items she'd helped carry here. There were preserves and jams in glass jars. On the floor were baskets of potatoes, carrots, beets and other root vegetables. Other baskets were filled with apples.

"In the winter we have to move some things from here that we don't want to freeze into the house. We put it into an insulated cellar beneath the cabin where it won't freeze up. Since the weather has started getting nice again, we've moved stuff back here. This cave keeps the food away from the house and it's better protected here from the animals. We use this mainly as a fridge in the spring, summer and autumn," he explained.

"My goodness, you can live out here forever," Milena whispered as she gazed around. There was so much food she would never have to see the inside of a prison cell again if she was allowed to stay here and live like a pioneer.

"Come on, let's get the rest of the bear packages in here before the wolves smell it."

Milena's eyes widened as fear raced up her spine.

"Wolves?" she squeaked.

He gazed down at her with a curious expression.

"Yes, there's plenty of wolves and coyotes too. They haven't taken down any humans that I know of, but you still need to be careful. Any cadavers can attract them and then they could go after the horses too."

"You certainly do have a lot of wildlife," Milena replied between her rapidly chattering teeth. She'd been so engrossed in inspecting the cave, she hadn't realized she'd gotten colder. Very cold.

She jumped as Daegen suddenly cursed beneath his breath.

"Sorry, didn't mean to frighten you. I just noticed you're freezing," he said.

To her surprise, he shrugged out of his coat.

"I should have realized you don't have a jacket on."

He looked downright distraught as he held up his coat. At first, she want to protest, but he was already slipping her arm into a balmy sleeve. The warmth embraced her and encouraged her to accept the rest of the coat around her upper body.

Blessed heat enveloped her.

She watched him gently roll up the sleeves until her hands showed.

"There, coat cuffs, the latest fashion statement," he said with a grin. A grin that made her insides jump like a live wire.

Mercy, she was certainly getting quite warm and so quickly! She liked this interesting...attraction she felt toward him.

"Thank you," she said. She didn't recognize her voice. It sounded soft and whispery. She cleared her throat and thankfully her voice sounded almost normal as she continued.

"This feels heavenly. I don't have a jacket so I'm sorry to be such pain."

"You're not a pain," Daegen growled with a shake to his head.

She held her breath as he began to button the jacket. Being in such close proximity to him had Milena enjoying his odor. He smelled slightly of soap, a hint of musky after-shave cologne and pine. She liked the scent, which made a curious question pop into her head. What would it be like to kiss him? Which led to yet another thought. Why *hadn't* she pursued him that one stormy night they'd spent together last summer at Moose Ranch?

Oh, now she remembered. He'd said he was gay. She'd found out shortly after he'd left that he'd been lying to her so she wouldn't be afraid of him with the two of them being all alone in the ranch house overnight.

Such a sweet guy, she thought.

She stared at his fingers as his hand reached under her chin and he pulled up the collar, touching her neck. His flesh sparked heat against her making her inhale.

"There...done. All warm and toasty," he whispered.

She noticed his breathing had become deeper and faster. Realized he was now staring at her, the pupils of his eyes wide and dark. Was that a sparkle of interest flashing in his gaze?

Oh no, that's more than a sparkle.

Something hot and needy ignited inside her. Instinctively she parted her lips and wished he would kiss her.

When he didn't, disappointment shot through her. He turned away and she had no choice but to follow him. She'd read too much into whatever had just happened. She must have. Why else would he behave as if nothing had happened?

That's because nothing did!

The jacket was truly warm, and she felt happy and grateful that he cared enough to give her his coat. What a chivalrous man.

Daegen didn't say anything as they made several more trips between the atv and the cave. When they were finished, he doused the light, locked up, and hung the lantern near the entrance. Before long they were racing along the trail once more, her arms wrapped around his midriff.

She sighed, happy to be away from that cold, damp cave.

It was heaven out here in the fresh air and impulsively she lay her head upon his strong back and watched the moonlight splash over the meadow.

Wow, but it sure was pretty out here at night. In the distance was the silhouette of pine trees pitch black against a dark blue satin sky filled with glittering sequin stars and a huge white full moon. As they neared the area where the moose had been, she noticed they were gone.

"To your left about a hundred feet is our smokehouse!" he shouted.

Milena looked over and spied a six-foot wide, six foot tall building with a long pipe coming out of a steep roof.

"Made out of solid rocks! Keeps the animals out!" he again shouted.

A moment later, Daegen plunged them down the embankment over the rattling planks and the dreaded black creek and then up the other side of the hill.

A few minutes later he'd parked the machine in the shelter, and they walked over to the cabin after making a quick pit stop at the outhouse, thankfully with the use of a flashlight that she remembered being on a shelf inside the little building.

When they entered the cabin, Paul was already asleep in his bed and Mitch was at the makeshift kitchen counter washing the dishes in a tub of soapy water and then rinsing in another tub of water.

"We're short one bed tonight," Mitch called out as Daegen closed the door behind them.

"She can have mine," Daegen replied. "I can bunk out on the porch."

"Oh, no. I can't take your bed away from you —"

Daegen held up his hand to quieten her protest.

"We've got warm bedrolls stored in a trunk right over here," he said as he strolled to a corner of the room, lifted a lid from a scarred wooden chest and dragged out a roll of what looked like a two-inch thick sponge.

"I have slept on worse when I was in the military," he said as he shoved the sponge beneath one arm and picked up a sleeping bag and pillow from a nearby shelf. Then he headed to the door.

"Don't argue with the man, just open the door for him and let the door hit him on the ass on his way out," Mitch called.

"Good! I'd rather be outside cause it gets too damned noisy with all that snoring in here anyways," Daegen replied and threw Milena a teasing wink and then nodded to the door for her to open.

"Hey! That's not nice! We don't snore!" Paul called sleepily from his bed.

Milena smiled under her breath at how these three men seemed to get along so easily with their teasing. No one seemed offended.

Daegen stopped in the doorway and gazed down at her. Then he smiled and her insides just went all electrical and she forgot how to breathe.

"Goodnight, princess," Daegen said softly.

Wow, such a wonderfully soft voice, she pondered. He broke eye contact and she suddenly remembered how to breathe again. He stepped outside and disappeared into the darkness of the porch. Guilt made Milena bite her bottom lip as she closed the door.

"I should be out there, instead of him," she said as she peered out the nearest window but saw no sign of Daegen.

"You wouldn't last half an hour out there, scarecrow. Too many night noises. The wolves howling, the racoons fighting, and the moose butting their antlers as they fight it out for a mate. Too noisy. I speak from experience," Mitch said as he turned off the lantern he'd placed on the counter. The cabin was plunged into semi darkness with the one remaining lantern set on the tabletop.

"Since you're already situated, you keep the bed you had last night. I'll take Daegen's bed. I hope you're tired because I for one am already sleepwalking."

He yawned and then joined her at the window and looked out.

With this new lighting she was able to make out the meadow beneath the spotlight from the moon. Nothing moved out there.

And for a moment things were so quiet she became fully aware of Mitch. His breathing sounded gentle, and she inhaled his scent. He smelled different from Daegen. There was a tinge of soap and a freshness from the outdoors and a hint of perspiration.

His odor made her feel very aware that she was a woman, and he was a man. The same way Daegen made her feel...yet different.

She wanted to touch Mitch just like she'd touched Daegen as she'd held him around his waist while she'd sat on the atv. She wanted to wrap an arm around Mitch's waist right now and hold him against her and feel safe just as she'd just experienced with Daegen on the ride back.

Mitch yawned again and Milena found herself following up with a yawn of her own. She was tired. Really tired.

"I restrung the privacy blankets while Sleeping Beauty Paul over there put down some fresh sheets for you, despite me warning him it was too soon for him to move around like that. So, of course he got dizzy and had to lay down."

"Oh no, is he okay? A head injury is really serious. Someone should get a doctor out here to check on him."

Mitch made a funny grunt and shook his head.

"No doctors around. Paul is all we got. Besides being a vet, he's a Wilderness Emergency Medical Responder, so following his instructions are the best we have right now. And there's that bush pilot midwife new in the area, maybe Paul would qualify as a baby."

"I heard that," Paul grumbled.

Mitch chuckled and happiness bubbled through Milena. She absolutely loved how they teased each other. Back in the prison, most of the women were hardened and didn't appreciate too much kidding around. Milena had discovered quickly who could take a joke, and who couldn't, and these three men were simply awesome.

"Come on, I'll show you how to turn off the lantern and how to start it up, then you can get to sleep whenever you want."

"Oh, okay, that would be great." That was a good idea because she had no clue how these gas lanterns worked.

A few minutes later, she'd learned how to work the lantern and both of them were brushing their teeth at the kitchen counter.

"Just spit in the sink and dump in some water to wash it away. The pipe goes outside to a small hand dug hole and into the ground. The toothpaste is green friendly biodegradable and so are most of the other products we use."

Milena spit into the sink, rinsed with a cup of cold water and splashed more water down the sink.

"Good job. You're a natural, scarecrow" Mitch praised.

To her surprise, Mitch smiled at her.

She inhaled at how sweetly his eyes sparkled and she impulsively smiled back. He wasn't such a nasty guy after all.

"Let's get under. Morning comes early around these parts. I put a candle and matches beside your bed too in case you need to get up at night to use the privy."

Oh? She had to go to the bathroom outdoors at night? Um, no way. She could hold until morning. She was not getting eaten by a bear or her head stomped on by a moose.

"Use the candle wisely. Make sure it's out before you fall asleep. You don't want your pillow to accidentally knock it over. I'll give you another lesson with the lantern tomorrow so for tonight you can use the candle. Head on in and light the candle and let me know when I can turn out the light."

Milena nodded, grabbed her toothbrush and once she was behind the privacy wall, she quickly lit the candle, which he had actually set in a cup full of sand. Then she called out so he could shut the light. When he did, the cabin was almost dark, except for the small flickering flame from her candle.

She removed her clothing and slid on her nightie. As she climbed beneath the cool sheets, she sighed and pulled the blankets tight up to her chin. She made sure the flashlight was within reach and then she blew out the candle.

"Goodnight," she called out into the eerie darkness.

Her answer was a soft snore.

Boy, he wasn't kidding when he said he was sleepy.

Milena snuggled deeper beneath her warm covers, closed her eyes and tried hard to fall asleep. But she couldn't.

She kept replaying the events of the day. Of what happened to Paul and then Mitch's close call with the bear. Then she remembered there was no lock on the door. Why didn't they have a lock on the door? Whomever had attacked Paul could walk in and slice their throats. The only semblance of relief was that Daegen was sleeping on the porch, unless of course, they slit his throat first and then came in.

Milena shuddered and took a deep breath in order to chase away the horrid thoughts.

Suddenly she realized someone had left the window slightly open beside her bed and she could feel a gentle cool breeze whisper against her face. She also heard thousands of frogs singing down by the creek. They were so loud, and they sounded so happy. She wished she could be so happy and carefree. Simply lying on the rocks beside a creek having no fear of anything.

For a split second she thought she smelled smoke, and alarm raced through her. But then the smell was gone. Surely it must have been from the candle she'd just extinguished?

Other smells embraced her. The scent of pine and earth and tangy aromas from tonight's dinner. There were sounds too. The nervous hammering of her heart. An owl hooted somewhere in the distance and then came a far-off cry of a loon.

Milena smiled and sighed.

Wow. A loon.

She had only heard loons on the television in the common room back at the prison. She inhaled sharply as she remembered the harsh clang of the cell door locking her in every night at eight sharp. She'd hated that sound.

It was the finality of another dreary day behind her, and another long night filled with women crying out in their dreams or whimpering as they masturbated or in some cases a woman climbing into bed with her cellmate and both of them making out.

Prison. Such a horrid boring place.

But this fledgling ranch was anything but boring.

She smiled into her pillow. She had learned how to operate an all-terrain vehicle, refreshed her nursing skills, learned how to use a gas stove, knew a bit about lanterns, and she'd realized too that she had one heck of an interesting sexual arousal system. Her sexuality was very much alive concerning *all* three men.

Thoughts turned to her ex-cellmate and now friend JJ over at Moose Ranch. She lived in the ranch house with three men, and she had an almost six month old baby girl. JJ didn't have to tell Milena that JJ loved all three men. It was written in the intense way she looked at them.

But Mitch's older brother, Brady must have captured her heart because she'd had a baby with him. She sensed Rafe and Dan must care for her too because she'd seen *something* in their gazes when they looked at her too.

And yet, there was only room for one man in a woman's heart.

What she would give to have a life like JJ. The safety of a strong man who unconditionally loved her, a baby of her own and a ranch to run.

But Milena knew a man could never be for her because she was damaged goods. There was no pardon for her like JJ had been given.

But...she could dream.

This morning's sex dream proved she was very much alive in the arousal department. But, oh she didn't dare dream naughty tonight, not with the men in the room.

Despite that last thought, Milena drifted off to sleep, totally oblivious of another whispery scent of smoke that drifted into the window.

· · ᴈᴆᴆ · ·

DAEGEN FROWNED AS HE stood completely naked in the meadow near the cabin and watched Milena's window. Watched as the light went out.

He really needed to get some sleep like the rest of them. Especially because when he got overtired, he was more prone to those annoying ptsd nightmares.

Damn memories.

Last year when he'd first come to Snowy Creek Ranch, he'd thought he'd be able to put his past to rest in this pristine peaceful environment.

Unfortunately, he'd been wrong and he'd brought his issues right along with him. Every branch that snapped had him on full alert. Every ear-splitting pound of a hammer as they'd forged the cabin walls made him tense to the point of agony.

Even the persistent cracking of a woodpecker's beak against the thick bark of a tree sent Daegen spiraling to that gut wrenching day when he'd received a telephone call and learned about his wife and unborn child's fate and that same day the one gunshot that had killed a close military friend right in front of him.

His flashbacks of helplessness and raw emotions of grief and anger had gotten so bad, he hadn't been able to sleep after coming here. He'd become irritable and lashed out at Mitch and Paul for every little thing.

He'd seen the concern in his friends' eyes, and he'd finally realized he needed to renew his visits to a shrink or he might lose this unique friendship with his two partners.

He'd found a good therapist in Thunder Bay. She'd helped him and she'd also hooked him up with a ptsd buddy.

Every once in a while he visited his ptsd buddy at his secluded cabin and they talked. It was good talking with someone who knew what it felt like to be out of control sometimes and bombarded by memories of bad things that had happened and feeling helpless and frustrated and angry.

He'd stayed overnight with him on several occasions, and they'd talked and Daegen had come away from the visits realizing he didn't want to be a hermit like his buddy had chosen to become.

Nope, Daegen wanted a life. And he was getting better.

So much better that he was reacting to Milena in the way a man who'd been without a woman for too long reacts to a woman. He'd been hiding his reaction toward her all day. The naughty things her sweet smile did to his body parts down south was pure torture.

He swore beneath his breath as just thinking about her made his penis throb with such an intense need, he had to grit his teeth.

He slid behind a nearby tree and gazed off into the moonlit meadow.

Nothing moved out there. But inside him, everything was stirring.

His heart smiled with an odd happiness that hadn't been there this morning when he'd left the plane and headed to the cabin. His senses pulsed with an erotic awareness and his cock a hardness he hadn't felt since being with his wife. His cock and balls were so tender, he knew of only one way to alleviate his need.

The cool night air blew against his scorching flesh making him shiver. He noted a whiff of woodsmoke coming in from the south, but there was nothing he could do about it now, so he ignored it and groaned as he slid his right hand up along his rigid hot shaft and allowed the memories of watching Milena in the shower this morning burst forward. He'd been aroused instantly when he'd seen her. She'd been totally oblivious that he'd watched her soap her luscious naked curves. Her breasts were pert and medium sized. Her nipples large and pink.

Daegen growled at the raging hunger that snapped like a whip within him as he imagined Milena dropping to her knees right in front of him at this moment.

His heartbeat faster as he rubbed his ultra-sensitive cockhead, fantasizing that Milena's soft, tender lips were wrapping around his rigid tip. White-hot lightning pleasure burst and zipped along the nerve endings wherever he touched his pulsing staff.

Hell, he'd wanted Milena the first time he'd met her last summer, but he'd had to put the brakes on by fibbing and informing her that he was gay. Now she was here.

And she thought he was gay.

Oh shit.

He stroked harder against his hands and gasped as more pleasure surged through him. He gazed down at his fully erect shaft. How *long* was he going to be able to keep up the disguise of being gay?

Man, this was going to get rough being around her and not being able to do anything. He swore he could *feel* her making love to his cock right now. She would drag his shaft deep into her mouth and suck and lick and...*oh man*.

His palms pumped his shaft. Muscles shivered and his hot penis jerked. He breathed faster. Moaned and groaned as fiery pleasures ripped with lightning speed through his penis and exploded like a bomb into his balls and lower belly.

The orgasm left him gasping, his thighs trembling and his knees so weak he could barely stand.

Suddenly he knew without a doubt, given a chance, he would make love to Milena Allen, and he'd make sure their first time together would never be forgotten.

Chapter Five

Even after having a wonderful restful night sleep, thankfully devoid of anymore hot sex dreams, Milena didn't feel too safe. She scanned every nook and cranny of the very high mountainous-like hill that Mitch and she ascended. She just wanted to make sure there weren't any intruders lurking around ready to bash their heads in.

Beneath the early morning sunshine, the upward route was rough, and she didn't even think she could classify this one-foot wide path as a trail but somehow Mitch knew where he was going. He'd said that once they reached the top, he would hopefully have cell phone reception and would report to his brother, Brady, about what was going on around here.

She just hoped he didn't talk to anybody else, like his sister, or the prison, or he could send her back.

She'd offered to remain at the bottom of the rocky outcrop because the climb had looked so daunting, but he'd insisted it wasn't safe for her to be alone, so here she was, climbing up a steep incline with the muscles in her legs utterly sore and she could barely catch her breath.

"Scarecrow, you're way out of shape," Mitch said with a chuckle as they *finally* crested the top of the gigantic hill, and he withdrew his cell phone from his breast pocket.

He gazed at her.

The early morning sun glinted against his blue eyes showing off some fantastic lime-colored specks that made breath catch at the beautiful play of colors.

"Is there anyone you would like to call? Your parole officer?" he suddenly asked as he held out the phone to her.

That question unexpectedly rocked her. Her parole officer had said to call once a week to report in, but it wasn't a week, and she wasn't eager to hear the woman's stern voice on such a bright, sunny morning.

She could call JJ, but since Mitch was calling Moose Ranch, he would tell Brady she was here and then JJ would know.

Besides, if she got on the phone with JJ, Milena would start crying when she heard her friend's voice. She'd missed JJ so much and the last thing she wanted was for Mitch to see her crying.

Milena shook her head.

"Okay take a few minutes to recuperate. There's a nice fallen log to sit on between those trees and a great view. Just don't fall over the cliff," he said in a stern voice.

She frowned. She felt dismissed as he punched numbers onto his cell screen.

This morning, over breakfast, she'd listened to the men discuss the smokehouse and how Daegen had put the bear meat in already and set the fire. He'd said he'd take care of the bear hide later today. Then they'd talked about letting their nearby neighbor Moose Ranch know what had happened. There had also been mention of informing an elderly lady, owner of Lamb Rock Ranch. Her place bordered their property to the north of Snowy Creek

Ranch. Unfortunately, the woman had no phone, so the subject about letting her know had been dropped.

Huh, it appeared this place was not as secluded as she had been led to believe by the parole officer. There were people in this wilderness. If she could call neighbors that lived many miles away as nearby. But still, people lived in this wilderness. If they could do it, she could too.

As Mitch began to talk to his brother, Milena wandered to the area where he had pointed. Pushing aside a few pine boughs, she gasped as she stepped into an entirely new world.

She walked to the edge of the towering cliff and her heart stopped as she gazed north to where the guys had said the elderly woman lived on her lamb ranch. There were miles upon miles of endless forest and yet she caught glimpses of several lakes.

She looked south and then west and saw sparkling green meadows and shimmering blue lakes and a dark dense forest way in the distance.

Wow.

Once again, she felt as if she had fallen into a wonderful dream. One from which she wished she would never wake up.

"Could be some trigger-happy wilderness campers doing shit they shouldn't be doing," Mitch said as he tried to keep his voice from getting too loud. When he got angry his voice always increased and he didn't want to scare Milena.

The phone crackled. He had a bad connection and could barely hear Brady.

"It's best to report it," his brother said. "What happened to Paul is assault. We've got a bad connection, so I'll call the police on your behalf and let them know."

Just then the phone crackled again, and Mitch couldn't hear was Brady was saying. Then he came back again.

"You there?" Brady asked.

"Yeah, cell phone keeps cutting out."

Suddenly the phone became clear again and he heard Brady talking.

"I'll give the cops a call for you, tell them what happened. I'll find out who is responsible for the wildlife in the area, and I'll give them a call too. Just sit tight. Keep eyes at the back of your head and..." The phone cut out again.

Shit.

A good half a minute later, Brady came back again.

"Hello? Hello? Hello? Are you there?"

"You're cutting out again." Mitch said.

"Ok, let's finish. I'll make all the calls. I'll be in touch. Take care, little brother," Brady said.

"You too, man. Oh wait..." He was about to tell him to contact Jenna and tell her about the mistake in sending Milena here and changed his mind. The last thing he wanted was for Brady to start laughing his ass off at being duped by their sister.

"Never mind. Bye."

The line cut had out again and Mitch reluctantly disconnected.

He gazed over toward where Milena had disappeared through the evergreens moments earlier. Then he looked back at his cell phone and quickly checked his voice mail.

Nothing from Jenna.

Crap.

He thought about calling his sister again and giving her tons more shit just so he could feel better, but he had the sense she wasn't going to be calling him back. Not for a whole hell of a long time.

Mitch cursed softly and placed his cell phone back into his breast pocket. He gazed down the trail they'd just climbed. Below, he spotted the meandering blue river he'd been getting water at when that wounded bear had shown up. He'd expected to dream about the encounter but had been surprised he'd dreamed about Milena instead. And those had not been professional dreams.

His cock suddenly thickened and pressed impatiently against his pants.

He blew out a tense breath.

A distraction like her was not what they needed here on the ranch. He should keep his distance from her, but it was hard when he'd been the one who'd pulled the shortest straw this morning when the three of them had secretly gotten together down at the creek and discussed what to do about her.

Pulling the shortest straw meant he'd be training her today.

This morning, when she'd been out in the shower, he'd checked the mail and seen the one from the prison.

His gut had twisted as he'd read it. It had outlined all the requirements of her being allowed to stay. One being if they didn't think she would work out, they were obligated to let her parole officer know and arrangements would be made to pick her up.

Mitch closed his eyes and cursed softly.

Hell, how could he send her back to prison?

She was already loosening up and looking less like a caged animal and more like a woman. Her cheeks were blooming with color too. It was a stark comparison to the pale faced, tense female who'd shown up here.

He'd wanted the guys to read the letter too, but they had merely shook their heads and said nothing. It didn't appear to matter to them that they had a serious felon living here.

Instead, Paul had taken a look in the mirror at the stitches she'd put into his forehead and told them she sewed better than he did.

Mitch shook his head. Paul wasn't easy when it came to giving compliments about medical stuff. He was a perfectionist in his trade, so Paul's approval was taken seriously by Mitch.

Paul also stated Milena had kept a cool head under pressure after finding him injured. She'd reacted quickly and efficiently, and he'd stated he had no doubt she would be a good asset to the ranch where emergencies were concerned.

Then Daegen had chimed in saying she was a fast learner, and very nice to look at and he had no doubt the four of them could have a professional relationship.

Paul had nodded eagerly. Too eagerly.

Mitch wasn't sure. Being around her made him pay more attention to her and not the tasks that needed doing.

He frowned. Time to get to work.

· · ❧ · ·

EIGHTY-EIGHT-YEAR-OLD Jane Sunflower caught movement just outside her kitchen window and without hesitation, and ignoring the arthritis paining her shoulders, she reached up and grabbed her .22 rifle from where she kept it on a gun rack above her kitchen door.

Quickly she stepped outside, pointed the rifle into the woods and snapped off a couple of shots.

"Sons of bitches! Get off my property!" she yelled as loud as she could.

She heard the cracking branches as whoever had been lurking around behind her log cabin ran for their life.

She would shoot to kill. She had signs posted all over her property warning of her intentions.

Living alone out here at Lamb Rock Ranch for fifty years had taught her to shoot first and never ask questions.

Had it been someone with good intentions, she had no doubt they would have called out to her. She could count the number of trusted friends on her right hand, which was less a little finger, compliments of accidentally chopping it off during her first year here while securing kindling.

She had tended the wound herself, sewed up the leftover stump and packed the injury in herbs. She'd been grateful it hadn't become infected. But chopping off a little finger was nothing in comparison to what she had endured from an abusive second husband who'd made her life a living hell in the city. Her family and cops hadn't been able to stop him from stalking her after she'd left him, so she'd disappeared without a trace and had come to live out here.

Since then, she'd been dishing out her own frontier justice, just as she was doing now.

She wondered who was sniffing around her place. This was her third sighting of someone in two weeks.

It was just shadows, probably cause her eyesight wasn't so good anymore, and she'd heard several gunshots about two miles out over the course of the days.

"This place is getting too damn crowded," she rambled to herself and went back inside.

Last year someone had leased the government land adjoining her ranch. Three men had come over and introduced themselves late last fall. They had been civil, calling out to her, letting her know she had visitors.

Hell, they'd even brought over a basket full of fresh fruits and vegetables that had come in mighty handy over the winter. They had been nice fellows and she'd put up tea and some shortbread biscuits for them.

She'd loved how the men appreciated her baking and had teased them by telling them they needed a woman to take care of them. She had sent them back to their place with some of her homemade biodegradable sheep milk soaps, shampoos and candles. Enough to last them a whole winter. She expected they would be by for more soon enough, if they'd used them.

Yes, they had been fine gentlemen and she hoped they would drop by again sometime. Preferably with wives. A good man needed a good woman to take care of him.

She grimaced at the soreness in her arthritic shoulders as she placed her rifle back in its place above the kitchen door.

She really should move the weapon into a more easily accessible spot, but she wasn't one for change.

Jane Sunflower returned her attention to the lamb milk she had boiling in her pot. She'd make some nice vanilla scented candles from this batch. She had plenty of them in storage, but candles always came in handy, especially since she had no electricity.

Nor was she going to have any electricity line put in either. It would cost too much money and she didn't want to waste her money on bills. She'd been saving her money for almost fifty years from the sales she'd made from her sheep milk products. When she'd reached sixty-five, she'd hired a private eye to investigate where her stalker might be. The bastard was in prison, for killing his wife. It could have been her, had she not left the abusive son of a bitch.

Sure, she could have come out of hiding, but well, she wouldn't dare leave her lambs. They were her family. Except when she needed some meat, of course. Then one came in real handy.

She'd applied for her Old Age Pension, and what little Canada Pension she'd accumulated during her years of waitressing before hiding out here. The money came in handy, allowing her to buy the supplies she needed to keep her little business going.

Yep, that direct deposit was the best thing that had happened to her. Since then, she hadn't needed to do her yearly trip to Thunder Bay with the checks that had been delivered via bush plane every month.

She hated the city, any city, and she knew in her heart she would die here when the time was right.

Last year, during her regular yearly visit to the city, she'd made a will with a lawyer, bequeathing her lambs and this place to a woman she knew would truly appreciate her little homemade ranch. A woman who would make Jane proud of her decision.

As Jane stirred her boiling lamb milk, she kept one eye on the window and beyond. Anyone showed up again and they were dead meat.

. . ᴔ . .

HARD LABOR OF CLEANING out the horse stables was just what Milena needed to keep her mind off the possibility that they would send her packing back to the prison. It was an awful miserable feeling of being unwanted, and she didn't much care for it, so she threw herself into the job Mitch had given to her.

Thankfully Paul recuperated well enough to be put in charge of having supper on the table when they got home tonight.

Milena bit her bottom lip as a rush of emotions clutched her chest. Paul being injured and alone at the cabin made her wish she could be back there to take care of him, but she also knew the horses needed tending and Paul was a doctor and he had reassured her he would be fine.

She slid the shovel into the half-filled pile of not so nice smelling horse manure and wiped the back of her gloved hand across her forehead to catch the dripping perspiration. Then she lifted the handles of the wheelbarrow and moved to the next empty stall.

This morning, Daegen had cooked them a large breakfast of scrambled eggs, canned ham and pancakes drenched with natural maple syrup that Mitch's brother, Brady, had made from syrup he'd collected and cooked off this spring from sugar maple trees on Moose Ranch property.

After breakfast, Daegen said he'd be in charge of the southern part of the ranch along with the smokehouse and left. Mitch had packed lunch for the two of them and then they'd taken the all-terrain vehicles to that godawful mountain-hill so he could make his phone calls that she hadn't been able to listen in on because she'd been infatuated with the scenery.

He'd seemed to be in a good enough mood after his calls, and he'd brought her to what he called the North Gorge Barn, where yet another old grey-planked barn with rusty spiral lightning rods set atop a steep roof was perched on top of a low rolling hillside, with a bunch of older horses housed inside the barn.

She had to admit the scenery in this valley was breathtakingly beautiful. Every chance she got she peeked out the opened windows of each stall and feasted her eyes.

Emerald colored grass waved in the mild breeze. Orange breasted robins, bright blue jays, tiny swallows and other types of birds she couldn't name fluttered about outside and sometimes inside the large two-story barn.

When she began cleaning out the stalls on the north side, she caught glimpses of several of the horses that Mitch had let out earlier this morning. All of the animals were gorgeous. She had no idea what breed of horses they were, but Mitch said they'd been retired from horse racing or breeding, and their owners paid to have them live out the rest of their lives here. Their owners were allowed to drop in anytime, and Mitch had told her there were a couple of rustic guest rooms inside this barn, as well as the other barn, somewhere in back for owners who wished to spend time with their horse or horses as the case might be.

He'd also said he was putting her in charge of keeping the guest rooms clean before and after guests! Did it mean they were letting her stay? Unless he was just saying that to avoid a scene. Surely, he'd read the letter from the penitentiary by now? She hadn't seen it or the rest of the mail anymore.

She didn't have the heart to ask if they were allowing her to stay so she'd kept her jubilant happiness buried beneath the what if they didn't want to keep her, scenario. At least if she didn't get her hopes up too high, they wouldn't be dashed if she got the boot.

After mucking the next stall, the wheelbarrow was full, and she pushed it outside and around to the back of the barn where Mitch had instructed her to go. The hill was sloped away from the creek and into a meadow back there so there wouldn't be any contamination issues. She dumped the smelly contents at the edge of an existing manure pile, wiped more sweat off her forehead, ignored her protesting shoulder muscles and pushed the wheelbarrow around to the front of the barn again.

Movement out of the corner of her eye made her stop. She gazed down the hill to where several black horses leisurely browsed.

She spied Mitch down there. He stood beneath a lone towering pine tree alongside a shiny white horse. The horse stood still while Mitch gently brushed the animal's coat. But that's not what grabbed her attention. What had her watching was the fact he was shirtless.

Even from here she could see he had a light dusting of brown-colored chest hair and plenty of well-sculpted muscles bulging in his shoulders and biceps as he brushed.

Watching him awakened a naughty need deep inside her. It was a desperate craving to run her palms over his sleek muscles. To feel the power this man must possess between his thighs. To have him thrust his cock in and out of her spasming vagina.

Heat and arousal swept through her like wildfire and she unexpectedly wanted to tear off her clothing and run naked to him.

Beads of stinging sweat dripped into her eyes. Quickly she closed them and wiped the perspiration away. When she looked again, Mitch was watching her!

Or dear Lord! The last thing she wanted was for him to think she was interested in him!

She threw him a quick wave, grabbed the wheelbarrow and swept into the safe interior of the barn.

Her heart beat insanely fast as excitement raced through her. Did he know how wantonly she responded to seeing him shirtless? Her reaction had been just as shameless when she had seen Daegen clad in just a towel and again when she'd cleansed Paul's head injury.

How in the world was she going to handle living here with these men when she was reacting this way?

She certainly could use another cold shower.

She really should ask for her own room, but where would they put her? Way out here in one of the barns? On her own? She'd be scared for sure.

Nope, no way was she going to get eaten by a bear out here. She had to find a way to handle these disobedient needs that were exploding through her like a long dormant volcano.

Milena cursed beneath her breath, picked up the shovel and headed to the next stall. Hard manual labor had to be the cure she needed, and she would follow up with a long cold shower when the work day was done.

Mitch closed his eyes and shook his head. Why in hell was he not fighting harder to get rid of Milena? He should have had her bags packed and on the fastest bush plane out of here. Yet here he was doling out responsibilities to her like she was staying here forever.

He opened his eyes and blew out a tense breath as he remembered watching her moments earlier. She was wearing that tattered old straw hat she'd found this morning in the barn. It had been left behind by one of their customers at some point and she brought new meaning to the abrupt nickname of scarecrow he had given to her.

Sexy, smexy scarecrow.

She was wearing a tight blouse and too tight jeans that illuminated womanly curves he hadn't really noticed when he'd been so angry.

But he was noticing everything about Milena today.

Jenna had put them into a very bad situation. What the hell had she been thinking?

"What the hell am I supposed to do with a woman around this place, eh, Misty?" he mumbled to the horse.

The horse snorted and seemed to roll his brown eyes, giving Mitch the impression that the old stud was laughing at him as if saying, what a stupid question.

"Yeah, I know what you would do. Follow your instincts and have your way with her and put out the fires flaming both you and your mate. But life as a human just isn't that easy, Misty. It's complicated."

Very complicated.

Mitch raised his brush and began grooming the horse's mane.

• • ⚬ • •

LUNCH TIME CAME QUICKLY and despite her protesting muscles every time she moved, Milena was eager to find a nice spot outdoors and away from the barn to have lunch.

After washing their hands with soap at a hand pump, complete with an old concrete sink, just inside the barn, she told him she wanted to go outside to eat. She was surprised that Mitch followed her, carrying the cooler containing their food and a large fleece blanket.

Thankfully he'd put on his shirt when he'd come to the barn, or she would have self-combusted seeing his muscles up close and personal.

He picked them a flat spot halfway up a nearby knoll where he spread out the blanket, and she kicked off her running shoes, stepped on the blanket and then sat down.

He sat across from her and looked up at the clear sky.

"We're lucky. It's not supposed to rain for a couple of days. We can get a lot of work done. But there's always a chance of pop-up storms, so we need to keep an eye to the sky."

Oh great. More manure shoveling. Not that rain would prevent that job from being carried out as it was indoors.

"By the look on your face, you're not pleased?" he asked as he opened the cooler and began to withdraw containers and a large Thermos.

She noticed laughter sparkling in his eyes and the sweetest smile kissing the sides of his mouth.

She loved this side of him, but she got the feeling he might be teasing her about something.

She may as well tell him the truth about how she was feeling.

"My arms and my back are killing me," she admitted.

His smile burst open, and he nodded with apparent understanding.

"Figured they might be. You're not used to this type of physical hard work. But you'll get used to it. How many more stalls do you have left?" he asked as he poured black coffee into two mugs and then handed her a container of food.

"Most of the stalls are all cleaned out. Clean straw is in, and I was generous like you said. Just have a couple more stalls to do and then I still have to place in some feed in all of them like you told me."

He chuckled, startling her.

"Wow. You work fast. A job like that usually takes us all day. Every day. Seven days a week and then there's the other barn to tend too."

Devastation rocked her. Every day? The other barn too? Oh my God! She wouldn't last here.

Tears built in her eyes and emotions welled.

Mitch suddenly looked horrified.

"Hey, don't cry. I was just kidding. It's my twisted sense of humor. We all take turns having a day or two off during the week. And you don't have to shovel shit all the time. We take turns doing that too," Mitch reached out and gently patted her shoulder.

The touch of his palm was hot and electric, yet she couldn't react. She wasn't cut out to be a cowgirl.

Sincere concern was evident in his gaze and suddenly she wanted to cry and cry and cry. Yet had he just said she would have a day or two off during the week? That sounded heavenly.

"Sorry," she mumbled.

She swore she had no idea how she managed to keep herself from falling apart. Through welled up tears, she took a bite out of the delicious looking sandwich that she'd removed from the container he'd handed her moments earlier.

"You'll feel better with some food in your stomach. Eat," he instructed.

She nodded jerkily.

Her momentary desolation was forgotten as the tangy flavors of mayonnaise, crispy bacon, lettuce, tomato, mustard and a meat that looked a lot like steak but had a taste she didn't recognize, yet instantly loved, exploded against her taste buds.

He was right. The food cheered her up and she made involuntary noises of appreciation, treasuring every bite.

"Truth be told, it takes two of us usually a couple of hours to do what you're doing," Mitch said. She noted there was that teasing grin again.

Two people? She was doing a job that two people usually did?

Son of a bitch!

"Since you're a rookie, I had to initiate you," he said with a shrug.

Relief swept through Milena. She should be mad. Livid. But she wasn't.

"Seriously? I'm not going to be stuck doing this every day? All day?"

His frown deepened. He truly did look upset.

"Geez, if I knew you were so sensitive, I would never have played this trick on you."

She wanted to tell him it was okay. She wanted to tell herself to suck it up and to be grateful he was pranking her. It meant he was already thinking she was one of the guys. She should be thankful and relieved, but suddenly she just couldn't let this go.

"You're mean. I quit," she stated in as serious a voice as she could get out.

Ha! So there!

To her surprise, his face went totally pale, and his mouth dropped open with apparent shock.

"Wow, I didn't know you took things so seriously. You're so sensitive," she stated.

But she couldn't keep a straight face any longer and burst out laughing.

Mitch rolled his eyes and muttered, "Payback is a bitch, you got me."

His frown dissolved, and then he was laughing right along with her.

"Well, I am glad we both have a sense of humor," she said after she stopped giggling.

He nodded but said nothing and then they both concentrated on eating until Milena complimented him on being a good cook.

"We have to be good cooks, or we'd kill each other," he explained. "And thank you for the compliment. We've kind of gotten used to each other and we've slacked off with praises, so it's nice to hear one."

"The meat in this sandwich. It's good. Kind of tastes like roast beef, but different."

Mitch nodded.

"It's bear meat."

Her eyes widened with horror. What? She stopped chewing. Surely, he was playing another joke on her? She forced herself to swallow and stared at the last bite she had left to eat.

Oh man, it tasted so good. Surely, he lied.

She stared at him, trying to read his face, as he stared back at her. There was no hint of teasing in his blue eyes. He kept as straight a face as he had a moment earlier when he'd told her they were eating bear.

"You are kidding, right?" she prodded.

"Seriously. I went on a bear hunt and got one. We're allowed to catch a certain amount of bear or deer per hunting season with our license. When the one I got yesterday is smoked, it'll taste just as good. I promise. Personally, I prefer beef. My brother sends some over once in a while from Moose Ranch, which is great. But other groceries and delivery by float plane are expensive and you can't eat beef all the time, so bear, deer and moose are on the menu."

Oh great. This just figured. She was in love with bear meat. Why couldn't something just go right?

His eyes narrowed as he gazed at her.

"Why the frown?"

"I'm not really into eating bear. Being chased by one, yes, I can understand that. Getting eaten by one, sure, if he can catch me. But me eating a bear. It's just so weird."

If she really thought about it, she just might make herself sick. She had bear in her belly. Best not to think about it.

"That's the city girl in you talking. You'll get used to everything out here. Now finish your lunch as dinner is a long time off."

Her heart almost exploded with joy at what he'd just said. She would get used to everything? They were keeping her?

Ask him, Milena. Put yourself out of your misery.

But she just couldn't bring herself to ask if they were truly letting her stay. What if he said her days were numbered? Or maybe he would lie and just be nice and he wouldn't tell her the truth because he feared she would run into the woods and disappear, and he wouldn't be able to send her back to prison.

"You've got some mayonnaise on your cheek," his soft voice broke into her thoughts.

He was staring at her in a funny kind of way that made her tense with awareness.

"I do?" she answered, feeling very self-conscious.

His eyes twinkled, and she realized that his eyes were the same color as the cloudless blue sky overhead. Cheerful and beautiful.

She was also noticing that the sunshine beaming down around her unexpectedly seemed so much brighter. The air smelled fresher. The birds sang louder.

Her mouth felt drier.

"Yeah, mayonnaise on your chin and mustard on your upper lip."

An awesome fluttery feeling swept through her as he reached up and lightly wiped his warm fingertip over her chin. Sure enough, his fingertip came away with a decent smear of mayonnaise, which to her surprise, he licked off. He had a very nice-looking tongue that instantly had her thinking about Mitch's head dipping between her thighs.

His hot mouth searing over her pussy and his tongue thrusting like a miniature cock in and out of her vagina.

Heat skewered her.

Oh dear, this was awkward and very intense.

She held still as he reached up and wiped off the mustard. He licked that too!

"Scarecrow, you're starting to look delicious enough to eat," he said in a tender voice.

Oh wow. Was that a seductive comment? Or was she seriously reading into something that did not exist because she had been without a guy for like ever?

His smile disappeared, and he focused his attention to the cooler. He hauled out water bottles and produced a couple of bananas and then apples. He handed her one of each.

"Eat up. I'm going to go check on Black Rex. He is the oldest of the horses and he needs extra special attention. I'll keep an eye out for any trouble. Stay here and relax for at least an hour. There's plenty more water in the cooler. Drink as much as you want before you head back in to work, okay? Make sure you keep your eyes open too in case there's trouble. I'll just be a shout away."

He peeled his banana and tossed the shell into his empty lunch container, then placed the lid and put it into the cooler.

"I'll be right down there," he pointed to the meadow where several horses grazed beneath the sunshine.

"Okay."

He stood and nodded to her.

"There's more food in the cooler in case you want some. See you later," he said in a firm voice.

He appeared tense as he turned away. His smile was gone, and he looked like a serious boss once again. She watched as he walked with confident strides down the hill, munching on his banana.

He sure did appear to be a different man than the angry one she'd met her first night here.

But doubts crept in again. Was he being nice because she was on her way out?

She bit her bottom lip and forced that thought away.

No, don't think so negatively. She needed to start thinking positively again. Somewhere along the way to Snowy Creek Ranch, she'd lost her positive frame of mind.

She watched as Mitch stopped by a magnificent black horse that was drinking at the river's edge. It lifted his head and brushed his muzzle against Mitch's shoulder. The horse watched as Mitch produced a knife and began cutting up his apple.

Milena was too far away to hear what he was saying, but she could hear his voice. He sounded happy and so was the horse as it neighed in between eating the apple chunks.

Milena smiled and drained the remainder of her black coffee. For a while she watched Mitch with the horse, and then slowly gathered the remaining empty containers and placed them back into the cooler. She debated whether or not to eat the last sandwich in there but decided not to.

She closed the lid and then lay on the blanket, placed her hands beneath her neck and continued to watch as Mitch grabbed the reins of the horse and began to lead him along the edge of the river away from her. Every once in a while he would look her way and her heart would thump just a bit harder.

The meadow was long, and she lost sight of man and horse when they disappeared behind a row of bushes. She turned her attention to surveying her surroundings. There was no movement anywhere in the far away tree line. She smiled and watched a couple of loons fly low overhead, their wings flapping mightily.

There *had* been something naughty there in Mitch's gaze when he had wiped the mayonnaise and mustard off her face, hadn't there? Or was it just wishful thinking on her part? What kind of guy eats off a woman's face?

She giggled and shook her head, allowing her mind to drift along to how she'd felt while imagining Mitch's head buried between her thighs...

"Hey scarecrow. Let me kiss you. Let me make love to you," Mitch's voice punctured through the many layers of Milena's erotic fantasy, and she stiffened.

Oh my, she'd fallen asleep? She opened her eyes and whimpered.

Mitch was lying on his side on the blanket right beside her, gazing at her. His eyes were dark and stormy. Filled with lust.

"I want to kiss you," he breathed.

"You do?" she whispered in disbelief. Was she dreaming?

His head lowered and her breathing grew rough.

"But we don't even know each other," she whispered.

He didn't seem to register what she'd just said as his hot mouth melted over her lips in a dominating kiss.

Her thoughts spun out of control and eagerness lashed her. His tongue thrust into her mouth and mated with her tongue. Touching, swirling, plunging until carnal sensations pounded through her pussy and anus.

"You taste so good," Mitch mumbled as he broke the intoxicating kiss.

Her lips tingled and her tongue pulsed wonderfully. She wanted him to kiss her again!

"Let's have a peek at the rest of you," he breathed.

His fingers worked the buttons on her blouse and in seconds her bra was fully exposed. He lifted her bra and her breasts spilled free of their restraints.

"Pretty, don't you think, Daegen?" Mitch mumbled.

Oh gosh. Daegen was here too?

"Beautiful," Daegen expressed.

She saw him now. He was lying on the blanket on her other side. His face was lowering to her left breast.

Mitch's mouth was zooming in on her right breast.

She jerked and cried out as hot lips covered her sensitive nipples. Their strong tongues lapped, and their sharp teeth nibbled. They sucked hard increasing the erotic sensations swirling through her and making her vagina and sphincter muscles clench with need.

They were unleashing something wild and exhilarating inside her. Something she really enjoyed.

Wow, these two men sure knew how to bring out the woman in her...she wanted more.

More!

. . ⚓ . .

DAEGEN STARED DOWN at the smoldering ashes of the makeshift fireplace he'd just found. After he'd taken care of the horses this morning, he'd decided to check around the barn where someone had clobbered Paul yesterday.

Whoever it had been, was either nuts, afraid of getting caught trespassing or afraid of getting caught doing something that was illegal. He didn't like what he was seeing here. Whoever had made this fire hadn't put it out properly.

Daegen lifted his canteen out of the pouch at his waist, grabbed a stick and poured water onto the smoldering ashes.

Fucking moron didn't even know how easily a forest fire could start. The campfire had been made about a mile outside their southern property line and two miles from the ranch house.

It was too close for comfort.

A good thing a lake was nearby. Daegen filled his canteen several times and put the campfire totally out.

He knew there were interior campers who used the crown land, but those people were usually careful, and they didn't go around whacking people over the head or leave smoldering fires.

Shit.

He had come out here to northern Ontario to find some peace from all that he'd experienced in his life the past few years. The last thing he'd expected was to use his learned tracking skills to hunt down another human in his own country.

And this guy who'd camped here was messy.

As Daegen looked around the site, he noticed several things. A few feet away there were trampled ferns where he assumed a tent had been pitched. Two tinfoil plates with pieces of aluminum foil were strewn around the ground by the campfire. He lifted one of the plates and noticed remnants of oil and unpopped corn.

There was an empty can of mosquito spray, a couple empty cans of beans and pork, several pop cans and two fish skeletons that had been tossed behind a fallen log. There had been more than one person here and the occupants of the camp had had a dinner of fresh trout and popcorn and most likely a halo of mosquitoes dogging their every move at night.

There were other things he'd discovered as well but he'd let Mitch and the others know about it later. After spending more than an hour investigating the area around the camp, he opted to head back. It would be a long trek to the barn, and he'd promised to get the bear meat into the smokehouse and to keep an eye on that pregnant mare. He hadn't anticipated being gone for so long.

Anger simmered through him as he hurried back the way he'd come. He just hoped that the assholes building fires out here weren't going to burn down this entire freaking forest and Snowy Creek Ranch right along with it.

. . ❧ . .

PAUL KNEW HE SHOULD stay at the cabin and take it easy, unfortunately he wasn't much of a patient, especially if he was both the doctor and the patient. He had asked Daegen to keep the old pregnant mare in her stall today and to keep an eye on her. With orders that if he thought anything was wrong with her, he should come and tell Paul right away. But Daegen wasn't a vet. How would he know if Brownie Belle was in distress? Besides Daegen had his own chores to do.

Brownie Belle would be alone for long periods of time while Daegen exercised the horses and Paul just couldn't sit around here playing cooking couch potato any longer. For some unknown reason he had a very bad feeling she needed him.

Brownie Belle was too old to have another foal.

He had been really pissed off when her owner, Everly Constance, had brought the horse here to have her foal. Everly was a stupid bitch in having the mare impregnated when she should have been retired long before now. He had warned her there was a good chance Brownie Belle and her foal would not survive. But she'd given him her instructions. Save the foal at all costs.

Everly's mare had been a profitable racehorse and then a lucrative breed mare. Brownie Belle's parents had been famous racehorses as well and Everly had made millions on BB as she was known in the racing circles. Yet the woman wanted to squeeze more money out of the twenty-seven-year-old horse.

Sometimes, especially in cases with older horses, which in his opinion this case he considered to be animal abuse, he wished he had never gone into this horse ranch business. He got tremendously sad when he had to put one down because of the stupidity of their owners.

Yet he knew the horses needed him and right now instincts were screaming that BB needed him. Maybe it was just his imagination because he'd been away from her for so long, but he preferred to be safer than sorry.

Due to his concussion, there were still bouts of dizziness. He'd just have to stop the atv if he had a spell. Besides, it wasn't as if there was any traffic way out here, except maybe a horse, but he'd be too far away from the ones roaming in the meadows to accidentally hit one.

He felt better once he had the machine, and he was on his way. He reached the barn without mishap and parked near the area where he had been assaulted.

Goosebumps crept up the back of his neck as he remembered stepping out of the darkness of the barn and into the bright sunshine. Someone had struck him so hard and so fast, he'd gone down like a ton of bricks.

With the anxious feeling he might get hit over the head again, he cautiously let himself into the cool barn and immediately went to the office and then the cage that had housed the injured gyrfalcon. He checked the lock, wondering if maybe it hadn't been working correctly and that's how the animal had escaped. But it was secure and worked well.

Strange. He could have sworn he had locked that cage after putting the bird back inside.

An alarming neighing suddenly shot through the interior of the barn, snapping Paul to attention.

Brownie Belle was in distress!

Paul made a grab for his black medical bag that he always kept on the nearby shelf, but the quick movement snapped dizziness through him and the interior of the barn began to sway.

Oh man! No! Not now! He managed to take a firm hold of the door handle to keep from falling over.

Brownie Belle must have known he was here. She was crying out to him for help, and he couldn't do anything with the barn swirling all around him.

Where the hell was Daegen?

.. ⌘ ..

"HOW LONG HAS SHE BEEN like this?" Daegen whispered as he and Mitch stared down at Milena where she slept on her back with her hands tucked beneath her neck.

Daegen had to admit, she looked sexy as sin in her rumpled clothing. The swells of her breasts peeked out at the top of her slightly opened blouse, and they erotically moved up and down with her every breath.

"Not too long, maybe an hour," Mitch replied in a low voice. "I expected she might drop off. She looked exhausted at lunch. I worked her hard this morning. Figured she should get a taste of ranch life and reality."

Disappointment grabbed Daegen.

"So, she can decide if she wants to leave here?" he prodded.

"So, we can decide if she's tough enough to be here. This ranch cannot be a babysitting service for ex-cons."

Man, he hadn't expected Mitch to be so serious.

"But she passed the test. So, we let her sleep for a while. I've already taken each of the horses into the river for a swim. Want to help me run some of them on the track? We can keep an eye on her from there, in case someone is still lurking around. Then later we can run the rest of the horses on the trails."

Daegen nodded.

"Good idea. While we work, I've got some discoveries to discuss with you. You're going to find them very interesting."

"Unless it's serious, let's save it for supper so we all can hear it together," came Mitch's reply.

"Okay, it'll wait. Let's head on down, and let her sleep," Daegen replied.

Milena waited impatiently until she didn't hear the men talking anymore, then she slowly opened her eyes and blew out a tense breath. The two men were down by the river with a couple of horses.

First, when she'd struggled to awaken from the layers of hot fantasies of Mitch and Daegen sucking on her nipples, she'd wanted to reach down between her tense thighs and put out the fire of arousal they were causing. But then she realized she'd fallen asleep and that Daegen and Mitch were now nearby and talking about her.

Thank heavens, she hadn't started to masturbate!

For a split second she'd panicked, thinking maybe she'd made sensual noises in her sleep, but it didn't appear as if she had, because they'd just been talking normally.

She knew it was rude to eavesdrop, and her face had flamed with heat knowing they were watching her, but she hadn't been able to resist listening in on their conversation and so she'd lain still.

Her heart had been crushed when Mitch said this wasn't a babysitting service for ex-cons. But then he'd said she had passed his test.

Milena thoughtfully chewed on her lower lip. So, it hadn't been an initiation as he'd said earlier. He *was* serious about his ranch. Well, so was she. She would show those cowboys exactly how good an asset she would be for them.

With renewed energy, and a naughty fire burning deep inside her pussy, Milena got up, grabbed the cooler and blanket, and then headed back to the barn. Hopefully the coolness inside the large building would dampen her growing sexual desires. But she had the feeling it wouldn't.

Next best thing, she'd have to work hard to distract herself from those hot images of the naked men that had followed her out of her sleep fantasy world.

Oh boy, she had lots of work to do!

. . ❧ . .

PAUL CURSED HIMSELF for not being stable enough on his feet to help the mare. She lay on her side, her swollen belly heaving, her eyes rolling in pain. He'd been able to make it to her stall, but he was still dizzy as hell.

Where the hell was Daegen anyways? Paul had called out a few times for him but there'd been no answer.

But Daegen had been here. The stalls he'd stumbled past had been cleaned. The water in BB's bucket and her food was fresh.

The only consolation was he didn't think the mare had been laboring for too long.

Impatiently, he'd waited for the dizziness to dissipate and then went about examining her.

It only took him a few minutes to figure out her heart was under stress and the foal was in the wrong position. Due to his sporadic dizziness, Paul was not confident he could do the task of repositioning the foal.

Man! Of all the times for no one to be around to help him. This was not that time.

Paul sighed and smoothed his hand over BB's swollen belly. He spoke gently but the horse was aggravated, and she kept struggling to get up.

Her legs were flailing too much, and he knew she could injure herself. He could give her a sedative, but it might relax her too much and she wouldn't be able to push. He could leave her and head to where Mitch and Milena were working at the other barn for help. But he would lose a good half hour.

He didn't want to leave a distressed, pregnant mare on her own. Anything could happen.

Her heart could fail, and she would go into cardiac arrest and he'd have to let her go and do an emergency C-section to save the foal. If it could even be saved.

But he wanted to save both of them. And right now, it looked like that might not happen.

Shit! He needed help and he needed it fast!

Chapter Six

"**H**ello! Paul? Are you in here?" Milena yelled into the barn. When she'd approached the large building with her atv, she'd spied another machine outside and knowing that Daegen and Mitch were still at the other barn, she knew it belonged to Paul.

But she'd continued to be cautious, leaving her atv far away from the barn so any intruders would not hear her coming. She'd grabbed a big piece of branch as protection and walked in the rest of the way. Upon entering the barn, she thought she'd heard Paul's voice from somewhere inside and so she'd called out.

"Over here! Quick! I need help!" he yelled.

She froze when she heard his frantic shout. Truthfully, she had not expected him to be here. Had not wanted anyone to know she was here. She had snuck away from the other barn with masturbating in mind. But it appeared that naughty bit of fun would have to wait.

When Paul gave out a second frantic shout, her gaze snapped to the wall where the first aid kit should be, and she realized it was back at the cabin.

Damn!

She didn't think twice before moving quickly yet cautiously toward where Paul continued to shout. Had he been attacked again? Her heart cracked insanely hard as she peeked into a stall, fully expecting to find him injured.

But when she saw him, she understood what was happening. It appeared both horse and Paul were in distress. The horse lay on its side, her belly swollen, her sides heaving. Paul sat weaving back and forth on a small stool with an open doctor's bag on the ground in front of him.

His eyes were closed.

"Milena. Is Mitch with you?" His voice was calm now.

"No."

"Then you'll have to help. Probably best too. You have smaller hands. I need you to wash your hands and arms all the way up to your elbows back at the water pump. Wash them like you've never washed them before with soap and water. You're going to have to go up inside her and try to turn the foal."

· · ᪣ · ·

WHAT? HER MIND SCREAMED as she rushed outside. There was a fresh unopened bar of soap there right beside a little piece of soap. In a fit of irritation, she opened the fresh bar and eyed the towel slung on the water pump. Was it clean?

No, she couldn't take the chance. She tossed it to the ground. She washed her hands and arms all the way up to her elbows as Paul had demanded.

Her heart thumped madly, and her mouth was dry. Treating a human's injuries she could handle, but a horse?

Oh, boy. Oh, man. Oh, shit!

She probably overdid the soaping and rinsing and was thankful when she was finished. But then a nagging question hit her. Shouldn't the water be sterilized? Boiled? Something?

She asked Paul when she got back, but he mumbled something about BB probably wouldn't make it anyways and if she did, he would dose her with antibiotics to prevent infection.

"Well, screw you, doctor," Milena snapped with defiance and enjoyed the surprised look wash over Paul's face.

"No one has ever died on my watch and I'm not about to let it happen now. Tell me what to do," she growled.

She ignored Paul's sad look and followed his instructions to the letter.

. . ❧ . .

TWO HOURS LATER, MILENA was staring at the exhausted mother as she weakly licked her black as coal baby who struggled to stay standing on shaking, thin legs.

Happiness bubbled through her. Such a beautiful sight to see new life in the world.

"Do you think they're going to make it?" Milena asked Paul as he returned with a large syringe filled with clear liquid.

Hope as bright as she'd ever felt in her life coursed through her.

"That she's standing and licking her foal is a good sign," Paul answered.

But he certainly didn't have the same optimism as she had. His frown cut deep lines into the sides of his mouth, and he appeared concerned and forlorn. Maybe even doubtful.

She didn't let his funk get her down. She'd just delivered a baby horse! And they were both alive. This was something to celebrate!

"The mare's heart is very weak. She's old and should have been retired years ago. She was in quite a bit of distress too. I don't see any signs of trouble, but we'll have to keep a close eye on both of them for the next twenty-four hours. I'll be sleeping here tonight."

"Then I'm staying here too," Milena said quickly.

She felt a strong connection to both horses now and she didn't want anything to happen to them.

"We can bunk in the guest rooms in back of the barn. Consider it another adventure as you seem to be having plenty of them since arriving," Paul said with a nod.

"I love adventures," Milena said and giggled.

Wow, she felt like a little kid. Free and without worry. It was a really nice feeling.

"Hey, Paul! Is Milena in here?"

Mitch's angry shout reverberated throughout the barn, sending birds chattering and flying out open windows.

Milena swallowed.

Oh crap! She'd expected to have returned to the other barn before they'd discovered her gone.

"He sounds like he's pissed," Paul said as he placed the syringe onto a tray.

"Oh. Oh. Busted," Milena whispered.

Worry pushed aside her newfound carefree attitude.

"Something I should know about?" Paul asked. His eyebrows were raised with curiosity.

"You'll find out in a minute."

Paul nodded.

"In here!" he shouted. He lowered his voice and winked at her.

"Just remember what I told you about him, his bark is much worse than his bite."

"Yeah, right," Milena mumbled and kept her gaze to the newborn.

Paul had said it was a girl. Milena wondered what her name would eventually be.

"Why the hell did you leave without telling us?" Mitch growled in a low restrained voice as he caught sight of her.

He stood in the stall doorway and his eyes blazed with anger and maybe even relief?

"I left a large note on the bulletin board just beside the desk I saw you using this morning in the office barn. Figured you'd find it; in case you came looking for me. I just wanted to see how Brownie Belle was doing," she said, quickly securing her cover story for coming here.

"Son of a bitch," Mitch cursed softly.

"I guess you didn't look there?" Paul asked with a chuckle.

"No, we were working the horses. Daegen noticed her atv was gone. I thought because of what happened yesterday maybe something bad—" He stopped short and fell silent.

The muscles in his cheeks clenched and he inhaled a deep slow breath, almost as if trying to stay in control.

Oh dear. Paul was right. He was pissed off.

"As long as you're safe. Just next time physically tell one of us, okay?"

Huh, was he seriously concerned about her? He didn't even know her. She was a virtual stranger to him and yet...he appeared anxious.

Milena nodded.

"Sure. Won't let it happen again." To her surprise, Mitch visibly untensed. His shoulders dropped and he smiled as he spied the foal.

"What a beauty. Everly will be pleased. Did Brownie Belle make out okay?" Mitch asked Paul.

Paul nodded to Milena.

"Once again, this one appeared like my knight in shining armor. I was having one hell of a dizzy spell. Figured I wouldn't be of any use to the horse cause of it. Then Milena showed up and I realized with her small hands, she could correct the position of the foal. It would have been much harder on BB with my big hands. I seriously couldn't have done it without Milena. She came to my rescue once again."

"Impressive," Mitch said as his gaze focused on her. His penetrating blue eyes appeared darker than she remembered, and they sparkled with interest.

Milena's breath backed up as her tummy made a wonderful dip like she was going down some wild roller coaster. If looks could talk, she bet he would be saying, "You can come to my rescue anytime too."

"Hey! Did you find her?" Daegen's concerned shout rocketed through the now quiet building.

"In here!" Milena called out as she forced herself to break eye contact with Mitch's constant intense gaze.

"Man, you gave us a scare. Thought maybe Mitch worked you too hard and you quit," Daegen said as he joined them.

His face lit up when he saw the two horses.

"Hey, look who's here? That's a nice foal. Shiny and black just like the dad. Girl or boy?" Daegen asked.

"Girl, but you all need to go and leave Mom and baby to rest. I've got to give BB a shot and I'll meet you out there."

He held up his syringe and the three of them moved like a well-oiled machine down the hallway.

"How is the mother?" Daegen asked her as the three of them left the barn.

Before she could answer and to Milena's embarrassment, Mitch told him about Paul saying praises for her as he explained how she had helped during the difficult birth.

By the time Mitch was finished Daegen was beaming proudly as he studied her.

Gosh, they were making her feel really good about herself. In more ways than one. But she needed the focus off herself. She wasn't used to all this kind of attention.

"I think Paul needs to get checked out by a doctor," Milena blurted.

She had concerns for him. He should have been able to handle the difficult birth on his own, despite singing her praises. She noticed how sometimes he had squinted while giving her instructions.

Just then Paul joined them and Daegen and Mitch frowned as they turned their attention to Paul.

"Thought you said you were feeling better this morning," Mitch said quickly.

"I was. I was. I just have to avoid sudden movements. I learned that the hard way," Paul replied.

"Okay, I'll get on the cell phone and call for a crisis ride over at Moose Ranch. I'm sure JJ can fly one of us with you into the city to Emergency," Mitch replied.

Paul looked shocked.

"No way. Hold on. I'm certain it's just residual from a concussion. I need time to recuperate. Give it a few days. Besides, I can't leave Brownie Belle. She needs constant medical attention, now."

"Paul, a head wound is nothing to laugh at," Daegen said.

"I'm sure Milena and JJ can take you in and accompany you," Mitch chimed in.

"I can do that," Milena said quickly. She sure would feel better if he agreed to go.

"Come on guys. Don't gang up on me like this. I am fine. But how about a compromise. Give me two days. Forty-eight hours. If I don't see an improvement, I'll go."

Mitch shook his head.

"In the meantime, if you drop dead?" Mitch asked.

"Then I won't have to go, will I?" Paul laughed.

"It sure would remove that constant pain in my neck," Mitch said.

Milena couldn't help but gasp at his sharp retort, but then she caught the tips of Mitch's lips upturn slightly.

Joking. My goodness.

"Okay fine, but if we notice anything off, we are contacting Moose Ranch and there will be no arguments if we do. Agreed?" Mitch said with a stern voice that made it sound like everything was final.

Irritation whizzed through Milena.

"You're not taking his life seriously enough, guys," she blurted.

She hadn't meant to voice her thought out so loud, and her outburst had all three men staring at her with what she assumed was surprise. A weird overwhelming sensual awareness crashed through her. It came strong and hard, and she was confused by its intensity.

These men are so sexy hot, she thought as heat melted through her.

"I didn't think you cared," Paul said in a soft voice, the sides of his eyes crinkled with humor...or was it happiness?

Oh dear. She didn't want them to get the wrong idea. Time to downplay.

"Of course, I care. If you guys are gone, who will pay me for all my hard labor?" she joked and struggled to fight the flames of desire rushing through her as the men continued to stare at her with interest now. Their bodies appeared tense and their gazes...forceful.

Her pussy trembled with unexpected visions of all three men kissing her upon her intimate body parts.

Mercy, what she wouldn't give for a huge bucket of ice cubes to be poured over her about now.

"She's got us there," Daegen said.

He broke the suddenly uncomfortable silence by clapping his hands together snapping Paul and Mitch out of the apparent trance they'd been under.

"I'll give the rest of the horses over in the North Gorge their workout. Okay Mitch?" Daegen continued. "Then I'll get them settled for the night and get the bear into the smokehouse. See you at supper."

He didn't wait for Mitch to answer and trudged off toward one of the atvs. A few moments later the engine roared to life and Daegen raced away toward the north barn which glimmered as a small grey speck on the hill far off in the distance.

Milena tried to ignore the intense way Paul kept staring at her, as well as her awareness of him, by abruptly rubbing her calloused hands together.

"So? What's next on our agenda? More stalls to muck here? I completed the ones at the North Gorge barn before coming here."

God, she hoped there weren't any more stalls to clean. She was exhausted.

Mitch smiled and tilted his cowboy hat back off his face.

"You are an eager beaver aren't you?" he asked and then inhaled deeply before continuing.

"There's nothing like some hard work, fresh air and open skies to put life into perspective," she said.

Keeps me on my toes, and my mind off wanting sex, she added quietly.

To her horror, her cheeks suddenly went really hot.

Lovely, was she blushing?

"You're looking a little flushed for work," Mitch said.

Great, he had noticed.

"Daegen's done all that needed doing here so why don't you head back to the cabin with Paul. I'll keep an eye on Brownie Belle and the foal. Then I'll bring in the horses and come back for supper."

Relief poured through Milena. Thank you! No more work today!

"I'd rather stay and keep an eye on them myself," Paul said.

"Are you sure it's wise to stay here alone? Something may happen again. What if you get dizzy?" Milena blurted.

"She does care about you, Paul," Mitch said and elbowed Paul.

"Nah, she's just interested in my money," Paul replied with a wink to her.

"You two are incorrigible," Milena shook her head.

"Okay, how about you and Mitch go back and start supper?" Paul suggested.

"How about you and Mitch stay here. He can keep an eye on you. I will go back and start supper. No arguments." The last thing she wanted was to hang around with Mitch or Paul some more today. She needed some space to think and to cool down. A cold shower was first on her agenda. Besides, cooking would be much better than cleaning out stalls.

"Only on one condition," Paul suddenly said.

Concern made his eyes darker, and Milena wondered why he suddenly seemed so serious.

"Since we don't know why I got hit and who might still be around, we're going to need to be very vigilant."

He turned to Mitch, who also toted a frown.

"I am not comfortable having her go off alone," Paul said.

Mitch nodded.

"Daegen did say he picked up tracks of two people leading away from our property, but that doesn't mean they won't circle around and come back," Mitch supposed.

Milena waved at them.

"Hey, hello. Quit talking like I am not here. I'm a big girl. I just spent thirteen years in prison and survived. If that didn't teach me to be careful, I don't know what will. Besides, I know how to work the rifle, thanks to some lessons yesterday. It's in back of our trailer. I'll keep it with me and shoot first and ask questions later. How's that? Can I go?"

Milena literally watched relief pour through both men.

"Point taken. She's not some innocent city girl," Mitch said softly.

"And she's tough under pressure," Paul added.

"And this ranch isn't a babysitting service," Milena blurted.

She took satisfaction in Mitch's eyes widen with surprise. Good, she was glad he knew she'd been listening.

"Okay you've sold us on you being a survivor. Still, be very careful. Take our atv and keep the safety catch on and keep the rifle close to you," Mitch muttered.

Milena rolled her eyes. Man, this coddling stuff was beginning to stifle her. The air was suddenly feeling way too hot. She needed to get away from them. Now.

"Will do. I'll get supper on."

Before she could turn and leave, Paul cut in.

"Hold on. Let me tell you that I've already done most of it. The roast is just inside the cooler beneath the cabin. Mitch put it in last night. Just move the carpet and tug on that notch. The roast has been marinating all night. The rest is all on the table,"

Milena held up her hand and she brushed past the two cowboys.

"No worries. I'll figure it out. Later, gentlemen."

She lifted the rifle from the trailer of Mitch's atv, holding back a groan as her sore fingers curled around the stock. With her other hand she checked the safety catch, just to impress the guys who were watching her again and to let them know she still remembered what she'd been taught about how to handle a rifle.

Then she placed the rifle back into its scabbard, slipped on her helmet and allowed herself a grimace at the newly formed calluses on her palms.

Man, her hands were sore, but in a really good way. She had done useful things today. Physical things.

Earned some respect too when she had to remind them, she was not a baby and had survived prison. She had seen impression flare in their eyes.

Yeah, she was a tough chick. She could handle anything. She was free now. She was going to live the dream.

Just to show off to them a little, she revved up the atv, slid it into gear and turned the machine in the direction of the cabin.

Milena smiled despite the aches nagging her shoulders and upper back as she held tight to the handlebars. She had cleared out a shitload from the barn and delivered a baby horse.

How cool was that? The ladies back at the pen couldn't brag about this kind of stuff. A momentary sadness enveloped her as she remembered a couple of her closest friends who were locked away. But she couldn't do anything for them right now.

She was here and they were there. She needed to concentrate on what was happening with her, here and now.

Warm spring air caressed her face and she sensed she was going to like it here at Snowy Creek Ranch.

She *really* was going to like it.

· · ✿ · ·

"INTERESTING LADY," Paul said beneath his breath as Mitch, and he strolled back into the barn.

"Uh huh," Mitch mumbled as he entered their small office area.

Paul grinned and stood in the doorway. He watched Mitch slump into the chair behind the desk. He pretended to be looking for something in one of the desk drawers.

Paul had seen that bulge pressing against Mitch's pants. Felt his own shaft throbbing at the sight of Milena acting all defiant and confident. Man, she straddled that atv really nice with her long legs. He bet a million dollars Daegen cleared out fast so he could get away from the woman screwing with his hormones.

"She's sexy as hell walking with a rifle. And that cute old straw hat too," Paul added.

"Yeah, well, cute and sexy ain't going to run this ranch," Mitch growled, without looking up.

Paul knew Mitch was sexually frustrated as heck. It was in the way he held his jaw, tight and tense and his voice was unusually husky beneath that angry tone.

Paul couldn't help but chuckle beneath his breath.

Mitch's head snapped up and his blue eyes shot daggers at him.

Oh. Oh.

"Back off with the jokes, Paul. Go tend to BB and her foal. I've got some paperwork to do, and I'll exercise the horses before bringing them back in."

Mitch was acting all business-like, but Paul could tell his friend was steaming hot. Perspiration beaded his forehead, and his face was flushed. Hell, he was hotter than hades himself.

Maybe having Milena around was going to be a bad idea. But that thought disappeared faster than it appeared.

"Okay, let me know when you're ready to go," Paul said.

Mitch merely grunted.

Paul left the doorway and headed back to the stall. Brownie Belle neighed a welcome when she saw him. He swore she already looked a little better. Her sides weren't heaving as much, and her dark brown eyes were filled with excitement instead of pain now. Even the foal was standing a little steadier.

He closed his eyes and sent up a prayer of thanks for Brownie Belle and the foal for still being alive.

And for all the naughty feelings running amuck on Snowy Creek Ranch. It was about time things on this boring ranch started to get interesting.

· · ⚓ · ·

MITCH SWORE SOFTLY beneath his breath as he found what he was looking for in the bottom drawer. The bottle of whiskey and a small glass. He rarely entertained a drink for himself. But today he needed one. Bad.

Milena was quickly becoming an asset that was getting increasingly harder to get rid of...and it was pissing him off.

He was losing control of the ranch and he was losing control of his hormones. Yeah, she looked really hot when she got all defiant and, in their face, and carried a rifle like she was some cowgirl born on the range.

Not to mention that straw hat. He didn't know why that tattered thing on her pretty little head made him so...horny. But it did.

He twisted open the bottle and poured himself a drink.

Man, he was going to kill Jenna. He seriously was going to kill his sister.

He tossed back the drink and sucked in a breath as the fiery liquid burned all the way down his throat, taking his mind off Milena for just a few precious seconds.

Then he poured himself a second drink. It was a good thing he knew how to hold his liquor, because he was going to need a few to take the sexual edge off his swollen cock and tight balls, compliments of Milena, before he headed back to work.

. . ❧ . .

SHE HATED IT HERE! Why was everything going so wrong with her supper preparations? Why had she volunteered to cook? She sucked at cooking.

Except maybe if there had just been one stupid cookbook around, then she might have been able to figure out what Paul had been planning to make when he had set out all these vegetables on the table. Milena stared through the thick blue smoke that permeated the cabin interior, and coughed, and rubbed her stinging eyes.

The pot roast she'd stuffed into the oven hours earlier, now sat on top of the stove, black as coal and smoking like a bitch.

While the roast had been in the oven, she'd been in the shower, thoroughly enjoying herself beneath the cool water. There had been no interruptions while she'd happily masturbated, and she'd gotten carried away...until there had been no more water.

Then she'd toweled herself off, sat in the sunshine to dry her hair and had been greeted to a smoke festival upon returning to the cabin.

Tears sprung to her eyes as frustration flooded her. She'd wanted so badly to make the cowboys a hearty meal, but even the chopped vegetables she had placed in the roast pan had burned to a crisp.

She stiffened as heavy boots suddenly pounced up the steps. Oh shoot! Where had she left that damned rifle?

The creak of the doorknob being twisted, made her freeze in fear.

Oh, no!

She'd popped a chair beneath the doorknob in hopes it would keep any uninvited trespassers from entering while she'd rescued the roast from the oven and then tried to figure out how to stop in from smoking so much.

The doorknob twisted some more. She swallowed against the alarm gripping her.

She spied the rifle on the kitchen counter where she'd left it. Quickly, she rushed over and grabbed the weapon. She unlatched the rifle's safety catch, then aimed the weapon at the door.

Terror rushed through her as the door cracked open an inch.

Her finger rested on the trigger. Should she shoot and ask questions later?

"What the hell? Milena? Is everything okay?" Daegen's voice erupted from the other side of the room, and she rushed over to let him in.

Thank God!

She trembled as she realized she had almost pulled the trigger! Almost shot Daegen.

Queasiness made her sick to her stomach. Anger uncurled throughout her.

A moment later, she had the chair aside and the door opened.

Blue smoke curled outside and around Mitch, Paul and Daegen. They stood there, concern marring their faces.

"What's going on?" Mitch asked as he stepped inside and took the rifle from her hands.

"I almost shot you guys. It might be a good idea to put locks on your doors," Milena blurted. She hadn't wanted to mention it. Hadn't wanted to appear weak, but this scare really jostled her.

"We just never got around to finishing things. Never saw the need," Daegen said.

"Well, there is need," she grumbled. She'd feel a whole lot better with some sort of security system here.

"We can see that," Mitch said as he gingerly removed the bullets, one by one, from the rifle.

"Just order the parts and I can put the hardware on," Milena snapped.

Great. She was volunteering to do stuff she really had no idea how to do. Just like supper. She was never going to learn to keep her mouth shut, was she?

Daegen brushed past her, grabbed a pair of oven mitts, took the roast pan, and with a pained expression on his face, walked back outside with it.

Mitch chuckled as he opened up the kitchen windows.

"A good thing we took the time to put screens on all the windows. You know in case of smoke emergency," he said. She didn't miss his smile.

Well, at least someone could have a sense of humor at a time like this.

"And we sure have had our share of smoke emergencies. Remember the time you forgot to shut off the stove after you baked a cake and the cloth that was sitting on top of the stove caught fire," Paul asked Mitch.

"A good thing we were in the cabin," Mitch said with a nod.

"Well, I don't know why it burned. Obviously, I don't know how to use an oven. I did take baking classes in prison and nothing like this ever happened.

"You forgot to take it off broil," Mitch observed and nodded to the dial with all the degrees.

Milena shook her head and crowded in beside Mitch. Sure enough it was set to broil.

"How is that possible? I turned it to four hundred degrees. Even I know that regarding a roast."

"You turned it, just to bug me, right?" she asked Mitch, who frowned at her accusation.

"No, I didn't," he replied.

"I know I put it to the correct temperature."

"Did you leave the cabin?" Paul asked.

"Yes, I took a shower. And then I sat under the sun in the meadow to dry my hair." A creepy feeling slithered through Milena.

"But I had the rifle with me at all times, except for in the shower."

Goosebumps rippled up her arms. Someone had probably been watching her. Probably seen her naked.

How horrible!

"Then an intruder may have done it. Maybe the same son of a bitch that clobbered me," Paul said as he pulled out a chair and sat down at the kitchen table.

"We're going to need to get locks," Mitch said. "They could have burned the entire cabin down had Milena not come in when she did. Whoever is out there is dangerous."

"And still around," Milena said as she moved quickly to the nearest window to gaze out.

Nothing moved, except the grass and the trees in the late afternoon breeze.

"They might do something to the barns and the horses," Paul said tensely.

"That possibility exists," Mitch replied as he placed the rifle into the plastic protective casing, locked it and then set it on the kitchen counter beside her.

"See anything?"

"No, nothing."

"Good. Then I suggest we eat because I for one think better on a full stomach," Paul suggested.

Milena wanted to throw her sore hands up in the air and simply cry and beg for forgiveness for ruining dinner. But these guys weren't even mad.

"But the roast is ruined," she complained.

"Daegen will fix it. He's had experience with our cooking. If he can fix our mistakes, he can fix yours," Mitch said.

"You'll like it, as long as you're into smokey flavoring," Paul joked.

"I'm so hungry I could eat the smoke!" Milena admitted.

The guys laughed and she found herself relaxing.

"We've got a pressure cooker too. I'll just chop up some of the potatoes and carrots and we'll have mashed potatoes and cooked carrots in no time flat," Paul said as he stood.

Thankfully he didn't sway from dizziness and Milena noted his face wasn't pale anymore. Maybe he *was* feeling better.

Mitch sat down at the table that she'd already set with the yellowware and patted the seat of the chair beside him.

"Come on, scarecrow, sit down. You must be beat. Daegen and Paul can serve."

Wow, she hadn't expected Mitch to have sympathy for her.

Milena flopped heavily onto the seat Mitch had indicated, suddenly realizing her feet were sore.

"I am kind of tired," she admitted.

"Did it kill you to say that?" Mitch asked with a warm wink that gave Milena encouragement.

"And I must admit I am not a good cook either. That's something that never really interested me. I only took one baking course."

She suddenly felt compelled to explain.

"I mean when you're stuck in prison, you get told to work in the kitchen. But food there is pretty much frozen or in cans. It's rare we get fresh vegetables or fruits. I mean just because I am female, doesn't mean I am naturally inclined to be domestic..." She stopped when she noticed Mitch staring at her, the sides of his lips upturned into a very sexy smile that she loved.

"Do you want apple juice or water?" Paul suddenly asked from behind her.

She twisted around to find Paul holding a can of apple juice and a pitcher of water. Condensation had formed over the glass of the water container. Yeah, she wanted something cold.

"Water, please," she replied.

She grabbed a glass in front of her and held it out for him so he could pour, but Paul suddenly cursed and to her surprise he sat down on a seat beside her and grabbed her wrist.

"What the hell happened to your hand, Milena?" he asked as he turned her hand, palm upward to reveal several blisters and her red skin.

Shock coursed through her at his concern. His eyes were dark, and he was mad. It frightened her.

"I...I..." Oh, she didn't even know how to explain.

The squeak of a chair rippled through the air as Mitch pulled closer to her. His frown was so severe she worried she had done something wrong, but what?

"I gave you gloves to prevent this. Didn't you wear them?" Mitch asked as his frown deepened.

"I did, but sometimes I took them off and I forgot to put them back on," she admitted.

"First aid kit is right here," Paul plopped the black bag onto the table in front of Mitch.

"Get her hands clean and put a light application of salve on them," Paul instructed as he reached down and grabbed the pitcher of water and apple juice.

Good Lord! she was not going to let Mitch touch her? She plopped her hands into her lap, hoping that was that.

Unfortunately, Mitch had other ideas.

"We always follow the doctor's orders around here, Milena. We wash and put salve on now," he said sternly.

"Oh, no, really I am fine. I can do it after we eat. Seriously I am fine."

To her surprise, Paul placed a basin filled with water beside the doctor bag. That was followed with a washcloth, towel and a bar of soap.

"We take care of our injuries right away," Paul said as he moved back to the stove.

"We don't want infections. Prevention is the cure. Place your hands in there and wash," Mitch said as he nodded to the basin.

Oh man.

Milena reluctantly nodded and tried to ignore how close he remained. His scent drifted all around her like a lasso. He smelled of pine, fresh grass and a hint of perspiration. He was a hard worker. She'd watched him several times today, peeking out the barn windows while he had brushed and exercised each horse.

He would be a very good catch of a man, her inner voice whispered.

Milena scolded herself for such horrid thoughts about one of her bosses.

Keep your mind on the job, girl.

On. The. Job.

She grabbed the soap and sighed as she slid her hands into the warm water. Wow, this felt heavenly. And the way Mitch was looking at her felt good too.

It only took a couple of minutes, and her hands were clean. Paul then supplied some warm rinsing water in another wash basin and Mitch placed the jar of cream in front of her. She liberally smeared it on with ease, loving the way it soothed her tattered flesh upon impact.

It was really nice how the two men doted on her. It was a good feeling to know someone cared about her and she found herself smiling inwardly and outwardly.

· · ⚓ · ·

"HA!" DAEGEN CALLED out as he entered the cabin with pot roast in pan.

Milena, Paul and Mitch all gazed his way, expectation and hunger brewing in their eyes. He could tell that they were impressed with the new look of the roast.

"Told you he would be able to fix it," Mitch chuckled.

"It's still nice and hot and pretty well cooked inside. I've already carved it. Let's eat!"

The group, including Milena, let out a chorus of cheers as he placed the pan onto a wooden board in the middle of the table.

Supper had always been a jovial time between the three of them and Daegen noticed since Milena's arrival, and the adjustment period of awkwardness, it appeared everyone was happy and at ease tonight.

He liked this friendly, carefree atmosphere. Too bad he was going to have to break it apart with the information he had discovered today. But he would wait until dessert. At least that way, their stomachs would be full.

As the plates were passed around, he gave everyone a healthy several thick slices of roast. They deserved it from another day filled with work. Especially Milena. He'd noticed her red palms, but also noticed salve had been put on. It appeared Paul had been aware also and had taken charge for her care.

Daegen enjoyed the mashed potatoes and carrots that Paul had created and he had to admit the roast was tasty too.

"This is the last of the potatoes from Moose Ranch," Paul said.

Mitch and Paul moaned and Milena, bless her heart, didn't appear to understand why. Over the winter, they had enjoyed the delicious, organic food that his brother had brought over late last fall.

"Moose Ranch donated a bunch of food from their garden last year," Daegen explained to Milena.

"The guys discovered food grown out here tastes better than the food we order in bulk and have flown in via plane," Mitch added.

Milena nodded, her eyes bright, her cheeks rosy from the outdoor air, as she helped herself to another slice of roast and mashed potatoes.

Daegen chuckled. She was too busy eating to care at the moment.

"You know what that means," Mitch said as he chomped on his food.

"Our turn to get started on a garden of our own," Paul replied.

Mitch moaned.

"More work for us all," Paul complained.

Daegen watched Milena's eyes widen and her mouth worked into a pretty little O of surprise.

Poor thing. She really had had a rough day. She'd even fallen asleep on that blanket on the hillside after she and Mitch had had lunch.

When they'd come upon her, she'd looked so angelic in her peaceful slumber. So attractive. So sexy.

As he remembered seeing her, her hands tucked beneath her neck, her breasts rising and falling slowly, her jean-clad legs spread...Daegen's shaft hardened against the sudden tightness of his pants, and he silently cursed. It was a similar response as to when he'd seen her on her first morning out there standing naked in the shower.

He inhaled sharply at the memory.

He knew without a doubt nights were now going to be filled with visions of her creamy smooth flesh and of him taking her up against the shower wall, hearing her gasps of pleasure as he plunged his swollen shaft deep inside her quivering wet, hot, tight vagina.

"Earth to Daegen. Earth to Daegen,"

Mitch's voice rushed up through the dark tunnel of steamy visions and slammed into him like a lightning bolt.

He blinked as a hand waved in front of his face.

Milena appeared across from him. She had a curious, maybe even knowing expression on her face.

Embarrassment made heat fuse through him.

"Where did you go, Daeg?" Paul asked with a chuckle.

"Yeah, man. You totally zoned out. Are you okay?" Mitch asked.

There was an underlying tone of concern in each of their voices and Daegen realized the guys thought he had drifted back to *that* day. Which he sometimes did.

Thankfully not this time.

"Sorry, was thinking about what I found this morning," Daegen said and then he suddenly wished he hadn't brought up the subject. There was something else he had discovered that he didn't feel was appropriate to discuss in front of a lady.

"Yeah, that's what we were asking about," Paul said.

He hoped his face wasn't flashing red in the lamplight. Maybe they would catch on that he was hung up on Milena. Man, he hadn't blushed since he was a teen.

"So?" Mitch prodded. All eyes were upon Daegen, eager to know.

He stared at his empty plate. He really should grab another helping of roast and potatoes, but maybe he would leave room for dessert.

He put down his utensils and quickly brought them up to speed about tracking the person who he assumed had been the one that had attacked Paul, to a camp over an hour away from here. He had discovered that the attacker had spent the night near a small lake, with another person. He had discovered casings from a shotgun.

"That's what the bear had been shot with. I dug shot out of its lung," Mitch broke in.

"Wow, this person could have very easily shot Paul too, instead of bashing him," Milena voiced out loud what Daegen had been thinking all day.

He realized things could have been a whole lot worse.

"Agreed," Daegen replied. "From here on out we work in pairs. Keep your eyes out for trouble."

"Did you find anything else?" Milena prodded.

Great. He had hoped to discuss the rest with the guys in secret, but maybe she should be in on the loop too. She worked here. She was now a part of everything, so best not to keep things from her.

Daegen nodded and sighed.

"From the couple of partial prints I saw, I believe it is a man that hit Paul. He was met by a woman at the campsite. Let's just say they were intimate."

"What do you mean, intimate?" Milena blurted with a frown. It appeared by her curious gaze that she wasn't the least bit embarrassed.

"I found protection. A couple of safes," Daegen admitted. His face grew even hotter.

"They might have been two guys," she pondered.

Daegen shook his head.

"I found a couple woman's feminine napkins."

"Oh," Milena replied and that's when he suddenly realized something. Milena would need feminine hygiene products. He doubted she had brought more than a month's worth.

Shit!

Milena's eyes narrowed with thoughtfulness.

"So, someone bashes in Paul's head, his gyrfalcon that had been shot disappears, a wounded bear with a bullet in it attacks Mitch. This guy meets up with a woman and they spend the night together. He leaves a trail and he's acting as if he's done nothing wrong."

Milena bit her bottom lip and made a cute little hmm sound. Daegen sensed she had already figured something out.

"What are you thinking?" Paul asked as he placed his elbows onto the table and leaned in with interest.

"I'm not sure, but, when I was in prison, I did a lot of reading and watched a lot of documentaries. This might be too far-fetched, but maybe, just maybe, you've got poachers?"

"Poachers?" Paul and Mitch replied in unison.

Daegen frowned. This was not what he wanted to hear.

"I've read that because of Canada's vast wilderness, it's easy for poachers to get away with catching and or killing animals. For example, a bear's gallbladder can bring up to $10,000 in certain overseas markets because it is considered an aphrodisiac. Some poachers even catch the bears. They keep them alive, transport them overseas and the captured bear is operated on, a device is placed around its gallbladder and then the bear is kept the rest of its life in a cage, where a couple of times a day, that device is twisted, and it squeezes bile out of the bear's gallbladder. It's a very painful existence for the bear and it sometimes even chews off its paws in order to try to kill itself. The bile collected is sold on the market and is used in medicines and aphrodisiacs."

Oh man, he was going to be sick.

Daegen gazed over at Mitch and Paul who sat quietly but appeared quite intrigued with what Milena was saying.

"And if I remember correctly," she continued. "Gyrfalcons are considered an exotic bird. It would bring thousands of dollars on the overseas markets."

Mitch broke in. "When I spoke with my brother, he said he was going to report what happened to Paul to the authorities, but I doubt anyone is going to come way out here to investigate."

"Yeah well, if someone is going around kidnapping and shooting animals then I think we need to figure out how we can bring them to justice," Paul snapped angrily.

"We don't need this kind of bullshit happening to defenseless animals just so some lazy assholes can make money."

Daegen could tell Paul was at maximum anger mode. There was a curly blue vein that popped out in his forehead when he got mad. And it was really popping now.

The veterinarian didn't get mad often, but when animals were concerned, he got pretty passionate.

"I gotta agree with Paul. We cannot let this go on around here," Mitch said.

"Or anywhere," Milena snapped.

Her pretty brown eyes sparkled with fire and Daegen liked the defiant side of the woman.

Sexy as sin in the shower. Sweet and vulnerable while sleeping and protective and passionate when awake. This pretty lady had many sides to her, and prison hadn't squashed her. She was strong and surprisingly did not appear bitter from years of incarceration.

Yet there was also a frightened, vulnerable side to her. He had seen it the first day while at the lakeside dock when she had panicked and taken off on an all-terrain vehicle. He had not seen her panic since, so it made him wonder what that episode by the lake had been about.

"Earth to Daegen, again," Mitch's amused voice snapped through his thoughts like barbed wire.

"What?" he asked and realized he'd been staring at Milena again and thinking about her.

Oh geez. He could tell in the way her eyes were downward and shy, she *had* noticed his attention on her. Were the guys aware he had developed the hots for her?

"Dessert time," Paul announced from the kitchen counter area.

Man, he had not even noticed that Paul had left the table.

"I was wondering if maybe one of these days I should take a trip and check in on Jane Sunflower," Daegen muttered, hoping to change the subject. Hoping to get a day away from Milena so he could collect his thoughts and do some heavy-duty masturbating.

"Who is Jane Sunflower?" Milena asked.

In her eagerness to learn about the woman, Milena was now leaning forward against the table. Daegen's gaze zeroed in on her breasts as the tabletop cupped them. Every part of his body was zinging it into full male awareness mode.

He was a breast man. He loved looking at a woman's breasts, whether in a guy's magazine or up close and personal. And right now, his imagination was going haywire at the thought of undressing Milena.

"She's a neighbor. An elderly lady. She's been living in the woods over forty years," Mitch explained.

"Forty years?" Milena gasped. The look of shock on her face made Daegen smile. She was so cute when she was surprised.

"You know what? I think that's a good idea. Best to tell her to keep an eye out," Paul said as he placed a plate laden with raisin cookies onto the table.

Mitch groaned as he gazed at their dessert.

"Oh, come on, like you can't make anything else but your concrete cookies?" he complained.

"Hey, beggars can't be choosers," Paul retorted. "Eat up. There's plenty where that came from. Who wants coffee to go with these delicious cookies?"

"You mean coffee to wash down those hard-as-a-rock, break-my-teeth cookies," Mitch winked at Milena.

Milena laughed, and he swore the sound of her laughter was like music. The melodic sound did some really nice things to his senses. He could tell in the curious way Mitch and Paul were smiling at her, they were experiencing similar emotions. He bet they liked the way she laughed. Liked it a lot.

• • ⌘ • •

PAUL HAD REALLY APPRECIATED Milena's gentle laughter during dessert. She'd sounded like one of those songbirds he enjoyed listening to when twilight descended over the barns. Those birds always made him feel peaceful and happy. But Milena's laughter made him anything but peaceful and happy. They made him aware of her. Very aware.

Tonight, the two of them were heading to the closest barn so they could keep an eye on the mare and her foal.

He sat upon the atv seat behind her, and sizzling heat wafted off her body melting into his flesh despite the couple inches he tried to keep open between them as she drove the vehicle along the meadow path.

But every time they hit a bump or dipped into a gully; he was forced against her. Paul swallowed and tried to pull himself away from her, despite wanting to stay right where he was, snug as a bug feeling her soft body press against his chest and...against very hard parts down south.

He sighed in relief when the silhouette of the barn appeared on the hill.

Being in such close quarters to her made him feel uneasy, but in a really good way. She smelled nice tonight. Clean and flowery. Probably from that afternoon shower she'd had while someone had snuck into the cabin and turned the stove to broil.

He sure hoped that wasn't the case, but she'd been adamant she had turned it to the proper setting.

After supper when everyone, including Milena, had pitched in gathering up the dishes, he noted that Daegen and Mitch had tried to act casual, as if nothing extraordinary had happened to their dimension with Milena being thrown into the mix. But Paul sensed an underlying tension in the cabin as they'd cleaned up the kitchen and dishes.

When Paul had mentioned that Milena and he would be spending the night out in the barn keeping an eye on the horses, Paul thought he might have detected some jealousy lingering on Mitch and Daegen's faces. Or maybe it had been envy?

Or maybe it has just been his imagination?

Oh hell, he didn't know. Suddenly he didn't care what the guys thought. He was just glad that Milena was here with him.

Chapter Seven

S ome weird inner happiness embraced Milena as she watched Paul hover around mother and baby horse. He appeared so attentive to his two patients. His large hands touched them gently and his voice was so soft as he talked to them.

When they had first arrived about an hour ago, the mare had appeared distressed, but Paul had calmed her down with an apple. Then he'd discovered her heart was racing again and he'd administered the appropriate medication which he assured Milena would not harm the foal through the mother's milk, after she had voiced her concerns.

"Okay, I am satisfied that mother is fine," Paul finally whispered and then he quietly motioned for Milena to leave the stall.

The foal was sleeping, but the mare watched Milena with bright brown eyes as she moved toward the door. Milena waved to her and to her surprise and excitement, the mare neighed.

Paul followed her, grabbing the lantern off the hook near the doorway as he moved into the hallway with her. He closed the stall door and motioned for her to follow him. She grabbed the bundle of clean clothing and the salve she'd brought with her from the bench where she'd placed them earlier and followed him.

"I'll show you to one of the two guest rooms that we have made up for visitors," Paul said as they moved along the corridor, past several stalls on each side, each pen filled with a quiet horse.

Near the end of the hall, Paul stopped at a large wood door. It creeped ominously as he pushed inward.

He held the lantern up high, and she saw a foyer. On each side was a wood plank door. Each door had a black-painted horseshoe nailed to it.

"Voila, the guest rooms," Paul said with a smile. "They come complete with beds, and I don't know about you, but I am sleeping while I am standing up talking to you."

"Another sleepwalker," Milena chuckled.

"You too?" Paul asked

Milena nodded and stifled a yawn with the back of her hand.

"You can take the door to the left. It's more feminine. Just stay here for a second, while I locate candles in my room, then the lantern is all yours."

Milena nodded sleepily and watched Paul disappear into his room, leaving her in the dark with only lamplight spilling into the hallway. A bit of uneasiness settled over her as she waited. It was pretty quiet in the barn except for an occasional neigh or snort from a horse or a sporadic creak or groan from the wind that pushed against the barn walls.

On the way over here, she'd noticed the wind had picked up. She'd anticipated a storm, but the black sky had been filled with bright white stars that sparkled above them as she had driven here. She wondered if the violent person who had attacked Paul was still lurking around tonight. She shivered at that thought. Prayed the intruder was gone forever.

"Okay, I'm all set with a candle," Paul said as he returned. He stood in front of the other guest room door and beckoned to her to come.

When she joined him, he swung open the door and handed her the lantern.

"What time should we check on the horses?" Milena asked, suddenly worried about them.

"With the meds, BB should be alright through the night, but I will check on her in about three hours. The foal is fine. She's a strong one and did you notice how she's taken a shine to you? Rubbing her head against your hand every chance she gets?" There was amusement in Paul's voice, and it made her smile.

"I noticed. I figured all baby horses did that?"

"They usually do that to their mothers. She figures since you saved his life, you can be her mother too."

Milena laughed.

"Seriously, if something happens to BB, you're the surrogate."

Oh mercy. For the foal's sake, she hoped nothing happened to its mother. Milena knew firsthand how badly it felt to have a mother die.

"Can you wake me up too so I can see them? Unless there's an alarm clock in there?"

She didn't own a watch or an alarm clock. Had never really needed one in prison. Large institutional wall clocks locked behind unbreakable glass were hung on prison walls pretty much everywhere, including in any cell she'd been in.

Paul chuckled.

"If you're a glutton for punishment, I can wake you."

Relief poured through her.

"Thanks."

She didn't know why she had become so quickly attached to the two horses, but call her silly, ever since she'd helped to deliver the foal, both mother and child just seemed to be like her family.

"Don't forget to put more salve on before going to bed. Goodnight," came Paul's whisper and Milena realized he'd already headed back to his room and was standing in his doorway.

"Good night," she called out.

There came a gentle creak as he closed his door, and a weird feeling of happiness crashed in around her once again. She really truly was not in prison anymore. There were no more harsh clangs of the metal doors slamming shut. No monotone voices yacking over the speaker system warning lights out in thirty minutes and then another warning at ten minutes and then a warning in the morning to wake up. On and on it went. She'd been a mindless zombie at times in there.

Milena shivered and she shook off the memories.

She was here. Not there.

Now all she needed to do was focus on keeping her thoughts in the present and not where she had spent so many years of her life locked up.

She lifted the lantern and stepped into the room. Her mouth dropped open with appreciation as she surveyed the rustic beauty of the small room. The walls were grey weathered wood planks, just like the rest of the barn, with several pretty watercolor paintings of horses hanging here and there. Near the white-painted iron wrought double bed was a white wood shelf with several novels, a candle and matches. There was also a white tallboy bureau pushed into the far corner and a quaint white painted oval mirror that had been hung on the back of the door she'd just closed.

A gorgeous black and red Navajo style rug covered most of the wood-planked floor and colorful Navajo style blankets were folded on a chair with more blankets covering the bed. The burst of colors brightened the dark room and made her feel joyful. But her happiness dissipated when she spied two long windows at one end of the room. There were no curtains.

Geez, what was it with these cowboys and no curtains? She noticed there were no locks on the doors or windows either.

Great. Just great.

Milena sighed and set the lantern on a cute little night table on the right side of the bed, then she plopped onto the mattress, which seemed firm and comfortable. She placed her nightie and clean underwear and salve, of which she had rolled up and tied together with a rope, beside her.

She shook her head as she looked at her simple clothing. She felt like she was the orphan Anne from the series of movies *Anne of Green Gables*. She'd seen the movies and the television series every time they had come onto the tv set in the common room of whichever prison she was being housed in at the time, much to the irritation of some inmates. But the women who'd protest, only did so for a short time and then they would join her in watching the story unfold of the elderly brother and sister who'd sent away for a boy to help out on their farm, only to receive a girl instead. Kind of like her story here.

She laughed quietly and quickly changed into her nightie. Then she tossed the blankets aside, gasping at the pretty pink and white heart patterned sheets. The material caressed nice and soft against her skin as she slipped between them. The pillow was plump and lush against her head. Everything felt so comfortable, and she had no doubt she'd sleep.

She smeared the salve on her hands, reached out and then turned off the lantern. The room fell into an almost complete blackness which immediately spooked her. Milena tucked the blankets up around her ears and stared at the windows. After a minute, her eyes grew accustomed to the darkness, and she could see the sky and the twinkling stars. As she lowered her gaze, she spied the dark silhouette of trees far off in the distance.

The room smelled nice. Of apple and she pondered if there was potpourri tucked away in the nearby dresser.

As her eyes closed, she wondered who had decorated this room. It couldn't have been the men. It had a feminine touch, just like Paul had said.

Her gut clenched. Was a girlfriend or maybe even a wife in the picture for one or all of them? She had just assumed all of them were single. Maybe she had presumed wrong?

Her heart sank. She hoped the guys didn't have girlfriends or wives or were in serious relationships. She smiled and snuggled deeper into the soft pillow. She liked it here with just the four of them.

She liked it here. A lot.

. . ⚓ . .

PAUL BLEW OUT THE CANDLE and wrapped the blankets closer around him. He'd forgotten how dark it was in this room, especially because it had only one small window compared to the other room which had two large ones that allowed plenty of moonlight to seep in.

The other room...Painful memories rushed over him. Everly had decorated that room. What a bitch she'd turned out to be.

She used the other room when she dropped by to check on her pregnant mare and her other horses. They should never have agreed to board her horses, mainly because of their past. But this ranch was just starting out and her father knew a lot of people in the horse business. And Everly knew them as well.

Had he snubbed her, he knew without a doubt she would turn the horse people against boarding their horses here and he didn't want this ranch to fail because of her.

Man, just thinking of that woman made boiling anger roar through him. Paul realized he'd clenched his fists and he forced himself to relax by inhaling deeply and thinking of something else or better yet, someone else.

Milena.

She was strong. She had to be to have endured prison for so many years and come out of it still being sweet. Sure, there was an edge of toughness to her, but there was something else about her that captured his attention. She had a helplessness hidden beneath her strong persona.

Every once in a while he caught glimpses of it and it made him stand up and take notice. It brought out his protective side.

Her helplessness had shone through when they'd returned to discover her holding the rifle, and she'd been ticked off because there had been no door locks.

Paul chuckled softly. He didn't blame her for being mad.

He had brought a loaded handgun along tonight without letting her know. No way was someone going to beat him up again or get near her without him killing them.

Her vulnerability went much deeper. Sometimes she got a lost girl look in her pretty brown eyes. A look that expressed to him that she felt like she didn't belong here. He hoped with time that would change.

Hell, he hoped she would stay. Forever.

When she had gone out tonight to the outhouse, Paul had walked her there, making sure no one or any bears or wolves were lurking around. But all had appeared calm tonight.

Maybe, just maybe, whoever had hit him and had screwed with the oven was gone for good.

He felt bad for the gyrfalcon though. He hoped that Milena's theory about an animal thief was wrong. He hoped that the bird had managed to break out of its cage, and simply escaped. It had been getting stronger every day, its appetite returning. He *truly* hoped Milena was wrong. But instincts told him that she was right.

Shit.

The three of them had come out here into the wilderness to get away from civilization and away from the stress that had been killing Mitch.

Paul's gut clenched as he thought about Mitch. Because of the sudden death of his parents, he had thrown himself into his work and an engagement. He'd been so stressed with his ultra-successful accounting firm and being engaged that his doctor had warned him if he kept up his brutal pace of being a workaholic, he would have a heart attack.

Paul had known Mitch and his large family since he could walk. Paul and Mitch had been inseparable since then, so the idea of Mitch dropping dead at such a young age unless something drastic happened like a slowdown in pace and a change in diet, the doctors had predicted Mitch would be dead of a heart attack by the age of fifty.

When Paul had suggested they both dump their jobs, set up shop in the wilderness like Mitch's brother, Brady, had done, Mitch had said no, at first. He'd said that "he literally would die of boredom out there in the desolate sticks", but when that heart attack the doctors had warned Mitch about, actually happened, it had changed Mitch's mind and his attitude in no time flat.

His friend had lost a lot of weight being out here working with the horses, eating wholesome foods, inhaling fresh air along with a different, more healthy kind of stress and lifestyle.

Daegen had joined them, because he'd thought it would help his ptsd. He said he was good with a hammer and carpentry, and he knew how to hunt so they'd invited him to be a partner here.

Paul had had his own reasons for leaving behind civilization. Avoiding Everly had been one major part and keeping Mitch alive had been the other major reason.

Too bad Everly was still in their lives. Thankfully though, in a minimalistic way.

Paul closed his eyes and wished Everly away. He did not want to think of her. He just wished she would stop popping into his head tonight.

He had been doing a good job in forgetting her, that is, until he had opened the room to show Milena. Everly had decorated it and claimed it as her own.

Paul smiled. He wondered how Everly would react when she discovered another woman was sleeping in her bed.

A small part of him wanted to see Everly's reaction, but a larger part hoped he would never see her again. But he knew that would not happen. At least not as long as he continued to board her horses and now also her foal here. He should contact her and let her know about the foal, but something inside him, something rebellious, just did not want her coming here and taking the foal to those cold training facilities they used to train horses. Maybe he never would tell her. Maybe he could pretend that Brownie Belle and the foal hadn't survived?

Oh crap, that was wishful thinking.

He cursed beneath his breath and forced himself to try to fall asleep. Despite his feeling very tired, he sensed sleep would be hard in coming tonight.

· · ⌁ · ·

"WHAT DO YOU THINK THE two of them are doing out there in the barn, all alone?" Daegen's soft question pierced the darkness of the cabin, making Mitch open his eyes.

It was darker than usual in here, probably because they had left the sheets strung up despite Milena not being here, and that was the window the moon would usually shine into at this time of the year. It was so weird not having her here. Even though she'd been around for such a short time, it felt as if she had been here forever.

"You know, Paul. He won't sleep until the mare is better," Mitch replied knowing full well his answer would not satisfy Daegen.

"Why didn't he ask one of us to go with him?" came Daegen's next question.

Hmm, so he was wondering if Paul and Milena might be getting close.

"I'm sure he wanted some alone time with her," Mitch teased

"Do you think that's why he asked her?" Daegen's voice was etched with excitement.

"Are you jealous? Maybe we should ask her to leave?" Mitch blurted. He wondered if Daegen was experiencing the same sense of loss as he was tonight.

"No, don't do that!" Daegen said quickly. Too quickly.

Mitch couldn't stop himself from laughing.

"What?" Daegen asked.

"Don't tell me you're already hung up on her?" Mitch asked.

"No more than you and Paul already are," he answered knowingly.

Shit!

Was he interested in Milena? Was Paul?

"Well, then maybe we have a problem," Mitch finally admitted, because he sure was interested in getting to know Milena more. Much more.

"Yeah, I guess we do," Daegen replied.

Silence followed and Mitch figured Daegen must've fallen asleep.

"Any suggestions?" Daegen asked after a few minutes.

"I suggest we all keep it strictly professional," Mitch finally replied.

Daegen chuckled softly.

"What?" Mitch growled, suddenly irritated.

"Like you kept it professional today? Lunch on the hillside on a blanket with her?"

Mitch noted the teasing undertone in his voice.

"Just trying to make her feel at home," he replied.

"You mean home, like in wife material?"

Mitch rolled his eyes, grabbed his spare pillow and whipped it Daegen's way hoping it hit him square in the face.

"Ompf!" came his muffled outcry.

Good. A hit.

"What the fuck?" Daegen laughed.

"Go to sleep and dream your dreams of Milena," Mitch said as he settled his head deeper into his remaining pillow and sighed.

"You just make sure you don't intrude on those dreams of mine or maybe a threesome might be something to explore," Daegen whispered.

Mitch stifled a moan and his cock jerked to full attention as visions erupted. Visions of Milena gasping with pleasure as he and Daegen made love to her.

"Shut up, man," Mitch warned between clenched teeth.

More laughter and then silence.

"Good night," Mitch finally whispered.

"Good night," came Daegen's reply.

Mitch resisted the urge to grab his hard shaft and stroke himself into an orgasm. He didn't want to give Daegen the satisfaction that a threesome with Milena turned him on. Bad.

Instead, he forced himself to think of all the work that needed to be done tomorrow. It took a while, but eventually he fell asleep.

. . ⚓ . .

MILENA KNEW SHE WAS dropping into a dream about her mother, and as always, she was helpless to stop it.

"She's slipping away, sweetheart, would you like to say goodbye to your mom?" The social worker's soft voice prodded Milena awake from the chair she'd fallen asleep on in the hospital's empty visitor's lounge.

A sudden coldness enveloped Milena and she couldn't help but tremble as fear wrapped its icy grip around her. She'd known this time would eventually come. Over the past year her mother had been sick off and on and Milena had learned that cancer and the chemotherapy drugs did that to people. Made them really sick.

Up until two weeks ago she had been able to stay home with her mom at their tiny one-bedroom apartment. They had been living there for a couple of years since dad had divorced mom. Then, they hadn't seen dad or heard from him again.

He hadn't even sent a birthday card. Nothing.

Mom said he had moved to a faraway country. In Dubai. Wherever that was.

At first, Milena had missed him. Had even missed his bad temper. But not anymore. She sure did miss mom though.

"Come. Follow me, hon. Let's go tell her goodbye."

The social worker named Mary held out her hand and for a second Milena didn't take it. She did not want to say goodbye to her mom. She was only eight years old. All her friends at school had their mothers and most had their fathers too. Oh, why couldn't she be lucky like her friends?

The social worker smiled. Milena liked her smile. It lit up her brown eyes and made her look really pretty. She had shoulder length dark brown hair that matched her eyes, and her voice was so gentle as she once again prodded Milena to come with her. The icy grip that had wrapped around her like a very bad coat, got worse as Milena grabbed her warm hand. On very shaky legs, she walked with the social worker down the quiet hallway to the room.

A nurse was sitting inside her mother's room beside her bed and when she saw Milena, she smiled. But her smile did not reach her cold blue eyes. Shivers raced up Milena's back and her mouth went frightfully dry when she saw how thin and white her mother looked. She looked even worse now than she had earlier this morning. The sight made Milena want to run away and never stop running.

"My Lena?" her mother whispered. Her voice was not her own. It sounded raspy, creepy.

Milena trembled as she stepped closer to the bed. Her mom's eyes were partly open but glazed in a weird way.

"Grab her hand so she knows you're here," instructed the nurse, who continued to sit at the other side of the bed.

Milena stared at her mother's hand. It was lifeless. Motionless. So thin.

Oh, please mommy. Please get better. I want us to go home.

"Take her hand, honey," the social worker prodded in such an ultra-gentle voice that Milena reluctantly did as she was told. She slipped her small fingers against her mother's outstretched palm.

Milena shivered. So cold. So, like ice.

"Mommy. I'm here. It's me."

She swore her mom smiled ever so slightly, but she wasn't sure. But her fingers gently curled around Milena's fingers.

"Be strong, My Milena. Be strong. Promise me."

Emotions, deep and raw ripped through Milena's chest. Suddenly she knew. Knew without a doubt that this was the last time she would see her mother alive. If she could call this state being alive. Her cheeks were sunken, and her lips were blue and parted as she struggled to suck in air.

"I love you, mom," Milena whispered.

She could hardly speak. Could hardly think as suddenly her mother's fingers went limp and an awful rattling sound ripped through the air. Suddenly there was no breathing.

Breathe, mom. Breath.

"She's gone," the nurse said in a monotone voice.

Milena could only stare at her mother. Could only will and pray and silently beg her to start breathing again.

But nothing happened. There was just silence. Complete and utter quiet. A silence she'd never experienced before.

She was alone now, and it was suddenly as if her mother had never existed.

"Come now, hon. Let's go," the social worker said as she pried Milena's fingers away from her mother's cold, lifeless hand.

Be strong. My Milena. Be strong

Milena's mother's soft, weak whisper broke Milena from her sleep and she opened her eyes to complete darkness and utter stillness.

For several long seconds Milena wondered if maybe she herself was dead. Maybe she was buried beneath the ground in a casket and had suddenly come back to life like she had envisioned her mother doing.

To her surprise, no panic hit her, as it usually did when she thought about her mom. There was just peace now and acceptance. For years, she'd awaken from nightmares, thinking her mother was still alive after they had buried her in that pine coffin. She remembered the single long stem red rose the social worker had given her to place on top of her mother's casket just before they had lowered it into the dark wet hole on that horrible rainy spring mid-May morning. Suddenly Milena remembered that her mom had died twenty-three years ago today.

Shit. This was the first time she'd forgotten the death anniversary. Every other year she'd been plagued with anxiety as she anticipated the arrival of this anniversary death date.

Surprisingly, sadness at thinking about her, didn't envelope her as it usually did. She felt strangely happy. Even hopeful.

How odd. Yet, how nice.

A soft thump echoed through the air from outside her room. Milena stiffened beneath her warm blankets.

What was that?

She tried to orient herself as to where she had left the lantern and realized it would be useless without the matches which were on a nearby shelf. If she moved, the intruder might hear her. But the intruder might also hurt Paul again. A surge of protectiveness for Paul forced her to quietly push aside her covers.

She sat up and reached through the eerie darkness. But before she could so much as locate the matches, a horrible howling erupted right outside the windows.

Oh my gosh! Terror raced through her in shuttering waves and she froze and stared into the blackness. What in the world was that?

Another spine tingling howl. This one came from somewhere further away.

Wolves? Although she had never heard them in reality before, she recognized the spooky sound from the wildlife documentaries she'd watched in prison.

As another spine tingling howl from the first wolf shattered the silence of her room it was at that moment she vowed to always carry matches with her from here on out. There was nothing worse than being caught in the dark without a light source.

Another howl. It was so close she wondered if maybe the wolf knew she was here and it would crash through the window to get to her.

More howls. Close and far.

Oh God.

Her heart beat in a maddening speed and her teeth chattered.

So much for being tough.

She leaned back against her pillow and pulled the blankets up around her neck and listened.

The howling continued, but there was another noise. A creak of the floorboards. Nearby. In the barn.

She stopped breathing and listened.

Another creak. Was that the outer door to this hallway creaking open? Was that footsteps she heard?

Yup! Someone was moving around in the back area of this barn.

Milena moved quickly. Blindly she ran her hand along the shelf. Her fingertips touched the candle and then the little box of matches!

Thank you, God!

Her hands shook wildly as she managed to slide open the box, and grab a match. She held the rounded end to the sandpaper side and then moved the match swiftly across. Pain sizzled through her thumb and forefinger as a tiny yellow flame flared and she immediately dropped the match onto the blanket. The light went out.

Her thumb and forefinger throbbed and felt awfully hot. She'd burned herself. She could smell the unpleasant scent of what had just happened to her flesh.

Shoot! In her panic she'd held the match too close to the sulphur end. She wouldn't make that mistake again. She grabbed another, and this time she held it properly. She struck the side of the box again and the match flared, illuminating the room with a tiny whisper of light.

Her gaze flew to the windows. Darkness loomed outside and her imagination conjured up a face in the window.

She stifled a scream. Chilly shivers scrambled across the back of her shoulders.

Nobody is there. Just your imagination.

She avoided looking at the windows again and quickly put the flame to the wick of the candle. Light flickered throughout the room and she swung her legs out of bed. The floorboards were ice cold beneath her feet. She shivered as the wolves howled some more. Back and forth they went.

She wanted to scream at them to shut up!

Okay. Calm down.

She just needed to cross the hallway and wake Paul and tell him there was someone lurking around.

Her heart beat even faster. Her knees wobbled and her legs threatened to give out as she stood. She had never been so scared in her entire life.

Well, that was not true. But this was in the top five for sure.

She reached the door, and opened it.

Someone stood right there!

She screamed and slammed the door shut. Hurriedly she gazed around the room for something she could use as a weapon.

Oh my God! There was nothing!

Had they already gotten Paul? Was she alone and at the mercy of a serial killer?

A brisk knock erupted at the door, making her jump and scream again.

"It's just me. Are you okay?" came Paul's voice.

"I was just coming to wake you up and check on—."

Milena whipped open the door and she swore if she hadn't been holding the candle she would have leaped right into Paul's arms. With him just being here and safe, some of her fear zipped right out of her. She peered over his shoulder, down the hallway into the darkness.

"Someone's inside the barn. I heard something."

"That was me. I dropped the flashlight. It rolled under the bed," Paul explained while staring at her with a curious expression. Did she see the sides of his lips twitch with amusement? Was he laughing at her?

"And I suppose you heard the wolves? Those creatures scared the daylights out of me," she confessed.

He didn't answer and she noted that his gaze now appeared hot and heavy and had dropped to her chest area. A hot blush whispered across her cheeks.

Her nightgown was old and threadbare and she just knew he could see the outline of her nipples and breasts. She resisted folding her arms over her chest. She liked the intimate shivers of excitement that coursed through her as he looked. It appeared he finally realized she'd caught him gawking and he quickly averted his gaze and cleared his throat.

Were his cheeks darkening? Oh my Lord, yes they were! She had embarrassed him!

"Do you still want to join me while I check on the horses? " he asked in a hoarse voice.

Milena smiled inwardly.

"You go ahead. I'll be there in just a minute," she answered.

He nodded and was about to go, then stopped.

"Could you bring the lantern too?" His eyes were bright in the candlelight and the angle of shadows played with Paul's facial features. Something nice and naughty fluttered deep inside her chest as she spied the dark five o'clock shadow hugging his cheeks and chin.

He really was cute.

She nodded jerkily.

Reluctantly, she stepped back into her room, set the candle on the lone chair and quickly slipped on her jeans.

Moments later, she was fully dressed and with glowing lantern in hand, she walked quietly past the stables so as not to disturb the animals further than they already were from the howling wolves.

Thankfully the wolves had stopped their noise. Perhaps her scream had scared them away?

She let herself into the stall and hung the lantern on the sturdy hook just inside the door and watched Paul's facial features as he sat on the stool with a stethoscope pressed to the new mother's chest area and the flashlight in his other hand.

Milena hadn't realized how much tension had been built up inside her until she saw Paul smile as he lifted the stethoscope and look up at Milena. His eyes sparkled wet with what she perceived as relief. Wow, he really got emotional with his patients. What an awesome trait in a man.

"Good news?" she asked as she gently stroked the foal's mane. The newborn whinnied in appreciation and then rubbed her face against Milena's hand.

"The best news. Her meds are working better than I expected. The foal is doing great too. I think it's best we just leave them be and let them get back to sleep."

Paul stood, picked up his black bag from a nearby shelf, placed the stethoscope inside and then headed toward the door. He grabbed the lantern and waited for her.

"Goodnight, sweeties," Milena said softly.

She wanted to embrace both of the horses, but she refrained herself. She could do the hugging in the morning.

Both of them watched her with dark brown eyes as she stood. The mare snorted and the foal neighed in protest.

Paul opened the stall door and she slipped past him into the cool hallway.

"It's a shame we got dressed for nothing," Paul said as he joined her. "Not that I'm complaining. How about we celebrate?" he asked in a most cheerful voice.

He was truly beaming.

"With what?" Milena asked, curiosity grabbing hold of her. They hadn't brought any food or refreshments along with them. The only thing she could think of was to drink some of that ice cold water that came out of the hand pump outside.

She shivered. And she wasn't about to go out there with wolves lurking around.

"Follow me," he instructed.

She followed him down the stable way and into the main front area of the barn. She remembered there was an office area just to the right near the door entrance and that's exactly where he headed.

Inside the office, he hung the lantern on a hook and the light splashed over the room to illuminate a rather large old oak desk that had seen better days. The top of the desk top was filled with nicks and cracks and it was overflowing with all kinds of paper paraphernalia.

Wow, it was a clutter, she had to admit.

"Excuse the mess. We've never gotten around to a proper filing system. But we always manage to pay the bills on time."

Paul sat down on a tattered office chair, leaned over, pulled open a drawer and to her surprise he hauled out a box of store bought cookies and then a bottle.

"My not so secret vices. Chocolate chip cookies and whiskey."

Booze. Oh. Oh.

Uneasiness assailed her as he brought out a couple of whiskey shot glasses, cleared a small spot on the table and placed the glasses on the desk.

"Um, I'm not allowed to have alcohol as per parole conditions," Milena said quickly.

Paul scrunched up his mouth and shrugged his shoulders.

"So, don't tell them. I won't," Paul replied. He poured one shot glass half full.

Nervousness burned through her.

"I can't lie when I talk to my parole officer when she asks me. But I can eat cookies."

She expected him to be irritated that she was raining on his celebration, but to her surprise, Paul chuckled.

"A woman who can't lie but can enjoy cookies is a woman after my own heart," Paul said, with a smile.

She smiled back at him, thankful for his easy going nature.

"Okay, sorry," he continued. "My bad. How about some water instead? I drew it from the spring just this afternoon. It'll wash down the cookies and believe you me, these cookies taste a heck of a lot better than my homemade concrete cookies."

"Sure, sounds like a plan."

"Grab a bottle. It's just in the corner there. Should be nice and cold from being on the ground."

There were several plastic bottles and sure enough the one she picked was nicely chilled. She twisted the cap open and poured water into her shot glass.

Paul ripped open the cookie package and set it on the table, then he lifted his glass and his eyes sparkled with such happiness, Milena felt it flow right into her like a river of joyfulness.

"Here's to a job well done with the horses. I can honestly say if you hadn't been here to deliver the foal, I doubt BB or her baby would be alive tonight. Cheers to a job well done."

Wow, she truly felt like a heroine at this moment.

Milena quickly grabbed her glass and touched it to his. A delicate clink echoed throughout the office.

"Cheers," she said.

She watched his lips curl over the rim of his glass and she enjoyed the way his eyes closed with appreciation and how his Adams apple bobbed as he swallowed the whiskey.

"You sure do take your job seriously," Milena said, as a moment later, his eyes popped open and she watched him pour a second glass.

"To tell you the truth, I get a high when one of my patients feels better."

He sure was flying now as he crunched on a cookie and then popped his head back and downed the second drink.

"How many drinks does it take for you to get drunk ?" she joked and then chuckled as he let out a long sigh of what she could only perceive as satisfaction.

"Not many. Mitch is much better at holding his liquor," he said with a smile and a wink.

She liked this easy going side of him, but that didn't mean she wanted him tipsy.

"I probably already am drunk," he replied, his grin widening.

To her surprise, he poured himself another shot and his hand was halfway to his mouth with the glass, when she grabbed his wrist, stopping him cold.

Surprise and confusion swirled in his now glassy eyes.

"When was the last pain medication you took?"

He frowned and looked up toward the wood planked office ceiling as if in deep thought.

"Hmm, this late afternoon. Or afternoon late...umm, just before dinner or maybe it was after? I'm not sure."

His gaze dropped to where she continued to hold his wrist and a sweet smile tilted his lips. Her breath caught at the wicked awareness zinging through her.

"Do you care?" he asked and lowered his arm.

Reluctantly she let go of him.

"Of course I care," Milena said quickly. Maybe too quickly. A hot blush of heat swept into her cheeks.

His lips parted slightly and he got a sultry expression in his eyes. She didn't have much experience with sex but instincts told her this was sexual awareness.

Oh boy.

"When was the last time you've been kissed?" he asked in a deep guttural voice.

"Excuse me?" she blurted, feeling confused at the rush of excitement shattering any caution she knew she should use.

"I want to kiss you. Can I kiss you?" he asked. His voice was soft now. Barely a whisper.

Suddenly she couldn't think. Couldn't even talk or form a thought. She wasn't even sure if she nodded permission for a kiss or if she had imagined doing so.

She held her breath as he moved his head closer to hers or maybe she was leaning toward him?

She wasn't sure, but suddenly at this moment, only one thing existed.

Attraction.

Searing lust flared and snapped to life the instant his hot mouth melted over hers and every nerve ending in her body fired up. She whimpered as his lips moved over hers and his tongue pushed past her lips. Without thinking she opened her mouth and his tongue played havoc with her senses as it dueled with her tongue.

Arousal burst through her like an untapped explosion. She wanted to grab his shoulders. Wanted to rub herself all over his body.

But before she could—.

He was pulling away.

"Wow," Paul breathed as he stared at her with appreciation and maybe even surprise?

Her lips tingled, felt so wonderfully swollen.

His kiss, how excruciatingly brief it was, had changed something inside of her. It had awakened something she hadn't realized she possessed. If there were words to describe it, she would say it was a primal need to have sex with this man.

And she wanted more. Needed more. Another kiss.

"I apologize. I shouldn't have taken advantage of you like that," Paul said.

His words were like a bucket of ice cold water dumping over her head.

Immediately she sobered. What in the world was she thinking? That he might be serious about her?

Oh my gosh. Fantasies, woman. Stupid fantasies.

"It must have been the booze. Yeah that's it. Has to be the booze and the meds mixture," Paul mumbled as he looked down at the shot glass full of whiskey sitting on the desk.

"I guess you're already drunk," she said with a forced chuckle.

But inside, devastation ruled. She had read way too much into this kiss. He was drunk, but she wasn't. So what was her excuse for feeling so wonderful inside his kiss?

"I think we better turn in. We have got an early morning," Paul said.

He avoided looking at her as he rewrapped the box of cookies and placed it and the bottle into the drawer.

"I'll take care of this in the morning." He waved to the glasses on the table.

As he swiftly grabbed the lantern, she thought she spied his cheeks were dark. Was he blushing?

No, it had to be the alcohol, just like he'd said.

Quietly she followed him and they returned to the guest quarters. He handed her the lantern, flicked on his flashlight and after a quick goodnight, he was gone.

Milena moaned inwardly as she slipped into her tiny room. Her body ached to be touched by Paul and her lips still tingled as she quickly undressed and donned her nightie.

A few seconds later, she slipped between the sheets and pulled up the warm covers. The air was chilly and she quickly reached out, made sure the matches were right there beside the lantern where she could reach them if needed, then she turned off the light.

The room plunged into darkness and Milena waited until her eyes adjusted to the night. She could see the outline of the windows and the stars sparkling in the black sky. There were no illusions of someone looking in. There were no sounds either. No wind clattering against the barn boards. The horses didn't neigh. Not even the wolves howled.

It was utterly tomb like.

It should make her feel scared, this desolation. But it didn't. Something wild had just happed between her and Paul.

Despite his protest that he shouldn't have kissed her, and despite her idea she was reading too much into the kiss, this wonderous quiet encouraged her to be in tune with her body and with her needs, her wants.

Dear heaven. She desired *sex*.

She closed her eyes and whimpered in frustration.

She needed an orgasm. She wanted to take off the sexual edge that Paul had created inside of her with just *one* itty bitty kiss. What would have happened had there been more kisses? Hot touches? Removal of their clothing?

Heat whispered into her cheeks. How would she be able to face him tomorrow in the light of day after that succulent kiss that had made her lose control so quickly?

She inhaled deeply and exhaled softly. She would think of how to handle the situation in the morning. Right now, she wanted some serious alone time.

And she was alone. Truly unaccompanied in her own room for the first time in like...many years. No one was watching her on a prison security camera. No men were listening beyond strung up sheets in a one room cabin.

She would just have to be quiet so Paul didn't hear.

Moaning softly, she raised her knees and spread her legs. Then she lifted her nightie and glided a hand over her right breast and gently massaged and pulled on her tender nipple.

She slipped her other hand between her open legs and stroked her ultra-sensitive clitoris. On the odd time when she'd masturbated in prison, it would take her awhile to become aroused. Not so tonight.

Behind her tightly closed eyes, she saw Paul. Envisioned him standing beside her bed, gazing down at her with a heavy lidded lusty look that told her he'd been lying when he'd said he shouldn't have kissed her.

Suddenly she just *knew* he had lied. *Knew* it hadn't been the combination of alcohol and pain meds. He *had* been acting on an attraction to her. Call it instincts and she had good instincts because she'd survived prison.

Giddiness at the sudden realization made her massage her clit more sensuously. Harder. Faster. And then without so much as a warning, she came on a moan, her body arching as destroying pleasure exploded through her.

Lightning bolts of erotic sensations slammed into her, making her writhe and buck. She thrust her fingers into her wet vagina and stroked in and out like a mini-cock. Wicked spasms had her jerking and whimpering shamelessly.

Too soon, the firestorm ebbed and she began working toward another orgasm. Her fingers worked their magic. Touching. Rubbing. Massaging.

The stirrings came again. And soon Milena was riding another wicked wave.

Oh yes! This was fantastic! This was how it should be!

This was the pleasure she'd been reading about in romance novels.

This was freedom!

Chapter Eight

P aul listened intently.

He'd been going over in his mind that intoxicating kiss he'd just shared with Milena, debating whether he should calm his naughty hard as a rock cock with a good old fashioned masturbation session, when he'd heard it.

A strangled cry? The creak of bedsprings? He should get out of bed and go and check. But out here in the wilderness there were all sorts of strange noises. Had someone come into the barn, the horses would have neighed or snorted. They were like that. In tune to people they knew and nervous around strangers.

But it was utterly quiet...except for those low interesting sounds.

A soft whimper? A creak?

Was Milena masturbating? Or was he just wishful thinking?

He should not have kissed her. Should have kept his head. But in the way she'd observed him with that vulnerable sexy as hell look as she'd watched him drink his whiskey.

His aching cock jerked at the seductive memory and his breaths became faster.

Oh damn! He wanted sex. Now.

His body was wound up too tight from the memories of her moist mouth opening so willingly beneath his prodding tongue and he knew he wouldn't be able to get any sleep unless he loosened up. And there was only one way he could think of to do it.

Have sex.

He lifted his ass and slid off his pajama bottoms. He preferred to sleep in the nude, had for many years, Mitch and Daegen did too. But with Milena here on the ranch, there had been a quiet mad scramble for pajama bottoms behind her back. Luckily Mitch had several, compliments of his oldest sister, Jenna, who sent a pair of flannel pajamas to him every Christmas. He'd had the foresight to bring several along to their ranch...just in case it got too damned cold, he'd explained to them.

Well, shit, being cold was the furthest thing on Paul's mind at the moment. His flesh felt hot to the touch as he wrapped his fingers around his penis, which was uncomfortably thick, but nicely heavy.

Oh, man, he was so damned hard with arousal.

Paul hissed through his teeth as he tenderly caressed the rigid throbbing length. His fingers swirled around his sensitive plum-shaped cockhead and already he could feel the electrical arousal shimmering in his balls. Making them pull tighter.

He barely realized he could no longer hear those interesting sounds. Had Milena brought herself to satisfaction? Was she sleeping soundly now while he struggled to keep himself from ripping away his blankets and going to her?

He massaged his cock harder, pulled on his scrotum, then slid his palms up and down his length causing an incredible friction. His noisy breathing filled the cool air. Perspiration whispered over his brow. He rubbed harder. And faster!

Before he knew what was happening, lightning shards of brutal pleasure snapped along his quivering penis and exploded into his lower belly. Paul shuddered and convulsed as the enjoyable bursts shook him to his very core.

As the climax slowly ebbed, Paul lay gasping.

Wow! He'd never gone through an orgasm this intense or this fast before! This was something he truly would enjoy experiencing again.

And again.

He could only imagine how it would be having Milena writhing beneath him, while he pleasured her and himself over and over.

To Paul's surprise, his cock started to harden again.

Oh man, he had the feeling this was going to be one hell of a long night.

·· ⚓ ··

MITCH'S GAZE DID NOT waver from the sheet of paper he was reading.

Daegen had noticed Mitch was once again reading the letter from the penitentiary as he sat at the kitchen table. Truth be told Daegen hadn't wanted to know what the correctional facility had to say about Milena. He knew she'd been in prison for a number of years and had done something bad and he'd told Mitch the other day he didn't want to know the details. He didn't need to know. She was an awesome woman and that was all that mattered.

He studied Mitch who continued to read. The frown on his face made Daegen's gut twist into one awful knot at the thought that there was something really bad in that letter. The last few days had been truly interesting and exciting with Milena around. Whatever bee was in Mitch's bonnet regarding the letter, Daegen hoped he would keep it to himself.

He turned over the bear steaks in the frying pan, then set about scrambling the eggs.

"She needs to check in with her parole officer by phone once a week. If she misses a call, that is a parole violation and she would be sent back," Mitch suddenly blurted as he slowly folded the papers and slipped them back into the envelope.

That was it? The crestfallen look on Mitch's face had made him believe something bad was going on.

"Kind of hard to keep a weekly schedule when the phones don't work half the time," Mitch muttered.

"That's what has you so upset? I thought you would jump at the first chance of sending her back? Having her miss a call would have her gone. This could be your ticket to freedom."

Daegen knew he was being harsh in his teasing, but he needed to know where Mitch stood on the Milena issue. He did not want to get too close to her if Mitch decided she was gone.

Daegen suddenly chided himself. He was not going to fall for Milena. Not a chance.

Too late for that, his inner voice chanted.

Daegen slammed down on that thought. He was not falling for the girl. No way.

When Mitch didn't answer, Daegen gazed over at him. Mitch wasn't sitting anymore. He was standing at the kitchen window gazing out toward the barn.

Daegen tensed.

"See something?"

"Yeah, they're coming back."

Just at that moment, he heard the rumble of the all terrain vehicle .

"Wonder if Paul got any action last night," Daegen teased.

He hoped his remark would get Mitch out of the funk he'd fallen into. Unfortunately Mitch didn't respond. From this angle, Daegen spied the scowl on his friend's face.

Despite Mitch's frown, excitement powered through Daegen. He couldn't wait to see Milena.

"Just in time for breakfast," Daegen called out as the door burst inward and Milena appeared.

She was like a beautiful ray of sunshine stepping into the room. She wore the same clothing she had worn last night and suddenly he wondered exactly how many articles of clothing she owned?

A woman fresh out of prison probably didn't own much. Why hadn't any of them even realized she would need certain things, especially since there was no store out here. He would need to talk to JJ or another woman to rectify the situation as soon as possible. Hell sooner!

· · ᪣ · ·

"LEATHER WORK GLOVES, post driver, fence stretcher, fence pliers, staple gun, staples, hammer, wire to tie fence ," Mitch looked over at Milena who furiously scribbled on a notepad what he was dictating.

Her forehead was scrunched up in determination and he had to admit she looked real cute when she was concentrating. He forced himself to keep washing the breakfast dishes and continued rattling off the list of items the two of them would need today.

"Bug spray, posts, wire cutters and water. Looks like a nice warm spring day full of sunshine. So yeah, include plenty of water, Paul."

He shot a look over at Paul, who was in charge of making everyone's lunch today. The man stared absently at the ham and cheese sandwiches he'd set into plastic storage containers.

Hmm, he had been staring far too long

"Almost finished?" he asked Paul, who didn't answer.

Paul hadn't put on any of the lids to keep the food fresh and seemed to be acting as if he didn't know what to do next.

What the heck?

Alarm sizzled through Mitch. Was Paul's head injury causing issues?

"Something wrong, Paul?" he asked quickly.

He didn't miss Milena's head snap up and she looked to Paul who frowned and placed the lidless containers into the bag.

Both of them had appeared way too quiet at breakfast and now Paul's screwup with the containers.

At Mitch's question, Paul's cheeks darkened.

Holy shit! Was his face flushed? No way.

Paul looked at Milena, who said nothing as she averted his gaze, then he looked at Mitch and shook his head, his frown turning into a momentary grimace.

"No. Nope. Not at all. I was just thinking about all the horses I have to check today. Lots of work. Lots on the mind. You know how it is. Nothing wrong. No, sir."

He had known Paul virtually all his life and when Paul denied something a little too vehemently, it meant the opposite.

And he *was* blushing. So was Milena. Her cheeks were unusually pink.

Had something happened between the two of them in the barn last night? Had Paul made a move on her?

No way. He wouldn't have the nerve. Paul was girl shy. Especially after what had happened with his last girlfriend. He'd sworn off women. At least that's what he'd said when they'd first moved out here last year.

"Doth protestith too much, my friend. By the way, lids are welcome on those lunch containers."

"Huh?" Paul looked into the bag, then realized what he had done. He swore softly and began to correct his mistake.

"We need to get out to the shed and grab the supplies and get on with the day. Milena you've got half an hour. If you need to take a shower, take it now. It'll probably take most of the day to build that paddock near the barn."

"Oh, I'm fine. I'll take one tonight," she said a little too quickly and gazed back down at the notepad.

Yep. Something had happened. The two of them were avoiding eye contact.

Had Paul made a move on Milena? Had she turned him down?

Ouch.

Mitch placed the last rinsed plate into the dish rack, removed his apron and hung it on a nearby hook .

"Okay then. Let's get on with it. Half an hour earlier start means half an hour earlier back here for supper."

"I like the sound of that. I'm already hungry," Milena chuckled as she stood, notepad in hand.

"You just had breakfast, " Paul laughed.

Mitch noted her earlier quiet mood had suddenly dissipated. Now her eyes sparkled with excitement. He liked her attitude toward a full day of hard labor. He supposed it beat shoveling manure all morning, which was Daegen's job today. That and letting out all the horses into the pasture and exercising them one at a time and then returning them to the barn so Paul could check them out.

Mitch enjoyed his time with the horses, but he suddenly realized he was looking forward to having Milena's company for the day. Much more than the company of the horses. He grabbed the cooler that Paul had just placed their lunch into, and smiled at the unusual lightheartedness he felt knowing that Milena was right behind him.

Strange, just a few days ago, he wanted her gone. Now he couldn't envision life here on the ranch without her.

• • ∽⊷ • •

MILENA COULDN'T HELP herself, but every time Mitch lifted the post driver, she got a really nice fluttery feeling deep inside the pit of her belly as the muscles in his chest and arms bulged and jerked.

Such eye candy. Have mercy!

She liked the way he smelled too. A faint aroma of spicy soap and perspiration along with a pine scent wafted off him. Sweat blistered across his forehead and drenched the back of his green muscle T-shirt. Wet wisps of hair peeked out from beneath that black cowboy hat he wore.

She was glad the salve she'd been using was doing the job. Sure her hands were a bit sore, but the soreness was tolerable and the gloves she wore were nicely padded. This morning when Paul had said he wanted to get a new paddock up for BB and her foal, Mitch had volunteered to do the work and she'd wanted to help too.

The guys had tried to talk her out of this job because of her hands, but she'd protested to the point they'd given in, which made her feel useful and good knowing that she could persuade them to see things her way.

"Okay, next post," Mitch said as he lifted the driver out of the hole he'd just made.

Milena moved quickly and dropped a heavy post into the hole and then shoveled the displaced dirt around to keep it nice and sturdy.

Mitch had already paced himself to the next spot and placed the digger against the earth, but he didn't start.

Instead, he leaned on the machine, frowned and stared at the ground.

"Did something happen between you and Paul last night? Did you two have a fight or something?" he suddenly asked.

His question stunned her. Had they been that obvious? How in the world could she tell Mitch that Paul and she had kissed? She felt her cheeks turn to fire.

Mitch looked up from the ground and his eyes darkened and twinkled in a teasing way.

"If Paul did something inappropriate, I can have a talk with him."

Horror swept through Milena.

"Oh no! Please, everything is fine. I don't want to cause any trouble. Nothing inappropriate has happened. Paul and I get along very well."

Mitch's eyebrows furrowed and he nodded, seemingly satisfied with her answer.

"Not the reaction I was expecting, but if you say so."

Thankfully he didn't say anything else about it.

Good heavens! That was too close.

"There is something else we need to discuss."

Milena sensed the seriousness in his voice and she instinctively knew he had read the letter from the prison.

Shit! She should have made it disappear!

She tensed as she watched him look across the lush green meadows. She followed his gaze to where several horses grazed near the winding creek. It was a picturesque sight. Serene. Peaceful. The feelings of calm and happiness flooded her and instantly she realized she never wanted to leave this place called Snowy Creek Ranch.

"A letter came from the penitentiary concerning you," he said.

Her momentary feelings of happy and calm were shattered. Oh darn! Just as she suspected.

She waited for him to continue, but he didn't. Instead, he turned on the digger and the lush dark earth began to mound around the quickly forming hole.

Suddenly she wanted to run away to the trailer as an excuse to grab the next post, but she needed to stay and find out what he had to say.

Several minutes went by and then he finally turned off the machine, removed his cowboy hat and wiped the perspiration from his brow with the back of his hand.

Her lower belly fluttered prettily. Mercy, he looked like some suntanned sexy cowboy God. She blinked away that insane thought when he spoke.

"We need to set up weekly phone conversations to touch base with your parole officer. Report cards, I guess." Mitch said with a wink.

Wow, she hadn't expected him to say that.

Immediately she relaxed. She had thought he was going to discuss why she had been sent to prison in the first place and then tell her he was giving her her walking papers.

"Since you arrived here on Thursday morning, we can call her this upcoming Thursday. Sound good?"

Milena shrugged.

"Whatever works best for your schedule. I don't want to be any trouble."

"You need to stop thinking that you're trouble," he snapped.

Then he cursed sharply and the piercing sound made Milena jump. He looked at her, the lines around his mouth giving her the impression he was not amused.

She suddenly realized she loved the sensual shape of his lips.

"You need to stop doing that too," he said gently.

Oh dear. How could he know what she was thinking? Did he know she thought he was sexy?

"Doing what?" she answered in a voice just as soft.

Have mercy, she had never sounded so sultry before. Milena swallowed trying to wet her suddenly dry throat.

"Looking at me like I'm going to bite your head off. I know we had a bit of a rough start. That would be my sister's fault, not yours. I don't want you to think you are any trouble, because you are not. Got it?"

"Oh, okay. Sure."

Wow, that had come right out of left field. His acceptance of her made all the difference and suddenly everything around her appeared so much brighter. She noted he had the most spectacular blue eyes. They glistened in the sunlight, much in the same way as the blue sapphire gems in her mother's engagement ring had shone beneath the lights.

"You have almost the same shade of blue colored eyes like your brother, Brady," she muttered.

He looked surprised and frowned.

"How do you know, Brady?"

"I ranch sat for them last summer over at Moose ranch. You guys were building a cabin for the fall roundup at some lake far away."

"That's right. We never did get to meet you. So you were that lady?"

"Yes. It was a trial run. Your sister pulled strings to get me a temporary gig with her Cowboys Online Program. I even met Daegen then."

His eyes widened.

"You met Daegen before here?" He sounded shocked. Obviously Daegen had not told them they had previously met.

Milena smiled as she remembered how they'd met.

"He rescued me from a bear who was intent on killing me and stealing the two buckets of blueberries I had picked."

Mitch's mouth dropped open in surprise.

"Seriously? He never mentioned it."

"I guess I'm forgettable," she teased.

She made a move to go and retrieve another post from the trailer, when his next words stopped her .

"You're definitely not forgettable, Milena. I think your confidence needs some heavy duty boosting."

His soft-spoken voice caressed her senses and she swore her knees weakened with desire as he strolled toward her. There was a look of intent in his gaze and before she knew what was happening, his fingers curled around her upper arms and his head lowered.

Oh my goodness! He was going to kiss her?

His eyes closed and so did hers. Butterflies flooded her belly and her heart crashed against her chest.

"Definitely not forgettable," he whispered.

His warm breath caressed her mouth and instinctively she parted her lips and slid her hands up and curled her fingers against the base of his warm neck.

Lightning heat sizzled across her mouth as his lips melted over hers. A flaming destructive need claimed her and she easily moved into the kiss. Moved against his body.

Moaned as she felt his solid erection press against her abdomen.

Lusty feelings gripped her and she boldly thrust her tongue into his mouth. She touched his tongue and he groaned and she whimpered at the naughty impact.

Oh, she could lose all control so easily inside these incredible sensations. Just like she had with Paul last night. The thought of kissing another man right after Paul should have stopped her. But it didn't. It aroused her with a dark hunger to think two men were wanting her.

Instinctively she arched her breasts against his hard muscular chest and she felt her nipples hardening with need. Anticipation roared through her as she slid her hands upward from his neck and cupped the back of his head, pushing his mouth harder against hers. Searing flames of heat lanced her pussy as he rubbed his erection against her abdomen.

And then he was pulling away...

He bit his bottom lip giving her a sheepish look.

"I guess the boss is going to have to have a talk with me about inappropriate behavior in the workplace," Mitch muttered as he swept up his cowboy hat and popped it back on his head.

Her body hummed with frustrated excitement. Oh lordy. She couldn't believe what had just happened. Her ears were buzzing and her lips were tingling much in the same way she'd reacted to Paul's kiss last night.

"Please don't apologize. We kissed and now that that is out of the way, let's get back to work," she murmured. She certainly didn't need another explanation like the one she had gotten from Paul last night.

It appeared as if Mitch wanted to say something, but instead he just nodded. She watched him stroll back to his job.

Inappropriate behavior? Give me more, please.

She felt aroused and hot.

Oh, so very hot. Just like after last night's kiss. Thankfully she'd been able to alleviate her arousal in her little room.

She gazed to beyond the fir trees lining the meadow. The forest appeared dense and dark. Probably nice and cool. She could excuse herself, go into the trees and pleasure herself, but with her luck, she'd get lost.

Oh boy. Within the span of twelve hours she had been kissed by two very attractive cowboys and she really liked the way those kisses made her feel.

The roar of the post digger being turned on ripped Milena back to reality.

Who cared about inappropriate behavior? She'd lost so many years of her life. Now that she was out, she just wanted to explore these naughty reactions.

In prison, seeing the rare male guard had done nothing for her. She'd pretty much only fantasized about movie or television stars and those had been pathetic fantasies compared to what she was experiencing now.

"You never said. Did the bear get your buckets of blueberries?" Mitch shouted as he operated the machine.

He was already perspiring again and she wanted to ask again for him to trade places and let her operate the post digger. But when she'd asked him several times this morning, he'd refused, stating that he needed to build up muscles.

"No, Daegen rescued them too. And they even survived the thunderstorm while he canoed me back to the ranch," she yelled back.

To her surprise, Mitch laughed.

"The things a man won't do for some blueberry pie. He did get some pie, didn't he?"

"Actually, come to think of it, when we got back to the ranch, the electricity went out shortly after, so we went to bed."

She had lied about the reason Daegen hadn't eaten any blueberries. Truth was he'd lost his appetite when she'd revealed she was a convict out of prison on a temporary leave.

Mitch's eyes widened.

"Out of power? Really?"

Milena immediately caught his meaning, and her cheeks warmed. Daegen had told her that he was gay to put her mind at ease about the two of them spending the night together alone. She later found out from JJ, that he wasn't gay. Had she known the truth, she might have acted upon the opportunity and had a one-night stand with Daegen.

"We slept in separate rooms. In the morning, he was gone."

And without so much as a goodbye, she added silently.

"So, you owe him a blueberry pie at the very least for all his trouble in rescuing you," he prodded.

She bit back a smile.

"Are you insinuating that I bake a pie for Daegen?"

"Hell no. Not just him. I want one too."

Milena laughed at his comment.

Mitch removed the post digger and placed himself at the next spot where he would dig another hole. Milena hoisted a cedar post out of the trailer, brought it to the recently dug hole and placed the post. She retrieved the shovel and heaped dirt around the post until it was solid.

Then she drove the all terrain vehicle to where Mitch was working. She hopped off the machine and went to the front part of the trailer where she opened the cooler and withdrew a plastic bottle of drinking water.

"Want some water?" she shouted above the roar of the post digger. She was pretty warm standing under the sunshine, so she could only imagine how hot he must be as he toiled.

His face was red from exertion and she wanted to keep him hydrated.

He shook his head.

"Not yet. You go ahead."

This is so nice and cold, she thought as she rolled the chilled bottle across her hot forehead.

"Oh, this feels fantastic," Milena called out as she closed her eyes and loved the cool moisture of the bottle of water drip across her warm skin.

"A blueberry pie would feel fantastic too!" Mitch shouted back.

He had already completed another hole and had started another.

Gosh, he worked fast.

"Do you have any blueberries? Ready made pie crust?" Milena yelled to him.

Certainly she could bake a blueberry pie. Her mom had bought those ready made crusts at the grocery store.

"Sorry, no. We would have to make our own crust but I don't have the ingredients on hand. It just so happens I know how to make crust. My mom couldn't keep me and a couple of my brothers out of the kitchen when baking desserts came around. So she taught us the instant we were old enough not to put our fingers near the electric mixer."

"Awesome!" Suddenly Milena had an urge for blueberry pie.

"Remember the hill we climbed the other day to make phone calls?" Mitch called out.

Milena nodded.

"Plenty of blueberries on the south side of that hill. But we will have to wait until late July or early August!"

"Oh shoot."

"Until then we have a short wait for wild strawberries. We get them late June into early July. That's followed by wild raspberries. Then the blueberries. Then after that come the blackberries. And then the apples. There's a few apple trees scattered here and there from previous owners. But the apples are not as nice and shiny as the ones you buy in the store."

All these fruits? Way out here? This was absolutely insane! But in a really cool way!

"It's a natural grocery store out here," Milena laughed and undid the bottle cap. She watched Mitch as he moved the post digger to another spot.

Yeah, he sure did look sexy drenched in sweat. He held the auger with one gloved hand and with the other hand wiped his brow. Her pulse pounded as his muscles flexed in his arms.

"When we get the garden going, we'll have an abundance of vegetables this fall," he said as he gazed at her, a smile on his face.

"But won't the animals eat everything?" Milena asked.

She took a few generous swallows of the cold water and truly enjoyed how it splashed into her parched mouth.

He shook his head.

"I was over at Moose Ranch a couple weeks back and Dan was showing me the cages he made to protect their crops. Moose Ranch has Internet access so while I was there I ordered the supplies to make the cages, ordered the seeds and a roto tiller and some tools. The order should be coming in via bush plane in a week or two."

Milena couldn't believe it.

"Amazing. You don't have to go to the city to shop. Everything comes to you via bush plane?"

Mitch nodded.

Suddenly he turned off the post digger, left it standing in the partially made hole he'd been drilling and strolled toward her.

She tensed. The last time he left a post, he'd come over and kissed her.

Her heart began to pound with anticipation. Her breath halted as he stepped beside her. Heat waves blew off his body and caressed her skin.

But he did not kiss her.

Instead, he removed his gloves and placed them on the edge of the trailer, opened the cooler and grabbed himself a bottle of water.

Damn.

"It's getting pretty hot," he mumbled as he twisted off his bottle cap.

Hot was an understatement. She was burning up just watching how sexy he looked shirtless with perspiration lashing his bulging muscles.

Suddenly she just didn't want to work anymore. She just wanted sex. With Mitch. With Paul. With Daegen.

Fresh perspiration blossomed across her forehead as her face heated.

Oh heavens!

Had all these years in a prison without a man screwed her up? Why did she want all of her cowboy bosses to have sex with her?

Impulsively Milena lifted her water bottle and allowed the rest of the contents to pour over her head. She gasped as the rivulets gushed down her neck, along her back, over her chest and between her breasts.

"I bet that felt good," Mitch laughed.

Her eyes snapped open. Mitch was staring at her with an interested grin as his gaze flew from her breasts to her face.

She didn't dare look down. The water would surely be outlining her bra against her t-shirt.

For a few precious seconds she'd simply immersed herself in the pleasure of the water cascading over her and forgotten Mitch was here.

"There is the creek to cool off in if you would like. I'll just keep working and give you some privacy."

Anxiety shot through Milena. The creek? No way!

Oh! But why couldn't she just be normal and not be afraid of water! How insane was she? Why couldn't she just jump into a lake or river or just sit beside a stream and stick her feet in the water without having an anxiety attack? She remembered doing it when she'd been little. Being carefree and having fun splashing in the water. But something must have happened to change it. She didn't know what. And now she just couldn't do it.

"Something wrong?" Mitch suddenly asked. His eyebrows were furrowed with concern and he was frowning at her.

"I don't have a bathing suit, so I can't." She hoped that would be the end of it.

But she was wrong.

"None of us having bathing suits. Just use your birthday suit. That's why I said I would give you privacy if you want to cool down."

Birthday suit. Wow. Wouldn't that be awesome. Splashing around naked with three cowboys. That *should* be an incentive to get into the water. It wasn't.

"Oh, I'm fine. I can keep working."

Working instead of sex...er, a swim? Stupid woman!

For a split second she had the feeling if he said he would join her in the water in his birthday suit, she just might have an incentive to overcome her irrational fear. But the daring feeling vanished.

"Are you sure? I don't want you coming down with heat stroke. You're not used to being outside in this kind of weather. I would totally understand if you want to take a plunge."

She shook her head.

No. she was tough. She would stay. She didn't want him to think she was a sissy. She wanted him to think she was a good laborer. Maybe even something more?

Stop with the crazy thoughts! You are a nobody. An ex-con. Just a helper.

"I'll take one when you do," she said and tossed her empty bottle into the trailer.

He chuckled seemingly happy with her answer. He lifted his bottle which was still half full and dumped the contents over his head, just as she had done.

She laughed as he gasped and danced around.

"Wow! Yep, that does feel good."

He looked real good too with wet hair and beads of water dripping off his luscious lips. Lips she really wanted to kiss again.

The inner fire stroking her need to have sex increased tenfold.

"Okay, let's get back to it, then," Mitch said as he grabbed his work gloves and headed back to his post digger.

Milena moaned inwardly. This was going to be one very hard day.

• • ᥡᦫᦾ • •

DO. NOT. KISS. HER. Ever. Again.

Mitch chastised himself over and over as they worked. He continued his mantra through lunch as they sat in the shade of the nearby pine forest. Then through the afternoon as they finished the paddock. When quitting time came around he was too tired to keep his Do. Not. Kiss. Her. Ever. Again. mantra going.

When she volunteered to drive, he was glad to sit behind her and enjoy the scenery.

The late afternoon sunshine splashed orange across the tips of the pine trees lacing the edge of the meadow they were travelling through. This part of the day was always his favorite. A day of work behind him and a leisurely evening with the guys in front of him.

But Milena was not just one of the guys. Not after that succulent kiss they'd shared. He closed his eyes and tried hard not to remember what had happened.

He had purposely worked his ass off in a desperate effort to keep his mind from wandering back to that damn toe curling kiss.

But as the sweat trickled down his back throughout the day, a wildfire had pounded through his veins. Every muscle in his body tensed every time he thought of how delicate and vulnerable her mouth had felt beneath his. Raw wanton need had kicked through him, just as it was doing now and with it came this weird protective emotion in his heart for her.

Shit. He should have gotten rid of her the minute she'd showed up. Now it was already too late.

Her mouth had felt so hot. So willing. So soft.

And she'd smelled so good. Like flowers and sunshine and—

"Hey! We've got company!" Milena's shout crashed through Mitch's thoughts and for a few seconds he had no idea what she was talking about. But when she slowed and then stopped the ATV, he spied three deer standing right smack on the rugged meadow trail not more than thirty feet in front of them.

The animals stood like frozen statues staring at them. Only an occasional ear twitched as a fly buzzed around.

"It must be a family," Milena whispered. Her voice was edged with awe.

Mitch kept his voice low as he answered her.

"The largest one is the buck. You can tell because his head on top is flatter than hers. The other larger one is the female. The smaller is their baby."

"They are so beautiful," Milena whispered.

So are you, Mitch thought.

"I can't believe people hurt these wonderful creatures," she said in a soft innocent voice that almost broke his heart.

He opted not to reveal to her that last autumn they'd shot and killed a deer for food. He hadn't liked doing it, but ordering meat via the Internet and having it flown in was not a viable option, especially when they had decided to learn to live off the land.

A faraway drone of a plane had the female deer sprinting off across the meadow, the white of her tail upward warning the rest to follow. And they did.

By the time a plane flew into sight the deer had disappeared into the surrounding wilderness.

"Plane coming in from Moose Ranch," Mitch said from behind her.

Milena squinted upward and saw the sunshine glint off a big white bush plane. Her heart crashed as she twisted the key into the ignition and within a second she was speeding them toward the cabin which was just a speck in the distance.

Moose Ranch! Maybe JJ was coming? Oh please be JJ! Last year she was the only pilot at Moose Ranch. It had to be JJ!!

She swore if she could drive this machine any faster without causing them to roll over, she would. The tense way Mitch was suddenly clutching his arms around her waist made her realise he probably thought she was a crazy driver.

Heck, she didn't even have a driver's license. Were people without a license even allowed to drive these machines?

Oh Milena, who cares. The men wouldn't let you drive if it was illegal to do so.

She blew out a tense breath as they neared the cabin.

Home, cute, home, Milena thought with a smile. She spied a spiral of white smoke billowing out of the chimney and realized it had gotten colder now that the sun was behind the trees.

As they drew closer to the cabin, she spied a couple of atv's erupting from the right side of the forest and she remembered that was the direction of the trail to the lake.

Paul and Daegen must have heard the plane too and gone down to meet their guests. Milena's excitement grew as several figures got off their machines and waited for them.

Happiness crashed through her like a torpedo the instant she recognized the pilot of the plane. It was her friend who she had not seen since last summer.

It was JJ!

"Jennifer Jane!" Milena called out and waved. JJ waved back.

Milena parked the machine and her arms ached to hug her old friend as they practically ran to each other. Tears of happiness streamed from Milena's eyes blurring everything as she swept her arms around JJ. Her friend hugged her back and they were both crying. They clung to each other for so long, and Milena felt her own tension leave her body.

Hugging people had always brought her comfort. It was a human contact that she craved and she reserved hugs only for people she trusted. And she trusted JJ.

"Let me take a look at you," Milena said between sobs as she reluctantly broke the hug.

JJ looked stunning. Her beautiful brown eyes sparkled brilliantly and her cheeks looked like blushing rose buds. She wore a light gray fleece hoodie, blue jeans and sturdy looking hiking boots.

"Oh my gosh, you look so healthy and beautiful. Rural life truly agrees with you," Milena praised.

"Hey, what about this one?" came Brady's gruff voice.

Milena snapped her gaze to Brady, who looked just as fresh and happy as JJ. But that's not what captured her full attention. It was what Brady held in his arms.

Her heart twisted at the sight.

A baby. And she was smiling at Milena as if happy to see her. Her blue eyes were wide as she gazed curiously at Milena. Then she cooed prettily which was followed by a bubble erupting between her rosebud shaped mouth.

"Milena, Meet Christmas. Or Christine or Chrissy for short."

This was JJ's baby. She'd had her last Christmas.

Happiness rocked through Milena. This was the first baby she had seen up close in years.

"Oh my goodness. Hi little Christmas. I heard that you had been born. Your mom wrote to me and told me all about you."

She resisted the overwhelming urge to reach out, grab the little baby and hug her.

"She is adorable. She's what, five months old now?" Milena asked. She couldn't take her eyes off the sweet baby.

"You can hold her." JJ suddenly said with an encouraging smile.

Without warning, terror raced through Milena.

She shook her head.

"Oh no, I couldn't. I might drop her."

Abruptly JJ laughed. It was a light hearted laugh that chased away Milena's momentary fear.

"Go on, hold her. It's instinct not to drop her," Brady prodded with a grin.

Brady held out the baby and Milena's lingering doubts vanished.

She accepted the soft bundle of warmth and was surprised at how heavy she felt and how wonderful she smelled. Fresh, and a soft baby powder scent.

Milena hugged her gently and instinctively rocked her quietly in her arms. She spoke softly to the baby and watched her eyelids flutter and then close. Within seconds she was fast asleep.

"Oh lordy. Am I this boring?" Milena laughed.

When she looked up she was shocked to see Mitch, Paul and Daegen watching her. Their gazes were curious, yet intense as if they were seeing her for the first time.

A sudden bout of shyness whipped through her and her cheeks warmed.

"You're a natural. She trusts you already. If she didn't, she wouldn't fall asleep," JJ complimented.

"Want me to take her back?" Brady asked.

"Oh no, I'm fine," Milena answered quickly.

She wanted to hold this baby in her arms forever and ever. She looked so sweet and innocent and she made Milena's heart sing with joy. Despite everything she'd been through, being locked up in prison, she realized there still was so much beauty and innocence in this world.

"Come on inside with us, Brady. Let's leave the ladies here to talk. Ladies, dinner is in fifteen minutes," Paul said.

He motioned with a wave for the guys to go inside.

A moment later, there was a flurry of excited men's' voices from inside the cabin.

"Come on. Let's go sit on the porch chairs," JJ instructed.

She grabbed a large duffel bag from the back of one of the atv trailers and headed up the stairs.

A moment later, Milena and JJ were talking quietly while they sat on the white wicker chairs and the baby slept in Milena's arms.

"I was absolutely over the moon when Brady told me he had spoken with Mitch and that you were here at Snowy Creek Ranch," JJ gushed.

"It happened so fast. I am afraid to pinch myself in case I wake up and all this is not real," Milena said truthfully.

"Oh, it's real. I had the same reaction when I first arrived over at Moose Ranch. Sometimes I still think it's a dream," JJ replied. She gazed down at her daughter and her entire face transformed into one of peace and unconditional love

Wow. I wonder if I will ever be so lucky as JJ, Milena thought as she lightly brushed a finger against the baby's cherub cheek. Her skin felt so soft, just like the red velvet dress her mother had made her when she'd been a kid

"I daydream that I'm in a magical wilderness that is making all my dreams come true," JJ said softy with a pensive expression.

Milena frowned. She wished JJ's magical wilderness would make her dreams come true too. At the moment she didn't feel fully comfortable about staying here, especially now that she had shared kisses with Paul and Mitch. Surely the guys would find out about the kisses. Men talked, didn't they? They'd get upset and maybe send her back to prison.

"Oh my God, Milena. Why such a sad face all of a sudden? Did I say something wrong?" JJ gasped.

Her friend reached out and tenderly placed her hand on Milena's elbow. Such a sweet gesture. She hadn't had so much human physical contact in years.

Men kissing her. A baby nestled in her arms. A caring concerned friend.

She wanted to blurt her doubts about not being allowed to stay here to JJ, but she didn't dare open up an avenue for questions.

Instead, she gazed at the baby and all her doom and gloom disintegrated.

She smiled reassuringly at JJ.

"Everything is fine. It's just like I said, sometimes I feel like I am dreaming and I get scared."

JJ breathed a sigh of relief.

"Whew! For a minute there I thought you might not be happy here."

"I am," Milena answered quickly. "I'm still trying to settle in."

But two men have kissed me and I enjoyed the kisses and I don't know what to do?

"Oh good. You had me worried. I want you happy, Milena. Just as happy as I am."

Milena bit back another frown. She doubted she would ever be truly forever happy, but she remained silent about the subject, opting to change it.

"Your daughter is so beautiful, JJ," she said truthfully.

JJ nodded and giggled tenderly.

"She can be a handful when she's awake. She's got Brady's curiosity and watches everything we do. And she's so smart. I swear she's already trying to talk despite the guys insisting it is too early. But enough about the baby. Before I forget, I brought you some lady supplies. Makeup, a compact mirror, and other items. It's all here." She pointed to the duffel bag Milena had seen JJ remove from the trailer earlier.

"You can take a look later," JJ said and then suddenly she was squirming with excitement in the chair.

"I want to ask you a question and you can't say no."

Milena laughed. "I can't say no? What kind of a question is that?"

JJ swept her hands over her mouth and Milena swore she had never seen her friend this ecstatic.

"What is it?" she prodded, feeling JJ's excitement pour through herself.

"In two weeks. Saturday late afternoon and into the night. I'm throwing a spring dance party. I want you to come. All our friends will be there and I would like to introduce you."

A bad sinking feeling crawled through my Milena and she shrugged her shoulders and shook her head.

"I'm not one for parties."

JJ blinked with obvious surprise.

"You're serious. Since when? You were the bubbliest person in prison. You were the welcome lady. That's what everyone called you. You made all the newbies feel just a bit better with your warm hugs. I cannot tell you enough how much help you were to me on the inside, coaxing me out of my cell every chance you got. Now I'm here to return the favor. Not that you're in a jail cell here. But a woman surrounded by men likes to get out once in awhile and have some fun, right?"

JJ winked and Milena laughed.

"You're talking about yourself!" she huffed.

"I cannot tell a lie, but yes I want to have my friends over and enjoy their company and have a night of dancing."

JJ settled her hand on Milena's wrist and squeezed gently, reassuringly.

"Please come. For me?"

Her friend's eyes sparkled with hope and Milena felt her resistance crash and burn.

Oh crap. How could she say no to JJ? Especially after everything JJ had done for her in getting her a ranch sitting job last year and then setting her up with the Cowboys Online program through Brady's sister. It was because of JJ and Jenna that Milena was here.

"Of course, I will come. But I don't have anything fancy to wear."

"I'm taking care of that. I will come early that day and get you ready. You will love it. I promise. Oh my gosh! You have made me so happy, Milena!"

JJ reached over and hugged Milena, being extra careful not to squeeze or wake the baby.

Oh dear. Talk about pressure. She doubted she would have a good time. She was regretting her decision already.

"Food is ready, ladies," Daegen said from behind a nearby open window.

"Be right in," JJ called out softly.

"Your cowboys are invited too," JJ added as she grabbed the duffel bag and stood.

Oh great. How in the world was she going to socialize with her three bosses being there?

The same way you're doing it now, a very naughty voice echoed in her head. Milena groaned inwardly.

Oh please, give me strength, she prayed.

With the sleeping baby cuddled in her arms, Milena got up and followed JJ into the cabin.

Chapter Nine

"And please give Miss Jane Sunflower this note from me when you go and visit her," JJ said as she handed Daegen a letter she had written for the elderly woman who was Snowy Creek Ranch's neighbor.

"And this present. It contains a jar of maple syrup that Brady and Chrissy made and some beef jerky which doesn't require refrigeration. It's quite light to carry."

Milena watched as JJ handed Daegen a package. He accepted it with a smile and she could tell Daegen really appreciated JJ's thoughtfulness.

Apparently Daegen had let Moose Ranch know that he was going to pay their elderly neighbor a visit.

"I'll make sure she get's it," he said with a nod.

Milena was once again holding the baby, who was wide awake and staring at Milena with the same curiosity she'd been portraying earlier before she'd fallen asleep. She really enjoyed cuddling little Chrissy. It was as if the baby had chased away all the dark corners inside of Milena.

"I had no idea we had another neighbour until last autumn when Blue called Brady and asked us to check on her. Her plane was having technical difficulties and she helps Jane at her ranch sometimes and she couldn't make it. But I was grounded due to my pregnancy, so Brady canoed over to ask the guys if they would mind checking in on her," JJ told Milena.

"She's done pretty good for herself living all alone out there with her lamb ranch," Paul explained. "She bakes some mean shortbread cookies and her lamb milk soap and candles came in handy. We had no idea she was there either."

"I think it is wise to check in on her, especially with her being elderly. The last of the snow has melted in the forest, so it should be easy enough for a two-day hike over and back," Daegen said.

Milena frowned but remained silent. They had congregated around the all terrain vehicles and the only source of light was the yellow glow splashing over them from a gas lantern someone had set on the porch railing behind them.

Brady and Mitch had disappeared in the darkness to head over to the shed with the excuse Mitch needed a part for the tractor and Brady had agreed to order it via Internet. He just needed the part number. But when they returned JJ would be gone and Milena suddenly wasn't looking forward to being alone with the three men.

She had noticed no one had brought up the real reason Daegen was going to the hermit neighbor, which she was sure was to warn Jane Sunflower that someone was shooting animals and attacking people. Milena figured maybe they didn't want to worry JJ due to her anxiety issues and Milena hadn't brought up the subject either because she figured it wasn't her place.

"Daegen! I have an idea!" JJ suddenly said in a flurry of excitement.

"Why don't you take Milena with you to visit Miss Jane Sunflower. I'm sure she would love some female companionship!"

Milena's tummy sank.

Her? Alone with Daegen? He suddenly looked just as uneasy as Milena felt.

"Well, it's almost a full day hike to get there and I'm not sure we can spare two people," Daegen muttered as he stared at the ground, seemingly unsure of what else to say.

"Sure we can," Paul broke in. "The only horse that needs tending to is Brownie Belle. I can help with mucking out the stalls and Mitch can let the other horses roam on their own for a day or two."

"Great! Then it is settled," JJ said. She turned to Milena and then lovingly gazed at her daughter..

"She's really taken with you," JJ said softly.

"And I'm taken with her too," Milena admitted.

"You're a natural with kids. Isn't she a natural with kids?" JJ asked Daegen and Paul who stood on each side of Milena, making her very aware they were here.

"Yeah, she is," Daegen replied in a soft whispery voice.

"A regular mom," Paul agreed.

JJ smiled and in the lamplight Milena wasn't sure if she caught a mischievous glint in her friend's eyes. She really hoped it was just a trick of the light, because Lord help her the last thing she needed was to have a matchmaker on her hands with everything else that was going on.

• • ～✤～ • •

"I STILL CANNOT BELIEVE Jenna would do that to you, even after she promised she wouldn't," Brady said.

Humor laced his voice as they walked along the edge of the forest, back toward the cabin.

Mitch bristled with anger.

"I hope you didn't have any input in this scheme of hers or I would disown you as my brother, just like I am going to do to Jenna the instant she returns my calls."

"I swear. When you first told me what she did, I just about fell off my chair I laughed so hard."

Mitch rolled his eyes and growled at his brother.

"Oh come on, little brother, it can't be all that bad?"

Mitch winced as Brady slapped his back in a sign of affection and continued talking.

"Sorry, bro, but seriously, things didn't turn out bad for me. We got JJ and we wouldn't trade her for anything in the world."

Truth be told he wouldn't trade Milena either, but he wasn't just ready to admit that yet.

"You said before supper that you heard back from the Ministry of Natural Resources about the injured animals? But you wanted to tell me after supper out of earshot of JJ?" Mitch asked.

In the moonlight, he noted his brother frown.

"They said there have been reports since last summer about suspicious activity in the area. The MNR suspects poachers and they are grateful you called it in. There have been cuts to conservation officers and that's why no one has checked it out yet. But they will send someone as soon as they can. I also contacted the Ontario Provincial Police about Paul being attacked. They said they would send someone out as soon as possible to interview him as to what happened."

Surprise washed over Mitch.

"Out here? Seriously?"

Brady nodded. "

"Yup, so keep an eye out."

"It's what we've been doing. Kind of hard to work thinking you have a target on your back."

"Poachers usually don't like to attract attention to themselves while being in an area they're harvesting animals, so they're curious as to why Paul was attacked."

"Well, the low profile part is good to know. I'm guessing someone was inside the barn and maybe panicked," Mitch said.

"Let's hope so. Looks like it's time to go. They're already outside waiting on us," Brady replied and nodded toward the cabin.

Mitch caught sight of the small group standing beside the all terrain vehicles talking and laughing. He noted Milena cradling the baby again. He could tell she really enjoyed the infant and he'd literally seen all the stress melt out of her the instant Brady had handed little Christmas over to her earlier when they'd first arrived.

"So, when are you two having another baby?" Mitch suddenly blurted. He hadn't meant to say it out loud, but too late to take it back now.

A really nice smile whispered across Brady's face and instinctively Mitch knew Brady wanted another kid.

"As soon as JJ asks," Brady replied.

"It's that easy?" Mitch joked.

"Well, no there's much more to it than that, bro. Didn't dad give you all the birds and the bees speech?"

Mitch couldn't help but laugh and enjoyed Brady chiming in as well.

"Oh man, do not remind me about that speech. Dad acted so awkward, it was so painful to listen to stuff I'd already learned in school."

"He was awkward with you too?" Brady asked. "I would have thought he would have improved after telling me about the birds and the bees. You would think it would have been easy for him to talk about such things having had so many kids of his own."

"What are you two boys talking about?" JJ called out as they strolled into the yard.

Mitch watched as Brady wrapped an arm around JJ's waist and brought her close to him.

"Man talk," he said with a smile and winked at Mitch.

"Well, mister man, are we going? We need to be going so I can get Chrissy to bed."

"That's my cue to drive you guys out to the lake," Daegen said as he started handing out the helmets.

"I'll just say goodbye here," Milena said and then she gently kissed Chrissy's velvety cheek.

The baby cooed happily.

"Here, I'll take her and settle her into the baby carrier," Brady said.

Milena nodded. A thick wedge of emotion clutched her chest as Brady emptied her arms of the suddenly wiggling baby.

She didn't want them to go. She already loved Chrissy so much her heart was near to bursting with grief at being separated from her.

JJ strolled forward and gave Milena are warm hug.

"Remember in two weeks. We'll see you for the party. I'm picking you all up," JJ said.

I'll be here earlier, she mouthed the words to Milena, who nodded and her tummy once again dipped in a frightened kind of way. Her going to a party? She just did not see it happening.

There was a bustle of activity as the cooing baby was placed into a papoose like cradle and hoisted onto Brady's back.

Then Brady climbed on an atv behind Mitch and JJ sat behind Daegen on the other machine. JJ waved to Milena and soon the vehicles were slowly motoring along the trail, their lights searing through the darkness.

"We had a long day. I'm toast. Let's go inside and get ready for bed," Paul said as he stomped up the stairs.

"I'll be in in a few minutes," Milena replied.

Paul didn't say anything as he slipped inside the cabin. Truth be told, she just wanted to stand out here in the meadow, inhale the fresh air and listen.

From the direction of the creek, the frogs sang and cool wind whispered through the nearby branches of a pine tree. Overhead, the stars twinkled brightly in the dark sky.

A few minutes later the rumble of the engines stopped. That meant they'd reached the lake.

The lake. That's the main reason she hadn't wanted to go say goodbye down there, due to her irrational fear of water. She didn't want to re-experience the panic. She knew it was unreasonable to think this way, but she couldn't help it.

Somewhere far off in the forest, an owl hooted. The eerie sound sent shivers racing up her spine. But she held steadfast. If she couldn't say goodbye down at the lake, then at least she could wait out here and watch the plane fly overhead. It didn't take long to hear the plane's engine prattle on. Then it grew louder and faster and Milena knew JJ was racing her plane across the dark waters.

Despite her anxiety and her fears JJ had managed to learn to fly a bush plane.

How cool was that?

JJ of all people. A woman who hadn't wanted to leave her prison cell except for meals and mandatory exercise was now a pilot flying free as a bird.

Milena smiled.

The sound of the plane grew louder and Milena ran further into the meadow and waved as the plane shot like a cannonball above the trees and flew right overhead. JJ must have seen her because she did a weird dip with one wing and then the other wing. She was waving back to her with the plane!

Oh dear, she hoped the baby didn't get sick from that gesture.

Milena watched as the plane disappeared behind the treetops on the north side of the meadow.

Her heart sank. JJ was gone. The baby was gone.

She hugged her tired arms and strolled back to the cabin. Towards the lake, in the woods, she spied the lights of the machines flash between the trees. Daegen and Mitch were returning. It was time for bed and suddenly she was exhausted.

No doubt, she would sleep well tonight.

. . ᘛ . .

"PACK YOUR STUFF. WHERE heading over to Jane Sunflower's place!"

At first, Milena thought she was dreaming Daegen's voice, but when sunlight suddenly shone at her closed eyes, she tucked her blankets over her head.

"Come on, sleepyhead. Breakfast is just about done and we need to catch the light," Daegen prodded. Amusement laced his voice and confusion snapped through her.

Catch the light? What in the world was going on?

She lifted the blankets off her face and realized it was still dark outside! A beam of light splashed against the sheets draped over the rope that separated her bed from most of the room. There was no sunlight, just a flashlight.

Jane Sunflower.

JJ had set it up. Daegen had taken her seriously.

Shoot!

"I'm...I'm coming," she managed to say as she tried to orient herself.

She flung her blankets aside and lit the candle beside her bed. She needed to hurry and get dressed and explain to Daegen that he didn't have to take her along with him. She really would prefer to stay here and just work.

She didn't hear Paul or Mitch talking. Where they still in bed? Or had they already taken off for the day? Reluctantly Milena got out of bed and started to dress.

· · ❧ · ·

DAEGEN WAS PLACING the thin strips of bear steaks into the frying pans when he noticed Milena had lit a candle behind the blankets. There was just one little problem. Okay, so it was a big problem.

By the angle the candle was shining and with her getting dressed in front of the light, he had no problem making out her curvy silhouette.

Mitch and Paul entered the cabin at that moment after having showered and attending to other necessities and they were as quiet as mice as well as very alert as they watched the show of Milena's sexy shadow behind the blanket slipping on her bra and then her top. Then she was bending over and removing her panties.

Oh man! Here we go!

His cock hardened and his breaths came quick as awareness flooded him. His nasty reaction was exactly why he needed to tell her to stay here without hurting her feelings.

How in the hell was he going to be able to control himself when they would be alone?

He caught Paul staring at him and he didn't like that grin plastered on his friend's face. Nor did he like the smirk on Mitch's face either.

The two of them were still laughing about JJ roping Milena to come along with Daegen. Sheesh, would those two guys ever grow up?

. . ❧ . .

"MAYBE YOU HAD BETTER stay here and help out the guys with the chores," Daegen suddenly blurted as Milena grabbed a second helping of Daegen's homemade hash browns. She'd been trying to figure out how to get out of this trip with him and he was presenting her with the perfect opportunity to opt out.

Thank you, God!

Before Milena could tell him not a problem, Paul chimed in.

"Nope, JJ insisted that Milena meet Jane Sunflower and it's best you do as she asks. I don't want to get on her bad side and get uninvited to her party. She cooks real good. And I for one am dying for one their delicious barbecued Angus steaks."

"Damn straight. No way can you two back out." Mitch added. "Let Milena have some lady to lady time and don't forget JJ's letter for her."

Damn them! If she had the nerve, she would have smacked both Mitch and Paul. How dare they gang up like this?

"JJ would do no such thing as to uninvite you to her party. She's not that kind of woman," Daegen replied.

"Why do I get the feeling no one wants my company?" Milena blurted.

Oh shoot! She hadn't met to say that out loud. The room fell silent as the men all turned to look at her. They appeared uneasy and shocked. Perhaps they had forgotten she'd been in the room?

"No, no, we don't mind having you here," Mitch blurted. He looked a bit pale and embarrassed.

"Just didn't want to wear you out. It's a really long hike," Daegen replied.

"Well I wouldn't want Milena to dishearten JJ. She would be really disappointed if Milena didn't have a story to share with her about Jane," Paul hedged.

Guilt powered through her. Paul did have a point. And she kind of would like to meet this elderly woman. She was curious as to how Jane had survived out here in the wilderness without stores.

"Besides it will give me some time to recuperate from the pole digging," Mitch said and he winced as he stood.

Another shard of guilt stabbed Milena. His back and arms must be quite sore today.

"Besides, having two people going is best. Especially with what's been going on around here."

And that was the final shard of guilt. She realized Paul couldn't go because of his head injury. It was best for him to not do too much. And Mitch was tired from yesterday and he needed to be here to feed and exercise the horses. She could keep an eye out so Daegen would be safe. She also realized she had some leverage.

"Okay not a problem. But on two conditions. The two of you stick together like glue. And when we get back I get to do some post digging on any new projects, deal?"

Mitch sighed. He said nothing for a good fifteen seconds, then he nodded.

Satisfaction shifted through Milena.

"Okay, deal," Mitch said.

Milena jumped when Paul gave his hands a quick slap onto the table.

"Good! Then it's settled. I'll pack you two some grub."

Mitch was already digging through a chest of drawers in a far corner of the room.

"I'll pack up one of those lightweight tents and a sleeping bag for each of you in case you run into bad weather on the way. "

"Oh and don't forget to pack a gun," Paul said quickly.

Daegen scowled and focused his attention to Milena. Her heart sank.

Wow, he really didn't want her to go along with him, did he?

"Looks like they're in one hell of a hurry to get rid of both of us, Milena," Daegen muttered and then to her surprise, he winked and raised his voice.

"Wait until you get a taste of Jane Sunflower's cookies. Do me a favor Milena and ask Ms. Sunflower for her shortbread cookie recipe so Paul won't have to make those concrete cookies of his anymore."

"I heard that," Paul mumbled. "And I won't be packing any cookies for you, Daeg. That will teach you to insult my baking."

Daegen grinned and his entire face transformed beneath that beard and mustache. Cute crinkles erupted at the sides of his eyes. Something lovely fluttered deep inside of her belly. She really liked this humorous side of him.

"Your cookies are too heavy to carry anyway," he said. He reached for a second helping of those bear steaks.

Suddenly Milena didn't feel as apprehensive as she had moments earlier about going on this trip alone with him. Maybe she was going to have a good time? Maybe one day she would be able to live on her own in the woods just like this Sunflower hermit woman. Blessed peace among nature. No twenty-four hour noise and lights like she'd experienced in prison.

Milena resisted the urge to hug herself as happiness flooded through her. Yes, she would make sure to learn as much as possible from the elderly woman.

Suddenly Milena couldn't wait to get started on her new adventure!

• • ➝ • •

"DO YOU THINK DAEGEN is going to be pissed off at us for making sure Milena went with him?" Paul asked as he closed his doctor bag and gave Brownie Belle's rump a gentle pat. The horse nayed and nuzzled her foal.

"He'll thank us," Mitch replied as he dumped another bucket of fresh water into the trough for the horse.

"What kind of answer is that?" Paul asked.

"She'll be watching his back. I didn't like the idea of him going alone. Bad idea of one of us going with him. You just had a head wound and had I gone it would set us back because she still needs to have more experience before she can be a solid asset."

Paul knew she was already a solid asset, especially in the way she made him feel when she was around him and in that innocent but sexy way she had kissed him back the other night.

"You certainly seemed real eager to get rid of her. Why?" Mitch asked.

"Just wanted to make sure JJ didn't get mad at us, like I said earlier," Paul replied. Truth was he needed to get his head wrapped around what to do about JJ and his developing attraction to her and he couldn't do it with her being a distraction.

"Uh huh. I am not buying that bullshit. What happened between the two of you when you spent the night together in the barn? It sounds to me like you're trying to distance her from yourself ."

Oh. Oh. Time to deflect. His cheeks began to burn as he remembered the kiss.

"We didn't spend the night together." Paul averted eye contact as he let himself out of the stall. Mitch followed right behind him.

"Something happened. You two were acting real funny the next morning," Mitch prodded.

"Let it rest, man. I've got to check on the rest of the horses and you need to clean out the stalls."

He had hoped Mitch would drop it at Paul's reminder of a full day of work ahead of them, but sometimes Mitch was like a dog with a bone and it appeared this was one of those times.

"Ha! Just as I suspected! What happened? Did you make a play for her? Did she turn you down?" Mitch laughed as he followed Paul into the barn office.

Paul set his doctor bag onto the desk and tensed when he noticed the two whiskey glasses, one still full, sitting on the desk.

Damn! He needed to get rid of the evidence before Mitch saw.

But before he could make the glasses disappear, Mitch was already chuckling and staring at the desk.

"You guys were drinking together. Holy, you got balls, man. Were you trying to loosen yourself up? I mean after Everly...what she did...geez, you would need an extra bottle to loosen yourself up."

At the mention of Everly, Paul smarted. Mitch had warned him over and over about her, but he hadn't listened.

"I'm over her. Time to move on. Lesson learned," Paul replied, truly impressed in the way he kept the hurt out of his voice.

"Thankfully Milena is way different," Mitch said. There was a softness in his voice that captured Paul's full attention.

He knew Mitch like the back of his hand, and he instantly understood why Mitch was badgering him about Milena. He was checking to see if Paul was interested in her, because Mitch was interested in her too!

Oh man! They both liked the same woman? Again?

Paul growled inwardly. It was time to set the cards onto the table, so to speak.

"We kissed," Paul blurted, feeling instant relief that the truth was out.

Mitch's eyes widened in surprise.

"Wow," was his reply.

"You did want to know if something happened. I kissed her and she kissed me back. End of story."

Mitch sore softly and Paul noticed his friend's cheeks flush and his eyes appeared a bit brighter than usual.

Interesting.

"I kissed her too," Mitch said.

What? Had he heard right?

Paul felt his eyes widen as surprised washed over him.

"Oh, man. You didn't."

But in the serious way Mitch was staring back at him, he knew Mitch was telling the truth.

"When?" Paul asked, suddenly wanting to hear all the details.

"Yesterday, while taking a break from the post digging. She was being down on herself and I just wanted to show her she was desirable. It was...impulsive on my part ."

Paul inhaled as a shot of anger rippled through him. He wasn't mad at Mitch, he was just ticked off at himself for liking the same girl Mitch did.

"Looks like we might have a bit of a problem," Mitch said slowly.

"Looks like," Paul admitted. He wasn't sure if he could be the man to bow out. He wanted Milena.

Damn, but that thought just hit him like a ton of bricks. He *did* want her for himself.

"What do you suggest we do about it?" Mitch asked, watching him carefully.

He shook his head. Did Mitch expect Paul to say Mitch could have Milena?

He didn't think he could do that. One little kiss with her and he was hooked. So he could totally understand why Mitch wanted her after a kiss.

"Don't know. But I know one thing."

"What's that?" Mitch asked.

" I think Daegen is carrying a torch for her too. I've seen him looking at her and I don't mean in a boss employee kind of way," Paul confessed.

Mitch swore softly.

"It looks like Milena is in trouble having three cowboys pursuing her at the same time," Paul pondered.

"When he gets back, the three of us are going to have to have a serious as hell discussion about Milena and what we should do about her. In the meantime, I'll start bringing out the horses."

Mitch left the office and a few moments later he could hear the cheerful neighs of horses being led out of their stalls.

Paul frowned as he grabbed the two glasses and headed outside to the water pump to wash them. He hoped that Mitch didn't decide to get Jenna to send Milena back to prison. That would solve the problem for sure.

But that is the last thing he wanted for her or for himself.

Until Daegen and Milena returned from their trip to Jane Sunflower, Paul would make sure he came up with an acceptable solution.

He just didn't know what it would be.

"Good heavens?!" Milena whispered from a crouched position right beside Daegen.

About forty feet in front of them on the virtually invisible trail that Daegen had been leading her along, stood a large black bear.

And Milena literally meant stood. The beast was huge as she reared up on her hind legs and sniffed the air with her wet black nose.

Nearby, two small black cubs were quickly climbing a tall pine tree. Daegen kept his finger to his mouth indicating she remain silent. She was anything but quiet.

Her heart crashed against her chest like a battering ram and she had no doubt the bears probably heard. She wanted to run from this black giant, but she knew the animal would take it as a sign of fear and then she would be prey. It would chase her down and crunch through her bones with her sharp gleaming white fangs and Milena would be history.

Today was not a good day to die.

As she stared at the bear, rays of sunshine streamed through the heavy canopy of pine branches and the air smelled fresh and clean. It was so different from the cleaning solution and stale air in prison.

No, she had just gotten her freedom and she was not about to let a mama bear steal it away. She turned her gaze to Daegen. His brown eyes were focused solely on the bear.

He didn't appear too concerned but for all she knew he could be hiding his fear so she wouldn't get scared.

Too late for that! She was terrified!

She looked back at the bear who let out a low warning growl. The sound sent creepy shivers up her back, along her arms and down her legs. She swore even the knapsack on her back was shivering in fright.

Oh darn! Her knapsack carried food!

Another volley of fear and adrenalin snapped through her. She pushed down on her need to scream hysterically.

Was the bear sniffing the air because it smelled the food in her knapsack?

She jumped when the bear growled again and suddenly the cubs, who had been halfway up the tree, came scrambling back down and ran off into the woods. Mother bear got off her hind legs and let loose a bunch of snorts that had Milena shaking all over.

Then the bear turned and quickly followed her cubs.

"Wow, that was close," Daegen muttered as he slowly got up.

He grinned down at her as he held out his hand, but she shook her head. She doubted she could stand, her legs were shaking so hard.

"What's the matter?" he asked and then began to laugh.

His laughter irritated her and she lost her composure.

"I am sure glad you find it amusing that we were almost bear food!" Milena snapped. She wasn't sure if she should smack that amused grin off his cute lips, cry or kiss him.

She sobered at that last thought.

Kiss him?

Oh my, where had *that* come from?

She bet if she had been standing, she would have kissed him.

Why? She had no idea. Maybe because she had just come face to face with possible death? Or this need to kiss him was a side effect of adrenaline? Maybe because he looked so adorable when he was happy? The crinkles lining the edges of his eyes made him look so sexy.

"Almost is the important word. Look at it this way, if she had killed us at least we would have gone to good use and helped to feed her babies."

Was this guy for real?

"You have a sick twisted sense of humor, Daegen," she murmured.

"I will take that as a compliment."

He winked at her and wiggled his fingers and she realized he was still extending his hand to her offering assistance in her getting up.

"Come on, daylight is burning. Let's get a move on."

"You're serious? I mean we could have been dead right now," Milena muttered. She grabbed his hand and he pulled her up as if she were a feather.

Wow, he was strong and his hand holding hers felt...perfect.

She sighed. It was a feeling of loss when he let go of her. She wanted him holding her hand again.

"You don't know what's going to happen to you from one minute in life to the next," Daegen said as he started forward.

"We could get hit by a falling tree branch two feet ahead of us and be killed. Or we could drop dead from a heart attack like Mitch almost did."

"What?" Milena gasped.

Daegen stopped cold and cursed softly as he turned around to face her.

He looked embarrassed.

"Sorry, my bad. That kind of just slipped out. I shouldn't have said that. Not my story to tell. Please, don't tell him I told you."

He started forward again. Right along the same path the bears had just gone down.

But that wasn't at the top of her priority list at the moment. She was still adjusting to what Daegen had just confessed and concern was snapping through her like a live wire.

Mitch had almost dropped dead from a heart attack?

This was a piece of news she simply did not like. She needed to find out more.

" I won't say anything," she said as she rushed to catch up to him.

"Is he alright? Should he be out here in the middle of nowhere without a hospital nearby? What if he has another heart attack? I mean is it safe for him to be post digging? That is brutal work."

She remembered how red his face had been and how much he'd been perspiring.

"Do you know what to do if he does have another heart attack? I mean there should be some precautions in place for him, shouldn't there be?"

She was firing her questions at him like missiles and she noted Daegen's shoulders tense with each question. But he didn't stop walking.

Instead, he picked up his pace to the point she had to jog to keep up to him.

"Mitch is fine. The doctor gave him a clean bill of health before he came out here. You don't need to worry."

Oh, but she was worried.

With Daegen's admission about Mitch, it opened the gates to more questions as to why were these three men living alone out here? Once again, she wondered did they have girlfriends? Wives?

Suddenly she wanted to know more about each of them.

Girl! An inner voice admonished. *They are none of your business! Their love life is none of your business! They don't belong to you!*

Milena blew out an anxious breath. Who knew it was so stressful caring about men she barely knew.

She forced any more questions back down inside of her.

Not. My. Business.

She focused her attention to her surroundings. They had been walking a good two hours through cute little green meadows and dense forests. She had seen marks cut into the bark of some of the trees and she figured the guys had blazed a trail to keep them from getting lost on their way through last fall.

She knew she would have no problem getting lost out here, despite the occasional cuts in the trees. Everything looked the same and yet it didn't. Every nook consisted of overflowing green ferns or clusters of white and purple trilliums or boulders laced with green moss. The creeks where thankfully small. Logs had been placed over them making little bridges that she was able to cross without freaking out, mainly because she did not look down.

"This lady...Jane Sunflower. Why is she living out here all alone?" Milena asked.

"I never asked her. But she didn't have anyone but herself and her lambs when we visited her last autumn. She's a friendly enough lady once she knows you mean her no harm," Daegen replied.

"That was nice of you guys to go over and check on her last year."

Daegen shrugged his shoulders.

"Wasn't a problem,' he replied.

She didn't even know the woman but she felt concern for her. What kind of woman would live out here all alone anyway?

Someone like yourself, an inner voice whispered to Milena. She nodded to herself. Yeah, someone who wanted to put her past behind her. Someone who didn't ever want to go back into that past. Or back to prison.

"So, what's your issue with water?" Daegen's question seared through her like an arrow.

"What?" she asked trying to inject surprise into her voice, but she sounded weak.

"Every time we go over a creek you get tense. It's like watching a carefree she-wolf suddenly go into alert mode because she realizes a bear is ready to pounce."

"Well, we do have bears, don't we now?" Milena snapped.

"The day I came back. When we are at the lake to grab supplies, you freaked out."

"I did?"

Shit. He'd noticed.

He didn't turn around, but she heard the confidence in his voice. He knew something was wrong with her.

"Yeah, you did. And last summer when I rescued you and your blueberries from the bears, it was hell getting you to hop into that canoe."

"Well, you were a stranger." A sex-on-a-stick stranger. Who wasn't gay as he pretended to be.

She was about to remind him about his telling her he was gay when he really wasn't, when he suddenly changed the subject again.

"I hope you're not afraid of rain," he said.

She noted his tone had changed from confidence to one of seriousness.

Milena involuntarily tensed. Her gaze snapped upward. The sky looked clear and blue. There was no sign of rain.

She frowned.

"No, why?"

"I heard thunder," he said.

"I didn't hear anything?"

"If we hurry, we might make it to the cabin at the halfway point. "

"A cabin?" Milena asked. The last thing she had expected out here in the middle of nowhere was a cabin.

Daegen didn't answer. He'd picked up his pace and now she was almost jogging to keep up with him.

Mercy, the man had a long stride.

"Are you teasing me?" She laughed. He had to be playing her.

"Unless you want to stop and pitch the emergency tent I brought along. But I wouldn't advise it with those bears around. I guess we should have brought raincoats, but I figured the tent was the best choice and wanted to pack light. But we'll have to move faster."

Faster? Oh geez. So much for a leisurely long hike in the woods.

His talk of bears sobered her and she kept glancing around expecting to be charged by a big black bear at any moment. She caught her breath as she spied dark objects, which thankfully turned out to be burnt tree stumps from a forest fire many many years ago.

If she wasn't careful, her imagination was going to go into overdrive.

"You're quiet all of a sudden," Daegen said.

She detected amusement in his voice.

So he *had* been kidding about the thunder.

She relaxed.

"Just keeping an eye out for trouble," she admitted.

"Good."

Awareness whispered through her as she abruptly realized it was actually quite hot. Sweat dribbled down her back beneath the knapsack and perspiration beaded across her forehead and under her arms. Her cheeks felt flushed.

Thunder rumbled softly from somewhere up ahead.

Oh, no.

"Told you," he grumbled.

From previous experience during her stay last summer at Moose Ranch, storms appeared quickly around these parts.

"We're not going to make it to that cabin, are we?" she mumbled.

"No, but getting wet is better than getting eaten."

"True," she laughed.

"I like the way you laugh. You should do it more often," Daegen said as he kept up a frantic pace.

He liked her laugh? Wow.

Thunder rumbled again. This time closer.

A loon cried from somewhere up ahead. It was a lonesome sound made louder due to the thick promise of rain hanging in the air.

"We may be closer to that cabin than I think. It's right near a lake. That loon is probably enjoying a nice leisurely swim while she waits on the storm."

A lake? Oh crap!

Uneasiness swept through her. Her knapsack felt damp and heavy against her back. The forest ahead began to look darker and spookier. Tree limbs looked like gnarled old hands reaching out to grab her as she passed.

She shivered involuntarily.

"The rain will make everything fresh again," Daegen said as another rumble of thunder echoed eerily through the too quiet woods.

What if Daegen lost his way? What if they got stranded in this desolation only to starve to death and their bodies never found? What if they got hit by lightning while they were moving around beneath all these trees?

She caught her breath as her tummy hollowed out. The sun disappeared. The wind picked up fast and furious. The creepy branches all around them creaked with ominous warning.

Heavy thick cold raindrops began to drop on her.

"Deja vu," Daegen suddenly laughed and her uneasiness dissipated.

"Yeah," she giggled as she caught his meaning. It was how they'd first met. Him rescuing her from bears in a thunderstorm.

Man, she had been so afraid then. Her fear was starting to creep up again as lightning suddenly flashed overhead.

"Oh shit," Daegen muttered.

He stopped abruptly and she almost crashed into him.

Tremors of fear raced up her spine as she watched his face. His eyes were narrow. His head tilted a bit as if he were trying to hear something. Another idea hit her and her uneasiness swept into anxiety.

"Are we lost?" she blurted.

He glanced at her, his lips were compressed.. He looked insulted at her question.

"No . But I can hear the rain coming. We can pitch a tent or aim for the cabin. Either way we're gonna get really wet. Cabin is secure from the bears and has a stove where we can dry off."

He was walking fast again and she ran to catch up.

"What do you suggest?" she asked.

"If I was alone I would make a run for the cabin."

She straightened, instantly alert.

Was he insinuating she was a burden? Defiance roared through her.

"Then we'll run for the cabin," she said.

"We have the emergency tent in the knapsack."

"But we'll lose time setting it up, and there are the bears and we're already wet." And she was feeling chilled already. She wanted to get undercover and near a fire as quick as possible.

The tips of his lips turned upward. His eyes sparkled. Did she detect appreciation?

He nodded and to her surprise, he reached back and grabbed her hand. His fingers were strong and reassuring and boy did she suddenly feel safe.

"Hold on tight. I'm going to start running. If I go too fast, just let me know. Try to watch for anything you might fall over."

She blinked. Was he serious? They were surrounded by rotting and burned out tree stumps, downed branches and rocks were scattered all over the place.

She didn't have time to respond as he pulled her along with him.

He moved fast. Mercy, did he ever move fast.

The wind increased. Branches cracked and then came the full force of rain.

To wash the spiders out.

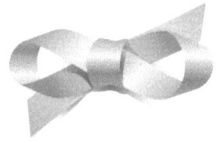

Chapter Ten

"Looks like the storm's going to be a bitch!" Paul called out as he watched Mitch lead the last nervous wide-eyed horse toward the barn. Behind his friend and the horse, the sky rolled with bruised blue-black clouds. Wind howled over that way and thunder crashed.

"Spring has finally graced us with her presence," Mitch said as he led the whining horse past Paul and into the safety of the barn.

Earlier, Paul had sensed a storm might be coming due to the unusual heat at this time of the year and so he'd opted to gather the horses at the other barn and bring them inside.

After feeding them and making sure they were all settled, he'd come to the other barn and found Mitch also bringing in the horses. The last one in was the oldest of the group.

He had been a racehorse, prime in his time, winning plenty of races that made his owners rich. Instead of shipping the horse off to the glue factory when he'd passed his prime, the owners had flown the horse here and now he was enjoying a leisurely retirement.

Paul shook his head. He didn't like the idea of animals being used to make people rich. But he couldn't say anything or he would be a hypocrite, because he was making a living off animals himself.

"Do you think they'll be okay out there?" Mitch asked as he joined Paul at the open barn door.

Because this building was set on the top of a hill, it gave them a good view of the surrounding meadows, the gorge with a river and the dense rolling forest beyond.

Trees swayed like blades of grass and Paul worried that Daegen and Milena might have been caught off guard.

"You're not answering. Your lack of reassurance is not a good sign," Mitch said.

"He's an ex soldier. He's used to roughing it. "

He heard Mitch inhale softly and slowly as if trying to calm himself.

"Milena is not used to roughing it," Mitch said quietly.

Paul couldn't help but to laugh.

"Oh, come on! Wake up, man. She spent years in a prison. Last I heard those places are not spas."

To Paul's surprise, Mitch looked relieved. Too bad he didn't feel the same.

"Yeah, you're right. She's tough," Mitch answered.

A sharp slap to Paul's upper back had him cursing from the pain.

"Come on. Nothing we can do. Shut the barn door before the storm rips it off the hinges. I've got lunch in the office. Let's eat."

Mitch headed back inside.

Paul stood there and listened to the barn sides groan as the wind and rain battered against it. He didn't worry about their safety. Whoever had built these barns had known what they were doing. The buildings were solid despite being old.

He took one more look out across the meadow at the dark forest beyond to where the trees thrashed about as if caught in a wild frenzied dance. He wished he had gone with Milena and Daegen, but realized if Milena was to get caught out in a thunderstorm, it was best to be with an experienced man like Daegen. He just hoped that Daegen's demons didn't surface because of all that noise.

Post traumatic stress was a bitch.

Paul exhaled, grabbed the door latch and slid the door closed.

Time for lunch. Too bad he wasn't hungry.

. . ᦢ . .

KEEP IT TOGETHER, DAEGEN. Keep it together. It's just thunder. Keep it together.

If he hadn't been holding onto Milena's hand and trying to keep a decent run so she wouldn't fall, he probably would have panicked at the too loud noise, as he sometimes did, and rushed like a madman to that cabin. Thankfully, she was here as it helped keep him grounded. The last thing he wanted was for her to see he had issues too.

He was grateful when the small board and batten cabin with rusty metal roof loomed just ahead. It was literally a beacon in the storm and thankfully still intact after the brutal winter.

When they rushed up the stairs and he pushed open the door, they were soaked to the skin.

Milena was shaking and so was he. Damn but getting wet sure put a chill to his mood.

"I'll get the fire started," he said.

But he didn't move as he watched her survey the dark, rustic interior of the old building. Her chest was heaving from all that running, and her breasts were showing off their seductive curves. He could even make out the silhouette of her bra and the bold nipples that poked against her top.

Daegen's cock tightened, and sexual tension zipped through him.

She looked like a fully clothed goddess who'd just stepped out of a shower. Her hair was a tangled mess and crystal-clear water droplets dripped down her cheeks, along the slope of her cute button nose and fell onto her pretty lips.

Man, how had he been able to walk away from her so easily last summer?

Truth was, it had not been easy. A piece of him had died when she'd told him she was a convict on temporary leave from a prison. That night at Moose Ranch, he'd even toyed with the idea of hiding her at Snowy Creek Ranch. But he'd had to think of his two partners and if he got caught hiding an escaped convict, a woman he didn't even know, he'd land years in prison. But that hadn't stopped him from dreaming about her almost every night since then.

His searing fantasies had him waking up hot and aroused. He'd taken many a cold midnight shower or swim in the lake last summer and autumn. This winter he'd dove naked into the snowbanks just to get her out of his mind.

Now she was here.

Daegen crashed back to reality when Milena suddenly removed her pack. The movement made her wet curvy breasts jut out even more.

His cock jerked at the erotic sight.

Oh damn!

"This is nice. How old do you think this cabin is? Maybe a century home?"

Her eyes sparkled with appreciation as she stared around the rustic interior, totally oblivious of the lightning flashing at the small paned windows giving him a great view of her wet curves.

A century home? She was kidding, right?

"The inside walls are logs. They'll last forever. I can see the chinking is made with moss. An inexpensive way to fill in gaps between the logs. But that sheet metal nailed to the roof looks rusty. I'm surprised the roof is not leaking," she said as she looked up at the dry ceiling.

He shrugged out of his pack and a moment later brought out a flashlight, a package of waterproof matches and a long white stemmed emergency candle.

He placed the knapsack upon the small wood table and quickly lit a match to the candle. A little yellow glow brightened up the room. He set the candle into an old tin he found on the table and tried hard not to shiver at being so cold.

"How did you find this place? Who in the world would build it here right out in the middle of nowhere?" she asked.

She was still gazing around the room. At the several shelves laden with tin containers which he knew contained dried food for emergency use and then to the two cots set in a corner.

"It actually belongs to Moose Ranch. One of their many shelters. It's on a piece of land that juts out between Jane Sunflower's place and our ranch. Moose Ranch uses it as an emergency cabin when they're checking on their Angus cattle housed in one of their fenced meadows about four miles south of here. They've got hundreds of acres and old and new shelters all over their property. They keep their more used cabins stocked with non-perishable foods, stoves and firewood," Daegen explained as he forced himself to keep his focus off her.

He grabbed some kindling and noted it was the same that they'd restocked here upon their previous visit. It was apparent no one had used this cabin since last time Daegen, Mitch and Paul had come through last autumn.

He opened the damper and set upon making a fire in the old cast iron stove.

As he shoved some old newspapers beneath the kindling and lit the paper, he explained what Jane Sunflower had told them about this cabin.

"Jane Sunflower told us about some of the history. She said many years back, when she first got to her place, there was a young man who lived here. A hermit, she called him. Didn't know his name, but he had been living here for several years. When he discovered she was living five miles away, he packed up and left.

She'd found a note from him pinned to her front door. The note said she could help herself to all the contents he had left behind and he wouldn't be back. He finished by saying the area was too crowded."

"Too crowded? Oh my God!" Milena laughed.

It was a deep laugh. Genuine and happy. The musical sound reached somewhere deep inside his heart to a place he had thought dead forever. He gasped as he felt something; an anguish, shift and rip apart. It was an emotional pain held hostage in his body and his soul right up until this very second.

For a few brief seconds, he couldn't even breathe as the suffering left him.

"Daegen? Are you okay?"

Her soft question shattered his momentary paralysis and he blinked into the fire he'd just created.

It was a nice fire. Beautiful colours of orange, yellow and blue. The flames hungrily lapped at the kindling and snapped and popped. Wow. He had forgotten how pretty a fire could actually be.

"Daeg?" Her touch to his shoulder had him sighing and relaxing.

"Yeah, yeah. I'm good." For a few seconds, he'd never felt better. It was a feeling he would like to hold onto forever, but he needed to get moving.

He grabbed larger pieces of wood and placed them inside, then shut the stove door and stood.

"Shall we eat? I'm starving. And it looks like the storm is already settling down," Milena said as she eagerly eyed the knapsack with their food and then at the windows.

Milena was right.

Instead of rain pounding the sheet metal roof, it was now just a pitter patter. The crackling in the fireplace quickly turned to a healthy roar and heat now wafted through the room.

"Let's eat by the stove. I'm hungry," she insisted.

"Get out of those wet clothes, first. Then we eat," he instructed. It was best she got warm and he didn't have to look at her luscious wet curves.

He strolled to where she stood. She'd already began to take the food items out of the pack and she stopped as he scowled into her empty pack.

"What's wrong? They didn't forget to pack the food, did they?" she asked.

"No extra clothes? Did we forget to pack extra clothes?" Daegen mumbled.

"Well, I didn't pack any. Except underwear. You said pack light."

Daegen frowned as he began to search through his knapsack. He thought he'd placed a bundle of extra clothing for himself at the bottom of the pack and it wasn't here. Had Paul or Mitch removed it? Or had he simply forgotten?

Now he remembered. He'd removed the bundle and put in the sleeping bag and then forgotten to place the clothing back in because he'd been in such a damned hurry.

"We'll have to use the sleeping bags."

"Okay, we can do that," she replied but she didn't move.

Instead, she looked at him as if *he* should be doing something. Then it suddenly dawned on him what she was waiting for.

"Sorry, I forgot you're a lady, not one of the guys," he chuckled.

"Is that a compliment or a question?" She laughed and the sound of her voice literally made his heart sing.

Wow, she really had an effect on him.

He cleared his suddenly dry throat.

"I'll step outside. You get out of your clothes and cover up in the sleeping bag. It's a good thing the bags were wrapped in plastic," he mumbled as he watched her lift a blue sleeping bag from the knapsack.

Man, she was pretty. He liked watching her fingers. They were slender and long. She wore no jewelry. Some day he would love to put a ring on her finger. Some day...

Snap out of it, Daegen!

He forced himself to stop staring at her and a moment later, he stepped outside.

"I'll hurry," she called out as he closed the door and entered a new world.

Everything sparkled as rays of sunshine streamed into the forest from the southwest. The trees glittered with wetness and silver drops fell from branches. The wind had eased and the sun was brightening. The air smelled fresh, crisp and cool replacing the muggy heat.

He stared at the trees. Really stared at them. He noted the white texture of a birch bark sapling that struggled to grow beneath the canopy of vibrant green pine trees. The ground was covered in brown pine needles and here and there were burnt out remains of trees from a forest fire years ago.

He also noticed stumps, their tops covered in green sparkling moss. Here and there, the relics were scattered for as far as he could see. Those had been trees once. Most likely cut down to make this cabin.

Huh, he'd never noticed those stumps before. Never really noticed how bright the woods looked when the sun was shining.

Past the trees, directly to the west, he spied the small lake. The water glimmered silver and a spooky white mist hovered over it.

Misty Lake it was called. He remembered seeing it on the map. It was an appropriate name for the lake.

A knock from behind him brought him back to attention. The door opened and Milena stood there clad in her blue sleeping bag. He caught glimpses of her long neck and smooth shoulders and upper chest as she motioned for him to come inside.

Her eyes were laughing and her cheeks were rosy pink. She appeared quite happy to be comfortable again.

"Go on in and change. It's so warm inside. You'll love it!" she squealed and came out in her bare feet.

He wanted to protest and send her back in but he realized she wouldn't feel relaxed having him change right in front of her as if she were one of the guys.

Man, had he really said that he'd forgotten she was a lady? He was an idiot.

He nodded and hurried inside.

She was right. It was already warm and he hurried to undress. Once he had the sleeping bag wrapped around him, he called her back inside. He gave her the one chair in the cabin and he sat on the cot close to the stove.

"Paul wasn't kidding when he said he packed light-weight food," Milena chuckled as she swallowed a delicious quarter slice of a peanut butter and strawberry jam sandwich.

"Personally I'm so hungry I could eat a bunch of bear steak sandwiches," Daegen muttered.

"Oh please, no bears. I have had enough of bears," she complained, immediately remembering what they'd experienced out on the trail with the mother bear and her two cubs.

Talk about terror of the highest degree!

She glanced over at him and caught his teasing smile. Her heart picked up a little too fast as she noticed he'd allowed his sleeping bag to fall off his shoulders and puddle around his waist.

Oh boy. It sure is getting hot in here.

Arousal snapped through her as she spied muscles galore rippling in his right bicep and shoulder as he closed his eyes and lifted the water bottle to his mouth.

Below his scruffy beard, she spied his Adams apple bob as he drank.

As she shoved another quarter of the delicious peanut butter and jam sandwich into her mouth, her gaze went straight to where she noticed his bare knees peek out from the opening of the sleeping bag.

She wondered how his thighs looked. She bet they were rigid muscles from all that working he did around the ranch.

The sleeping bag she'd wrapped herself in was making her way too hot. She swore she was going to self combust!

What would Daegen do if she just let the sleeping bag drop off her body? Would he still think of her as just one of the guys?

She grinned. Maybe she should just drop the bag? Just for the hell of it. Just to prove a point. Just to see his reaction.

Her breath caught as she imagined him gasp in surprise at her boldness and then stand and then drop his bag. Would his erection be big and thick and oh, so hard and...

"Now who is zoning out?" Daegen's chuckle sobered her and heat flushed into her face as he gazed back at her with a very sensual smile.

He'd caught her staring at him. How embarrassing!

"Sorry. I was just thinking..."

Oh dear. She couldn't tell him what she had been thinking.

"About?" His head tilted in question.

Gosh, he looked so cute when he did that gesture with his head.

"About how long before our clothes are dry? I'm getting way too warm wrapped up like a cocoon."

"I'll open the door and the windows," Daegen said.

He stood quickly and strolled over to the door. She noted he'd lifted the sleeping bag and wrapped it around his upper body.

Oh pooh.

"I'll grab us some desert," Milena said, trying to get her mind off Daegen.

She retrieved a couple of brown-spotted bananas from the knapsack and brought the fruit over to him where he stood in the open doorway.

He muttered a quiet, almost bashful thanks as she handed him the banana.

Hmm, was he shy?

Oh my gosh. She hadn't even thought that he might not have desired to bring her along because he just wanted to be alone. She fell silent as that thought began to take hold.

On the trail he hadn't said much. Maybe a couple handful of words until he'd spotted the bear and urged her to get down and keep quiet. Come to think of it, he was a quiet man compared to Mitch and Paul. Why hadn't she noticed that before?

She stood beside him and enjoyed the mild air that blew against her face. She also realized that just having him here made her feel...sexually aware and safe. He didn't have to do small talk because she felt comfortable with him.

The air was refreshing and she loosened her grip on her sleeping bag, allowing some of the air to enter her hot cocoon.

"You never did answer my question," Daegen suddenly said as he calmly peeled his banana and nodded at the forest.

Milena searched her memory wondering what he meant. She followed his gaze and tensed at the sight of the lake that shone between the trees.

"Why you're so afraid of water or is it just lakes and creeks in general?"

Oh crap. That question.

"I don't know why," she blurted.

She hadn't meant to admit her issue but it had just come out.

"Exposure is one way to overcome your fear. At least that's what my shrink tells me."

Milena almost choked on the piece of banana she had just been swallowing.

"A shrink? You're seeing a shrink?" she blurted.

To her dismay her voice sounded shocked and maybe even a little judgemental?

"Don't look so horrified," Daegen chuckled as he turned from the doorway and walked toward the tattered rope they'd found in the cabin and strung over the stove to hang their wet clothing.

From this angle she couldn't see his face, but she assumed her reaction must have upset him.

"I'm so sorry. That was rude of me. I didn't mean to offend."

Daegen gazed over at her, a genuine smile tilted his lips.

"You didn't offend me. I have a problem that I wasn't able to solve on my own, so I went to a professional to get help. No shame in that, right?"

Now she really felt bad.

"No, not at all," she replied.

She wondered why he had felt the need to see a shrink?

Oh Milena! This is none of your business!

"Anyways she said changing the way you react to a stressful situation, or in your case the way you react to your fear of water is the best long term solution. Of course drugs are available to help, but I chose the cognitive way, meaning changing the way I think about something."

"Has it worked?" Milena asked and rolled her eyes at her outburst.

"I'm sorry. None of my business. Forget I asked."

He didn't say anything and she joined him to check on her clothing.

"Hey, they're already dry," she laughed. Even her bra and panty, which she'd tried to hide between her shirt and jeans, were almost dry.

"Probably another half an hour and then we can head out," Daegen nodded to the nearest window where to Milena's surprise a cheerful ray of sunshine streamed into the slightly smoky room.

"Half an hour to kill. How about you tell me why you're so afraid of water and maybe we can figure out how to tackle the problem?"

Irritation swept through her. Why was he pushing her so much?

"I've lived with the problem for as long as I can remember. It's just a part of me. I'll deal with it," Milena stated.

She hoped her firm voice would give him the hint to back off.

"You've never tried to address it? Professionally?"

"Kind of hard to deal with it when you're stuck in prison. But I did try, on my own, when I was younger, before prison. I just..."

Milena sighed in frustration. She didn't have the money to see a shrink. Then or now.

"Can we please get off the subject?"

Daegen shrugged.

"Sure, how about we toss some more wood into the stove and then go outside and wait for the clothes to dry. I'll put a pot of water on and we can have coffee."

Excitement whipped through Milena.

"Coffee? You brought coffee?" He was kidding right?

"If Paul knows what's good for him, he will have packed up some instant coffee, some cups and his cement cookies, despite saying he wouldn't give me some."

"Well, you're not getting my share," Milena said with a giggle.

"We'll see about that," Daegen replied. Then he chuckled as he peeked into the knapsack and made an O shape with his lips. A second later, he lifted out two large baggies containing cookies and held them up.

He wiggled his eyebrows

"See? He has to force them on me."

Milena laughed again. Paul was such a sweetheart. And so was Daegen.

"See, he cares about you," Milena teased.

"Too bad he doesn't care about my teeth. Damn cookies are so hard I wouldn't be surprised if I break a tooth one of these days. Let's make sure we leave some for the bears. They won't be able to eat us if they have no teeth."

Milena couldn't help but laugh again and she suddenly realized she enjoyed laughing. A lot.

Yup, she needed to laugh more often.

. . ⚓ . .

"WHAT'S WRONG?" PAUL shouted as he brought his atv up beside Mitch who had stopped in the meadow.

Mitch pointed south, toward their cabin.

Paul stared until he caught sight of some figures standing on the veranda about half a mile away. He counted three people.

"Are you expecting anyone today?" Mitch asked.

A slice of uneasiness whispered through Paul. He was not eager to get hit over the head again.

"Not today. Too soon for all the supplies we've ordered. Maybe Brady came with Dan and Rafe?" he answered.

"You need to get your eyes examined, my man. That's two guys and a woman," Mitch clarified with a chuckle.

Paul squinted through the late afternoon sunshine, but couldn't make out details.

"How can you tell from here? Paul asked.

"I eat my carrots. You don't," Mitch chuckled.

"Where is your gun?" Paul asked, realizing that maybe they should get locks on those doors. There were plenty of unexpected visitors lately.

Mitch patted his jean jacket.

"In the shoulder holster. Yours?" he questioned.

"In the doctor's bag. In the trailer behind me."

Mitch shook his head and frowned. His frown made Paul see the error in his ways. Guilt rippled at his insides.

"You're slacking, bro. I thought we were supposed to be watching each other's backs?" Mitch chided.

"Hey, I'm a veterinarian. Not a gunfighter," Paul answered with a touch of annoyance.

He had come out here so he could concentrate on doctoring horses. This wild west scenario of shooting someone who might be dangerous just wasn't his thing.

Mitch must have seen his irritation and chuckled.

"I doubt the bad guys would be standing out in the open ready to bushwhack us. Let's go and see who has graced us with their presence."

"I'll get my gun first," Paul said.

He didn't wait for Mitch to reply because his friend was right. Paul should have kept the gun closer at hand today.

Seconds later, he had his weapon nestled on his lap with the safety catch on. At least if there was trouble he could protect himself and Mitch.

"Ready?" Mitch asked.

Paul smiled and patted his pistol.

Mitch shook his head, and Paul caught a teasing glint in his eyes.

"You might want to turn the barrel outward. You don't want it going off accidentally and shooting something off that can't be replaced."

Paul was too tense to laugh at Mitch's jab.

"Safety catch is on," Paul reminded him.

"Yeah, well I hate to break it to you but safety catches are not always a hundred percent reliable."

"Oh come on! Seriously?" Paul gasped. He was about to curse his friend but Mitch was already pulling his machine forward.

He was teasing him, wasn't he?"

Paul gazed down at the gun and decided to reposition it. This time with the barrel pointing straight ahead, away from his private parts and right at Mitch's back.

Paul chuckled. If Mitch hadn't been kidding, then Mitch would pay.

As they drove closer to the cabin, Paul's tension eased as he recognized the woman. She was one of North Country Air's bush pilots.

It was Kaley.

She was a mysterious one. Quiet to the point of irritating and she never volunteered any information about herself. But Brady had mentioned that Kaley had been helpful to JJ in overcoming her fear of flying so she could follow her dream of becoming a bush pilot. So, in his book, he would make an effort to keep being welcoming to her.

However, the two men who had come with her, he didn't recognize. Both wore uniforms. One man, the taller one, appeared friendly as he waved to them.

He was dressed in black and the word POLICE was emblazoned in yellow across his chest. An arm badge said OPP which meant Ontario Provincial Police. He was most likely here due to the assault on him.

The other man didn't look so pleasant as he scowled when Mitch and himself approached on their vehicles.

Paul didn't like him right off the bat. Even from the distance of twenty feet, Paul could see the man's eyes were a very light blue and appeared squinty and suspicious. He wore a tan and green camouflage top and pants. Most likely a wildlife person who wanted to know about the poaching.

Boy, had these two men come to the right place.

. . ❧ . .

WITHIN THE HOUR MILENA and Daegen were back on the trail that Milena still could not see, despite Daegen insisting one did exist. Every once in awhile, he would point out a piece cut out of the bark of a tree and reassured her they were not lost.

His assurances gave her little comfort. Too bad her running shoes were not participating in the comfort level. Something on the rear part of her shoe was rubbing along the back of her right heel and she suspected a blister was forming from all this walking. Her prison issue runners had not been the best fitting in the first place and were lousy for this rough terrain.

To fight the increasing discomfort, she kept reminding herself that being out here in the fresh crisp air was a zillion times better than being incarcerated.

She glanced at the clear blue sky. The sun was getting lower on the horizon so she figured it must be around four o'clock. It would be dark in about three hours. They'd been walking off and on for several hours. Her thighs and her calves were sore and damned if a blister wasn't forming on her other foot too!

"Oh. crap," she whispered.

Daegen must have heard her for he immediately stopped.

"What's wrong?" he asked with a frown.

"Nothing," she said brightly. Maybe too cheerfully.

Daegen's frown deepened.

"The sound of your voice tells me different."

"Oh, crap," she blurted again.

How the heck did he know something was wrong? Could he read her that well?

"Tell me," he said in a commanding tone.

"How long before we get there?"

"Another four hours."

Horror flooded her.

"Oh my God, are you serious?" She was going to turn around. She had to. She couldn't go on like this with her body and feet now aching.

"No, but you should have seen your face," he laughed.

Milena slapped his arm. Hard.

Daegen danced away, clutching his bicep.

"Ouch. You pack a powerful punch for a scarecrow princess."

"Seriously, how long?"

"About ten minutes. I bet she already knows we're here. Last time when Mitch, Paul and I came over, she had intercepted us a mile back. She must be losing her touch."

"Who's losing her touch?" A woman's shout came from somewhere behind them.

Milena whirled around, but she could see no one.

Daegen laughed.

"See? Told you she probably knew we were here." Daegen said softly.

He turned around and shouted into the trees.

"Jane Sunflower? Its Daegen. I was here last fall with my two partners!"

Silence followed.

Milena strained her eyes, but she could see no sign of movement. For as far back as she could see there were only tall pine trees and white trilliums peeking out of a green carpet of ferns and moss-covered boulders scattered here and there.

Suddenly a woman stepped out from behind a large tree around thirty feet away. Milena's eyes widened in surprise as she surveyed the new arrival.

The woman was elderly. Maybe eighty years old, maybe even older. She had very long white hair that flowed down out of a cowboy style straw hat. She wore a dark green knit wool sweater, a pair of green track pants and muddy boots.

Milena swallowed as she spied the long rifle the woman held in her hands. Thankfully, the barrel of the weapon was pointed at the ground and not at them.

"Hi," Milena called out and made sure not to move.

The last thing she wanted was for the lady to shoot her for fear that Milena might be going for a gun.

To her surprise, the old woman smiled to show only a couple of teeth. One on the bottom left and one on the top right. Despite her lack of teeth, the woman's wrinkled, weathered face transformed from one of seriousness to one of friendliness.

"So? You took my advice and got yourself a wife," the woman said.

"Oh, I'm not his wife," Milena laughed, feeling self-conscious.

The woman shook her head and looked somewhat disappointed.

"So, you're living in sin, are you?" The piercing question was directed at Milena, not Daegen.

Dear Lord. How embarrassing.

Thankfully Daegen came to her rescue.

"This is Milena. She is an employee over at Snowy Creek Ranch."

"Never heard of it."

She walked toward them and then extended her right hand in greeting.

"Pleased to meet you, miss."

Milena shook hands with her. The woman had a strong grip and her little finger was missing. To Milena's surprise, she was immediately embraced by a feeling of warmth and something deep in the back of her mind sizzled to life. Suddenly she remembered her grandmother who had died when Milena had been around three years old. Huh, she hadn't thought about Gram in years.

The woman let go of Milena's hand and her gaze dropped to Milena's shoes.

"Those have got to go. I've got an extra pair, I never use. They'll fit you good."

"Oh, I can't—"

"Tut!" Jane Sunflower lifted her right hand and shook her head. Her brown eyes twinkled.

"No arguments, miss. I'm too old and I'm too wise. You won't win any arguments with me," she replied and then she wiggled her fingers.

"Give me your knapsack. You've carried it long enough."

Surprise washed over Milena. The old lady wanted her knapsack?

"Oh no, I couldn't let you—"

"What did I just say?" Her eyes flashed with defiance.

Milena sighed. It was useless to argue with the woman. Reluctantly she removed her knapsack.

"I'll take it," Daegen volunteered.

But before Milena could hand the knapsack to him, the woman snatched it away.

"Here, hold on to this," she instructed to Daegen, who looked as if he wanted to argue, but quickly decided against it.

He accepted her rifle and while the woman struggled into the knapsack, he winked at Milena.

"What brings the two of you by?" she asked as she unexpectedly grabbed Milena by her hand and began leading her forward.

"We wanted to check and make sure you were okay," Milena volunteered.

"Yeah, figured there was trouble."

"How so?" Daegen asked from behind them.

"People been creeping around. Came too close for my comfort the other day. Thought you might be them again, but you weren't. So I've been following you a good mile."

"Damn you're good. I didn't even notice, " Daegen chuckled.

"Watch that swearing, young man. Especially when in front of ladies."

"Yes, ma'am." Daegen replied quickly, but Milena could hear the amusement in his voice and when she glanced over her shoulder at him, he gave her another wink.

There was something about his winks that made a really nice feeling sweep over her. It felt as if he cared about her, but that was a crazy idea because they barely knew each other.

A moment later they came to the edge of the forest where they were barred by a waist high split rail fence. Beyond the fence Milena spied acres and acres of lush green meadow with bursts of white birch tree saplings here and there and snowy white lambs munching on the greenest grass she'd ever seen. The sight was so beautiful that for a few seconds she realized this must be how Dorothy in the Wizard of Oz movie might have felt after being dropped into a magical land of color.

"Welcome to Lamb Rock Ranch," Jane Sunflower said as she reached down and unlatched a wire from the top of a post. A gate swung open and she ushered them through.

Many of the woolly sheep were curious and lifted their heads to baa at them.

"They're adorable. They look like giant cotton balls," Milena laughed. Some of the sheep had black faces and some had baby lambs near them.

"They're friendly," Jane simply said.

She relatched the wire and pulled Milena along. They followed a fence that meandered along the edge of the forest and a few minutes later they turned a corner and Milena gasped as she saw a cute log cabin set at the edge of the meadow.

It was a simple little house. Very old from the look of it. The roof was a rusty looking sheet metal similar to the cabin they'd taken refuge earlier in the day.

But this building was a story and a half. It had a steep roof and dark green shutters hung at the small white-frame windows. A couple of grey antlers were set at each end of the cabin and there were several rusty metal watering cans filled to overflowing with green ferns, and white and purple trilliums, set upon the veranda.

The porch was made of wood planks with no railing. Set at one corner was a rocking chair with a colorful quilt draped over it. The door was knotty pine wood.

And it had a lock.

She also noticed a big wood-planked barn. It loomed spookily behind the house in the forest. Milena figured that was were the sheep from the meadow must get housed.

"Let's go inside. You've arrived just in time for supper. I've got lamb stew cooking in the pot and more than enough for all of us. And since you'll be staying the night, I've also got plenty of candles. I just finished up a batch the other day," she said as she let go of Milena's hand and opened the front door.

The wonderful scent of herbs teased Milena's nostrils as she and Daegen followed Jane inside.

It was a little cool in the cabin and Milena wished for a sweater. Absently she rubbed her arms to get warm.

"I'll set the table and call when dinner is ready. Have a seat on the couch." She pointed to a sofa laden with more colorful quilts.

"I can help, Miss Sunflower," Milena volunteered.

She loved the woman already.

To Milena's surprise, the lady held out her gnarled, wrinkled hand to her.

"Call me, Jane. Come along, we can chat in the kitchen. I have the stove going in there. It will be warm for you. Your young man can stock the fireboxes."

Milena caught a grin from Daegen as the woman wrapped her hand around Milena's hand and held tight.

Jane turned to look at Daegen who was setting his knapsack on the living room floor beside a quaint wood rocking chair, near the stone fireplace.

"You do remember where the woodpile is?" she asked him.

Daegen nodded. "Yes, ma'am."

"Good. I expect a nice toasty room in here ready for us after supper."

"Yes, ma'am. I will get right on it."

"Good. My old arms are getting tired of bringing in the wood," she said and then she pulled Milena along with her. She opened a wood-plank door and a burst of warm air welcomed them as they stepped into the kitchen.

"I almost didn't recognize him beneath all that scruffy hair when I first spotted you two miles out," Jane muttered as she let go of Milena and nodded for her to sit at the small round table.

"I've got carrots you can peel. Hold on a minute while I get the supplies," she said.

It felt good to sit down. Her feet were aching and her tummy growled with hunger. As Jane went about grabbing items, Milena took the opportunity to gaze around the room.

There were plenty of copper pots, pans and kettles that hung from hooks here and there on the walls and from the lone rough hewn ceiling beam. There were no kitchen cabinets, just shelves laden with white dishes, pale green cups, a pretty teapot, and some drinking glasses.

"Now, here, this is for you," Jane said as to Milena's surprise she held what appeared to be an almost brand new pair of hiking boots with a pair of thick black socks protruding from each boot and a cute white knit cardigan that was too fancy for the wilderness.

But Milena fell in love with the cardigan right away.

"Hardly been used. Sweater has been on the hook near on a year. Never used it. Was a present but I don't really want it. It's yours. From the looks of you, you need it more than I ever would. The boots here, they've been sitting here near on five years. A friend flew them in, but I just don't have the heart to part with my old ones."

Jane pointed to the boots she wore. They were old, tattered yet appeared in well working order.

But still...

"Oh my gosh. I really cannot take these. You need them for emergency."

The woman looked shocked, maybe even offended. She shook her head and went to a black cast-iron woodstove in a corner of the kitchen. A black round pot had been set on top and steam erupted from the sides of a lid. Milena figured that was the supper she'd mentioned and it sure did smell good.

"Like what kind of emergency? You will take them and I'm so happy Daegen brought you along. It's not too often I get womenfolk company out here, except for Blue of course."

"Blue? The bush pilot?"

"Yes, do you know her? She's a lovely young lady. Reminds me of me at that age. She brings her daughter sometimes. Such a sweet baby."

"Yes, she is a nice lady," Milena agreed.

"Now I want you to get out of those shoes and socks. I've got a first aid kit for those blisters on your heels."

Milena's mouth dropped open in surprise.

"How did you know?"

Jane laughed.

"I know everything."

A moment later she was placing a small cardboard shoebox onto the table. The box was filled with band aids, rolls of gauze, painkillers, scissors and there were several jars marked with labels that said first aid cream, calendula cream and plantain cream.

Jane lifted one of the jars, opened the lid and placed the jar onto the table. Inside looked to be a light green ointment.

"Smear this on your blisters right now and go barefoot the rest of the evening. It will soothe the ouch. More later and then more in the morning."

"Thank you, so much," Milena whispered as she fought back a burst of emotion. She couldn't believe how nice this woman was being to her, a person she didn't even know. Most of the older women who had been imprisoned for many years at the prisons she'd been in had guarded their emotions. They'd acted so tough or bitter by being on the inside and Milena had struggled to not become like some of them.

And now meeting Jane Sunflower was like a beautiful breath of sunshine.

$\cdots \infty \cdots$

"SO YOU HAVEN'T NOTICED anything else since?" The police officer who had introduced himself as Officer Kyle Green asked Paul as Mitch set a second pot of coffee in front of the four who sat at the kitchen table, talking.

Kaley had brought over a delicious chocolate cake from Moose Ranch, compliments of JJ due to the fact the officers had gone over there to speak with Brady first because Brady had been the one who'd reported the incident.

"Daegen did mention he smelled smoke one night, but we couldn't find anything suspicious aside from what we already told you."

The men nodded. Both were frowning.

"Unfortunately the Canadian wilderness is so vast and desolate that the poachers and animal hunters have a field day killing or taking our bears and other wildlife to other countries in exchange for money," Officer Green said.

"Milena had mentioned about seeing a documentary on that," Paul replied.

"Well, unfortunately it is true," the other officer, the one with the squinty eyes who'd introduced himself as Officer Rob Peel, said.

Both men pocketed their respective notebooks and stood.

"You're welcome to stay and have more cake and coffee," Mitch said.

The officers hesitated, both eyeing the cake.

"It was really good," Officer Green said. "But I don't want to make an enemy of your partners. When they come back and find out there was cake and they didn't get any because we ate their share...I would be in trouble. I don't like being in trouble."

They all laughed at his joke.

"Well, I need to get back to Thunder Bay as soon as possible anyway. I've got a client for a night time learning flight," Kaley said.

She'd been her usual quiet self and Paul had almost forgotten she was here.

Paul nodded.

He wished he had the balls to become a pilot himself, but he would prefer to keep his feet on the ground as much as possible. He knew Daegen had his pilot's licence but a few conversations over the winter between the three of them had made them realize that they didn't think it was feasible for the fledgling ranch to invest in a bush plane just yet. But when they became as prosperous as Moose Ranch, then they would revisit the subject.

"Okay, we'll drive you out to the lake," Mitch volunteered as they headed outdoors.

Paul frowned as he followed them into the twilight.

Too bad their peace had been shattered by those abusive animal poachers. If he were a betting man, he would swear the person who smacked him over his head had taken the gyrfalcon from its cage. Poor bird. He'd nursed it and it had been healing perfectly. He'd have set it free in a couple of days.

He wondered what fate awaited it.

He shook away the sharp pang of guilt and sadness and watched Mitch hand out the extra helmets for them to wear. There was room for only four of them, so one of the officers volunteered to drive and Paul said he would walk out to the lake to pick up the other machine.

He stood on the porch as they motored along the trail and into the woods. A few minutes later, he didn't hear the motors anymore.

He should start walking, but he decided to wait and listen.

Out toward the creek the frogs sang cheerfully. An owl hooted somewhere to the south and the wind whispered through the branches of the nearby pine trees in the forest.

This was peace. True peace.

Suddenly he had this overwhelming longing for Milena to be back here safe and sound, standing right here beside him. He wished he had been the one who'd gone with her to visit Jane Sunflower.

He wished it.

A lot.

He sighed, walked down the steps and headed across the meadow toward the trail that would lead him to the lake.

Chapter Eleven

"That was the best meal I've had in quite some time," Daegen praised Jane Sunflower as he walked beside her toward her rustic barn.

"It's mutton. I have it once in awhile. You got lucky. You should have come yesterday. I had lamb fries. Very tasty," she said with a knowing nod.

"Lamb fries? Never heard of that." Daegen replied.

"No? Well, quite delicious. They're lamb testicles."

Daegen started and the old woman laughed at his reaction. Her high pitched squeals of delight burst through the quiet of the twilight sending a nearby owl soaring into the sky.

"Sometimes I need to castrate. It don't go to waste. Nothing goes to waste out here. I've got a mighty fine garden growing in a nearby meadow. Use my lamb's dung for manure, but it has to be aged and dry so it gets into the soil nice. Your horse do would come in handy for that garden you say you're going to make this Spring."

He nodded politely at her word for horse manure and wished he hadn't asked the question about the lamb fries in the first place. Wished he'd remained back at the cabin with Milena.

But after supper, Jane had insisted that Milena rest by the fireplace and for Daegen to accompany Jane to the barn to check on a couple of pregnant lambs she had housed there.

As they approached the building, he moved ahead and opened the door for her.

"Thank you. I am glad that chivalry is not dead," she said as she entered.

Daegen couldn't help but smile. She was an old fashioned lady, that's for sure.

During supper, she'd told them tales about her time living here. About the hungry wolves that came howling right up to her doors at night in the winter and how the bears came right into her yard sniffing the air when she made pie. They'd become so lost in her stories, that twilight had fallen.

It felt different here than over at Snowy Creek Ranch. No frogs sang as they did back home, but there were the calls of several loons from a nearby lake.

It was dark and quiet in the barn as they entered and within seconds she had a lantern lit, had grabbed a stethoscope from a hook and led him past the numerous empty pens.

"I keep the sheep outdoors most of the time during the spring, summer and autumn. Sometimes I lose one or two to the wolves or bears but that's the hazard here in the north. During winter it gets kind of hard for my joints traipsing back and forth through the snow drifts so they stay inside the barn. Their body heat keeps things nice and toasty for them and I keep them well fed. Water comes in through insulated pipes from a windmill out behind the barn," she explained.

A few moments later, she stopped in front of a door, turned to him and placed her finger to her lips.

She spoke in a quiet tone.

"This section behind here is the nursery and maternity ward. I have two young ladies ready to pop. I find the lady lambs like it nice and quiet in back when their time is near."

They entered a warm room where Daegen spied two large white woolly lambs with black faces in separate pens. Each lay on an abundance of straw. They both let out baas of greeting as Jane clucked at them. It was obvious by their shiny eyes that they were glad to see her.

"Here, hold this while I check my sweeties."

A moment later she'd entered one of the pens and placed the stethoscope to the chest area and listened. She made a satisfied grunt and then went to the other pen to check the other lamb.

"Good. They're doing well," she said with a smile and then she ushered him back out into the main barn area.

As they walked toward the entrance she suddenly stopped and gazed up at him with a squinty suspicious look.

"You didn't come all the way out here to pay a visit, did you."

It wasn't a question.

"No, ma'am." He figured it was time to warn her, but she was way ahead of him.

"You're here about those people been creeping around. Almost shot one of them the other day,"

So, it seemed the bastards were lurking around here now. Concern for her safety shifted through him.

"What happened?" he asked.

"Nothing goes on around here without me knowing about it," she muttered in an angry tone. She turned away from him and hung up the stethoscope.

"There are three of them. They enjoy stealing my food when I'm out working."

"You said there are three people. Can you give me descriptions?"

"Oh sure, I got all the information written down. But I'll give you their descriptions only on one condition."

Daegen's tummy hollowed out in not such a nice way as she looked at him with the cutest smile that gave him the feeling he might not like what she was going to ask of him.

· · ❧ · ·

HAVING AN OPEN FIREPLACE and a fire to stare into while she waited for Daegen and Jane to return, was heavenly. Not only did the blaze blow an abundance of heat against her, but the roaring flames had the most intriguing relaxing effect on her as she stared at them. They danced in an abundance of colors; blue, yellow and red. The wood snapped and crackled as it was attacked by the fire.

Man, she sure had been missing a lot being stuck in prison. A gut wrenching sense of loss that she thought she'd conquered over the years suddenly slammed into her and she bit back a tortured sob.

She *had* lost so much time.

Maybe she would have been married by now if she'd been on the outside? Maybe she would have had some kids. Maybe she'd even be divorced like her parents?

But she'd ended up in the foster system after her mother's death. Her father and relatives hadn't wanted her.

In prison she'd dreamed about helping troubled kids at risk, just like she'd been at risk. She knew if she'd had someone to steer her in the right direction, or someone to look out for her, she would not have ended up in prison. She would be a part of their lives, like a mentor, and steer them away from trouble.

Maybe a social worker, or some sort of youth councillor, but those dreams had been squashed because she knew no one would hire an ex-con to look out for troubled kids.

A noise at the back door toward the kitchen area broke Milena from her thoughts. Fear and panic snapped through her like a live wire. Were the poachers breaking in?

She grabbed the fireplace poker, but before she could so much as stand up, Jane Sunflower had strolled into the small room with a stranger right behind her.

No, not a stranger.

"Daegen? she whispered.

She'd forgotten how sexy he looked without a beard and moustache. Not that he didn't look hot with all that scruffy hair on his face.

But without...yeah. Nicer.

"You see? I told you she would prefer you without the hermit look," Jane chuckled as she sat down in a padded rocking chair and clutched her gnarled arthritis riddled hands upon the armchairs.

Her smug smile illuminated her wrinkled face and Milena's cheeks warmed as Daegen glanced at her .

"I thought he was an intruder," Milena blurted, trying to change the subject.

"Believe me, he'd be dead now if he was," Jane said with a wink. "I like your reflexes. You were fast with that poker. That's how I am. I put someone out of commission first and then ask questions. Hold onto those reflexes you'll need them out here."

Milena nodded and placed the fire poker where she'd found it. Then she turned her attention to Daegen as he reached for a couple split logs near the hearth. She liked the way his fingers gently wrapped around the wood. Noted how the array of muscles bulged beneath his shirt as he tossed them onto the fire.

Her lower belly fluttered with awareness. How would his hands feel sliding over her body? His palms cupping her breasts as he lowered his luscious lips and kissed her nipples. She swallowed against her suddenly dry mouth and tore her gaze from him to Jane who stared back at her.

She was nodding slightly as if knowing that Milena was interested in Daegen. Thankfully she said nothing as she closed her eyes and rocked gently.

Daegen moved to his knapsack and withdrew the letter from JJ as well as the present she'd sent along.

"Here's a present from your next door neighbour, JJ. She didn't know you existed until recently and when she found out you were out here, she wanted us to bring you a gift from her."

Jane's eyes opened wide and she looked surprised as she accepted the gift and the envelope containing the letter.

"Oh my, a lady neighbour?" Jane mused as she opened the envelope.

She squinted as she read and then she smiled. Her eyes glowing with excitement as she withdrew a photograph.

She held it up for Daegen and Milena to see. It was a picture of JJ holding Chrissy.

"She wants to be my pen pal. Isn't that something? What a lovely little baby and such a pretty lady. And she invited me to a party. But there is no way I could go. I'm too old for parties and I won't leave my lambs. I did that last year when I made out my will and when I came back three of my lambs had been attacked and killed by wolves."

Jane placed the letter into the envelope, but held onto the photograph.

"No, siree," she said with a shake to her head.

"I won't let that happen again. I must write her back something. Will you be able to get my response to her?" She looked at Milena hopefully.

"Of course I can. JJ is coming to Snowy Creek in a couple of weeks, but I can let her know by cell phone that you won't be able to make it. Are you sure you won't change your mind?" Milena asked.

Jane pursed her lips and shook her head.

"Nope, but she was awful sweet to ask. Now let me see what's inside the box?"

She let out a gleeful yelp as she withdrew the mason jar of maple syrup. And another yelp when she unwrapped the beef jerky.

She grinned widely showing off her two remaining teeth.

"Oh goodness! It's like I have died and gone to heaven. Such precious gifts. I know I am lacking in the teeth department but I surely can suck on this beef jerky and make French toast with this syrup. Such a thoughtful lady, this JJ is."

Jane's happy reaction brought warmth cascading through Milena.

"Both are homemade," Milena said.

Jane nodded. "Yes, JJ says so in her letter. I haven't had beef in awhile." She stuck one of the several strips of dried beef into her mouth and closed her eyes.

"Oh, so good. So good," she muttered.

Milena looked over at Daegen who was smiling at the elderly woman who quietly sucked on the beef. When he spied Milena looking at him, he winked at her.

Milena winked back and returned to looking into the fire again.

It was so nice and peaceful here in Jane's cabin. The warmth felt wonderful and the relaxed silence was broken only by an occasional crackle and pop from the fire.

"I'll be bunking down in the barn tonight. I'll keep an eye on the two mothers-to-be," Daegen said after several minutes.

Jane nodded, but kept her eyes closed and continued to suck on the stick of beef jerky which hung out of her mouth about six inches.

"I'd appreciate it," she mumbled around her treat. "But before you do head out don't forget to grab some blankets on the table there by the window. And that gun you brought along too. Might want to keep it handy."

Alarm swept through Milena as her gaze flew to the closest window. She half expected a bear to be pushing its black nose up against the dirty pane, watching them. But there was nothing there. Just the blackness of the night.

"Are the bears around?" she asked tightly.

"Bears? I ain't afraid of no bears. It's the two-legged ones you need to be scared of," Jane muttered.

Her eyes were open now, but drooping with sleepiness.

"She's seen people around here. Chased them off with some shots from her rifle," Daegen told her.

Conflicting emotions sifted through Milena. Concern that there were intruders who could injure her like they did to Paul and also pride that Jane had the nerve to point a gun and shoot at people.

A soft snore erupted from Jane. Her mouth was slightly open and the beef jerky sat precariously on her lower lip.

"She's fallen asleep," Milena whispered.

Daegen nodded as he stood to one side of the fireplace and stared at the crackling flames.

"It's too much for an older lady to be working out here all on her own. She's got quite a few sheep to tend. We need to figure out some way to help her," Daegen said softly.

" I could stay here and help her for awhile," Milena volunteered.

She would love to help Jane out. It would give her a chance to gather her thoughts about wanting to have sex with all three of her bosses.

Daegen frowned. `

"No way," Jane suddenly growled.

Oh, she was awake again. She was holding her beef jerky in her hand and staring back at the two of them with defiance flashing in her eyes.

"I've been living out here on my own since before the two of you were even born. I have my sheep here and I will care for them. I will not leave them. Not until I'm dead. And even then, I have made preparations for their care after I leave this earth."

"Ma'am, forgive me for saying but—"

Jane stopped Daegen with a cutting motion of her hand slicing across her neck.

"Listen, I have had this conversation with Blue too many times and I'll tell you both what I told her. I may not look like I can take care of myself, but I can. And when the time comes when I need help, I know where to get inexpensive help. Until then..."

She nodded toward the kitchen area.

"Got my rifle all loaded and ready for trouble. Got another gun upstairs in my bed and yet another in the barn where I showed you. My eyes and my ears may be getting old, but the rest of me is still good enough to handle any shit, pardon my language, that gets thrown my way."

Her cheeks were flushed with anger as she stood.

"I'm heading up to bed now," she grumbled.

Then suddenly her demeanour changed to a friendly smile that lightened Milena's heart.

"Milena, I give you my couch. Spare pillows are with the blankets over there on the table. The couch is old but it is comfortable. I have spent many a blizzard nestled on that couch, listening to the wind battering my windows and the wolves howling at my doors. There's no fireplace upstairs but every spring I move up there until it gets too cold. I feel safer up there."

"Perhaps you should stay here where its warm," Milena suggested. She felt bad chasing Jane up to a cold room.

To Milena's surprise the woman came over, swooped over and hugged her with a warm embrace.

She smelled nice. Of beef jerky and happiness.

"Nonsense. I can tell you have had a rough life. Rougher than most, I can tell, but good times are here and in your future, I just know it," she whispered into Milena's ear.

She didn't know what to say, so she merely gave Jane a smile as the woman pulled away.

Jane then gave Daegen a hug.

Then she grabbed one of the several lit candles that Milena had set earlier along the mantle.

"Goodnight, children. Don't stay up too late. Morning comes quickly in these parts. Breakfast at sunrise."

"Goodnight," Daegen and Milena said in unison.

They watched Jane walk slowly up the steep steps that lined the back wall of the living room.

A moment later, boards creaked softly as she moved around upstairs.

"She's a very nice lady," Milena said as she returned to staring at the fire.

For some strange reason she felt embarrassed to look at Daegen, especially now with his new sexy look.

"Why didn't you tell me you were hurting?" Daegen asked.

He stared at her bare foot where she was unconsciously rubbing the ointment she'd lathered around a small blister earlier. Then his gaze went to the jar of ointment she'd left open on top of the small coffee table in front of the couch where she sat.

Oh shoot! She'd forgotten to put it away.

His expression was dark and his eyes were glazed with anger and concern.

Concern for her?

That someone should care about her, felt foreign. But in the intense way he studied her face, expecting an answer, she knew he did have concern about her.

Her breath caught as he sat down on the couch beside her. There was something intoxicating about the way he looked at her and it just about took her breath away.

"You need to smear that ointment all around the injured areas...like this."

Milena swallowed as he dipped a couple of his fingers into the jar and brought out a generous amount of ointment.

"Put your feet up on my lap," he said tenderly.

Oh my goodness! She shouldn't.

The soft lure of his voice had her doing exactly as he instructed and before she knew it, she had her calves settled over his strong thighs. She twisted her legs a little so he had easy access to the backs of her ankles. The heat of his thigh on her flesh made her feel hot and she was losing herself in the most incredible sensations of lust as he gently stroked the ointment over the raw areas.

She closed her eyes and melted against the sofa and then alongside his body.

Wow, she really liked the way he touched her. So gentle. So tender. Like she was a treasure.

It was such a nice bubbly feeling, to think she was important to someone. Disappointment shot through her as he moved his fingers away.

Her eyes popped open and she watched as he scooped more ointment and then gently stroked it onto the back of her other ankle. She closed her eyes again and a weird purring sound erupted from her. It was a sound she'd never heard before.

It was erotic and primal and suddenly his massaging stopped. She could feel the heat of his gaze upon her face and she opened her eyes. He was smiling at her. His eyes sparkled with...need?

Her heart became suspended in her chest as intense emotions snapped through her. All her senses snapped to alert mode.

His eyes darkened.

Her breaths came faster.

He was giving her a look she was beginning to recognize in the men at Snowy Creek Ranch. A similar kind of scorching gaze Paul and Mitch had given her before they'd kissed her.

Her thoughts wobbled. Was Daegen going to kiss her? Shock and disbelief and even hope roared through her.

Instinctively her lips parted. She became lost in his succulent gaze as he continued to watch her.

Suddenly he leaned forward or maybe she was leaning toward him? She wasn't sure. She didn't care.

She just wanted him.

She closed her eyes and felt a hand slide against the nape of her neck. He held her firm as his mouth melted over hers.

Her mind shattered and all she could do was feel.

He kissed firmer than Paul, but gentler than Mitch.

His warm mouth possessed hers. Kissed her and loved her.

She purred her approval and slid her hands over his taut shoulders. She loved the firm warm feel of his muscles beneath her fingers. Hard. So different than her body.

Her fingers moved up the strong column of his neck and then sifted into his fluffy hair. His strands felt like silk, a direct contrast to the hardness of his body.

She cupped the back of his head and kissed him back harder.

An awakening rushed through her. It was a deep seated hunger. An intense need. Powerful and raw. It blossomed and grew and instinctively she understood the meaning of attraction.

She'd felt it with Paul and then with Mitch and now with Daegen.

Yet with Daegen, it was profounder, harsher.

Emotions she had never experienced before tugged at her heart. *This* is what she had been missing in her life.

He kissed her harder. His guttural moans rippled upon her ears like music. She loved the spicy smell of him. Soap and pine and the coffee they had with dinner wafted off him.

So yummy.

She breathed him in like he was an addictive drug. Moaned in protest when he broke the kiss. The blissful connection shattered.

"Oh, boy," Daegen breathed.

He avoided eye contact as he uncupped his hand from the back of her neck.

His eyes were glassy in the firelight and their breaths shot through the quiet air like the motor on the post digger she'd been using with Mitch the other day.

"I shouldn't have done that," Daegen said quietly as he gazed at her.

Gosh, why did all the Snowy Creek men say that?

"It won't—"

She cut him off by leaning forward and finding his mouth again. She hadn't even realized she'd done it until his tongue thrust into her mouth creating an awesome buzz that hummed along her bloodstream right into her head and snapped through the rest of her, bringing an aching demand for more.

His thrusts into her mouth were sensual and she met his tongue with sensual movements of her own.

Pleasure and excitement and urgency all tumbled together. She arched against him, rubbing her breasts against his arm creating a wonderful friction upon her ultra sensitive nipples.

She spiralled into a thoughtless vortex were only her mouth existed. Pulsing pleasure. Intimate need.

Her lungs shuddered as she fought to breathe. Struggled to form a thought. Something deep in the back of her mind warned her that she should not be kissing him so passionately. So intimately.

Then all at once it was as if both were on the same wavelength and they pulled their mouths apart.

But not far.

She wanted to be near him. On him. Under him. Loving him.

"Bad idea," he whispered.

But his eyes were on fire and somewhere deep inside of her, something naughty and intense threatened to break free and crash through what little self-control she was holding onto.

"Very bad idea," she teased. "Especially since last summer you told me you were gay."

Suddenly he appeared bashful. He pursed his lips and shrugged his shoulders.

"Yeah, well, you were a damsel in distress. I didn't want to add to your distress."

Well, he certainly had created more suffering by kissing her, hadn't he?

Her mouth felt bruised yet tingled with awesomeness. Her body craved for him to kiss her again. All over her this time.

"I think we had better turn in, before..." He left his sentence hanging like a wicked invitation.

Maybe she should go out into the barn with him? Spend the night with him ...

Give your head a shake, woman! Have you lost your mind? Her sensible inner voice shouted inside her head.

Yes, I have lost my mind! And I love it! Her naughty side answered.

But this *was* wrong. Yet it felt *so* right.

Reluctantly she lifted her legs off his thighs, and he slowly stood.

His stare was so hot, she swore she could feel the heat of it raging into her as well.

"Goodnight," he said softly as he broke eye contact.

"Goodnight," she whispered back in a husky voice she barely recognized.

She watched as he strolled to the small pile of blankets and pillows that Jane Sunflower had arranged on a nearby table after supper. Nice muscles bulged in his biceps as he picked up what he needed. Then he turned to her.

A hot fire snapped in his eyes and naughty sensations whipped through her most intimate parts. She wanted him touching her breasts, sucking on her nipples, thrusting his shaft into her pussy. Her mouth felt ultrasensitive from the kiss, and she ached to stand up and go to him.

But his next words stopped her.

"I left the gun in my pack," he nodded to the knapsack beneath the table. "It's right on top. The safety catch is on. Jane showed me where the rifle is out in the barn, so I can use that if needed."

Alarm raced through her.

"Are you anticipating trouble?"

He shook his head. The sides of his luscious mouth tightened. It was nice to see his full lips now that his beard and moustache had been shaved. The mountain man look was gone, and she liked him better with his clean cut appearance. She wondered why he'd suddenly shaved it all off.

"No, so don't worry. I just wanted to let you know. Lock the doors once I'm gone."

Milena nodded jerkily and shivered as the door closed behind him. She stood and winced at the shakiness in her legs and the soreness in her wounded heels as she padded barefoot to the door.

Thankfully Jane Sunflower had outfitted the door with a deadbolt. Milena slid it into place and then went around to check the window latches which were secure and then to the other door near the kitchen.

It also had a deadbolt and was already locked. She gazed out the kitchen window and watched Daegen walk toward the barn. It was already dark outside, but streams of white moonlight bathed him in its brightness.

She liked his confident strides. He appeared to be a man who knew where he was going in life. A man who knew how to kiss. Boy, did he know how to kiss.

Excitement dashed away her momentary fear on the talk of guns as she remembered the seductive way his mouth had melted over her lips.

Sweet, yet demanding, his mouth had left an imprint on her. Her lips felt raw and nicely swollen. Her body felt all tingly and needy.

She bit her bottom lip as she pondered on following him and joining him for the night.

Good heavens, Milena! What in the world is wrong with you? Her inner voice admonished.

Now, she'd been kissed by all three men. How was she going to keep this a secret between the men?

Milena swallowed back a welling of nervousness at the thought of the men telling each other about kissing her.

What was she going to do?

. . ∾ . .

PRIMAL. THAT'S WHAT it was, Daegen thought as he stared up at the wood-planked ceiling of the barn. He'd gone primal out here in the wilderness. Outdoor living was bringing out the barbarian in him.

Earlier, when he'd come over from Jane's cabin, he'd climbed into the hayloft, tossed a blanket over a flattened area of hay, removed his clothing and lain down in the hopes of just forgetting what had happened between Milena and himself.

And just go to sleep.

Yeah right. Like that was going to happen.

He'd had a loss of self-control where Milena was concerned. He just couldn't get her out his mind! Her kiss had destroyed him in a really good way. Had breathed life into the fantasies he'd had about her since meeting her last summer.

Exhilaration raced through him as he remembered seeing her naked in the shower her first morning at Snowy Creek. Her sexy curves dripping with beads of moisture. Soap suds hugging her pert breasts. Long luscious legs.

Legs that would wrap around his waist as he plunged his penis deep within her, claiming her as his own woman

Daegen squeezed his eyes shut and panted as he reached down under the blanket, he'd dropped upon himself, and wrapped his hands around his solid, throbbing erection.

Man, Milena had really turned him on letting him kiss her. It had been hard leaving her in the cabin when every male instinct had urged him to push her down onto the sofa and take her hard and fast.

Or bring her out here where Jane couldn't hear Milena's moans as he made love to her.

Excitement ripped through him when he remembered the velvety feel of her skin as he'd rubbed ointment around her injuries. Her beautiful brown eyes had watched him with curiosity and her unique scent had wafted deep within his lungs making him so aware of her.

She smelled like a lightly scented lemony perfume. He hadn't been able to get enough of inhaling her. Hadn't been able to stop himself from kissing her.

He stroked his pulsing cock as he recalled how her silky mouth had parted and he'd thrust his tongue inside the hotness of her cavern. He couldn't remember ever being so aware of a woman, with the exception of his late wife. Usually, thoughts of Karen brought a knife of pain to his heart, but not this time.

This time it felt right that he'd kissed another woman.

Milena. Sweet, sensual Milena.

He wanted to kiss her everyday from here on out. Wanted to wake up beside her. Make love to her.

He imagined her being in bed with him. Her head lowering. Her sweet mouth taking his shaft, wrapping around his hardness like a velvet-encased steel glove.

He inhaled a sharp breath and caressed his cock harder.

She'd suck him hard and then soft and then she'd kiss his cockhead.

Erotic, almost painful sensations teased his flesh and he fought back the hard push of an oncoming orgasm.

Her mouth would play with his erection. Hard squeezes and indulgent licks and quick sucks.

Sensations were spiralling throughout him, and he could barely think now. He shuddered as the muscles in his lower abdomen knotted with tension.

He massaged himself harder. His hands moved faster and faster and his self control vanished. Fiery sensations lanced his cock and balls and destructive quakes exploded through him. He thrust heavily against his hands letting out guttural moans as all thoughts disintegrated and his body convulsed with uncontrolled abandon.

His head and back arched into the blanket-covered straw bedding as pleasure shook him.

He slipped inside the frenzy of hot tremors and kept his hands working along his sensitive shaft keeping the climax going for as long as he could.

When the spasms ebbed away, he lay there panting, staring up at the ceiling once again.

Perspiration caressed his brow and his body, and he enjoyed the after shudders of his climax.

Wow, that had been mind blowing. He could only imagine how good it would be with Milena physically being here.

Touching him, making love to him.

A new thought suddenly jolted him. How in hell was he going to keep his hands off her when they got back to Snowy Creek Ranch? How would he be able to keep his feelings about Milena a secret from the other guys?

Oh no, what was he going to do?

• • ❧ • •

MILENA SWORE SHE'D just fallen asleep when a rapping sound snapped her awake. Her heart pummelled against her chest as she stared into the darkness.

Confusion gripped her.

What had woken her? And where was she?

And then she remembered she was at Jane's place and that she'd kissed Daegen. How long had she been asleep?

She tensed as she heard the floorboards creak overhead. Jane was walking around upstairs.

"I'm coming! I'm coming!" came her shout as another rapping sound erupted from close by.

Oh my God! Someone was knocking at Jane's door? Out here in the middle of nowhere?

She grabbed the box of waterproof matches and a candle she'd brought along with her and left within easy reach on the table beside the sofa. She had it lit in a flash and quickly tossed the blankets aside.

On the mantel was an old-fashioned clock. It was twenty minutes after four in the morning! She'd been asleep for seven hours straight.

Cool air brushed against her bare flesh. Her old nightgown just wasn't any use out here in this kind of environment. She'd have to figure out a way to order clothing for herself. Quickly she slipped on the knit cardigan Jane had given her last night. Warmth instantly embraced her. Hurriedly she slid on the socks Jane had also given her. She headed toward the knapsack and the gun Daegen had said he'd left in there.

At the same time, she noticed a yellow light shine down the staircase. Jane was descending.

"One of the ewe's is in labor. She doesn't sound too good," came Daegen's shout.

Instantly Milena relaxed. It was Daegen.

No intruders. Thank God!

But there was a lamb in labor, and she would need help.

Milena met Jane at the bottom of the stairs and she was carrying a gas lantern. She quickly unlocked and then opened the door.

Daegen stood there. His hair was rumpled, and a sexy dark stubble shadowed his chin and upper lip. He looked sexy, and he also looked concerned.

Alarm bells shifted through Milena for the poor lamb in labor.

"It's her first time, so she's most likely upset. Doesn't understand the pain. But there's always a chance for a breech. So, I'd best check," Jane muttered.

She was wearing a red fleece robe and matching red slippers and Daegen wore his jeans and an open shirt giving Milena a glimpse of his heavily muscled bare chest.

Something naughty stirred deep inside of her and she wished she could run her fingers over those muscles.

But mercy! Why was she turned on by men's chests?

"Boil some water, please, Daegen. Don't come until we send for you. Milena come along with me. I may need your help," Jane Sunflower instructed.

There was no time for good morning greetings as Milena quickly brushed past Daegen. She sensed the tension of concern emanating from both of them.

"Anything else you might need?" Daegen asked as he slipped inside.

"Yeah, pray," Jane answered.

She grabbed Milena by the hand and pulled her along.

"Been worried about Missy. She's barely two. A bit young to be having her first one, but the males got loose out of their meadow due to a broken-down fence awhile back and had their way with the girls before I was able to get them back to their place."

Oh, my goodness! Those poor lambs. But Milena tamped down on her sympathy realizing that Jane was running a business and lambs were bred this way, even if by accident.

"Usually, I prefer to have my lambs born in the summer when it is nice and warm for my old bones. But the boys had other ideas. Been dealing with the lambing for the past couple of weeks because of their rowdiness. Just two ladies left to give birth inside. I didn't expect to get a full night sleep tonight. But it was close," she said.

Milena sensed the worry in the elderly woman's voice. Felt it in her strong grip.

The instant they entered the barn, Milena could hear the laboring lamb's cries of pain.

"I'm coming, darling Missy. I'm coming," Jane called out as she handed Milena the lantern and asked her to hold it up.

Set on a bench were two stainless steel buckets of water, a fresh bar of soap and a couple of towels. It was obvious she was prepared for a birth.

Jane dunked her hands into one of the buckets.

"Ooooh so cold," she complained as she wiggled her entire body and laughed.

She withdrew her hands and grabbed the bar of soap and began washing her hands.

"Sometimes I wonder why I am crazy enough to think of them lambs as my children," she muttered. "But they're my companions. They're all I got."

Sadness swept through Milena. Perhaps living all alone out here deep in the forest wasn't as nice as Milena had thought it would be.

"I'm sure the lambs think of you as their mother. They're lucky to have you," Milena said as she tried to comfort the old woman who furiously lathered her hands.

The sides of Jane's eyes crinkled, and a small smile came to her lips. She made a cute little grunting sound before dumping her hands into the second bucket of water to rinse off the soap.

"Should I get some more clean water? Did you want me to wash my hands too?" Milena asked.

"Nope, not yet. Gotta see what I'm dealing with first. Get off the sweater. You don't want it getting dirty and put this on," Jane said as she reached for a flannel shirt hanging on a nearby hook and handed it to Milena, who quickly changed.

"Here, just hold onto the lantern. When we get back into the maternity ward, I'll need you to place the lantern up nice and high on the hook so I can see."

Milena nodded and followed Jane to the back of the barn. She was surprised to find another room back here. It reminded her of the night she had spent with Paul in back of that barn with the two rooms.

The nice kiss they'd shared in the barn office.

And the kiss with Mitch out in the paddock they'd been building.

And last night's kiss with Daegen.

Oh, dear Lord.

Milena blew out a sharp breath and focused on Jane who stood in front of a pen. From somewhere in the darkness the ewe continued to bleat, calling out her distress.

"I'm here, Missy. Could you open the gate for me, Milena? Don't want to contaminate my hands. Usually, I bring the towel and use it to open, but I forgot."

Milena opened the latch and swung open the gate.

"Come on in. Gonna need your help." She nodded to a nearby wall. "Hook is up there."

Milena placed the lantern on the hook, turned and spied a white woolly lamb with black face nestled on the straw in a corner of the pen. Her eyes shone glassy with pain; her mouth was open as she kept doing a baa baa baa that grated on Milena's nerves.

"I'm here, Missy. It's alright. Mommy's here," Jane cooed as she patted the lamb on her head. The lamb kept complaining.

"Gonna need you to hold her neck firm, Milena, so as I can do an inspection and see how the baby is positioned. Make sure you hold tight, keeping your hands away from her mouth. Don't want her biting you or me in her pain."

Milena nodded, stepped forward and kneeled down beside the lamb who had stopped her crying and was eyeing Milena with curiosity.

"Just talk to her and then hug her neck. Keep her occupied," Jane said.

"Hi, sweetie. You're about to have a baby. That's why it's painful," Milena talked to the ewe as she wrapped her arms around its neck, not too tight as to choke her, but tight enough to keep her head from swinging around to nip at Jane who was already bending over at the backside of the ewe.

"Okay hold onto her. Nice and tight. I'm going in," Jane said.

Milena did as she was told and a second later the ewe squirmed wildly, thrusting out her back legs, but Jane had positioned herself in such a way as she wouldn't get kicked.

"Just another minute, Missy." Jane cooed and to Milena's surprise the older woman began to hum a tune that Milena remembered from the movie *The Sound of Music*.

Milena bit her bottom lip and wondered nervously if this was going to be the same nerve-wracking experience as what had happened with Brownie Belle and her foal.

To her surprise the ewe seemed to relax as she listened to Jane and Milena found herself relaxing too as she mentally put words to the song Jane hummed.

"That's the song *Something Good*, from The Sound to Music," Milena whispered.

"I hum and sing songs to my babies all the time. They love it," Jane said as she worked her hands at the back end of the ewe and continued to hum.

Milena joined her and began to hum softly.

They hummed the tune over and over for several minutes and then finally Jane stopped, and Milena did as well.

"Okay, I have found the problem and its fixed. Missy is going to be fine now. The baby is in the correct position, and it will be here in a minute."

Milena blinked in surprise. She'd expected to be out here for hours as she helped this ewe through a rough labor just as she'd done with Brownie Belle and Paul.

"Here it comes! Keep holding her neck, Milena. Keep humming! The lamb is almost here!" Jane hissed with excitement.

"Here? Now?" Milena asked.

Goodness, she hadn't expected it to happen so quickly.

She began to hum as waves of excitement gripped her. A new life was coming into the world, and she was here to watch and help. How cool was that!

"Hey, when it's time. It's time. Just keep holding her."

Milena nodded, her humming growing louder as she wrapped her arms tighter. She loved the warm soft wool of the ewe brushing against the side of her face. The animal continued to struggle, but not as bad as earlier.

She watched Jane's face twist in concentration, her arms pulling, her mouth set in a grim line.

Then she suddenly smiled and nodded.

"It's here," Jane said softly.

She began humming right along with Milena.

She was able to see the newborn now as it dropped into the straw. Its black face and scrawny body was wrapped in a watery, bloody membrane, which Jane quickly tore off.

"Hand me that bottle up there, please, Milena," Jane pointed to a nearby shelf that held a glass spray bottle with the words Iodine scrawled on the label.

Milena handed it to Jane and watched as she ripped the umbilical cord and squirted a good deal of iodine on the end of the cord still attached to the baby lamb with a stream of yellow-brown liquid.

"That'll help prevent infection. Okay, let her go. She'll want to start cleaning her baby."

Milena did as instructed and they watched as the ewe slowly got to her feet and sniffed the newborn. Then she started licking it.

"Good job. Missy," Jane said as she patted the ewe's head like it was a dog.

"It's a girl," Jane said to Milena. "Sometimes ewes don't take to their babies. That's when I bring them inside my cabin and set them in a box by the fire. Gotta keep them warm and I gotta feed them. Come on, I need to check on Twinkle next door."

"Twinkle? Like in twinkle toes?" Milena asked.

"Nope, like in twinkle twinkle little star. Was singing that song when she was born. Unfortunately, her mamma didn't make it. So, I had to take care of her like she was my own. Milk from a bottle, keeping her warm in the cabin with me. The ones without mom's are called bums. When that happens I gotta get another ewe who has lost her baby and try to see if she'll be a surrogate to the bum, which is rare for me cause I don't have such a huge flock. Like I said, if I have a bum, I have to keep them alive and nurture them myself."

Emotions, thick and raw erupted within Milena. She truly wished she'd had someone like Jane to look after her when she'd lost her mom. The elderly woman was so caring.

Milena grabbed the lantern and quickly followed Jane who had led her to the next pen and instructed Milena to lift the lantern higher so she could see.

As they peered in, Milena saw another ewe. But this one was bigger than Missy. She had a cute black face and looked like a puffy woolly cloud. She was standing in the straw and licking her newborn.

"Ahh, just like the last time. She's done the birthing all on her own. Twinkle is a pro. She knows what to do. Our job is done here."

"Don't you need to spray the iodine on the umbilical cord?" Milena asked as concern for the newborn gripped her.

"Nope, not right now. She'll lick that area on her own and I will do it later. Will do Missy's baby again too. Okay let's leave the mothers to tend to their babies. I need coffee and breakfast. How about you?"

Milena nodded, feeling stunned that one ewe had needed help and yet another had a baby all on her own.

"Good. Let's go," Jane said.

Oh my gosh. I cannot believe what I just witnessed, Milena thought as followed Jane out to the front area of the barn where she quickly washed up and Milena exchanged the flannel shirt for her pretty cardigan.

Milena felt as if something had changed within her this morning after seeing those animals. Jane had hit a sore spot reminding her that animals lost their mothers too, just like humans did.

But what happened to those babies when no one was around in the wilds to care for them? How could they survive? Suddenly she felt overwhelmed at that idea of helpless creatures being exposed to the elements and to other animals who'd just prefer to eat them.

So many orphans out there. Milena had to suck back her tears.

"My goodness, I am so glad that's over," Jane said as she towel dried her hands and gazed at Milena.

Her face dropped into a frown.

"What's wrong? You look sadder than I've seen anyone in a long time."

"How do you do it, Jane? Living out here all alone taking care of orphan lambs? I had ideas of living out here all alone just like you but now I realize I'm a chicken. I don't think I could do it."

"Oh, tonight was nothing. When the birthing season hits, I am living out here day and night assisting the lambs and taking care of bums all at the same time. Talk about multi-tasking. But quite rewarding when things work out."

Milena shook her head. She wasn't sure she would be up to a task having animals so dependant on her.

Jane smiled.

"Besides, a young lady like yourself should not be alone. You have Daegen and..." she paused to think.

Milena wanted to jump in and remind her that she worked for him, but she just couldn't quite do it. Maybe not protesting out loud might make it real somehow that she did belong to him.

Quit dreaming, Milena, she chastised herself.

"And Mitch and Paul. For a second, I couldn't remember their names. I am getting old," Jane said with a heavy sigh.

"But you came out here around my age, right? You said you've been here for over forty years. So why did you come out here if I can ask?"

Milena wished she hadn't asked as she spied a bitter smile touch the tips of Jane's lips and then it was gone.

Jane frowned. Her bushy grey eyebrows scrunched together.

"Well, I had troubles. Man trouble. My first husband died of throat cancer before we were married even a year. Smoked way too much. Thought he was invincible. But he wasn't. Well, then I hooked up with an acquaintance of his who turned out to be one nasty son of a bitch, pardon my language. I divorced him, but he became my stalker. The police could not help me, so I took care of removing myself from the toxic situation. I made myself get lost in this forest. I'm pretty sure had I stayed with him I would be dead now. Had I left him and not gone into hiding I would be dead. He's that type that would never have let me go. Do you know what I mean?"

Milena nodded, suddenly remembering how she had ended up in prison. It had been because of a poisonous relationship with a man who'd hooked her on drugs.

"Yes, I understand," she whispered.

She didn't want to remember that part of her life and over the years she'd done a pretty good job at shoving those memories deep down inside of her.

"I think you do. I can see it in your eyes. You have experienced something tragic in your life. Maybe even more than once."

The woman grimaced and grew silent, then she stared at the open door of the barn. Milena followed her gaze and noticed Daegen was out there chopping wood beside Jane's cabin. A couple of oil lamps were set nearby on a couple of logs. Above him, the sky was starting to brighten into a dull grey.

"I'm sorry about your first husband," Milena whispered, feeling bad that Jane had gotten such a bad break in life.

"He was a good man. You know sometimes things happen for a reason. Had my first husband not died, I wouldn't be out here taking care of all my wonderful lambs. And your Daegen here is a fine man. All three of them are fine men. I appreciate that they were worried about me, but I can take care of myself."

She tossed her towel onto a nearby hook and slapped her wrinkled hands together.

"Now! How about that coffee? We got lots of hot water, I am sure. Glad we didn't need it. I'll make us some breakfast. I have some fresh baked bread from yesterday, I have some blueberry jam preserves left from last year and some freshly churned butter from my lambs."

Shock reverberated through Milena.

"You make it all yourself?"

"For sure, young lady. Living out here, one learns to become self reliant in order to survive and making tasty food sure does help to keep yourself a man. It didn't work in my case but I'm the exception. That's why I'm going to share some recipes with you. I'll write them out and find some way to get them to you. Don't you worry."

Jane slipped her arms around Milena's waist, hugged her, then grabbed her hand and led her towards the open barn door.

"All is well with the ewes, Daegen! Breakfast in fifteen minutes! "she shouted to Daegen who was now piling the wood he'd chopped onto a stack of firewood set at the side of the cabin.

Daegen waved acknowledgement.

Jane Sunflower lowered her voice so just the two of them could hear.

"He's a handy and strong man and he looks so nice without that scruffy beard and mustache, don't you think? I cut it all off myself with an old razor blade I brought along and keep out in the barn. Was still as good as new. Belonged to my first husband, bless his soul. I used to tell my first husband that a woman doesn't want a mouth full of hair when he kisses her. Told Daegen that too."

"You did?"

"I did. And he complied albeit reluctantly. I expect he was hiding himself behind all that hair."

Milena smiled and gazed over at Daegen who was wiping sweat from his forehead with the sleeve of his still open shirt, giving her a glimpse of solid abdominal muscles.

Heated interest made a mad scramble through her. She looked away before Daegen realized he was being watched.

"You two make for a nice-looking couple. Have I told you that already?" Jane Sunflower peered at Milena as they walked up the front steps.

"Yes, you did. Several times last night when we were in the kitchen getting supper ready," Milena acknowledged, understanding the woman was trying to make a point.

"And there is nothing going on between us. He's just my boss," Milena said as they entered the cabin.

"That was some mighty big 'there is nothing going on between us kiss from just a boss' last night," Jane chuckled.

Milena stopped short. Her cheeks flushed with heated embarrassment.

"You saw!" she gasped.

"I had forgotten my presents from JJ on the table. I was coming down the stairs to fetch them. Wanted to see that picture again. I thought the creaking floorboards overhead and the squeaky stairs would tip off you two as to the fact I was coming back downstairs but I quickly realized an explosion would have gone off and the two of you would not have heard."

"It...it just happened. There is really nothing going on. I hope you don't think I'm a liar," Milena blurted.

Jane turned to Milena, her hands clutched to her chest and a genuine smile brightened her face.

"No, I don't think that at all, sweetie. Besides, it's really none of my business. But I think all of the men at Snowy Creek Ranch would be suitable for you. They are all upstanding young men. Now, if you wouldn't mind setting the table, I'll get the coffee and breakfast going. You will find everything you need in those shelves and that drawer."

She pointed to the areas where the items she wanted Milena to get were located and then she began gathering pots and pans.

"Over the years I have mastered this cooking wood stove like a pro," Jane said. "You have to be a fast learner out here where there are no stores, especially when you are out of your element on your own. Can you open the stove door and place in some bark and kindling? Do you remember how I told it to you?" Jane asked.

Milena nodded.

It was a good thing Jane had explained yesterday how to start a fire in the stove after Milena had asked her. She'd also watched how the men started their cast iron stove at Snowy Creek and saw how Daegen had piled the wood into that cabin stove yesterday or she would be inviting a bunch of smoke in here.

Milena checked the damper to make sure it was open, then grabbed some kindling and some bark from a large box nearby. Within a minute she had a small cracking fire and a touch of smoke billowing out of the open door. When the fire was big enough, she placed some larger pieces of wood on top and closed the heavy door.

"I'll put some logs in once it's fully caught fire," Milena said.

"Good job," Jane praised as she placed a pan with butter onto the stove. A few seconds later, the butter was sizzling.

"Homemade butter from my sheep," the elderly woman said with a proud smile.

"I didn't know you could make butter from sheep milk?"

"You have so much to learn," Jane said with an easy-going chuckle. "I have homemade sheep cheese, homemade bread, those blueberry preserves and some tasty thinly cut lamb chops for breakfast."

"Lamb chops for breakfast?" This was interesting.

"When I don't have eggs or bacon on hand, which is often, I use lamb chops. They go very well with the cheese and bread."

"I think this is awesome," Milena replied.

She spied the meat was already on the counter. It appeared fresh.

"Where was that stored? The guys use a cave in the side of a rocky hill. Do you have one too?"

"I took the meat out last night right after supper when I sent you two into the living room. Since it is early in the season, the area beneath the cabin is still frozen, so is my meat. I have a trap door right here beneath this rug."

She pointed to an area near the back door where a tattered rug was located.

"It's a caged box lined with Styrofoam and doesn't attract animals. But the bears and wolves suspect something is here, so I do get visitors."

Milena eyes widened at the mention of bears.

Jane laughed.

"I'm under the impression you've encountered bears already?"

Milena nodded.

"On the way over."

"Ah yes, Big Mamma and her two babies. They visited here earlier in the day yesterday. One of the babies tried to steal the bread right off my windowsill while it was cooling. Good thing I was cooking my lunch and saw him or her."

Fear shifted through Milena.

"Oh my God! Are you serious?"

"I smacked its nose with the broom. It ran so fast, and I laughed so hard. I really need to get the screens in before it gets too hot. It will be any day now if this warmth keeps up."

Jane was already back at the counter puttering around her meat.

Milena simply could not believe the woman was so casual about bears as if it was perfectly normal for a bear to steal her food. Just hearing about her close encounter had the chills of terror racing up her spine.

Milena shivered and hurried to set the table. When she was finished, she returned to Jane who was placing thin bacon-like slices of meat into the frying pan.

"Do you...do you kill your own lambs?" Milena asked as she watched the meat sizzle.

"Oh yes. No butchers around here. I have to do it, or I don't eat," Jane Sunflower said easily. "But I only kill one if really necessary. I put off the chore until I get really hungry for lamb. Since I'm not much for fish, or bear or moose, then I kill my oldest lamb."

Milena nodded and swallowed a grimace.

Oh, God. Nope, living on her own like this and killing creatures in order to survive was not going to be her cup of tea. She would stick with the cowboys and let them provide the food. She would be perfectly happy remaining to be a work hand, thank you very much.

Chapter Twelve

"I swear that was the best breakfast I ever had," Daegen said as they walked back along the edge of the meadow with the milling white lambs and rickety wood fence, following the same way they had come through yesterday.

All Milena could muster was a choked mutter of agreement. She'd barely been able to keep herself from breaking down into a washer full of tears after reluctantly accepting more presents from Jane Sunflower.

Jane had given her a gorgeous lightweight handmade quilt with a sunflower pattern. The colors of the material were breathtaking. An arrangement of yellows, browns, greens, bordered by sky blue. She had also given her a knitted blue and white scarf as well as a brand-new straw hat, insisting she get rid of the old one she'd worn here as it didn't make her look attractive to men. So, Milena had left it behind, at Jane's persistence. Jane also included the cardigan and scarf, insisting Milena wear them on cool mornings, such as this one.

At first, Milena had refused the gifts, but Jane had asserted to the point Milena had been afraid she would have offended the elderly lady. She hadn't known the woman twenty-four hours and it felt as if she were losing her best friend as she walked out of sight of the cabin with the woman still standing on her porch waving good-bye.

"She'll be fine," Daegen said as he slowed his pace allowing her to catch up.

Thankfully he didn't look at her. For if he did, she would probably lose it if she saw humour in his eyes about her blubbering over a lady she barely knew.

But it just didn't feel right leaving her here all alone, despite knowing she'd been on her own out here for decades.

Now as she walked, with the chill in the early morning air, Milena was so grateful for the warm attire she'd been given.

Listen to your elders. They are wise, her grandmother used to tell her. She hadn't remembered that until just now. Her grandmother had been so right, especially where Jane was concerned. Giving her sturdy boots and nice warm clothing.

"I can't wait to show Paul the cookies she gave us. Or maybe we'll just eat them all up before we get back home?" Daegen chuckled after a few minutes.

Despite feeling awful for leaving her newfound friend, the word home tugged at her heart.

Yes, Jane had been living here for so long that Milena should feel okay about leaving her. Yet the violent poacher might be around, and she could not shake the uneasy feeling she would never see Jane again. She resisted the overwhelming urge to run back and beg Jane to come with them or for her to let Milena stay with her until they knew for sure there was no more danger.

But Milena knew it was fanciful thinking. She'd always had a habit of getting attached to certain people in prison and her heart had been broken many times when they'd transferred them, or she'd been sent to a new prison.

JJ had been one of the inmates she'd liked very much, but then Milena had been transferred out without any warning. She'd learned her transfer had been to accommodate an incoming prisoner who had family nearby.

Milena shook her memories of prison life away. She was out now. There was no need to dwell on what was in the past.

Besides, it was beautiful outside. Even her feet were snug and warm and comfortable in the boots Jane had given to her. The blisters on her heels barely hurt and Jane's instructions to stop often to air out her feet and put on ointment was fresh on Milena's mind.

What a wonderful caring woman. She would miss her terribly. Not only did Jane remind Milena of her grandmother but also of her own mother who had always looked out for Milena's comfort and safety.

Emotions once again swirled in her chest and Milena drew in a deep breath of fresh pine scented air to calm herself.

Such a sweet smell. Such lovely shades of green everywhere she looked. Emerald, pickle, mint green colors. Dark green ferns were uncurling here and there. Bright olive-colored leaves waved from the branches of small saplings. Areas of the ground were covered in shamrock colored moss.

Over the next few hours, she distracted herself with the scenery. They stopped often so Milena could air out her feet and apply ointment and band aids that Jane had given her. Daegen didn't offer to play doctor as he had last night. Maybe he'd been serious when he'd said he shouldn't have kissed her? She knew he'd been about to say he wouldn't do it again, when she'd cut him off by kissing him again.

So maybe he wouldn't?

Maybe it was better this way? Maybe none of her bosses would kiss her again? Or maybe they would?

Elation sizzled through her at the idea that maybe this was the beginning of something very naughty. Why else would all three men be kissing her?

A knocking sound from nearby ripped Milena out of her thoughts.

"Hey, piliated woodpecker alert," Daegen called and pointed upward.

Milena continued walking and looked up. She caught sight of the large cat-sized black and white feathered woodpecker with a red crest on the top of its head about ten feet up a large pine tree that was full of rotten holes. The bird pummelled its long chisel-like beak against the bark making an unbelievably loud rat-a-tat sound.

Without so much of a warning Milena hit a brick wall, bounced away and her feet went right out from under her. She landed flat on her butt, thankfully it was a soft landing on a puffy mattress of moss.

The accident happened so fast all she could do was blink up at Daegen who cursed softly and quickly crouched beside her.

Concern marred his eyes.

"Oh man, I am so sorry. I didn't realize you were so close behind me. Are you hurt?"

Her heart fluttered wildly.

Oh boy. He was seriously worried about her. She just wasn't used to this sort of...caring from someone. And he really looked cute. Was she crazy thinking how attractive he looked when he appeared so worried for her?

"Milena? Talk to me, sweetheart. Are you okay?"

His strong hand was on her shoulder squeezing gently.

Wow, he had just called her sweetheart. Boy, she had never noticed the sparkling golden highlights in his eyes. Or how long his eyelashes looked. So dark and dreamy.

"Milena? Why aren't you answering me?"

Such a serious look he had now. So adorable.

She blinked, forcing her thoughts away.

"I'm fine. Would you feel like striking up a conversation after falling on your ass?" she muttered.

He laughed and embarrassment fused through her.

Reluctantly she accepted his outstretched hand and he pulled her easily up to her feet.

"You're sure you are okay? No broken bones?"

She touched along her backside and her pants felt a bit wet on her bum area.

"Just a wet behind."

"Moss will do that," he said with a chuckle.

A sudden jolt of alarm raced through her.

"Oh no! Did I get anything on the sweater?" she asked and grabbed the hem to pull the sweater forward. Thankfully she didn't see any dirt.

"Looks okay," Daegen reassured. "It's a good thing it is short. We'll have to dry your pants at the half-way cabin. It's not too far ahead. I don't want you catching a chill."

"I'm fine. It's not bad. I'm not fragile. I won't catch a chill. We can just walk fast and I can stay warm that way. Come on. Let's keep going," she urged.

Suddenly she just wanted to get to that cabin and make a little fire.

Man, talk about being a creature of comfort. A wet behind on a cool spring morning was not the most comfortable feeling. So much for claiming she wasn't fragile when suddenly all she wanted was a nice toasty fire to stand beside.

The concerned look had disappeared from Daegen's face. Perhaps she'd imagined it?

Yep. Must have.

Daegen nodded and started forward.

She followed him. But this time, she made sure she stayed a few paces behind him just in case he made another sudden stop. Besides, the hairs on the back of her neck were suddenly sticking up giving her the feeling they were being watched.

In the prison system, she had learned to heed the warning of following her instincts of danger. It had usually involved another inmate or a guard watching her, but there weren't any prison people out here, so maybe the poachers or bears were around?

Shivers raced up her spine.

Warily she gazed around as she walked, but she saw nothing out of the ordinary. That woodpecker flittered past them and settled on another tree nearby and was battering its beak once again. Cool wind rustled through the pine branches overhead.

The peace she'd been enjoying while observing all the different colors of nature, was gone, replaced by some weird unwanted worry about Jane and their own safety out here in the vast wilderness.

She worried her bottom lip and wished she could grab Daegen's hand as they had done when they'd run through the woods yesterday.

Was it only yesterday?

Gosh, so much had happened since then. She'd watched Jane deliver a baby lamb into the world and last night she'd been kissed by Daegen, and she'd so boldly returned that kiss.

Milena blew out a tense breath and tried really hard to disregard that creepy feeling of being watched. But try as she might, she just couldn't ignore it.

. . ~⚓~ . .

"I COULD PICK THEM OFF so easily," Bertris muttered as he aimed his .22 rifle at the man and then the woman who walked past them about a hundred feet away.

"You do that stupid and people will come looking. Then our entire project is finished because we can't work with the place crawling with cops," Sally grumbled as she stood behind the idiot she had been stuck with on this pouching run.

Bertris grunted softly.

"There is one way you can make sure I won't hurt them or that old lady."

Sallie rolled her eyes and shook her head. She should be disgusted at what he was suggesting, but hell, that's what she was here for and that's why she got paid the big bucks.

Keep the boys happy, her boss always said.

The promise of gratuitous sex was what kept most of the poachers she ran with in line. Most of these ruffians thought with their dicks and not with their brains, so they were easily handled by her mere suggestions and her body offerings.

Once the man and woman were long gone and Bertris appeared satisfied they were not coming back, he lowered his rifle, turned to her and smiled.

She recognized that lusty look. The creep wanted sex. She'd keep him occupied for the next little while so he would drop that animalistic need to kill. The last thing she wanted was to lose this gig. Her boss paid handsomely for bears and there were plenty of them here. She unloaded her knapsack and began unbuttoning her blouse...

Aside from Milena having that tumble and Daegen having an uneasy feeling they were being watched, probably by bears, they took many breaks. Milena followed Jane Sunflower's advice on foot care to the letter, while he'd kept an eye out for trouble.

At the rustic cabin, she volunteered to build a small fire in the stove, which she did without a problem, then she'd hung up her pants and panties to dry while wrapping herself in the sleeping bag.

He'd stayed outside on the most part, telling her he wanted to keep an eye out for the bears. But truthfully, seeing her panties hanging on the line by the hot stove had been an intriguing tease to his cock and balls. Staying outside had quelled his urges to some degree. After her clothing was dry, she'd called him in, and they ate the lunch that Jane had prepared for them.

Thick slabs of homemade bread with lamb butter and heaps of strawberry jam. Shortly after, Milena insisted they leave. He noticed she was preoccupied, and he figured she was emotional over leaving Jane.

Had it been up to him he would have left Milena at the lamb ranch with his gun. The two women had bonded so quickly, and he'd figured the elderly lady might be able to give Milena tips about living out here in the wilderness. But he knew the conditions of her parole because he and Paul and Mitch had discussed it one morning while she'd been in the shower.

Had he let her stay there, and someone found out she was not where she was supposed to be, they would take her away. That's the last thing he wanted. Besides, leaving her alone with Jane would have put Milena into danger as well if those poachers were still around.

Jane had insisted she had eyes at the back of her head, and he need not worry, but he'd told the elderly woman they were leaving under protest and he would report everything she had told him to the authorities as soon as possible.

She hadn't liked it and he assured her that he would not reveal her identity. She'd seemed satisfied with his promise.

He did have a bit of relief knowing that in a few days Jane expected her monthly supplies delivered through a bush pilot and she would report anything unusual to the pilot, who would come and tell him if something happened since their departure.

Upon secretly talking with Jane, he realized she felt relatively confident the poachers were no longer in the area as they would most likely keep a low profile after she'd fired at them the other day. But, she admitted, there was always that chance something bad might happen.

Poachers would be unpredictable, especially when large amounts of money were involved. It appeared Jane knew exactly what those bastards were up to and how much a bear, or a gyrfalcon or other wildlife would bring on the overseas market.

Man, just thinking about the wildlife being caged up almost drove him nuts. Too bad he had such spotty cell phone service, or he would have put a call to the authorities right now. But he hadn't bothered with the phone on this trip.

He wondered why Milena hadn't asked him or Jane of what Jane knew regarding the poachers. She'd been unusually quiet since leaving several hours ago, and her quietness rattled his nerves. He had gotten used to her being bright and cheerful. He realized she was upset about leaving Jane, but maybe she was upset about that spectacular kiss they had shared last night? Maybe it hadn't been so great for her?

Daegen frowned. Maybe he should apologize to her before they got back? He could tell her it would never happen again.

Hell, he couldn't promise her that, especially since he wanted it to happen again. Man, how was he going to explain to Mitch and Paul, he had kissed her? Not saying anything to them just didn't sit right.

They left the cabin after her clothing was dry and awhile ago, he'd let her know they were on Snowy Creek Ranch land again. Since then, she'd insisted on leading the way, telling him she recognized the landmarks. But night was descending fast now, and he hadn't thought she would be able to see the way in the twilight, but she had surprised him and she hadn't veered off the virtually invisible trail.

He watched her as she walked. He liked the cute sexy way her ass wiggled with her every step. He enjoyed the golden highlights of her hair as they shone beneath the rising full moon and every now and again her unique scent drifted along the gentle breeze teasing his nostrils and making his cock harden.

He kept remembering last night's kiss. How her warm curves melted against his lap as she'd settled her injured feet over his thighs. Yeah, she'd felt really fine.

"I see the light from the cabin," Milena suddenly called out.

Her voice rang with cheeriness, and she stopped and pointed through the darkness across the misty meadow where they'd been walking.

A lone light twinkled about half a mile away. They still had a good walk to get there, but he was glad they were finally home. The cabin wasn't much but it was where they belonged.

He smiled as welcome warmth enveloped him.

. . ❧ . .

MILENA WAS SO TIRED she could barely eat the hot stew Paul and Mitch had waiting for them. But before she'd sat down to eat, she'd removed her scarf and cardigan and folded them nicely in one of the drawers. Then she'd placed the gorgeous quilt upon her bed.

The guys had paid Jane's quilt many compliments and Milena had to admit, the quilt really added color to the cabin.

Although she just wanted to drop into bed, the guys, between kidding jabs at Daegen for shaving off his beard and moustache, had insisted they eat first.

Apparently, Paul and Mitch had been waiting on them and hadn't eaten any supper themselves. She had to admit their jovial company was nice and the food tasted pretty good. The savoury spices and salty flavors made love to her taste buds as she chewed on the soft carrots, potatoes and tasty meat. She really should ask what kind of meat was in the stew, but she figured if she knew it would just ruin her appetite. She'd just enjoy her meals from here on out without questions.

"Jane Sunflower sure did dress you up nice. That was a pretty knit sweater and scarf," Paul complimented between bites. The tips of his lips were upturned into a sweet smile, but his eyes were dark with interest.

Milena's face grew warm. She wasn't used to compliments. Especially from a man.

"Yeah, and she was very kind to give you a fancy new straw hat, Miss Scarecrow," Mitch teased with a wink.

Oh dear. She'd forgotten the hat. How rude of her. She reached up to take it off when to her surprise all the guys protested.

"Oh please, leave it on," Paul begged.

"Yeah, gorgeous scarecrow, leave it," Mitch said.

"Don't take it off. You look so cute with it," Daegen complimented.

Her cheeks burned hotter.

She wanted to tell them to stop with the compliments, but she didn't want to bring more attention to herself.

Quickly she reached for the glass of water. It was ice cold and so refreshing. As she drank, she tried to avoid eye contact with them. It was kind of hard when she had three sets of sexy guys watching her every move.

Mercy, but it was getting so hot in here. Sure, it could have something to do with the woodstove pumping out the heat on this cool night, but she'd been fine a moment ago. She wished she could roll the ice-cold glass across her warm cheeks, but she didn't dare.

Why were they watching her so intensely?

She swallowed and tried to keep eating and acting as casually as she could, but it was hard. She could *feel* their gazes on her. Could feel herself reacting as she remembered those scorching ménage dreams and fantasies she'd had since coming to Snowy Creek Ranch.

Oh boy. Oh boy. Was she in trouble living here, or was she in trouble?

Finally, Daegen cleared his throat and dove into revealing what Jane Sunflower had told him.

"She actually shot at them?" Mitch asked wide eyed.

Daegen nodded.

"She thinks if they think she'll shoot them then maybe they won't come back," Daegen continued.

"I hope she's right," replied Mitch.

"She thinks they're taking deer and bears. Says some of the deer who dropped by nightly in the meadows have not been around. And she found a baited cage a couple of miles away from her place. A cage big enough to catch bears. She was able to remove the bait and the next time she went back the cages were gone. She also found some fox carcasses in another area. They'd been skinned and their tails removed."

Sickness clawed at Milena's tummy. She dropped the fork and pushed her plate away. She suddenly couldn't eat anymore.

The guys peered at her. They were all frowning.

"Sorry, I guess we should have discussed it another time," Daegen said.

Meaning when she wasn't around.

Milena forced herself to pick up her fork and pulled her plate back in front of her.

"I can handle it. I am going to have to if I live out here, right?"

Milena forced herself to smile, but it felt shaky.

Daegen nodded in satisfaction and continued.

"She also said she heard a plane coming in low a couple of times."

Daegen dug into his shirt pocket and drew out a small, wrinkled piece of paper that Jane had given him with the description of the poachers. Mitch leaned across the table, snapped it up and read it.

His eyes twinkled with excitement.

"If it wasn't this late, we could have gone to the hillside and catch a signal and call Moose Ranch and let Brady know about these descriptions."

"Which reminds us, we had company while you two were away," Paul said.

Company? Excitement rushed through Milena. Had JJ returned with the baby?

"A cop and a fish and wildlife officer were here following up on Paul's assault and the poaching."

Oh, thank God! Maybe this place wasn't so backwards after all.

"What did they say?" Milena asked.

"Not encouraging. According to the fish and wildlife officer, resources are limited where the poaching is concerned. They'd look into it when they had time. As to the assault on me, without a description of the assailant, the cop figures we'd best keep our eyes open and report anything else suspicious directly to him."

Milena's hopes deflated and a sudden anger burned through her.

"So, nobody is going to do anything?"

"We'll report what Jane said and saw. I'm sure that will help," Daegen said in his soft tone that sucked some hostility out of her.

She wanted whoever had attacked Paul to go to prison and she wanted the people hurting and killing the animals to be fried in the electric chair.

How could anyone hurt defenceless animals? What was going to happen to that mother bear and her cubs if they got caught?

A really bad feeling slithered through her as she remembered watching a documentary on poachers and what happened to the trapped bears sent overseas.

Horrid things were done to them. They were held in cages for the rest of their lives.

"Who wants coffee?" Mitch suddenly asked and stood.

The men gave a round of affirmations.

Milena frowned. How could they have coffee when such an awful thing was going on somewhere in this forest? Were they so cold-hearted?

Oh gosh, she wanted to cry for the animals. She jumped as Paul placed his hand over hers and squeezed gently. Sorrow shone in his gaze.

"You cannot take what's happening out there so personally, Milena. We'll concentrate on the things we can control, like reporting everything to the authorities. You'll make yourself sick with worry if you let your mind go to what might be happening to them. I speak from experience."

"Boy, does he ever speak from experience!" Mitch called out from where he was grabbing the steaming coffee pot off the propane stove.

"When we were kids, Paul went through a phase where he literally watched every step he made because he refused to step on an ant, a spider, worms, hell, anything that moved," Mitch said with a chuckle.

Milena smiled as she envisioned a young Paul stepping carefully over anthills or crickets or grasshoppers.

"To this very day he refuses to cut the grass out in the meadows because he's afraid he'll chop up a frog," Daegen chuckled and winked at Milena.

"Well, I say chop them up. Frog legs soup for supper!" Mitch laughed heinously as he poured coffee into the cups.

"Oh, you shut up," Paul said with a smile. "I see you stopping and picking them up and bringing them to the creek, so you don't run them over."

"Yeah, yeah, okay. You caught me. I just want to make sure they grow nice and fat so we can eat them," Mitch replied.

"Who wants some of Jane Sunflower's shortbread cookies?" Daegen called out as he headed toward his knapsack where it sat on one of the beds.

Both Paul and Mitch cursed happily and beamed as Daegen dug out a large tinfoil wrapped package.

"No concrete cookies for us tonight," Daegen laughed.

He tossed the package Jane had given him onto the table. Mitch grabbed it first and unwrapped it, stuck one rectangular-shaped cookie in his mouth and began to hand out the rest of the cookies.

Paul was right. There was no reason to get herself sick over the animals. But she would wrack her brains out trying to figure out how to help them.

In the meantime, she would find comfort in a cup of coffee and a couple of Jane's cookies.

. . ⚓ . .

"WHAT DO YOU MEAN YOU kissed her?" Mitch asked Daegen the next morning as the three of them were getting the vehicles in the shed ready for work.

Daegen shrugged.

He had expected them to be surprised or maybe angry with him. They were neither. They appeared...amused.

Embarrassment lashed him like a whip. He should have kept his mouth shut but it wasn't fair to the guys to keep his kissing Milena a secret.

"Like he means he kissed her," Paul said with a laugh as he hooked up a trailer to one of the atvs.

"Hey, I'm trying to be serious here," Daegen said as he checked the fluid levels on the atv Milena would be using today.

"Serious is how delicious Jane Sunflower's cookies were last night. They come a close second to kissing Milena," Mitch replied.

He caught Mitch wink at Paul, who smiled and kept working on hitching the trailer.

Irritation nabbed Daegen.

"How the hell would you know?" Daegen snapped. Why were they being such assholes?

When no answer came, Daegen lifted his gaze from the oil dipstick he had been checking and found Mitch and Paul staring at him with weird expressions.

He couldn't understand why they were looking at him like this.

"What?" Daegen asked between gritted teeth.

"Do you seriously think you're the first one who has kissed, Milena? She's a very attractive woman," Mitch replied in a matter-of-fact voice.

Disbelief rocked him like an exploding bomb.

"Which one of you kissed her?" Daegen asked.

He tried to appear casual and was surprised that he wasn't angry. Instead, he was curious, interested and...aroused?

"Actually, both of us have," Paul answered.

What the hell? Why hadn't Paul told him this before? Paul was watching Daegen carefully. Maybe he was expecting Daegen to be upset? Maybe Paul figured he had first dibs on Milena because he'd kissed her first?

"Okay, so both of us kissed her," Daegen said slowly. He was beginning to feel awkward at the weird way the two men kept looking at him.

"Why are you guys still staring at me like this? What am I missing?"

"What Paul means by both of us is he and I have kissed her," Mitch explained.

Daegen felt his eyes widen in surprise.

"At the same time?" he blurted.

Erotic scenarios began to dance in his head. Paul kissing her while Mitch watched. Or Mitch kissing Milena while Paul watched. Or Daegen making love to Milena while both men watched.

Woah, man. Reign it in, Daegen. Where were these thoughts coming from? He'd never thought about sharing a woman before.

"When I kissed her, it was a spontaneous thing," Mitch's voice broke into Daegen's thoughts.

"She was being down on herself. She looked so vulnerable and it just kind of happened..."

"Same here," Paul added. "It wasn't planned. I just needed to kiss her..."

"Yeah, that's what happened with me. Something about her just made me want to kiss her," Daegen admitted.

"And one kiss just isn't enough, right?" Paul asked.

"No, it isn't," Daegen admitted.

"And you want more. Want to take it to the next level," Mitch stated.

"You too? Both of you?" Daegen asked.

Paul and Mitch nodded. Their gazes were determined and serious.

Damn, it looked like he had some mighty stiff competition. Or was Mitch now going to get rid of her?

"Hey, don't look like a beaten dog. Milena is not going anywhere," Paul said, as if reading his mind and then Paul looked at Mitch for apparent confirmation.

"Right?"

Mitch scratched his forehead. He was frowning. Daegen didn't like it when Mitch frowned. It meant he was about to be serious.

"She could be trouble," Mitch said slowly. "She could rip us all apart, because she's that kind of girl. I don't mean in a bad way. I mean in a keeper way. She is a keeper. She's a good woman. Strong in a crisis," Mitch said.

"And she's tender and caring where animals are concerned," Paul commented.

"You've seen how Chrissy took to her. So, she's good with kids," Mitch added.

"She's not a pet you know. We can't keep her like she's a pet that we can share..." Daegen stopped as an idea grabbed hold.

"It's not like civilization would judge us," Paul mused.

Holy smokes! Was Paul thinking what he was thinking? Share her?

"She would have to be willing," Mitch said softly.

Daegen could barely wrap his thoughts around what Mitch and Paul were saying.

"It's not like we've never shared a woman between the three of us," Daegen heard himself say and then he continued.

"But that woman was just a one-night-stand no-strings girl who was the one who suggested it in the first place. Milena is..."

"Different," Mitch said.

"Serious," Paul added.

"Not a one-night-stand kind of girl," Daegen said aloud when he understood that all three of them were thinking the same thing.

"It does look like we have some serious thinking to do, doesn't it, boys?" Mitch asked.

Yep," Paul replied.

Daegen nodded, feeling kind of shell-shocked at this turn of events.

Some serious thinking. And the idea of the three of them pursuing Milena all at the same time was suddenly playing havoc with his cock.

Why in the world was the idea of sharing her with Mitch and Paul turning him on so much?

Man, he wished he had the answer to that million-dollar question.

• • ⚓ • •

THE NEXT MORNING MILENA couldn't wait to get to the shower. She felt different. Needy. Sensually hot.

Her ménage dreams were back. Big time. They had tormented her throughout the night and a couple of times she'd awoken on a gasp, her body unbelievably sensitive and her clenching pussy and ass throbbing with need. But instead of men making love to her, double penetrating her, kissing her, she'd heard soft snores from Paul and Mitch.

Frustration had clawed through her. She'd been restless and debated sneaking outside to do some heavy-duty masturbating, but Daegen was sleeping out on the porch. Surely, he'd awaken and ask what she was up to.

She could tell him the truth.

Three men had kissed her and unleashed some naughty desires for more. She could beg him to put her out of her misery, but she just didn't have the nerve to say, please fuck me, sir. So, she'd forced herself to go back to sleep and had always drifted back into her naughty fantasy dreamland.

When the guys left for the vehicle shed after breakfast, she'd hurried out to the shower.

Now she embraced the cool water that splashed over her hot body. Her soapy hands caressed her breasts, plucked her nipples, and then slipped between her thighs to stroke her ultra-sensitive clit in an effort to try to relieve the pleasure trapped inside her.

Suddenly she imagined movement at the open doorway and found Mitch standing there. She jolted with shock.

He wore no clothing. His penis was erect, swollen and ultra long.

"Don't use all the water, scarecrow," he mouthed.

Milena trembled as she lifted her stare from his erection, her eyes travelling over his taut abdomen, muscular chest and then to his face.

His gaze was smoldering.

"I think we'd better share the water," he muttered and stepped into the stall with her.

Oh my!

"You're so beautiful, scarecrow. I want to taste you," he whispered in a dark, sultry voice.

He reached out and settled his thumb and forefinger beneath her chin, tilting her head upward. Tremors of eagerness thumped through her as he lowered his head and kissed her lips so gently that her mouth quivered when he pulled away.

"We've been wanting you, Milena," he breathed against her mouth.

"We?" She could hardly hear her own voice.

"Us," came Paul's voice from the open doorway.

Milena looked over and found Paul and Daegen standing there. Both men were naked. Each man stroked his own erection as they stared at her with molten expressions.

"We want you bad," Daegen muttered as he stepped into the stall with her and Mitch. Paul followed.

She'd no idea the shower could accommodate all of them, yet here they were.

Here she was, sandwiched between Mitch and Paul, while Daegen watched with hungry eyes.

Her breath caught as a hand caressed the curves of her buttocks. She cried out as Mitch lowered his head and sucked a nipple into his hot mouth. She ached as she felt a cockhead brush teasingly back and forth over the curve of her left hip.

Suddenly Daegen's face appeared, and his mouth melted over hers, his tongue pistoning between her parted lips.

Hands touched her everywhere. Travelling over her belly, her back, her breasts, her butt. Fingers stroked her labia folds and massaged her ultra sensitive clitoris.

Her hips jerked and she moaned as sensations zipped through her bloodstream and pleasure waves cascaded over her like a sparkling waterfall.

A mouth kissed her pussy, and she went wild.

Pleasure unleashed like a storm, and she writhed and bucked within the hard convulsive shudders. She loved the incredible sensations and became lost inside the flames of her orgasm. Lost within the firestorm of release...

"Oh my gosh!" Milena muttered as she heard an atv roaring toward the cabin, breaking her out of her fantasy.

She grabbed her towel and began to dry herself.

"Hey! Don't use all the water! Be ready in fifteen!" Mitch's shout came a moment later from the direction of the cabin, after the machine had been turned off.

Her cheeks grew warm. Oh darn! How much water had she used?

"Coming!" she called.

Quickly she slipped into her clean clothes. Then she slathered on some of Jane Sunflower's ointment to her quickly healing foot wounds, ripped open some band aids that she'd brought out with her and placed them lightly over the small blisters.

She tugged on some clean socks, thanks to JJ who'd left her several pair in that bag she'd brought the other day.

Then Milena slipped her feet into the boots, grabbed her other clothing, raced out of the change area and almost smashed into Paul.

"Woah don't rush. You'll end up breaking your pretty neck," he said in a guttural voice she found quite sexy.

There was something different about him as he gazed at her with sparkles in his forest green eyes. She couldn't put her finger on why, but suddenly she felt an awareness rushing through her. It was not a frightening feeling, but something exciting and maybe even naughty.

She sensed he was attracted to her. Big time.

Oh Milena! Come off it! It's just the remnants of your fantasy.

"Mitch said he's going to show you how to tack a horse today," Paul said.

He leaned casually against a nearby tree, and she noticed a long piece of straw dangling from the side of his mouth.

He was grinning. Seriously grinning. Like he was really happy about something.

Oh God! Had he heard her masturbating? Had he been here watching her shower? Those thoughts actually thrilled her.

Her cheeks flamed.

"I didn't hear you guys come back," she blurted as the rest of her body grew warm. She wanted to pass him, but he was blocking her and it appeared he wasn't in the mood to move out of her way.

"I decided to walk back. Daegen is bringing your vehicle over in a minute. He said you had some blisters from yesterday. Let me take a look."

"Oh, I'm fine. Really."

Paul shook his head.

"I'm a vet, but I'm also a certified wilderness technician. And as I've said before, the last thing we want is for anyone to get an infection out here. Have a seat on the bench," he ordered.

"I don't have any extra band aids," she lied. She did have a box tucked away inside her dirty clothing.

"It's ok. I have some here."

He held up a box.

Oh crap. He was not moving, and he was not taking no for an answer.

She hesitated.

He nodded to the makeshift bench in the so-called change room beside the shower.

Reluctantly she sat, undid her boots, slipped off her socks and gently pulled off the band aids covering the blisters.

Paul crouched down in front of her.

She lifted her right foot so he could take a look.

He didn't hold her ankle like Daegen the other night, but she wanted him to. Boy, did she want him to.

He just gazed at her wounds and didn't touch her.

He nodded.

"Looks good. Now the other foot."

Milena lifted her other foot and he visually surveyed it as well.

"Good. Looks like Jane knows her stuff."

She held her breath as he ripped open a package and tenderly placed the band aid over one wound and then another band aid over the other one.

Wow, he certainly did have a soft, caring touch. She wondered if the animals appreciated his touch as much as she did.

"Tonight, when you get back, smear on more ointment and band aids and then by bedtime, no ointment and no band aids so the wounds can air overnight. In the morning you can put more ointment on and cover them. If anything starts to go red, let me know right away."

To her surprise, he reached for her sock, then gently peeled it over her foot. Then he slid her boot on to her foot, being very careful as to not cause any pain with her blisters. He did the same with her other foot and then tied her laces.

"The shoe fits, Cinderella," he whispered.

He gazed up at her and her tummy flip flopped in a really nice way as she spied cute twinkles of happiness in his eyes.

Goodness! He really made her feel...needy.

She swallowed as he broke eye contact and stood.

"Have a nice day, Milena," he said in that sexy guttural voice.

She watched him as he strolled away. He had such nice wide shoulders. Narrow hips and very nice buns. A very sexy gait.

He was a man with a purpose.

A man who knew what he wanted, and she knew without a doubt now, he wanted her.

Confusion rocked her. How did she know it with such certainty? She had no clue how she knew, but she'd always been one to follow her instincts. They'd kept her alive in the prison system and they were rarely wrong.

She just had no clue how to handle this situation that she suddenly found herself in.

Three men were interested in her. She would never have thought that would ever happen to her. Not in a million years.

Chapter Thirteen

"That's awesome, you got it," Mitch praised as he inspected the job Milena had done on Willow.

Earlier, he'd shown her how to tack a horse. He'd gone over the steps with her several times with another horse and then he'd led Willow out of his stall and left Milena with him with instructions to tack him while he brought the horse they'd just tacked together out for some exercise.

When he'd returned she'd had Willow ready for his inspection.

Damn, but she learned fast. And she'd done a perfect job too.

He looked up from his inspection to find her gazing at him with a confidence he found attractive. Not too long ago he'd just wanted her gone and now he just...wanted her.

"So? What's next? Want me to muck out the stalls? Or tack another horse?"

Man, this woman was eager. He wondered if she would be just as eager in bed.

Silently he cursed himself for thinking about sex. He needed to keep his mind on the job at hand!

"Okay, you can tack Star, her name is right above her stall entrance. You'll find all her gear in the tack room just where I showed you."

"Yes, I remember. All the equipment for a specific horse is stored in a cubbyhole with the horse's name. Don't interchange equipment. Check for fraying, cracked leather, sharp metal bits, fractured rings—"

"Okay, okay. I'm impressed," Mitch chuckled.

"You should be."

His gaze swung to her face, and he found her laughing.

The sound of her amusement had his heart clenching with happiness. She was adorable wearing that straw hat. And so pretty when she laughed.

"Your sense of humor is cute. Now I'm going to take Willow on a short run down to the creek. He needs small amounts of exercise due to his arthritis. Then when I bring him back I'll expect Star to be tacked and then you can untack Willow and then drop that rope around his neck and tie it to the post there."

He showed her the soft rope they used for leading the horses and the post near the barn door.

"I'll lead him to the meadow so he can graze, when I get back," Mitch said.

Her eyes were sparkling with enthusiasm, and he knew she was happy to be given more jobs besides the mucking out of stalls.

"We'll do the same with the rest of the horses. You tack and untack and clean out the stalls in between when you have time, and I will exercise and for today I will release the horses. Another day I will show you how to exercise them and lead them. Take your time this morning. After lunch I can show you how we split firewood. We can do that until it's time to bring the horses back inside. First horse out is the first one back in, in that order. It gives them equal time."

"Firewood? Now? Isn't it too early in the season?" Milena laughed.

"We'll be splitting wood off and on all the way to and through winter. When it gets hot, you'll be glad some of it is done. Besides, the barns need to be kept warm in the winter. The stoves need to be stoked when it gets really cold."

She frowned, settled her hands on her hips and gazed back into the barn.

"How do you keep a barn this size warm through all the cold winter months? There are a lot of cracks between the wooden walls, and I can see the outside."

"Cracks are good for ventilation and the horses generate a lot of body heat, but when it's really cold outside, we fire up the outdoor ovens out back. Did you notice them? And the vents and ductwork inside?"

She frowned. He liked the charming way she scrunched up her eyebrows in question.

"I wasn't paying much attention to the duct work or the ovens. I kind of throw myself into a job and just concentrate on that, like mucking the stalls and replacing their water and food. No time to look around."

"Come around back, I'll show you."

"You will do more than show me. I want you to explain to me how everything works so I can be a valuable asset."

You're already a valuable asset, Mitch thought silently as he led her to the back of the barn.

. . ⌘ . .

"I HAD NO IDEA THIS place was so complex," Milena muttered after Mitch had finished explaining how the wood-fired ovens pumped heat through a ventilation system throughout the barn. One load of wood into the outdoor oven kept the horses reasonably warm through the cold winter days and another load of wood in the evening kept the horses happy and warm through a frigid night.

Nearby she spied a huge shed, partially stocked with neatly piled firewood.

"The trick is to make sure it doesn't get too hot inside the barn. Like I said, horses generate a lot of body heat on their own, so overheating them in the barn is not ideal. You need enough warmth to keep them comfortable and to make sure their water troughs don't freeze. As autumn approaches, we'll show you how it's all done. We've also got wood splitters and conveyor belts for the firewood, so labor isn't as intense as it would be using an axe," Mitch explained as he pointed to the woodshed.

"I'll show you all that later. Let's get the horses on the go. They like to socialize with each other during the day," he said, and they headed back around to the front.

She watched Mitch's eyes shine with pride as he continued chatting.

"Staying off the grid lets us keep more money for the horses special feed and care. We want the retired ones to have a nice retirement and the temporary stays to have a great place to relax."

"Do you rescue old or abandoned horses too?" she asked.

"Not yet. But Paul has mentioned he'd like to do that, so maybe down the road when the money becomes more consistent, we can accept neglected horses. Currently we house mostly racehorses or show horses. Remember the rule. First one out is first one back in. Try to remember the order which I take them out. That way the horses get roughly the same amount of free time outdoors."

Milena nodded. Man, this was awesome. She clapped her hands together to show him how eager she was to get work.

"Okay, let's do it."

Her heart leapt happily as he smiled.

"See you in a bit," he said.

He grabbed Willow's reins and led the horse out of the barn.

Mercy, he looked hot leading that horse. Like a real cowboy. The only thing missing was his black cowboy hat, which he'd left hanging on a nearby hook. She watched as he effortlessly stuck his foot into the stirrup, grabbed the pommel on the saddle and easily swung himself onto the horse.

He gave her a wave and then the horse and man trotted off.

Truth be told, she wasn't keen on mucking out the stables, but she knew she had to carry her weight out here.

But she really liked tacking a horse. Liked the smooth way the horse's coat felt beneath her hands as she placed a blanket on its back. Warm and soft. And the trusting way the horse stood and watched her with inquisitive eyes and sometimes neighed as she talked to it.

Milena smiled.

The way the horses listened to her, reminded her of a cat she once had when she was five years old. The cat had always watched her and purred as she'd talked to it.

Sassafrass had been her name. Milena had loved that female cat with all her heart. Had loved snuggling her and enjoyed the adorable way it had looked at her. It had been a stray and Mom had allowed her to keep the cat.

Then one day, Milena had heard mewing in her partially opened closet. Fear for her feline friend had made terror claw through her. She'd opened the closet door and discovered three little black newborn kittens lying on some dirty clothes that she had tossed into the closet after wearing them.

Sassafrass was lying on her side. Her eyes were closed, and Milena had known instinctively her cat was dead.

Milena had screamed in horror as helplessness raced through her. Her mother had come running and thankfully had known what to do. She had called an animal shelter and they'd come for the little newborn kittens and had also taken Sassafrass.

Milena had stopped eating for five days after her mother explained that sometimes animals and people died during birthing. It was just the way it was.

After that, she had not wanted another cat. Or any pets, for that matter. Life was too cruel. Too heartbreaking.

Thankfully though, she was mature now and understood what her mother had been trying to tell her.

Sometimes death just happened. That's the way it was. You just didn't see what was coming around the next corner, so it was best to live everyday as if it might be your last.

Milena also knew if they'd had the money and had known Sassafrass was pregnant, things would have turned out differently. A vet like Paul would have been able to save her cat.

Milena grew warm as she thought about Paul and how tenderly he'd checked her feet and how molten his eyes had seemed this morning.

Her pussy quivered as she imagined him kissing her again. Just like the other night.

Oh boy. Just thinking about having sex with one of her cowboys was making her way too hot and way too eager. Suddenly she wished she could pull off her clothes and run naked through the cool interior of the barn.

Or go into one of the empty stalls and...masturbate...while thinking about all three of the men, taking her. One by one and then together.

Milena blew out a tense breath.

In your wildest dreams, girl.

She rolled her eyes and shook her head.

Stop thinking such nonsense! Men did not share their women. Men were territorial and possessive and demanding.

At least that's what she'd experienced before being put behind bars. Her boyfriend had been really territorial, to the point of her being afraid of him if she even dared speak to anyone, especially to the opposite sex. To the point of letting him hook her on drugs. To the point of allowing him to make a criminal out of her.

Milena cursed softly beneath her breath. She had not thought about Dwayne in years. Since the last time she'd had a visit from him about ten years ago, when he'd promised he would wait for her to get out.

She'd realized it was her own fault for allowing him to crap all over her. She should have walked away from him at the first sign of him being trouble. But it hadn't been that easy. She'd been young and desperate for attention. Any kind of attention.

Milena sighed and frowned.

Dwayne was a disgusting man and she hoped she never saw him again. She prayed he never found out she was out of prison and that she was out here.

She shivered at that creepy thought of him showing up and still wanting her.

No way was she ever going back to that kind of trapped life with him.

Milena turned and went to get the next horse, her earlier happiness and arousal squashed.

. . ⚓ . .

THE MORNING FLEW BY relatively uneventful as Milena followed Mitch's orders to the letter. The two of them worked well together, she had to admit. Like a well-oiled machine or like an old married couple. Milena smiled at that last thought as she towel dried her hands after washing them at the pump. Then she went back into the barn, grabbed the lunch cooler and a clean horse blanket.

She'd finished mucking out the stables already because this time she'd known what to do and aside from sore arms due to lifting all that poop and maneuvering the wheel barrel out back, she felt pretty cheerful again feeling the sunshine on her face as she stepped outside.

She waved to Mitch as he returned from releasing the last horse into the meadow. She noticed that he'd put on the black cowboy hat. Now he really looked like a sexy cowboy.

As he neared, he lifted off the hat and with the back of his hand he wiped sweat off his forehead.

He smiled gratefully when she opened a chilled water bottle and handed it to him.

"Thanks, you don't know how much I need this," he said. "It's getting hot. Gonna be a nice spring if this weather keeps up."

Milena watched as he lifted the bottle to his sweet-looking lips and closed his eyes. Chords of muscles erupted in his neck as he drank. Rivulets of perspiration dripped down his face and disappeared beneath the collar of his blue and white checkered shirt. Sweat stained his entire chest area and beneath his arms.

Wow, exercising the horses must be harder work than she'd thought.

A tinge of alarm whispered through her as she remembered what Daegen had inadvertently confessed during their trip to Jane Sunflower's place.

Mitch had had heart trouble in the past. Was that why he was sweating so much now? Was he having a heart attack?

"Hey, what's the matter? You look like you're looking at a ghost," Mitch said with a laugh.

He had completely finished the water already and didn't wait for her to answer as he grabbed the horse blanket and cooler from her.

"I don't know about you, but I am starved," he called out.

He was already walking along the left side of the barn, and she had to run to catch up to him.

Mercy if the man was having a heart attack, surely, he wouldn't be hungry or moving so quickly?

She was dramatizing.

It was hot today, and he'd been outdoors under the sun while she'd been inside a nice cool barn.

Hmm, was that why he had made her work in the barn?

Oh, good grief, she was reading too much into everything again. She needed to relax. But that just did not seem possible when she was aware of his every movement.

Mitch walked past the area where they had eaten lunch the other day and headed toward the dark forest a quarter mile away. She stayed back a couple of steps and admired the way his dark hair curled against the nape of his tanned neck. She was intrigued in the sexy way his jeans cupped his plump ass cheeks and how long his stride was as he strolled with determination and excitement.

"Our previous woodlot," he explained as they passed an area with a bunch of what appeared to be recently cut tree stumps.

"We plan on putting grazing grass here as soon as we pull the stumps. That will make room for a few more horses."

Mitch sounded really excited, and his emotions swept her right along with him.

"And see over there, right at the far end behind the stumps? Just inside the tree line?"

She followed to where he pointed and gasped when she made out the silhouette of a small log cabin. Much smaller than Jane Sunflower's or Snowy Creek's cabin and about the size of the one she and Daegen had taken refuge in during the thunderstorm.

"It used to be a lumberjack cabin. The railroad is just on the other side of that strip of trees. There are abandoned cabins all along the railroad. Back in the thirties and forties there was clear cutting done through here and no transplanting of trees. That's why there are so many meadows and smaller trees."

"Really? Wow," Milena said as she surveyed the landscape.

Now that Mitch had mentioned the clear cutting, she could see many overgrown mounds of moss-covered stumps behind the tree lot he had mentioned. She also remembered back at the prison Officer Brown mentioning the railroad that ran through the property.

She'd thought of the railroad as her escape route, despite her parole officer saying it would take days or even weeks of walking to get out of here.

The thought of escape was fleeting now. She had no desire to leave but knowing a possible escape route existed on the off chance things went south and they came to take her back to prison, made her feel a little better.

"We plan on turning that cabin into a guest cabin. Sometimes the horses' owners like to drop in and spend time with their horses. The guest rooms in the barns are sufficient for now, but we would like another cabin in case one prefers not to lodge in the barn. Gives them more privacy.

"Sounds like a good plan. I like it."

"Really?" Mitch asked.

"For sure. If you need me to help decorate, I know how to sew. I can make curtains, bedspreads, couch covers. I like to sew."

Mitch stopped suddenly and turned to her. He had a really cool surprised expression on his face.

"You know how to sew? That is awesome. My mom was a fanatic with a sewing machine. She made clothes for everyone. There were a lot of us."

"Oh wow, how many siblings?"

"Seven kids. Lucky seven Mom used to say. Four girls and three boys. Let's see, there's Jenna, she's the oldest girl, then Carly, Megan and Ginny who is the youngest girl. Then Brady who is the oldest boy. Boone is the youngest boy and then me. It's hard to get any of us together at one place. We're pretty much scattered all over Canada and the U.S.," Mitch laughed and then started walking again.

"Sure, when we get the cabin fixed, you can be in charge of all the sewing and decorating. Would that be okay with you?"

"I'll need material. Lots of pretty material. Well maybe not pretty. I can sew by hand but having a sewing machine hooked maybe to a generator or solar would make things faster. I will have to get neutral tones so men and women both love it. And the color theme will have to match nature's colors of course. Blues, browns, greens and shades of white and maybe some yellow."

Mitch grinned as he listened to Milena design the interior of a cabin she hadn't even been inside yet.

Man, the way she was describing the plain rustic blue and green floral pattern curtains she'd hang up on the windows and the matching bedspread on the bed, he could see it so clearly and it was really nice. It made him want to get that cabin fixed right now.

She really did have a way with describing things, right down to the honey stain wood plank floorboards. He didn't have the heart to tell her the existing floor had porcupine nibbled holes in it and it would need to be replaced due to safety concerns.

When they reached the cool shade of the treeline, he spread the blanket and set the cooler in the middle.

He watched as she removed her boots and then sat cross legged beside the cooler. That she was so down to earth and not even bothered that she had to sit on a horse blanket instead of at a table for lunch, truly made him happy.

The city women he'd dated were always so...well-manicured, well-mannered and wanted to be treated like prima donna princesses. He hadn't minded when it was city life. He'd enjoyed wining and dining potential mates, and yet a part of him had always wished for a girl next door type like his mom.

Easy going and not picky.

Like Milena.

She was gazing up at him with her pretty eyes and patting the blanket beside him.

"Come on. Take off your hat and sit. I thought you were starving. I sure worked up an appetite."

He removed his hat and tossed it into the nearby grass. The whisper of wind blew against his damp hair cooling him a bit. He kicked off his boots and sat down beside her. She had already opened the cooler and to his delight, Paul had packed them turkey sandwiches. He was not about to tell her that they had shot and killed several turkeys during hunting season.

"Mmm, this is really tasty," she said after a few bites.

"Paul sure knows how to make a mean sandwich, doesn't he?" he asked.

She nodded vigorously and wiped away some mustard from her upper lip with the back of her hand.

He almost laughed. So much for napkins. So much for having an excuse to lick it off her face.

They did not talk as they ate. She was too busy enjoying the sandwich and surveying the scenery. And he was too busy watching her.

They had plenty of scenic spots on their property. This was one of them and why he'd brought her here for lunch. From the cool shade beneath the towering pine trees, they were able to see the closest barn and the rocky cliffs way off to the right where they were able to get cell reception at the top. They'd been up there this morning, before work, and he'd been able to get Brady on the cell phone and relayed the descriptions from Jane concerning the people lurking around in the woods. Brady had said he would take care of it from his end.

His brother was such a great help. He'd lucked out coming here and being his brother's neighbor, that's for sure.

Mitch focused his attention back to the scenery. There were rolling hills devoid of trees, green meadows, wood fences and grazing horses.

The scene was peaceful, quite the contrast to the towering office buildings of Toronto, the traffic congestion and the rushing people. While living in the city, he'd barely slept. He'd always stayed busy with work and women.

Not too long ago he'd thought he'd been satisfied with his job and his condo. He'd assumed he would live in the bustling city for the rest of his life. However now that he had a taste of outdoor living, he wouldn't want to be anywhere else but right here on Snowy Creek Ranch with the horses and with Milena.

Oh, man. It was so not good in the way she made him feel so good just being near her. He wondered if Paul and Daegen felt this way too? They must if they were kissing her too.

He helped himself to a second turkey sandwich and started munching on it while he watched her.

She was quiet. Still gazing around with that cute new straw hat on her head. Her eyes flicked to the barn, to the horses, and then to the rolling hills and back to the barn again.

There was a nice smile on her face. She appeared serene and satisfied. It was a totally different look than the one she'd had when she'd first shown up here looking scared, defiant and nervous.

Scarecrow.

He chuckled to himself at that last thought.

When she had shown up yesterday evening after visiting Jane Sunflower, wearing a new straw hat, he'd just about laughed. He'd wanted to kid her about it, but he'd held back. The old hat had fit his scarecrow profile of her perfectly, but now with the new one he sensed how proud she was to have been given it and the other attire by Jane.

He realized how hard it must have been for her in prison. Of course, he had no real clue having never been incarcerated himself, but his sister Megan, was another story. She'd been in prison for so long, he'd forgotten how she looked like. Jenna had been working from day one to get her out. It had been the main reason she'd created Cowboys Online. At least Megan had family who visited her often.

For Milena to have no family as per the profile they'd been sent in that letter, she must have felt very alone behind bars.

He would never give up his sometimes pain-in-the-ass siblings for anything.

Sure, they were all scattered to the wind, except for Brady being close and Jenna with her lousy two-timer husband being a few hundred miles to the north on their own little ranch, just knowing his siblings would have had his back in a crisis, made him feel strong and confident.

"You said earlier that the trees had been clear-cut around these parts. I'm assuming the old barns came after?" she suddenly asked, keeping her gaze to the barn.

"Yes, according to property records there were homesteaders who tried farming the land, but they couldn't seem to make a go of it, couldn't make the lease payments to the government and they left. The farmhouse fell apart. Our cabin sits on top of the rock foundation of the original farmhouse.

We had the water tested several times last year and it has always been fresh and drinkable. There's plenty of game for food too."

"Modern pioneers we are," she said with a grin.

"Yup, pioneers that never have a minute rest. Should we get started on the firewood? We can cut out half an hour earlier tonight, unless you're tired. If you are, you can stay, and rest and I can start."

To his surprise, her hand curled over his shoulder, and she held fast.

"Oh no you don't. You will stay and rest. I don't want you to have another..." She let her words trail off.

She suddenly looked horrified.

He didn't know how he knew that she knew he'd had a heart attack, but she knew. Irritation snapped through him. Who had the hell told her?

"I'm sorry. I shouldn't have said that," she whispered and looked away.

"Said what? You haven't said it."

Who had told her? He should let it go, yet he couldn't.

"I won't have another heart attack if that's what you're thinking," he said.

He felt the heat of her hand like a brand on his shoulder.

"I'm sorry, but I worry about you. You were sweating and your face was flushed, and I thought..."

"You thought I might be having one? I didn't know you cared," he teased, shaking off his irritation. Had it been Paul? Or Daegen who'd told her?

She frowned and let her hand drop away.

"Of course, I care," she snapped.

"But you hardly even know me," he replied, suddenly wanting to know exactly how much she did care.

She shook her head and laughed. It was a hearty laugh. Musical. Very nice. It made him feel...happy."

"But now..." she said softly and then stopped and bit her bottom lip.

Her cheeks reddened.

How interesting.

"And now? What?" he prodded.

He liked the way she rolled her eyes at him and then shook her head acting like she'd been caught about to say something she wasn't prepared to say.

He had to smile as he watched her squirm, and his heart was laughing in a really nice way.

Maybe she liked him? Man, why was he feeling so good?

"Now you're not such an asshole as I had first thought."

Yeah, he had behaved like an asshole when they'd first met.

"What made you change your mind about me?"

She continued to look at the scenery and shook her head.

"Oh, for heavens sakes, Mitch. Had I known you were going to waste your rest time with a bunch of questions, I would have sent you on your merry woodchopping way."

He laughed.

"What?" she snapped.

"You're cute when you're mad," he said.

A touch of a smile edged her lips. She liked his compliment. He figured that was a good sign.

"You're irritating when you're irritating," she spat. "Now shut up and rest, because I am going to."

He watched her lie flat on her back, her hands settled over her belly, and she closed her eyes.

Yep, she was tired, and she was pretty. He didn't say anything as he decided to lay down beside her. He plunged his hands over his belly and reluctantly closed his eyes.

He would much prefer to keep his eyes open and stare at her, but he didn't want to push his luck and have her catch him watching her.

He smiled and listened to her soft breathing. It was gentle and relaxing. Like a lullaby.

So very nice.

. . ≈ . .

MILENA HADN'T REALIZED she'd fallen asleep until an odd sound rattled through the cobwebs of her blissful oblivion sleep.

At first, she hadn't wanted to wake up. It was so peaceful wrapped inside the snug darkness. It was as if she had no care in the world.

She didn't know how long she stayed swathed in peace, but suddenly she realized she shouldn't be asleep. She should be working!

Her eyes popped open.

Pine tree branches gently swayed high above.

A strange sound flowed through the air. She turned her head and saw Mitch. He was asleep and the sound that had awoken her was his snoring.

Now she remembered. She'd insisted he rest, and they both must have fallen asleep.

She recalled their earlier conversation about his heart attack.

Man, she had blown it big time hovering over him like a mother hen. That must have been a turn off for him, but she hadn't been able to help herself. Her concern for his health had just come out of nowhere and grabbed onto her.

She'd been thankful he hadn't prodded further with his questioning about exactly how much she did care for him and she'd been relieved when he'd lain beside her.

The man had actually listened to her. Who would have thought?

She wondered how long she'd slept. Couldn't have been too long as the sun seemed to be in almost the same position in the sky as before when she'd first lain down.

A power nap. They were good for him. It would relax his heart.

In prison she'd taken a nap every afternoon. She'd always felt relaxed and more able to cope after a short sleep. She knew some of her fellow inmates hated them. They said if they took one, they'd wake up feeling sluggish or lazy. But she always felt refreshed. Just like now.

She turned to her side, facing Mitch and tucked her hands beneath her cheek. He looked so boyish when he slept.

Innocent. Vulnerable.

Yet the rest of him...such powerful looking arms. Wide chest. Lean torso. Nice long legs and a nice bump between his thighs.

She bit her bottom lip and wondered how big he might be, *down there*?

Embarrassment lashed her.

Oh no! Stop thinking this way!

Her breaths became quick, and she toyed with the idea of leaning over and pressing her lips to his mouth.

Would he awaken?

Would he kiss her back? Would his kiss be as intoxicating as the one they'd shared the other day while post digging?

For sure she would love to find out.

Have mercy, there she went again with her daydreaming. She should wake him. There was work to be done.

But she decided to wait and watch him sleep.

. . ❧ . .

HE SHOULDN'T BE DOING this with Milena. She was his employee, and he was her boss, but he just couldn't stop himself from watching her as she undressed in front of him.

"What people don't know won't hurt them," she whispered.

She dropped her blouse, and she was now lowering her bra straps.

Mitch, leave. Get out of here! His inner voice urged.

He couldn't. She was like the flame, and he was the moth. He was going to get burned.

Her breasts spilled free from her bra. The sultry curves grabbed his full attention. His mouth watered as he gazed at her plump pink nipples.

His cock jerked to attention.

Oh, man.

"Make love to me, Mitch. Make love to me, here. Now."

His breath caught as she slipped her fingers into the waistband of her jeans and slid them down over his lush hips.

Longing thundered inside of him.

Lower. Lower. She stepped out of her jeans.

Arousal roared through him as she did the same with her panties. Slid the garment down those long, luscious legs. And off.

He let his gaze wander over her body.

She was perfection. Sexy. He wanted her so bad.

All his mental restraints dissolved. The flame was burning him, and he was on fire.

"Touch me, Mitch," she whispered. Want smoldered in her eyes.

He reached out and touched her face. She was so soft. So beautiful.

He smoothed his fingertips over her silky eyelashes, then caressed the curve of her nose, across her plump quivering lips.

"Make love to me, Mitch. You know you want to. You know I want you to..."

He trembled as he smoothed his hands along her naked hot sides and settled his fingers upon the creamy curve of her hips.

Her mouth parted.

"Mitch. Mitch. Time to wake up."

Mitch came awake on a jolted gasp.

He blinked up at the blue sky then Milena's face moved into view.

For a few glorious seconds he thought he was still in his dream. His shaft ached. His body was tense. Arousal coursed through him.

He needed relief. He was about to reach out and grab her and bring her down beside him so he could make love to her, like she wanted. Like he wanted.

But she was smiling down at him in a curious, innocent kind of way wearing her cute new straw hat and the last teasing fragments of his dream disintegrated.

"Hey, sleepy head. We need to get back to work, remember?"

She was standing. Waiting. Not undressing. Not asking him to make love to her.

Shit. It had felt so *real*. So damned *good*.

"Right. Yup," he muttered, feeling the lusty heat push through him like a blow torch.

Holy cow! He was on fire. Sexual fire.

He let his gaze wander over her as she turned and squatted over the picnic cooler. She began putting the items back inside. He loved the way her jeans cupped her smooth ass cheeks. He would love to take her from behind.

His penis swelled even harder. He was going to be so sore down there when he got up, he just knew it.

Mitch swallowed. Every muscle in his body felt tense. Too tense. Perspiration blossomed across his forehead. Reluctantly he rolled onto his side and yup his shaft was really rigid.

Solid for her.

He needed to do some mighty hard work this afternoon to get his mind off Milena. There was only one problem. She was working with him.

· · ❧ · ·

MAN! This cutting wood business is crazy, Milena thought as she lifted the final twenty-four-inch length log and set it onto the log splitter like Mitch had shown her to do earlier in the afternoon. She flipped the switch, the machine grumbled, then the splicer moved and sliced through the middle of the log, splitting it in half. The divided parts fell onto a conveyor belt and were carried about ten feet away where they were dropped onto a pile they'd already split this afternoon.

The sun was hot but thankfully sinking lower in the sky, which meant it would soon be time to get the horses inside the barn and go back to the cabin and get supper.

She was so glad Jane had given her this straw hat. The edge was wider than the old one she'd been using and it provided shade to her face and when she bent her head, the brim of the hat hid her from seeing Mitch. Much earlier, he'd removed his shirt and sweat shimmered on his body.

Everywhere.

On his muscular arms, his back, his chest. His brown chest hairs sparkled with moisture and there was a rivulet of wetness arrowing along the hairs to his belly and abdomen and then descending into his jeans. She wished she could pull his pants down and get an up close and personal look at the rest of him.

He was a powerfully built man. She could see it in the intoxicating way his muscles bulged in his shoulders as he lifted the split logs from the heap after they came off the conveyer belt. He then carried the wood a few steps to the shed and stacked them onto a pile.

They hadn't said more than a handful of words since returning from lunch, aside from his instructions in showing her how to operate the wood splitter, which got its power from large batteries hooked up to several solar panels hanging on the back wall of the barn. After that, he'd remained quiet, kind of brooding, as he worked, stopping occasionally to drink from his water bottle or to wipe sweat from his brow.

She enjoyed watching him work. He moved gracefully with that confidence she liked about him.

She was watching him so intently that she hadn't realized he'd turned around and was looking right back at her. She tried to look away, but his gaze latched onto hers with what her instincts told her was a predatory stare.

Her breath halted as something nice, and naughty fluttered deep inside of her pussy.

Woah. Something had changed about him since his nap. He seemed so...intense.

"I dreamt about you at lunch," he said in a husky tone.

"Oh? You did? Should I ask what about? Or do I want to know?" she teased, trying to lighten the sudden heavy sexual tension zipping between them.

"It might be best if you don't know," he murmured in a throaty voice.

It almost seemed as if he was trying to decide on something. As if a war raged inside him. Like he wanted to do something, maybe say something else, but he wasn't sure if he should.

Her lips went dry as nervousness whispered through her.

She felt her eyes widen as she noticed the bulge between his thighs. It was much bigger now than when he'd been sleeping.

"Or maybe you should know," he suddenly said.

She'd just slid another log onto the splitter and flipped the switch, but he walked over to the splitter and shut it off. Almost complete silence suddenly permeated the hot air. She heard a blue jay squawking somewhere far off. Heard a bee buzz by. But nothing else, except the hammering of her heart.

She licked her lips and noticed that his gaze followed her movement. His eyes were dark. Dangerously dark. Sexy dark.

"I dreamed you were taking off your clothes," he said hoarsely.

She swallowed.

Okay.

He walked around the splitter to stand in front of her.

Something was happening between them. Something big.

Yup, definitely a sultry change in him after she'd woken him up from his power nap. She had noticed something in Paul this morning too. She hadn't seen Daegen after Mitch and Paul had returned from the vehicle shed, but all three of them had gone down there after breakfast.

Had the three men talked about the kisses they'd given her?

"Um, it was just a dream," she whispered. Was she having a fantasy? Was this real? She wanted it to be real.

"Was it?"

His big size almost overwhelmed her. He peered down at her and she was lost, but in a really good way.

He was a tall man. She'd have to get up on her tippy toes to kiss him.

Is that what he wanted? A kiss? It was what she wanted.

Her body coiled with sexual tension. She could smell his male scent wafting off him in waves. Raw, freshly cut wood, a tinge of sweat.

Need. Anguish. Hunger.

"I know we barely know each other. I know this is supposed to be a working relationship," he growled.

There was indecision in his eyes. She wanted that confidence that she loved to be back in his gaze.

She had the feeling he was trying to talk himself out of whatever he wanted to do to her. She could hear a "but" coming. She didn't want to hear a "but".

She wanted action.

She reached up and ignoring the surprised look in his ravenous gaze, she cupped the sides of his face and kissed him smack on his warm, sensuous mouth.

There was no going back. She knew it the instant he returned the kiss with a force that unleashed all her primal needs. She undulated against him and opened her mouth. He entered, their tongues clashing together causing all kinds of electrical sensations to cascade through her.

His hands settled upon her waist, and he pressed his body against hers, making her butt push up against the metal of the wood splitter.

She was trapped. She couldn't run away even if she wanted to, and she did not want to run. She wanted to have sex.

Exhilaration pummelled her as he kissed her harder, his body pressing into her. She could feel the heated imprint of his bulging erection against her lower abdomen. Could hear his low groans of anticipation against her trembling lips. He ripped his mouth away and started kissing her chin and then down the length of her neck.

She quivered as he nipped and licked along her collar bone, and she realized she was highly sensitive in this area. His hands had slipped off her waist and he was sensuously massaging her hips.

Then his hands were pulling up her shirt and she broke away from him lifting her arms allowing her shirt to come over her head and off. Her breaths were coming so fast she thought she might pass out. His gaze was so dark she swore she'd never seen anything so powerful.

He pulled up her bra and her breasts spilled free.

Heat and cream drenched her vagina as he lowered his head and kissed one nipple and then the other. She cried out as he sucked one into his hot mouth. The pressure of his lips around her sensitive bud created sizzles of pleasure, making her heady.

To keep her balance, she slapped her hands over his bare shoulders, her fingers digging into hard hot muscle. Her need for him grew. She wanted his mouth all over her.

She gasped as he let go and then sucked her other nipple between his hot lips. Incredible sensations exploded through her and she dug her nails deeper into his flesh.

"I want to see the rest of you," he whispered against her breast and then began lapping and sucking her throbbing nipple.

This was happening so fast. It was way out of control now, but she knew she was helpless to stop it.

She nodded jerkily, managed to reach down and lower her pants and underwear. They dropped and puddled at her feet trapped by her boots. She tried to kick them off but her balance was so off she slapped her hands onto his broad back, feeling the muscles flex beneath her palms. She splayed her fingers across his taut flesh, touching and caressing him.

He kept sucking on one nipple until bursts of pleasure pain had her panting. Then he moved his head to her other breast, nipping her tender tip between his teeth until she was yelping at the erotic pain. He followed up with a seductive lapping that had her keening from its burning intensity.

By the time he was finished, both her nipples were on fire. It felt fantastic!

Then he was untying her boots. Mindlessly, she kicked them off.

To her shock, Mitch moved his head lower, giving a hot string of kisses vertically down her belly and over her abdomen. Instinctively she spread her legs and moved against him, panting with excitement.

No man had done this to her. Ever.

His hands cupped her ass and he held tight. Suddenly he buried his face between her thighs. His tongue swiped between her labia, and he licked her sensitive clitoris. She couldn't stop herself from bucking. Her body became tense with arousal.

She grasped his steely shoulders. Held tight as he ate her.

She threw her head back and cried out as his tongue sucked on her folds, massaged her clit and then thrust into her vagina.

Hot moisture slid down her channel and she could hear him slurping her pleasure-soaked cream into his mouth. Then his lips stroked her clit and her belly tightened.

She shuddered and moaned as her body throbbed with hunger. Incredible sensations were mounting throughout her. He was taking her somewhere she'd never been. Somewhere thrilling. Somewhere so naughty.

Sharp teeth nibbled on her sensitive labia, and she jerked from the splinter of pain. His moist bristly tongue soothed the hurt. Then his mouth was slurping on her pussy again, making her frantic with the need for release.

She realized she was keening his name, over and over, like a song of defeat. He had her. She belonged to him.

When his mouth tenderly sucked on her clit, she exploded into an uncontrollable dance of pleasure, unleashing a wildness inside of her that she hadn't known existed.

She cried out and gyrated like a woman possessed. Pleasure rocked her like a ragdoll. Shuddering waves gripped her. Held her. Made love to her.

She spread her legs wider, loving his mouth sucking and licking and lapping at her pussy. The mind-numbing pleasure burst over her and around her, embracing her, never-ending.

Intense. Beautiful. She was hooked. She wanted this to go on forever.

And she wanted more.

· · ❧ · ·

DAEGEN AND PAUL WATCHED as Mitch moved his mouth from her pussy and licked his lips with obvious enjoyment.

"Ah man, that kind of desert I can use everyday," Daegen muttered from beside Paul.

"Mitch always moved fast on a lady when he wanted her," Paul replied.

Yeah, what he wouldn't do to be in Mitch's shoes right at this moment, Paul thought.

"It looks as if things are going to go at a faster pace than we had planned," Daegen said softly.

"Hell, the faster the better. It was a good thing Mitch pulled the shortest straw this morning or I would have taken her right there and then against the shower wall when I was examining her feet. Never seen such sexy feet. Man, she is so damned irresistible and innocent." Paul said,

After what Paul had just witnessed with her enjoying Mitch so much, he knew she was ripe for some burning hot pleasure. He would make sure she was glad she came here, and he meant that literally.

Daegen elbowed him gently, grabbing his attention.

"Come on, let's get out of here before she catches us watching. We don't want to scare her back to prison."

Paul nodded and they both headed back up the nearby hill to an area behind the trees to retrieve the horses they'd been exercising on the trail when they'd spied Mitch going down on Milena out here in the open.

That sexy scene they'd just witnessed was going to be scorching his brain for a very long time. A long time indeed.

· · ↬ · ·

MILENA COULDN'T STOP panting. No man had ever gone down on her. This had been her first time and it felt fantastic. She wasn't sure how to act now that Mitch was casually gazing at her, acting as if he went down on a woman every day.

He appeared so confident, and she felt so nervous and inexperienced.

Oh boy, was she ever inexperienced.

"I guess I should apologize? he asked and smiled.

Her pussy clenched with an intense need that had her wanting him to bury his face between her thighs again.

Milena smiled sheepishly as she shoved her breasts back into the cups of her bra. Oh dear, how her nipples looked so red and how wonderfully they throbbed from his suckling lips. She wanted his mouth upon her nipples again. She was about to blurt out for him to do her again, when a low rumble of thunder from somewhere south shattered her almost request.

Mitch swung his attention toward the sky. He frowned. She followed his gaze, but everything looked blue and clear.

"Time to gather the horses and get them to the barn. Storm is coming," he instructed.

"Sure," she answered in a breathy voice she didn't recognize.

Thankfully he didn't say anything else about what had just happened because she was feeling unbelievably self conscious.

He walked toward the tarp that had been covering the machines earlier and began unwrapping it. She dressed quickly and helped him secure the cover over the wood splitter and conveyer so they wouldn't get wet.

She wished she could do the same thing about herself, because her pussy was soaked just thinking about what had happened!

It had happened so fast. One minute they'd been working and the next he'd gone down on her. And she'd loved it.

She couldn't wait for it to happen again.

No siree.

Chapter Fourteen

A few days went by, and Milena didn't have the opportunity to work with Mitch again, but she wanted to. Oh, how she wanted to experience more pleasure at his hands and mouth, but he had acted pretty much normal. He was treating her just like one of the guys again, yet she was burning up inside. Yearning for more of Mitch's mouth seducing her body.

She wanted sex so bad, she realized she was making stupid little mistakes because her mind was wandering all the time.

Yesterday and today, she worked with Daegen at the north gorge barn doing most of the same as what she had done with Mitch, tacking the horses and helping to lead them out as well as cleaning out the stalls.

Minus the sex.

Daegen gave her a new job. He'd shown her how to brush the horses' coats until they shone beneath the sunshine. He even asked her to braid a couple of the horse's manes, right before a horse had his or her picture taken. Daegen explained that every few weeks they took pictures of some of the horses whose owners requested frequent updates.

A few days ago, they'd caught good cell service on the hill, and Daegen emailed the pictures of the horses he'd taken and sent updates to the clients. And Milena was able to touch base with her parole officer, assuring her that everything was going well and letting her know they had sporadic phone service out here. The parole officer wasn't too happy about that news, and so Daegen got on the call to confirm, and the woman seemed to relax, allowing Milena to call every month instead of every week.

With that call out of the way, Milena could relax too.

What she loved most was seeing the new mother and her foal, which Milena had named Long Legs because of his extremely long legs. Both horses were thriving and every chance she got she gave them extra grooming, extra feed and of course plenty of hugs.

"Are you ready for JJ's party? It'll be in just under a week," Daegen asked as he joined her outside at the hand pump where she was washing her hands.

"Oh no, already? Time flies too fast around here and no I am not ready. I doubt I will ever be," she admitted.

She moved aside for Daegen to get access to the pump, and she realized he'd removed his shirt! Muscles laced his arms and they bulged as he pumped. Water gushed from the cast iron spout, and he then cupped his hands catching the sparkling liquid to splash it over his sweaty chest.

Mamma Mia, she would love to do to Daegen what Mitch had done to her the other day. She struggled to squash her urges to suck his nipples into her mouth, then kiss her way down his belly, pull down his pants, grab his shaft and start sucking!

Her cheeks heated. She had to stop thinking such naughty things. She was not a wanton, or a free-spirited sexual woman.

But she wanted to be.

"Earth to Milena."

Daegen's voice made her tear her gaze from his chest and to find him staring at her with what she perceived as a knowing grin as he continued to splash water over his chest.

The water was staining the front of his track pants too, illuminating a very large bulge.

Oh, heaven help me.

"What did you say?" She managed to mumble. She pulled her gaze from that very nice bump between his thighs.

"I asked how come you don't think you'll ever be ready?"

His eyes twinkled with such heat as he studied her.

"I've been in prison. Kind of got used to not going to social events," she said and forced herself to rip away from his intense gaze to look out across the green meadow.

"I like it out here. Being free and being away from people."

"You can't hide out here for the rest of your life, Milena. Eventually, when your time is served here, you're going to want a life. Maybe meet a man. Get married. Have children."

Milena shook her head and handed Daegen a towel that they kept near the pump.

"I'll be too old to have kids when my sentence is up. I'm not even sure I want any either."

Daegen frowned as he dried his scrumptious bare chest.

"Why not? You were really great with Chrissy. That little kid bonded with you instantly. I have seen how the foal you delivered follows you around just as much as he follows his mother."

How in the world could she explain to Daegen that there was no opportunity for her to meet men out here. Besides what decent man would want an ex-con girlfriend or wife?

"Maybe there will be some eligible bachelors at the party?" he suggested.

Milena's tummy plummeted.

"I hope that's not why JJ is throwing the party. I couldn't go if that's the case."

To her surprise, Daegen laughed.

"I doubt she's throwing a party for that reason. The only eligible bachelors would be Mitch, Paul and I. I could say Dan and Rafe too, but I have my suspicions they only have eyes for JJ."

Shock reverberated through her at his words.

"What are you saying?"

Daegen shrugged.

"Use your imagination, baby. You haven't been around long enough to see the four of them together. I've seen the way the three men look at her. Like she's their goddess. They worship her."

Disbelief made her speechless. JJ was their goddess? Was JJ having sex with all three of them? Was JJ experiencing what Milena had been fantasising about doing with her three cowboys?

No. Not possible.

"Don't look so shocked. There's no one around to judge them. Out here we can do whatever we want, right? Nothing like living in the north country with no prying eyes on you."

She realized Daegen was watching her carefully. Was he studying her for a reaction? Maybe scouting out her opinion?

"Well, if what you say is happening then it would be none of my business. So, I wouldn't be able to judge. To each his own," she blurted.

You lie, stupid woman. You just had your chance of airing your sexual fantasies.

Milena tried hard to act like his near nakedness and this conversation wasn't affecting her, but she felt jittery and excited.

She wondered if Daegen was somehow picking up on her secret fantasies?

"We'll have a great time at the party. JJ cooks good. And they all barbecue up the best steaks. Man, I hope they have steaks," Daegen was saying as he headed toward the barn.

"Let's give the horses their feed and then call it a day. All this talk about food is making me hungry."

"Be right there," Milena called out.

She waited until he disappeared inside the barn and then swore softly beneath her breath.

Oh my God! *Was* JJ having sex with the other two men besides Brady?

She would never have guessed such a thing. That is, if it were even true.

When she'd housesat over at Moose Ranch last year, she hadn't spent much time with the four of them together. JJ had gone off with them to help build a cabin deep in the forest and Milena had spent only a couple of days with the four of them when they'd returned.

But the men had always been busy running the ranch and she'd seen them only at breakfast and then supper a couple of times and then she'd gone to bed early every night in order to give JJ and Brady their privacy.

Of course, there had been that plane crash she and JJ had been involved in and all the men had been *very* happy to see JJ.

Milena frowned.

Now that she thought about it, they had been overjoyed to see JJ when they'd discovered her alive. Not just friends happy either. Each of them had hugged her and kissed her...on the lips.

Milena swallowed against her suddenly dry mouth.

Oh my God. Why hadn't she thought of that before now? Was Daegen right? Was JJ sleeping with three men?

Suddenly she couldn't wait to get to that party. She would be keeping a close eye on JJ and her three cowboys.

A very close eye.

She realized something else. If JJ was sleeping with all three of them, then maybe Milena could start to make her own naughty fantasies come true too. But she would need to be very careful. She was out of prison on parole here. There was always a chance something would happen, and they might send her back to prison. She did not want to get pregnant. She would never want to leave her daughter or son as her mother had done to her.

But how could she send a message to the cowboys that she was ready to explore sex with each of them! Thunder mumbled bringing her back to her senses and she hurried into the barn to help Daegen with the remaining chores.

. . ⚓ . .

"JUST THOUGHT I WOULD swing by and let you know that Jane Sunflower said she has not seen anything suspicious since you guys left her the other day," Blue said as she and Milena sat on the wicker chairs on the porch.

Upon returning from the barn with Daegen, they'd found Blue chatting with Paul and Mitch on the porch. Shortly after, all three guys had disappeared into the house leaving Milena to entertain Blue.

"Jane gave me this to give to you. She told me you were very concerned for her well-being, and she really appreciated it," Blue said with a smile as she handed Milena a shoebox.

"She said this will come in handy for you."

Milena accepted the present. She couldn't believe that Jane was giving her yet another gift. Concern for her new friend pummelled her.

"How is she? Is she okay? I don't like the idea of her being alone out there," Milena confessed.

Blue smiled with reassurance.

"She's fine."

"Really?"

To her surprise, Blue laughed.

"Of course. Why not? She knows those woods like the back of her hand. She's made friends with all the animals in the area. They think she's one of them. And she has her eyes peeled for the poachers. She said the next time she sees them she'll shoot them and bury their bodies. She said no one would ever know."

"Oh, my goodness," Milena whispered. Was Jane so capable of taking care of herself to the point of killing someone?

"Supper is ready. Come on in and grab some grub," Paul said from the other side of the screen door.

"Oh, my goodness, I'm forgetting my manners. Please come in and join us for supper," Milena gasped. How could she be so rude and not invite her to stay earlier?

Blue nodded and laughed.

"Wow, I was not expecting an invite but sure I could stick around for supper."

"Great, come on. The guys are great cooks."

"As long as desert doesn't include Paul's cement cookies." Blue whispered and then winked at Milena.

A strange uneasiness whispered through Milena. How did Blue know about the cement cookies joke? Exactly how many times had she been here for supper in the past? Come to think of it, they all seemed to know each other quite well. Did any of the men have an interest in Blue?

Milena's unexplained uneasiness crept up a notch.

Had one or all of them been intimate with her?

Blue was blonde and so pretty and she complimented the presented meal quite freely as she sat down at the table.

Yes, she did appear quite at home here. She acted as if she were part of the family. She even laughed hysterically as Daegen spoke about the bears they had encountered on the way to Jane Sunflower's place.

A tinge of anger zipped through Milena. It hadn't been funny for her being terrified of the bears.

Was Blue flirting with Daegen in the way she was laughing?

You're jealous, Milena! An inner voice chastised.

No, I'm not jealous, she shouted back at herself.

Just immature. Oh yes. She was thinking very immature thoughts. But she couldn't seem to help it.

She carefully watched the guys.

Hmm, they seemed brighter, more cheerful and happier than usual with Blue being here.

Earlier, Daegen had been tired from their long day, but when he'd seen Blue, it appeared his weariness had vanished and he'd been quite cheerful.

Interesting.

Irritation continued to grow as she watched Paul scoop a helping of mashed potatoes onto Blue's plate. That was followed by Mitch placing a plump piece of meat onto her plate and then Paul poured her some wine into a wine glass.

Wine? Where had that come from? And where had the wine glasses been stored?

"I'd give you some, Milena, but I know you're not allowed," Paul said with a wink.

Well, sure, Paul. Share her parole requirements to the whole world. That she wasn't allowed to touch any alcohol.

Milena's cheeks grew warm as frustration gnawed through her.

Man, how embarrassing.

Blue looked at her with curiosity and thankfully said nothing.

"I spent this afternoon with Jane," Blue said. "She showed me how to make some soap from her lambs' milk. I'm planning on purchasing some land as soon as I can find something suitable and raise some lambs too. I have fallen in love with her woolly creatures. I want some of my own, and my daughter I am sure will love being out here in the wilderness," Blue gushed.

There were sparkles of excitement in her eyes and envy flooded Milena.

Blue was free to do whatever she wanted, and Milena was...

She stopped short.

Why in the world would she be envious and jealous of Blue?

Why was she experiencing such horrid emotions toward a woman who'd only been nice to her? Why in the world would she even consider Blue a threat?

Because she's pretty and she's free and she's a pilot. Men liked confident women and Milena was none of these.

"Hey, aren't you hungry? Milena? Are you not feeling well?" Daegen's concerned voice crashed through the walls of her thoughts and she was whipped back to reality to find four sets of concerned eyes upon her.

Shame on you, Milena. You're dragging these people down to your level of feeling sorry for yourself.

Before she could so much as come up with an answer, Mitch stood and started walking over to the kitchen area.

"I've got just what she needs. We were going to save this until later but..."

He grabbed something from beneath the countertop and hid it behind his back as he returned to the table.

Her breath caught at the sweet sexy smile on his lips as he gazed at Milena. Oh boy, she did like the way he looked at her.

From behind his back, he brought out a plain white ceramic vase containing a bunch of the cutest most breathtaking white daffodils she'd ever seen.

"Ta da! Our very own Poet's Daffodils," Mitch said.

Milena couldn't believe her eyes as she stared at the most beautiful flowers she'd ever seen.

The flowers were perfection. On each flower luscious white petals surrounded a yellow cup tinged with orange-red and inside the cup was a green throat. Slender green leaves protruded from two-foot-long stems. Their fragrance permeated the air and embraced her. They smelled of...freedom.

Instantly her spirits lifted.

"They are beautiful," Milena whispered and reached out to touch one of the daffodils.

She was mesmerized by how velvety the petals felt beneath her fingertips.

"They're already out?" Blue asked as she too reached out and stroked one of the petals.

"I just came upon them this morning. More will be blossoming in the next few days," Mitch answered.

"Snowy Creek is going to live up to its name again this year, compliments of the white daffodils," Blue laughed.

"Snowy Creek? I thought it had to do with snow?" Milena asked suddenly confused.

Paul shook his head.

"Every year for a few days, the banks of the entire creek which runs a good two miles from Snowy Lake, our lake nearby, to the next one called Owl Lake, becomes abloom in white," Paul explained.

"When I brought the fellows here last year we flew over the creek, and they were convinced there was snow lining the banks. They didn't believe me when I told him they were white daffodils and not snow," Blue added.

"Until we saw the flowers firsthand," Daegen said.

"Snowy Creek Ranch is what we came up with after seeing the flowers and learning the name of the creek is Snowy Creek," Mitch said with a chuckle.

"You're very lucky, Milena," Blue said softly. "Very few people have seen the flowers when they are all in bloom out here. You'll be in heaven. It's a rare sight."

You're very lucky. You'll be in heaven, Blue's words rang in her head.

Suddenly all Milena's jealousy and irritation melted away.

Blue was right. She was very lucky, and she was in heaven being surrounded by nature and not metal prison bars. She needed to remember that. Had it not been for these three men deciding to keep her, she would be back in prison.

Guilt slammed into Milena. She had no right to be upset or jealous of Blue. Not even for an instant. Blue had been kind to go out of her way and to come here with a gift from Jane. Milena owed Blue a debt of gratitude and not malice, bad thoughts or immature emotions.

"Ok, let's put the flowers into the middle of the table and finish eating. I haven't told you yet, but Jane sent me over with more of her shortbread cookies. I have them on the porch in my bag. But no one gets any until supper is all finished! So, eat up!" Blue said with a laugh.

Everyone's laughter and jokes about being saved from Paul's concrete cookies drifted through the air and Milena smiled as she placed the gorgeous bouquet as a centerpiece.

Blue was right. They needed to finish supper. She needed to remember that Blue was a guest in her home and the guys were being courteous and friendly. Milena needed to think and act appropriately also.

She caught herself. She'd just said her home.

Her home.

Dear Lord. She had a home.

Emotions swelled thick and raw, and Milena sent up a very happy thank you to heaven and also a please forgive me for my bad thoughts towards Blue and it won't happen again, she added.

She hoped He was listening, and she hoped He forgave her.

. . ⚓ . .

"ARE YOU SURE YOU WON'T stay here for the night?" Milena asked Blue as they climbed off the four wheeler not so near the lake and removed their helmets. She tried to keep her gaze away from the water and since there was no moon tonight to illuminate the waters, she was able to keep relatively calm.

Blue handed Milena her helmet and she quickly secured it to the back of the seat. When she looked back up, Blue had placed the headlamp on her head that Mitch had given her with instructions she could keep it. Reluctantly Milena placed hers on and they both switched on their lights allowing them to see each other as they talked.

Lightning flickered in the north sky and Milena didn't feel comfortable sending Blue off with the oncoming storm.

"Why don't you spend the night? We can send the guys out to the barn and have a girl's night in the cabin. The guys will be fine. There are cozy beds out there."

It would be kind of fun having a woman to talk to and she would love to get away from the lake.

Milena's fledgling hopes for a girls night plummeted as Blue shook her head.

"I'm heading south so I'm okay. I'm not much for flying in storms so if I thought I would run into trouble I'd bunk with you. Which makes me ask how do you handle it with all of you under the same roof? I noticed three beds. One of them has Jane Sunflower's quilt. She told me she gave it to you. Such a sweetheart, don't you think?"

Blue didn't wait for an answer before continuing.

"I mean you must run into each other in such close quarters...you know...kind of like changing clothes and stuff?"

Milena's cheeks warmed and she was so glad there was enough darkness to conceal her reaction. If only Blue knew what went on not under the cabin roof but away from the cabin!

Like getting kissed by all three of them and Mitch going down on her.

Whew, suddenly she was feeling too hot!

"We put sheets up at night, so we don't see each other changing so we don't really have no issues," she said quickly.

Although she could sleep in the barn instead of the cabin, but she'd be afraid of the wolves, bears and poachers.

"I'm happy to see that you are happy. That's all that matters."

Lightning flickered again.

"Well, that's my que. I'd best get going before it gets here," Blue said as she stepped onto the dock and Milena caught glimpses of the mirror-like water. That creepy panicky feeling accompanied by visions of a water monster hovered at the back of her thoughts and she immediately regretted volunteering to accompany Blue out here.

She wanted to leave, but she forced herself to stay and watched as Blue quickly untethered the lines that held her float plane.

Then she stepped onto the bottom step of the ladder and turned to gaze at Milena.

"Thanks again for the invite to supper. The food was great, and the company was even better. I'll take a rain check on that girls night too. We have all summer to get together."

"You're welcome here anytime, Blue." And she really meant it. "And bring your daughter some time. I would love to meet her."

"One day I will. See you at JJ's party!" Blue said with a wave and a moment later she disappeared into her plane, shutting the door.

Milena forced herself to stand there and watch as the lights flicked on one by one and then the engine roared to life. Milena spied Blue through the windshield.

She was checking her instrument panel in the cockpit, making sure everything was in order. Then Blue waved to her again. The engines roared even louder, and the plane moved forward and away from the dock at a slow pace, heading into the deep darkness of the lake.

Crawly shivers zipped up Milena's back and that spooky stupid idea of a monster erupting from the dark waters urged Milena to jump onto the four-wheeler. She had the vehicle started in record time and quickly turned it around. Without looking back, she rushed along the rugged trail through the eerie dark woods.

The headlight beams from the atv illuminated the way allowing her to see numerous frogs jumping out of the way. Devastation rocked her and she cringed and cried out as she ran over one frog and then another before she forced herself to slow down.

Damn! Because of her recklessness she had killed innocent animals. By the time she reached the cabin, she was weeping from the guilt assailing her.

She wiped away her tears, turned off the machine, grabbed the tarp off the side of the stairs that one of the guys had left out and secured it over the vehicle with the hooks attached to the tarp.

Down at the lake the plane's engines roared louder and she imagined Blue skimming across the water, picking up speed. A few moments later, Blue's plane soared over the treeline directly above the cabin and then Blue was gone over the treeline.

Silence followed and then thunder grumbled urging Milena to move up the stairs.

A low buttery glow of light splashed out of a nearby window and movement on the porch made Milena jump.

For a split second, she thought about screaming, but realized her headlamp was still on and as she looked up, the light splashed upon Daegen, who sat on one of the wicker chairs.

"Hey, are you okay?" he asked tenderly.

Emotions thick and raw bubbled up and she fought back the tears and switched off the lamp.

"If you call feeling awfully guilty for running over frogs okay, then I am fine."

To her horror, he chuckled.

"Hell, if I cried every time I ran over an innocent by accident, I would be right nervous about what I might say at the pearly gates when the time comes."

Milena couldn't help but laugh.

"I don't see you heading to the pearly gates willingly," she teased.

"When the time comes, the time comes," he stated with a slow easy shrug to his broad shoulders.

"Yeah, that's true. Where are Mitch and Paul? It's awfully quiet inside"

"Mitch went to the creek for a quick clean up and Paul got the shower. Looks like a storm is coming our way. I'm surprised Blue still headed out. I'd heard she was afraid of flying in storms. She must be working on her fear..." He let the sentence fade away. Silence followed.

She wondered if he was hinting at her working on her own fear of water.

"I am proud of you for bringing her down to the lake. It must have been difficult," he said.

"It wasn't...until I got near the lake," Milena admitted. She hadn't meant to confide in him, it had just happened.

"Well, you came back alive. That must stand for something." His teeth flashed white in the darkness as he smiled.

Milena shrugged.

Daegen inhaled and let out a slow long breath and then he spoke again.

"I thought I could live with some things. I thought I could handle it on my own. Sometimes you need help. My offer still stands."

"Offer?" She should not pretend. She knew what he was saying.

"It would be nice to go swimming with you in the lake, especially on hot summer nights. We don't have air conditioning out here so swimming at night helps to cool down a hot body before bed."

Oh my! She doubted she would ever go for a swim, although she did remember splashing carelessly in the water as a child.

"My mother told me that I was a water baby when I was little. She said during the summer months I lived and breathed in the apartment swimming pool where we lived. But I don't remember much of it. I guess I was too little."

Daegen rose from the wicker chair and stood in front of her. To her surprise, he took her hands into his.

His gaze was sexy, and she craved a kiss from him. A succulently sweet kiss like the one they'd shared at Jane Sunflower's cabin.

Heck, she wanted more than a kiss...

"Whatever water demon has got ahold of you, I'm sure you can conquer it. You're a strong woman, Milena. Stronger than you think. I believe you can do anything you set your mind to."

Milena laughed, feeling anything but strong. She'd just broken-down running over a couple of frogs.

"I wish I had your confidence," she blurted.

"Don't undersell yourself. You strike me as a woman who goes after what she wants..."

His voice had lowered into a husky tone and Milena couldn't help but wonder if he was talking about her wanting him. Or was she again reading into something that wasn't there?

Gosh, why couldn't she just have confidence in herself and do what she wanted to do with her three cowboys?

"A woman who follows her instincts..." he added.

She swallowed.

He *was* talking about her. And him.

Oh boy. It suddenly was getting very warm standing so close to him.

His fingers squeezed hers again. A gentle maybe even encouraging squeeze?

She should kiss him. She should show him he was right. She did want him.

"I..."

She was about to tell him just that when he suddenly let go of her hands.

Frustration gripped her. She almost reached out to grab him, but then sensed someone was walking up the path from the shower.

It had to be Paul.

Suddenly Daegen was pulling out the mat for his bed from behind the wicker chair.

"Time to turn in sweetheart. Plenty of work tomorrow," Daegen said quietly.

Milena nodded.

Quickly, she slipped into the cabin and hurried to the kitchen to brush her teeth. She realized someone had already strung the sheets up between her bed and the other two.

Maybe you should take down the barrier...invite them into your bed.

One by one by one, a naughty voice whispered.

Heat fused her as she grabbed her toothpaste and toothbrush. She spied Jane Sunflower's gift still on the counter where she had left it earlier. She would open it later. In private.

As she brushed her teeth, she could hear Daegen and Paul talking in soft tones. She couldn't make out what they were discussing, and her thoughts flew back to Daegen.

Had she just imagined being out there on the porch with him? Had she misread what he had said? He'd said she was a woman who followed her instincts. A woman who goes after what she wants.

Need erupted deep inside of her. A need for sex. With Daegen. At least to start.

Milena caught her reflection in the kitchen window and gasped. She didn't recognize herself. She had a tortured look. A woman of indecision.

She didn't like feeling this way. Off balance. Not in control.

Sure, in the penitentiary she'd been told what to do, what to wear, what to eat and when. But at least in prison she'd been in control of her emotions. Here, her emotions were all over the place.

She finished brushing her teeth. Using the basin of clean warm water that someone had set by the sink for her to use like they did every night, she quickly washed her face.

Since the storm was coming, she would shower in the morning. She could hear Mitch's voice now as he joined the other two men out on the porch. Time for her to head off to bed.

Hurriedly she gathered up her toiletries and grabbed Jane Sunflower's gift and glanced at the bouquet of white daffodils.

Just looking at their perfection made a wild inner happiness blossom inside of her.

Snowy Creek Ranch was named after white daffodils. Who would have thought that?

"Goodnight!" She called out giving the men their que that she was heading off to bed and they could come inside.

"Goodnight," Mitch answered.

"Sweet dreams," Daegen said in a deep voice.

"Have a nice sleep!" Paul called.

With all three of the men protected here at the cabin, she felt wonderfully safe despite the thunder and flashes of lightning. She slipped behind the privacy sheets and lit her candle on the shelf behind her. As she began to change into her nightgown, she heard Mitch and Paul call out their goodnights to Daegen. She hoped he didn't get wet out there on the porch.

Maybe you should invite him into your bed tonight? Her naughty inner voice teased.

Milena blew out a tense breath as arousal swept through her. She hadn't been with a man since she was a teenager, and it hadn't been anything special. At least not for her. He had been quick and selfish...and gotten her a long stay in prison.

Milena pushed away the thoughts of her old overbearing boyfriend.

She grabbed Jane Sunflower's gift and placed the box on her lap. It was an unusual box. A very pretty flowery wallpaper had been glued to the sides as well as the lid.

Milena grinned. It was a handmade box!

How sweet.

The lid lifted off easily and there was a note on top of a bunch of recipe style index size papers.

My dearest Milena,

It was a pleasure to meet you the other day. I'm sure your injuries have healed by now and I am pleased to offer you some of what I call my miracle first aid recipes so you can make your own healing ointment.

I'm also enclosing some of my favorite baking recipes. Daegen mentioned you were not much into cooking, don't tell him I told you. This is between us women.

I'm very old fashioned and there is one thing I know to be true and that is the way to a man's heart is through his stomach. Cook for your man, Milena. Make your man happy and he will give back tenfold. I wish you the best.

Always yours,

Jane Sunflower.

Milena grinned as she reread the letter. What would old fashioned Jane say if Milena told her she wouldn't mind cooking and baking for all *three* men on this ranch? The woman would probably have a heart attack.

Milena lifted the recipes out of the box and was impressed. Jane had recipes for every imaginable meal, from moose lasagna to cold weather chili. She read a few of them and then was about to place them back into the box when something at the bottom caught her eye.

It was a red Swiss army knife and there was another note beneath it.

Milena,

I'm sure you will find this knife handy.

I received it as a gift many years ago, but never used it because I already have one. I am gifting this knife to you.

Love, Jane.

For sure this knife would be helpful with her ranch chores. She would make it a point to carry it always knowing that someone cared enough to give her such a lovely gift.

Which reminded her. She hadn't had a chance to go through the entire bag of items JJ had brought over days ago.

She listened for Mitch and Paul and realized the gas lamp had been turned off and she now heard gentle snoring.

A rumble of thunder drifted through the partially opened window. She thought about closing it but then remembered they had told her at one point not to worry about leaving the windows open during storms because the overhangs on the cabin were quite wide preventing rain from getting to the windows.

She smiled and watched the lightning flicker. It appeared these three men were pretty smart. She liked smart. It made her feel safe.

She wondered where the poachers were tonight. Had they moved out of the area? Had they taken the bears and

Paul's missing gyrfalcon? She wished she could hunt those bastard poachers down and shoot them.

And end up in prison again.

Actually, yes. She would do anything to protect the innocent wildlife.

Milena sucked on her bottom lip and pushed aside the burst of anger and anxiety that claimed her whenever she thought about helpless animals getting abused. There was nothing she could do about it right now, so she needed to concentrate on something she could control.

Her gaze dropped to the duffel bag JJ had brought her. It was still on the floor where she had placed it. Quietly she got out of bed, set Jane's gift into the second drawer of her dresser and grabbed the bag. A moment later, she was back under her blankets with the bag nestled in her lap. Excitement pummelled her as she reached inside. Previously she'd removed socks and underwear, a top and a pair of pants that JJ had given her, but at that time Milena had had to get to work and knew there was more in the bag.

She lifted out a couple of months worth of feminine products. These would come in handy. She had one month worth from the prison and now a total of three months. She also pulled out a hairbrush, deodorant, toothbrushes and toothpaste and...heat shot through her face and then the rest of her as she pulled out several different packages and sizes of condoms.

Oh, my goodness!

Instantly she remembered what Daegen had told her earlier today about JJ being sexually active with all three of the men she lived with. Was this some kind of a hint from JJ that maybe she should have sex with more than one man?

Milena shook her head. No, right now it was just a comment by Daegen. There was no truth to it, was there? Maybe JJ had given her several different sizes so when the time came, Milena was prepared with a size that might fit in case the man or men didn't have any? That was a good idea.

She placed the condoms and other items back into the bag. Tomorrow, she'd have to find a safe place for those condoms. Hide them somewhere the guys wouldn't find them by accident. She slid the bag to the floor beside her bed and let out a slow breath.

With those condoms right there beside her, how in the world was she going to sleep tonight? But she had to.

Gosh, she wished she could masturbate right here and now. But she didn't dare. They might hear and she didn't want that. Or did she?

No, she couldn't. She'd have to endure. She'd have to force herself to get some sleep. She didn't want to jeopardize her job here.

She twisted around and blew out her candle. The room fell into darkness.

She slid lower beneath her snug blankets and stared at the nearby window. Occasional flashes of lightning lit up the room and thunder continued but at a lower growl than before. It appeared the storm was not coming this way after all.

Milena closed her eyes and listened to the men snore softly. Soon, she was asleep.

• • ☙ • •

THE NEXT FEW DAYS FLEW by and to Milena's disappointment the men continued to be perfect gentlemen.

How annoying! How frustrating! And how irritating!

They treated her just like one of them. They gave her an equal share of the work and no more, which of course, forced her to fantasize about them while she worked despite her beginning to think that maybe they'd lost interest in her? Maybe they'd decided to keep the relationship strictly professional from here on out?

That would suck.

"Plane coming in. Probably JJ," Paul's shout snapped Milena from the planting she'd been doing in the garden.

A few days ago, all the supplies for the garden had arrived. The guys and herself had worked tirelessly every evening and early in the morning to ready the soil for the seeds. They'd given her a couple of days off and instead of relaxing, she'd plunged her skills into planting. She absolutely loved working her bare hands into the dirt, mixing the manure and soil, then planting the seeds. She couldn't get enough of it.

She'd been glad they'd only worked half a day today, so she didn't feel tired. In order to keep her mounting anxiety about the party at bay, she'd busied herself doing some more gardening.

She'd also been so deep in her thoughts; she hadn't realized Paul had returned from his shower so that meant

Mitch and Daegen would be back soon too as they'd gone down to the creek to wash up.

"You head on over to the shower; I'll go down and pick her up. Here's a clean towel and washcloth for you," Paul called.

He stood at the edge of the veranda and smiled at her as he draped the items over the railing.

"This party is going to be fun. Gonna do a lot of dancing. Do you know how to dance?" Paul shouted at her.

Gosh, he was so happy. She wished she could be so carefree too, but the thought of going to a party was daunting.

Milena shrugged her shoulders.

"It's been a long time. I have forgotten, I'm sure."

"That's okay, we can teach you."

She wanted to protest, but he was already scrambling down the steps, whistling and rushing to the nearby four-wheeler.

Milena sighed, covered up the last of her seeds and stood.

She wished she could be happy about going to this party, but she wasn't. She'd grown used to the work routine here on the ranch. She wanted to stay here and just relax and stay inside her comfort zone.

Going to a festivity just seemed...frivolous. There was still plenty of seeding to do and the horses had gotten ripped off a couple of hours of outside air and sunshine because the humans wanted to go to a stupid party.

She shook her head and reluctantly walked over to the railing. She wished today was over and she was tucked back in bed, dreaming her dreams of her forever cowboys.

She shook her head, grabbed the towel and washcloth and started toward the shower.

Dream on, Milena. Dream on.

They'd all kissed her. Mitch had gone down on her and then nothing...

They were not interested in sex. At least not with her. She just wished she was experienced in the sex department. Then she'd know how to stir up some interest in them for her.

Yup, she sure had a lot of dreams. Too bad none of them were coming true.

· · ⚜ · ·

"OH, MILENA," JJ SAID softly as Milena came out from behind the sheet one of the guys had strung up by her bed while she'd been showering.

Upon returning to the cabin, after her shower, she'd found JJ waiting inside for her with several packages on the table. The men had been nowhere in sight and JJ had been so giddy with excitement Milena hadn't had the heart to lie and tell her she wasn't feeling well so she couldn't go.

"You look so beautiful," JJ whispered as she clutched her hands to her chest.

Disbelief rocked her.

"I do?" She wasn't beautiful. Not at all.

"Yes, you do. You look perfect. Too bad there is no full-length mirror here. But I must say the dress I picked for you fits you better than I could have ever have imagined."

Milena gazed down at herself. She wasn't much for fashion. Never had it in prison. Everyone wore the same thing.

But this dress...was a crinkly soft material. Country-like and beautiful. It fit her slender figure and embraced her breasts.

It had puffy short sleeves, with a lovely sky-blue shade decorated in a pretty dark blue bachelor button flower print. Big white buttons dropped from the cute square neckline right down the middle of the front of the dress to the hem which ended at her knees.

"And here," JJ said as she opened a small bag and lifted out a tiny black velvet box.

"Jewelry for your attire. Another gift from me. Repayment for always being so kind to me in prison."

Milena shook her head in protest as JJ opened the box and removed a sparkling gold necklace with the cutest gold heart locket.

"Oh no, JJ, please you have spent too much on me."

To Milena's surprise, JJ laughed.

"I must confess, I used you as an excuse to go to the city on a shopping spree. I had so much fun being on my own for the day. One day I will take you with me and you could buy me lunch as thanks?"

JJ's enthusiasm had Milena's protest caving. She wouldn't mind going to the city with JJ. She hadn't done something like shopping in years. And Mitch had told her they'd set up monthly automatic deposits for her at a bank in Thunder Bay. She still couldn't get over how much money they were paying her for her labor. She was going to be rich and there would be money in her account to go out shopping with JJ and repay her for her thoughtfulness and kindness. And she would love to buy gifts for Jane and the other ladies in thanks for their kind-heartedness too.

"Of course, I will. I would love to go with you sometime," Milena replied.

"Great! Okay, now turn around so I can put this necklace on you."

Milena did as she was instructed and within seconds the delicate necklace dangled from her neck. The gold locket glistened up at her awing her with its beauty.

"It sure is pretty," she whispered.

She'd never owned anything so beautiful.

"Now, for shoes," JJ said.

She pulled a pair of glittering beige sandals from a box.

JJ blinked at its beauty and newness. It smelled of leather.

"And a purse to match."

She brought out a glittering beige purse that matched the shoes and quickly stuffed the makeup and lipstick that she'd used on Milena into the purse.

"In case you need to touch up your makeup," JJ said, and then she went back to talking about the shoes. "I'm guessing your feet are a size eight. And I went with low heels because I figured high heels might not work for you yet, since you aren't used to them. Besides for a party, you want comfy but fashionable too. Put them on. We need to

be going. I still have to get ready myself. Oh, my goodness!
I am so happy you are here!"

JJ left no room for argument on getting out of this
party as she rushed around the table collecting the empty
plastic bags and Milena didn't have the heart to chastise her
for giving her all these extravagant gifts.

"I do wonder where the men have gotten off to. If they
don't show up soon, we'll have to leave without them," JJ
gushed and motioned to Milena to put on her shoes.

To her amazement, the pretty sandals fit her perfectly.
She grabbed the purse, slung the strap over her shoulder,
and followed JJ, who pushed open the screen door and
suddenly stopped.

"Oh, my goodness," JJ whispered.

There was both shock and surprise in her voice as she
remained immobile.

Curiosity at JJ's reaction had Milena gazing over her
friend's shoulder.

"Oh my gosh," Milena whispered as something akin to
appreciation flooded through her.

Mitch, Daegen and Paul stood side by side by side near
the bottom of the stairs looking up at them.

The three men had their hair combed, they were clean
shaven and dressed casually, yet not so casually, if that made
sense.

Mitch looked quite elite and handsome in a pair of
white slacks, a light blue dress shirt that brought out the
blue in his eyes and a midnight blue jacket. A fresh white
daffodil peeked out from the breast pocket.

Paul was just as handsome wearing black slacks, a white dress shirt and a rusty brown jacket. A white daffodil peeked out from his breast pocket as well.

And Daegen looked breathtaking in a pair of jeans, a black polo shirt and a tan colored casual blazer. A white daffodil peeked out from his breast pocket too!

"Wow, you guys sure do clean up," JJ laughed as she walked onto the porch and then stepped aside so Milena could also come out. When she hesitated, JJ grabbed her by the hand and ushered her outside.

"What do you think?" JJ asked as she squeezed Milena's hand.

She saw their eyes widen with apparent surprise and the late afternoon air was filled with whistles.

"You look great," Daegen said in a deep voice that sent exciting tingles up and down Milena's back.

"I want to be your first dance," Paul said in a dominant tone she found exhilarating.

"And I'd like the pleasure of being your last dance," Mitch said in a husky tone that demanded her attention.

"And I'll take all the dances in between," Daegen said with a wink.

All kinds of emotions flipped through her as she followed JJ down the stairs. All the guys were watching her every move and she suddenly felt unbelievably self-conscious. Her cheeks grew hot as Daegen gingerly placed the helmet onto her head, being careful not to mess up her hair, and secured the flap.

"Your chariot awaits," Paul said and bowed to Milena.

Daegen did a similar gesture for JJ, who giggled and hopped onto the atv after securing a helmet upon her head.

This was all happening so fast.

Paul started the machine and minutes later they were at the lake. That awful feeling of foreboding captured her as she gazed at the glistening blue waters but before she could state that she was not going, Daegen grabbed her by the elbow and firmly led her down the ominous dock to the tiny ladder that was set at the open floatplane door.

"You can do this. Just breathe nice and slow," Daegen whispered so only the two of them could hear.

Reluctantly Milena inhaled and exhaled and grabbed hold of the ladder. Her hands shook like leaves in a fierce wind, and a moment later, she was inside the plane with everyone following.

They hadn't even caught on that something had just happened inside of her.

"Everyone buckled up?" JJ cheerfully called out from the cockpit a minute later. There was an echo of affirmatives.

But Milena just wanted out!

In her rising panic she barely saw Paul, who sat across an aisle from her. Mitch was in the cockpit seated beside JJ and Daegen sat beside her, buckling her seat belt and then holding her hand, gently squeezing, which prevented her from literally jumping out of her seat and out of the plane.

"Paul tells me you might have forgotten how to dance. We'll have fun teaching you," Daegen said kindly.

Milena ignored him as she closed her eyes and practiced breathing slowly.

Paul and Mitch were chatting and hinting about how they hoped there would be some of Moose Ranch's angus steak at the party and JJ reassured them there would be plenty.

JJ's plane smelled faintly of fuel and oil, but it was nothing compared to the bush plane she'd come here in not so long ago. Gosh, it hadn't even been a few weeks!

The plane roared to life and then started to move.

Oh damn! No escape now!

She squeezed Daegen's fingers so tightly she was surprised he didn't cry out.

"Easy, everything is fine," Daegen reassured.

Yeah, right! Poor JJ. This must be how her anxiety attacks felt. So not fun.

The plane moved faster and then she felt it lighten as they soared into the sky. Thankfully no queasiness assailed her, but apprehension sliced through her like a cleaver as she anticipated getting off the plane in just a few minutes.

She forced herself to open her eyes and gaze around the interior just so the others wouldn't catch on she was panicking.

Everyone was so happy as they chattered about the party. JJ described that the guys had decorated the barn with bales of hay and cute lanterns and there was a platform for the dancers. They all had smiles and she had to pretend everything was so normal.

Yes, everyone was happy. Except her.

She wished she could look out the window. She'd enjoyed the aerial scenery when she'd first been brought to

Snowy Creek Ranch. Had loved the endless blue sky and green forests.

But now she just didn't want to look.

"Okay, everyone, we'll be down in a couple of minutes. Make sure your seat belts are secure," JJ called out after a few minutes.

Already? Oh no!

Her heart began to pound. Her breaths came too fast.

"You look really beautiful," Daegen's quiet voice snapped through her nervousness, bringing her immediately back to reality.

She wasn't used to compliments. She was not used to this anxiety.

"Everything will be fine. In a few minutes we'll be on solid ground again."

He squeezed her hand.

"It will only get worse as you get older. I'm thinking you should accompany me on my next trip to my doctor. I'll call her and ask her to squeeze you in."

She couldn't go on this way. He was right. Her fear of water was getting worse. She just wanted to be normal. To be happy, like everyone else.

She looked at him. His eyes glistened with warmth.

She nodded numbly.

"Good, I'll set it up."

For some crazy insane reason, just knowing she would have a professional to talk with soon, diminished her anxiety.

As the plane began to descend, excitement from the three men and JJ permeated the interior of the plane and whispered over Milena. She forced her breathing to slow again and felt better.

Moments later, the plane was aside the Moose Ranch dock.

JJ, Mitch and Paul were quick to exit and assisted in securing the bush plane and Daegen quietly encouraged her as he helped Milena down the steep ladder.

She couldn't get to land fast enough.

Using the excuse that she wanted to see the baby, which was true, she grabbed JJ's hand and quickly pulled her up the trail.

. .⚓. .

"DAMN BUT SHE SURE DOES look good in a dress," Mitch mumbled as he, Paul and Daegen stood on the dock and watched Milena and JJ stroll arm in arm up the trail toward the two-story ranch log house.

This is the kind of house that Milena should have, Mitch thought as he gazed upon the nice building. This was something she could be proud of. She could have a room of her own and her own bathroom.

Mitch shook his head and cursed beneath his breath.

"Hey man, take it easy. She's ours," Paul said from behind him.

Obviously, Paul had mistaken his curse that some man would scoop her away from them, and he didn't have the nerve to tell them that she deserved a better place to stay.

"She looks more than good in that dress. She looks hot," Daegen muttered as he suddenly pushed past them and headed up the path toward the back of the barn where Dan was waving for them to come over.

"And hotter out of that dress," Paul said with a wink and quickly followed Daegen.

Oh man, Paul's words were putting some mighty fine images of the lusciously naked Milena into his head. He felt his cock jerk with awareness as he remembered going down on her. Her tight pussy clamping around his tongue as he'd mouth fucked her.

That same night, Daegen and Paul had confronted him down by the creek where he'd been washing up. They'd confessed that they'd seen what he'd done to Milena.

They'd all agreed to back off her and give her some space. See what she did. See how she reacted.

It had been pure hell staying away from her. But he'd observed her. They all had.

She tried to act casually but there was a hunger in her eyes. She wanted more.

She would get more.

Soon. Very soon.

His cock hardened some more and pressed tighter against his pants.

Down, boy, down, Mitch chastised himself and quickly followed the guys.

Chapter Fifteen

"Oh my gosh, JJ, has she ever grown since the last time I saw her!" Milena whispered with excitement as they both watched Chrissy sleep. Sure, it had only been a couple of weeks since she'd first seen the baby, but she *had* grown.

When they'd first arrived at the ranch house and Brady told them Chrissy had just been put down for a nap, Milena had been disappointed. But JJ had insisted they pop upstairs so Milena could take a look.

Chrissy was lying on her stomach, her face turned toward them. Her cheeks were pudgy and pink like rosebuds. Her blushing mouth was slightly open and pursed into a pretty pout. Long, dark eyelashes framed her cheeks, and she wore a cute little yellow crochet hat while the rest of her was hidden beneath a soft yellow knit baby blanket.

The slow rise and fall of her chest reassured Milena she was in a deep sleep.

"Brady loves dressing her in matching clothes. Everything has to match," JJ said with a soft laugh.

"She's the cutest thing I have ever seen. The instant she wakes up I want to snuggle her," Milena whispered back.

She just could not stop looking at the baby and memorizing every detail from her tiny eyelashes to the cute miniature heart-shaped birth mark on her neck.

"You know, sometimes I worry myself into an anxiety attack because I'm so happy I have her and then I get afraid something bad will happen to her or to me," JJ whispered.

Milena instantly recognized her friend's worried tone. She reached out and curled her arm around JJ's waist and squeezed her gently.

"I'm sure lots of mothers worry themselves sick about their children," she reassured.

She'd expected JJ to smile back at her, but she didn't. Instead, her friend's frown deepened as she watched her daughter.

Oh, wow. JJ was really serious.

"Come on now, sweetie. Don't go looking for things that are not there. Stay in your happy place. Unless there's a real problem?" Milena squeezed her harder.

Immediately JJ shook her head and chuckled.

"You're right. I'm making things up that don't even exist."

She wiggled away from Milena's grasp and nodded.

Thankfully she smiled and her eyes twinkled happily.

Whew, Milena had said something right. JJ appeared to have snapped herself out of the funk she'd just been in.

"Any non-existent problems are of my own making. Sometimes I just can't seem to stop myself from thinking doom and gloom thoughts. I've been practicing in changing the way I think, but sometimes I slip. That's the main reason I decided to throw this spring fling for everyone. Party planning helps keep me grounded. It was a great distraction."

Milena could understand that JJ would be worried about her baby, but it wasn't healthy to literally make herself sick over problems that just were not there.

JJ needed a distraction right now too.

"Speaking of the party, let's let sleeping babes lie. I would love to see what you've been up to in your spare time with your planning," Milena coaxed.

But neither of them moved as they gazed down at the baby again.

When Milena looked at JJ, she was frowning again.

Oh dear.

"She's an angel, JJ. She'll be fine. You'll be fine," Milena whispered.

JJ nodded and her smile was back.

"You're right of course. I just needed someone to talk to about it. Thanks for lending an ear and setting me straight."

Milena understood where JJ was coming from. Since Milena had come to Snowy Creek Ranch there were numerous times she'd wondered if she really was out of prison or if this was all some sort of dream that she'd wake up from. That Paul, Mitch and Daegen were just some sexy dreams with hard labor.

"Just remember with everything you've been through in your past, it will take time to move your thoughts into a new, healthier way," Milena advised.

Man, if only she could take her own advice.

Milena inhaled deeply and committed Chrissy to her memory. Without warning, wonderful emotions tumbled through her.

Happiness. Love. And suddenly she yearned to have a sweet baby of her very own.

The thought of being a mother rocked through Milena like a bolt of lightning. Weird foreign ideas and feelings of nurturing and belonging began to blossom. Dreams she'd long dared not to think about. But here they were bubbling up from deep inside of her like an untapped well of delights.

Having her own children. Having a house of her own. Having a husband.

No, actually not a house. A quaint little cabin in the woods like the one over at Snowy Creek Ranch.

Milena smiled and nodded.

Yeah, that's what she would want for herself and her children. A simple, natural, carefree life.

Maybe she would someday.

Maybe.

· · ⚜ · ·

DAEGEN STOPPED ABRUPTLY when he walked around from the back of the barn and reached the top of the pathway. He noticed several people milling in the sunshine at the entrance of the barn. One of them was Milena and she was laughing with some strange guy.

"Oh, shit," he muttered.

"What?" Mitch and Paul both asked at the same time from immediately behind him.

The three of them had chatted with Dan for about half an hour about how to plant their garden before he'd excused himself saying he needed to get started on the steaks.

The steak comment had gotten Daegen's mouth watering. He sure did enjoy a good barbecue, but not when there was a potential threat regarding his woman, Milena.

"Competition at three o'clock," he muttered and nodded toward the small group.

He didn't recognize the man, but he sure was making Milena giggle. He was a very tall, very good-looking man around their age. He seemed quite animated with his hands and cheerful talking to the ladies and making them laugh.

"Who's that?" Paul asked the question that was burning through Daegen.

"Why is he wearing a suit?" Mitch questioned.

"The more urgent question is why is he staring at Milena?" Daegen pondered as uneasiness fizzled through him.

"Maybe he's looking at JJ or Blue? They're standing with Milena," Paul volunteered.

"Maybe he wants to be introduced to Milena?" Mitch suggested in an irritated tone.

"Maybe we should get our asses over there and make sure he knows she's taken?" Daegen said and started forward.

He was glad that Paul and Mitch were flanking him. They would make sure this stranger knows Milena was off limits.

. . ⚓ . .

FROM THE CORNER OF her eye, Milena could see Daegen, Mitch and Paul approaching. They appeared tense and maybe even hostile? They had weird glares in their eyes, and they said nothing as they milled around her.

The man she'd been introduced to did not appear to notice their dominating behavior as he was chatting about the skunks the two dogs he'd been dog sitting had tangled with last night. He'd been so descriptive in the way the poor dogs had howled after getting sprayed and his refusal to let them into the house that his story had made her laugh. Then he'd suddenly turned the conversation to ask Blue how her daughter was doing when the guys showed.

"Want to go inside?" Daegen suddenly asked.

She didn't even get a chance to answer as his firm hand settled against her lower back like a hot brand and he expertly steered her toward the barn. Paul and Mitch were quick to follow.

Irritation snapped through her. Why had they been so bad-mannered? She'd wanted to introduce them to the man. My goodness, he must think the people from Snowy Creek Ranch were so rude.

Her irritation was quickly forgotten as she stepped into the cool interior of the barn and was greeting by a delicate flowery scent.

A long table decorated with red and white gingham material lined one side of the barn. It was laden with generous bowls of salads and baked goods. Small metal pails held forks, knives and spoons. There were several piles of different sizes of white plates and cute red and white gingham napkins. Near the end of the table were the refreshments which included a large metal tub that had been filled with ice cubes and bottles of beer. The word BEER had been painted in black across the tub.

Wrapped around the overhead beams were white miniature lights and hanging from those same beams were red lanterns, which cast a bright glow upon the interior. Several hay bales were covered with soft-looking blankets so people could sit on them. There were several smaller foursome tables with blue and white gingham tablecloths and in each centre was a mason jar with a votive candle flickering inside.

It was all so visually stimulating that for a moment she'd forgotten she stood inside a barn and not in a genuine party room. Her breath backed up at the beauty as she continued to gaze around. White wicker baskets had been set on wall shelves and were filled with red and white tulips with yellow daffodils interspersed between the tulips.

Tucked in a corner was a large, raised wood-planked dance floor with hand railings and a set of steps up to the platform. She spied a record player perched on a bale of hay with records to go. Country music was playing.

"Shall we dance?" Paul asked.

He held out his hand and she reluctantly took it.

"I'm pretty rusty," she reminded him.

"Not a problem," Paul smiled as he led her up the steps onto the dance floor.

"Did I tell you how beautiful you look this evening," he whispered as he settled his palm on her hip.

Milena felt her cheeks heat at the compliment.

"Slow dance, follow my lead," Paul said as he pulled her closer. She trembled when she felt the large outline of his shaft press against her lower belly.

Oh my. He certainly was huge.

She tried to keep her focus on dancing, but his cock made it quite hard to concentrate and she stepped on his toes several times.

"I'm sorry," she apologized.

"Don't worry," Paul whispered against her ear. He wore a gentle aftershave tonight and it mixed quite nicely with the flowery scent permeating the barn.

She really liked the combination of smells and enjoyed the way he danced in a sexy rhythm that made her body hum.

"This is nice. Getting away from work and just having some fun time," Paul murmured.

Milena nodded.

Despite her not wanting to come to the party, she was actually enjoying herself. When the music stopped, she realized that Blue and Rafe had joined them on the dance floor. Suddenly Daegen tapped Paul on the shoulder, who reluctantly gave her up. Then Daegen asked her to dance.

The record player was playing another slow dance.

"Hey, how is it going?" Daegen asked as he held her just as close as Paul had. She swallowed at the impression of his shaft against her lower belly. Just as big and as hard as Paul's.

Why were they doing this to her? Teasing her in such a sexual manner after ignoring her for so long at the ranch.

"Good," she answered, surprised at the breathiness of her voice.

"Are you glad you came?" He pressed his cheek against hers.

"Yes," she said truthfully.

The brush of his flesh against hers was erotic and she found herself wanting to kiss him. His mouth was right there. No more than two inches away.

But she didn't dare.

Paul and Mitch would see, and she didn't want to hurt their feelings. Not in any way.

Oh, how was she going to handle these three men? She wanted to have all three of them all for herself. Not just one.

Was she being greedy? Sexually deviant?

Daegen took the next several dances with her and she melted against his strong body with each dance. They were joined by JJ who danced with Brady and then Rafe and then Dan which had Milena struggling to keep an eye on her friend as she also loved the strength of Daegen's body against hers.

Yes, Milena was beginning to see that JJ was into all three of her cowboys. She didn't make it apparent. None of them did, but Milena could see how protectively each of the men held her and how the three men gazed lovingly into her eyes while they danced with her.

Had Daegen not mentioned it, would she have noticed?

She noted that the man she'd been introduced to outside the barn was also on the dance floor with Kaley and then Blue. But he seemed to take a particularly intimate interest in the bush pilot, Kelly.

As they danced, Daegen spoke about his time in the military and his family, and she talked about her prison life. By the time they broke for a bite to eat, Milena was famished.

At the table she was almost drooling as she looked at all the different types of salads JJ had made. There was mixed vegetable salads, potato salads, egg salads and cucumber and tomato salads. Cute little tuna and salmon sandwiches that had been cut into quarters were perched like miniature high-rises on pretty floral plates.

"Brady and Rafe have the barbecue all fired up. I gave them your orders for steak awhile ago. They should be almost ready," Mitch said as he sidled in between Daegen and Milena.

"Great! Thanks, man! I'm going to run out and get them. Do you want yours too, Mitch?" Excitement flared in Daegen's eyes.

"Sure, I'll heap stuff on a plate for you."

Milena smiled. She loved how these guys got along so easily. It truly warmed her heart, and her mouth was watering up a storm too just looking at all these goodies and how delicious they would taste with some steak.

"You clean up really well," Mitch said as he handed her an empty plate and grabbed two more.

"Why, thank you. You don't look too shabby yourself," she grinned as she plopped some potato salad onto her plate.

"Thought you were rusty with dancing? You look pretty hot on the dance floor," Mitch complimented as she scooped some salad onto the two plates he was holding.

Her cheeks warmed at his praise. She hadn't realized he'd been watching.

"It's just like riding a bike. It came back naturally once I started. Reminded me of how much I love dancing. It's been quite awhile."

"I bet," he chuckled.

She scooped several more salads and some of the tiny sandwiches onto his plates and her own.

"Where is Paul? I haven't seen him for awhile."

"He's tending to a sickly calf. Rafe mentioned he hadn't been able to figure out what was wrong, and you know Paul and animals, like fruit flies to fruit."

"The calf is in good hands," Milena replied.

"Too bad the wild animals are not in good hands around these parts," the man she had been introduced to earlier said from behind them.

Beside her, Mitch visibly tensed.

Milena frowned. What was his problem with this guy anyway? Sure, he was handsome, and he was wearing a really nice suit. Overdressed for the occasion, but who was she to judge?

"Hi, Jay. Sorry I couldn't make introductions earlier. This is one of my bosses, Mitch, over at Snowy Creek Ranch...and Mitch, this is Jay. He's a firefighter and a smokejumper. He just got engaged to Kelly."

Milena noted Mitch's disposition changed immediately from one of what she had perceived as irritation to one of relief.

"To Kelly? Really? Wow. Congratulations on your engagement."

Mitch quickly placed the plates he'd been holding back onto the party table and pumped Jay's hand.

"Well, I certainly understand why you're surprised. I did ask her about five times before she finally said yes," Jay said and then laughed.

"Kelly is a great lady. She brings in our food and other supplies sometimes with her plane. Very helpful," Mitch complimented.

Hmm, Kelly had turned down a proposal five times?

"Thanks. I think so. But I have to marry her fast before she gets cold feet. I've been told she has an aversion to firefighters."

Mitch winced.

"Yeah, I heard her late fiancé was a smoke jumper like yourself."

"Yep, Luke was my best friend."

Mitch grimaced and shook his head.

"Ah shit man, sorry for your loss."

"It's still raw. Been a couple of years, but it's time for both of us to move on, you know? Time flies and before you know it, you're dead."

Mitch nodded.

"True. Let us know if we can help with the wedding or anything. We don't have a reliable phone, had a used satellite radio but it died. Still have to get a new one. You can text us. Might take awhile before we get the message though. Before you leave, I can give you the number. JJ knows where to find us."

Jay grinned.

"I've got a pretty good memory. Just give me the number and I will remember it."

"Cool."

Mitch gave him his cell number and Jay nodded.

He seemed quite pleased with Mitch's offer to help.

"Thanks. Appreciate that. I may take you up on your proposal. Pardon the pun."

Milena couldn't help but laugh. Jay was a funny fellow.

So why had Mitch, Paul and also Daegen, acted so weird earlier where Jay was concerned? They'd seemed hostile toward him, and they didn't even know each other, yet now Mitch was acting as if Jay was his newest best friend.

"So, you're the one that almost got eaten by that bear?" Jay inquired with wide eyes.

Mitch laughed.

"Had to play dead, before I truly was dead. The bear was literally breathing right down my neck."

Jay grimaced.

"So, you can see what I'm saying about not waiting on things that you're serious about," Jay said.

"Point well made," Mitch replied with a nod.

Milena hadn't forgotten Mitch's close call with the bear and wondered every day who had shot that animal and who had clobbered Paul and mostly likely taken that gyrfalcon. She didn't believe for a moment that Paul had left that cage door unlocked or ajar.

"Kelly was saying she saw smoke from a campfire a few days back, about two miles south of your cabin. She reported it to the authorities, but they said they'd have to have proof it was the poachers as it could just be interior campers," Jay said.

"Hmm, not too far from our place, eh?" Mitch suddenly had a worried expression that alerted Milena. She wondered if Mitch might be thinking the same thing she might be thinking. That maybe one of them should go south for a closer look.

She was about to ask Mitch if that might be something they should try when Daegen returned with their steaks. She was stunned to see his tight expression as he approached them. His intense gaze was fixated on Jay and a muscle jumped in his right cheek as he clenched his jaw.

Seriously? Why was he acting so...jealous?

Thankfully Jay's back was to Daegen so Jay could not see the hostility quite evident on Daegen's face.

No way was she misreading him. Now that she thought about it, wariness must have been what the men had been exhibiting earlier. It had to be.

But why against Jay?

Daegen was frowning as he placed a large platter of steaks onto the table. Thankfully Mitch was quick to make introductions. She watched Daegen's reaction change the instant Mitch mentioned Jay was Kelly's fiancé. He appeared relieved.

How odd.

Was she being naive in thinking the three men were jealous?

"Jay was saying Kelly spied some smoke from possible campers near our land," Mitch said to Daegen.

"Is that right? I think I'll go and talk to her and get the direct coordinates. Thanks for the tip, Jay. Congratulations on your engagement. Kelly is a great catch. Talk later."

Jay nodded as Daegen left and then turned his attention to Milena and Mitch.

"Well, I'll let you guys get to your grub and I'd best be getting back to my lady. Word has it she's engaged to me, and I don't want to give her an excuse to kick me to the curb already."

Mitch chuckled and Milena threw him a wave as he left.

"What an odd thing for him to say. I wonder why she turned him down five times," Milena pondered when Jay was out of earshot.

She reached for a fork and stabbed a delicious looking steak and set it on her plate.

Her tummy growled.

Mitch laughed.

"Dig in and I can tell you all about the gossip about Kelly."

"Gossip? You listen to gossip? Really?"

Mitch shrugged as he helped himself to a steak.

"Well, actually Brady told me awhile back about it."

"Oh, ok. So, I don't think that is gossip then."

Mitch laughed.

"Well, a couple years back Kelly was engaged to a smoke jumper."

"Dangerous job," Milena said as she began cutting the ultra juicing looking meat.

Spicy smells wafted through the air and teased her nostrils, making her mouth water.

"It is a tragic story, actually. Maybe I'll tell it to you after you eat? I don't want to spoil your appetite."

Milena shook her head and stuffed a piece of steak into her mouth. Flavors exploded against her taste buds, and it took everything for her not to moan out loud at the enjoyable taste of salt, barbecue sauce and spices. She chewed the delicacy as long as she could and swallowed, surprised that Mitch was watching her.

"By the look on your face, I'd say it's good?" he asked.

"That's an understatement. Do tell the story, it won't ruin my appetite. I've just spent years in prison, and I've heard all kinds of tragic stories. Things happen and people are devastated. It's a really rough world. Those who tell you different, have been very lucky. From your earlier conversation with Jay, I take it Kelly's fiancé died."

Hmm, maybe they should wait until after dinner for him to tell the story. He was looking kind of sad.

Mitch nodded and inhaled softly, before he continued.

"Well, the way Brady tells it, it was the day before they were to get married, and it was his last day on the job for a couple of weeks cause they were going to honeymoon at the log cabin they'd just had built in the woods...when his team got called in to fight a forest fire. He had the option of going in with his crew or staying back and doing paperwork."

Milena followed up the delicious piece of steak with some absolutely fantastic potato salad.

"I take it he didn't choose the paperwork?" she asked between bites.

"He went in with his crew. He got caught up in a firestorm. Never made it back to Kelly. Never found his body. Kelly told JJ she had sworn off men forever, so I think Jay must be a very special guy to have won Kelly's trust and her heart because he's a smoke jumper just like her fiancé."

Milena's tummy clenched in compassion for Kelly.

"Oh wow. She really must love him to be putting her heart out like that again."

"Yup."

"No wonder Jay is nervous. I would make the engagement as short as possible, so she doesn't turn into one of those runaway brides-to-be," Milena said as she enjoyed some cucumber salad and followed it up with another chunk of mouth-watering steak.

"Kelly must be a tough chick to go down that road again," Mitch said solemnly.

"Or she's in love. Love blinds people," Milena replied.

"Are you speaking from experience?" Mitch had such an innocent grin that she did not want to burst his bubble of happiness.

She'd thought she'd been in love with Dwayne, but she'd been used to carry out a horrible tragedy. Back then she'd mistaken domination and abuse for love, mindlessly doing what he told her to do.

"Just what I've heard," she replied.

She forced the thoughts of her past behaviour from her mind. Over the years in prison, she'd become an expert in burying her past deep inside her brain. It was too painful to relive her foster years after the death of her mother and the tragedy that had brought her to prison.

She also pushed aside the awful thing that had happened to Kelly because it appeared after what she'd gone through Kelly was going to have her happy forever after with Jay. That was kind of cool.

"Man, this steak is so good."

Mitch's praise burst through her thoughts, and she looked up to see juices dribbling down the sides of his lips.

Mmmm, he has such a yummy mouth, she thought as she began to eat again.

Mitch was right. The steak was so good, and she swore the salty and spicy flavors made love to her taste buds. She'd never tasted such a good steak. Heck, in prison any steak they'd been given was in name only. Meat, when they had it, had been tough to cut and even tougher to chew, but this steak quite literally melted in her mouth.

"So yummy," Milena agreed.

"Didn't we say Moose Ranch has the best steaks?" His eyes sparkled as he watched her eat.

Gosh, he was so cute. So sexy.

"We should get our own beef cattle and have steak everyday," she suggested between bites.

She grabbed a napkin and wiped away the juices sliding down her own chin. She would prefer to lick it off herself or better yet have Mitch lick it off for her.

She moaned at that thought. Moaned out loud.

Mitch stopped chewing and tensed.

"You don't like the idea?" she said quickly as she spied his eyes getting darker.

Sexy eyes. Predatory eyes. She recognized that look. It was the same one he he'd had that afternoon...when he'd gone down on her.

Oh boy. Right now, she wished they were back at Snowy Creek Ranch. Alone.

"It's actually a very good idea, but right now we've got plenty of work with the horses," he answered.

She would have to make it a point not to moan out loud anymore. The sound seemed to grab his attention. Or maybe she should do it more often? Maybe hint to them that she was ready for some hot and heavy sex! Her naughty inner voice teased.

Her cheeks warmed and the heat spread throughout her body.

Had she just thought *them?*

Oh boy!

"I'm thirsty. Want something cold?" Milena asked. She was even on her feet before Mitch could answer.

"I'll bring you back something cold."

Despite not wanting to leave the ultra delicious steak, salads and sandwiches, she needed to calm down. Once she reached the table, she moved in beside a woman who was helping herself to salad, and was able to calm down, especially when she spied a large crystal bowl filled with ice cubes and orange punch.

Goodness, how could she be reacting like this to Mitch right here at a party with so many people around?

"You look flushed. Taking a break from dancing?" A voice said from right beside her. Milena looked up from the table to find a woman who looked kind of familiar, but she couldn't quite peg where she had seen her before.

"I'm Kayley. Remember me?"

"Oh my gosh! I am so sorry. I didn't recognize you. You look like a totally different person all dressed up," Milena gushed.

"Thanks. I think."

Oh dear, had she just unintentionally insulted her?

Kayley did not look at all like the quiet bush pilot with the straight blonde hair. She was all dolled up with curly hair, makeup and a pretty yellow sundress.

"I am so sorry, Kaley. I didn't mean the way it sounded."

"No worries, hon. To tell you the truth I did not recognize you at first either," Kayley laughed.

"So? How is it going over at Snowy Creek? Are you all settled in?"

"Oh yes, the guys are fantastic."

"That's great. I apologize for just dropping you off and just running. It was so unprofessional of me. Had you disappeared I would have been in trouble, but I sensed I could trust you."

"I made it there alive as you can see," Milena laughed and did a happy twirl.

She opted not to tell Kayley how she had been terrified in the darkness walking that trail after she'd left. Or that she'd been welcomed to an empty house and later a hostile

Mitch had frightened her. But it had all turned out okay. Boy, had it ever turned out okay. She had three men interested in her.

"They are obviously taking very good care of you. You look wonderful," Kaley commended.

Milena's face grew even warmer. She wondered if she would ever not blush when someone gave her a compliment.

"Why don't you try the strawberry juice?" Kayley nodded to another crystal bowl that contained a light red liquid with small bobbing ice cubes.

"JJ made it from early strawberries in her garden. It will cool you right down. You look a little hot."

Oh great. My blushing is that noticeable?

"How about a dance, Kayley? I need to pump you for more information on Kelly," Jay's gruff voice cut into their conversation. He'd lost his suit jacket and his tie was also gone. He wore his white shirt open to the chest and seemed quite flustered.

Kayley smiled at Milena and winked.

"We're planning the wedding behind Kelly's back. Don't tell her. Duty calls. I'll grab some grub later. See you later, Milena."

With a goodbye wave of her hand, she was led onto the dance floor by Jay.

Milena watched them for awhile, until her cheeks didn't feel so hot anymore and then she turned her attention to the punch bowls.

She grabbed a ladle and scooped the strawberry juice and some ice cubes into a tall glass and gulped the delicious drink. It was icy cold and really hit the spot.

After a second glass, she poured one for Mitch and another for herself and returned to their table.

Mitch was still eating and most of his food was gone.

"Hey, missed you," he said with a smile.

Mercy, she'd missed him too. Come to think of it, she missed Daegen and Paul too.

She placed the glasses onto the table and joined him.

"Hurry and eat so we can get onto the dance floor again. I feel like dancing you to the moon."

Milena laughed and watched him as he grabbed the glass and closed his eyes and drank.

Her breaths came quicker at the sexy way his lips curled over the edge of the glass. Her cheeks grew warm again as she remembered how his mouth had worked such wonderful magic between her thighs.

Mercy, this was going to be a long evening.

·· ᥴᕽᵒ ··

"I RECOGNIZE THOSE LOOKS."

Milena stopped abruptly at JJ's voice as Milena stepped out of the bathroom to find her friend standing off to the side, a wide smile on her face, her arms crossed over her chest. She'd changed into a pretty country style dress that accentuated her figure. She looked very nice.

"What looks?" Milena asked.

Confusion rocked her. She had no clue what JJ was talking about. Had something gone on at the party that she had missed? She'd only come into the ranch house a few minutes ago to use the bathroom. She shouldn't have drunk so many glasses of that yummy strawberry punch, because now she was paying for it.

"Your cowboys."

Her confusion only increased.

"My cowboys? I don't understand."

"Mitch, Daegen and Paul. They're jealous."

"Jealous?" Milena asked dumbly. How could JJ know about Jay and the guys?

JJ giggled and hooked her arm with Milena's, leading her into the kitchen.

"I have been watching the way they look at you throughout the afternoon and evening. I recognized something was going on when they saw you with Jay when they first arrived. They're not jealous of each other when they are around you."

Suddenly she remembered her conversation with Daegen the other day saying JJ was most likely in a relationship with all three of her cowboys.

JJ laughed again.

"Why are you looking at me like that, Milena? Surely you must have noticed how they behaved before they knew Jay and Kelly were engaged."

"Yes, but I didn't know why—"

"They want you, Milena."

Milena's thoughts whirled. Someone was actually saying out loud what Milena had started to suspect. She didn't know what to say, so she remained silent.

"You must have picked up clues that they want you. I mean even prison life cannot kill a woman's natural instincts towards the opposite sex."

JJ was now speaking loudly and freely. Hopefully that meant no one was in the house. She needed to change the subject and fast, in case someone was listening.

"Where is the baby? Is she awake yet?" she said lamely.

"Brady may have taken her out and no changing the subject."

Milena's cheeks grew hot.

"I knew it," JJ laughed freely.

"I couldn't do anything with any of them. They are my bosses. I need to keep it strictly professional..."

"Oh, come on, sweetie. Who's gonna find out way out here? Who's gonna tell? We're free to do whatever we want," she stopped abruptly.

Milena noticed her friend's sudden rosy appearance.

"Are you...and all three of them?" Milena blurted.

She knew the answer just by looking at JJ's expression. Her face was flushed pink, and her eyes sparkled with excitement.

JJ nodded and bit her bottom lip and beamed.

So, what Daegen had said was true. She really was having sex with three different men!

"Oh, my goodness," Milena gasped as she grew hotter. She swore even her ears were blistering.

"And all of them at once with you too?" The question was out before she could even stop it.

JJ nodded and then rolled her eyes.

"Girlfriend, you need to unstick your head from the sandbox and start building sandcastles."

Milena couldn't help but laugh.

"Sandcastles? More like sand penises. And thanks for the condoms you stashed in the bag. I haven't had a chance to use them, but maybe...soon."

JJ looked stunned.

"Condoms? I didn't put any condoms in the stuff I gave you."

"You didn't? But then who?"

JJ's mouth dropped open.

"Use your imagination. Must have been one of your cowboys."

Milena worried her bottom lip.

"Come to think of it, there had been three boxes. Three different sizes. Three different brands," she whispered.

"Oh, my Lordy, woman. I cannot believe how lucky you are. How lucky we both are. Three men all to ourselves."

Milena jolted at the clumping sound of someone ascending the stairs to the mudroom down the hallway.

"Just keep those condoms on you at all times, girlfriend. The fresh air does something to the men out here. They get really frisky at all times of the day and night," JJ said and then winked.

Milena nodded jerkily.

Keep those condoms on you at all times

Who had given her the condoms? Paul? Daegen? Mitch? All three of them?

"Hello!" Blue called out as the mudroom door squeaked open.

"Right here in the kitchen, Blue!" JJ's shout snapped Milena back to reality and she watched as JJ headed toward the refrigerator.

JJ and three men? How did that work? Rafe, Brady and Dan, all seemed to get along so well...

Milena swallowed. So did Mitch, Paul and Daegen.

Dear Lord! Is that what had been happening lately? Were all three men interested in her? Did they want to share her? Were they going to bring her naughty fantasies into reality? Was she mad to even entertain such thoughts of sleeping with three men? She'd sworn off men knowing how much trouble one could get her into. How much trouble would three men get her into?

But these men were nothing like Dwayne. There was no comparison. These men would have her back no matter what. She knew that without a doubt.

"Everyone loves the steaks. Rafe needs some more to barbecue," Blue gushed as she entered the kitchen. She quickly turned to Milena.

"Daegen was looking for you," she said with a smile. "Wants to square dance with you."

Square dance? She didn't know the first thing about square dancing.

"Thanks. I'm heading out just now. JJ give me something to carry out."

Milena laughed. JJ was already handing her an extra-large platter filled with cold cuts and cheese and an arrangement of crackers.

"Wow," Blue said as she accepted a large tray colorfully decked out with slices of lemon cake and brownies.

"Does this lady know how to bake. Or does she know how to bake?" Blue laughed.

"I must admit I do have trouble keeping up feeding the guys," JJ replied as she removed a platter of raw steaks from the refrigerator.

"But it makes me so happy to see them eat what I make for them. They have such great appetites, especially after a hard day of working outdoors."

Milena caught JJ winking at her and instinctively sensed she wasn't talking about food, but about sex instead. Thankfully Blue hadn't noticed the wink.

Milena suddenly realized that maybe she should learn a thing or two on how to cook for her men too. She'd have to read more of Jane Sunflower's recipes.

"I'll get these out onto the table," she said and headed down the hall.

A moment later she was bathed in the evening sunshine as it descended toward the towering pine trees surrounding Moose Ranch. The sky was clear and blue and down at the lake, beyond the floatplanes at the dock, the waves were sparkling as if someone had thrown white diamonds across the waters.

A woodpecker did a rat-a-tat nearby and a cow mooed from the direction of the barn. The air was wonderfully mild and a gentle breeze that smelled of baking pine needles blew over her.

She exhaled a tense breath as she realized what she'd just thought moments earlier.

Her men.

Condoms and *her* men.

Suddenly she felt as if an entire new world had been opened up to her. A world of sexual exploration possibilities. She'd been in prison for so long. Had missed so much, especially in the sex and relationship department.

Oh dear. She had a lot to think about.

· · ❧ · ·

BRADY TIPTOED DOWN the stairs after the three women had left the house.

He'd been upstairs keeping an eye on Chrissy while she slept. He'd promised JJ that today she wouldn't have to worry about their baby. He was in charge of her.

But he hadn't meant to eavesdrop. He'd been at the top of the stairs about to come down for a coffee, when he'd overheard JJ and Milena talking.

He grinned. Odd, that JJ had spoken loud enough for him to hear about Milena's situation. She'd known he was upstairs.

Suddenly a lightbulb went off in his head.

Of course, JJ had wanted him to hear the conversation. She must have picked up on something happening between Milena and the guys.

"So little brother, you want to share a woman, just like your older brother. Maybe one day I'll have to give you some pointers. Or maybe, I'll just keep my mouth shut and let nature take its course. You sure don't need another awkward birds and bees talk like the one dad gave us," he chuckled to himself.

He was about to head into the kitchen to get that coffee when a cute little cry came from the nursery.

His daughter was waking up and he always loved the cheerful way she smiled when she saw him. All happy and so full of joy.

Yep, being a dad was such a cool job.

He turned around and hurried back upstairs.

．．⚭．．

"SQUARE DANCE IS UP next! Be my partner?" Daegen called to Milena as she stepped off the dance floor with Mitch. His eyes blazed with excitement, and it floored her that he truly wanted to dance with her.

Mitch made an excuse that he needed to go to the bathroom and then Daegen's hand settled along the curve of her right hip.

She trembled at the intimate gesture.

"Sure, just let me grab a quick drink?" she whispered.

Yep, she needed a cold drink. She was getting all hot again with just being near the guys.

Daegen led her toward the refreshment table were several happily chatting people had already formed a line.

"You certainly are enjoying yourself," Daegen said in a low tone as he spoke close to her ear.

Milena nodded, felt her face flame as she remembered her earlier conversation with JJ back at the ranch house.

"You're really throwing yourself into dancing. I knew you were a quick learner," he continued.

Quick learner?

She wondered if she was imagining the sensual undertone in his voice regarding the last two words.

Oh my gosh! Could she do what JJ was doing? Sleep with three men?

"What's your pleasure? JJ's homemade blueberry juice, homemade strawberry juice, some iced tea, pop or coffee?" Daegen's question broke into her thoughts.

She hadn't even realized they were now in front of the area at the long table where the refreshments had been placed.

He had already grabbed a glass and a ladle in hand and looked at her expectantly.

"Blueberry juice, please," she answered, remembering that they had first met last year over blueberries.

She could not help but notice how big his hands were or how long his fingers looked. Strong hands to cup her breasts. Long fingers to piston into her vagina as Paul and Mitch suckled her nipples.

She stifled a moan as her pussy clenched. Or maybe she hadn't stifled her moan?

Suddenly Daegen seemed...tense as he handed her the glass filled with blueberry juice.

He looked at her kind of funny. Like he was really aware of her. Like he was truly noticing her.

It appeared her head had finally unstuck itself from that sandbox JJ had suggested.

Milena swallowed at her very parched throat and couldn't get her glass to her mouth soon enough. Her mouth was rewarded by a spectacular burst of blueberry sweetness. Cold liquid kissed the insides of her cheeks, and she moaned her appreciation, not caring that Daegen heard or that he was still staring at her.

"Good?" he asked in a deep, guttural tone that breathed over her senses like an erotic breeze.

"Very, very good," she answered, feeling the sweetness pucker the insides of her mouth.

"Of course, it's good!" JJ laughed as she sidled in between them.

"These are the blueberries you picked last summer when you were here."

"Really?" Both Daegen and herself asked in unison.

"Yes, I froze a bunch of the ones that were left over from what Milena picked. The guys and I picked more after you had left too. Every once in awhile I bake a pie during winter. These berries are the last so drink up and enjoy. Oh, and I need to let you know that Kelly and Jay will be bringing you home tonight, instead of me."

JJ's gaze captured Milena's attention.

"And I will be dropping in for a visit soon and we can finish our earlier conversation."

Milena's face flamed. She swiftly sipped more of the cold juice.

JJ winked at Milena and quickly moved on to her other guests.

"Our blueberries. How cool is that?" Daegen said with a smile as he ladled himself some juice too.

Suddenly he held up his glass.

"Cheers. Here's to second chances," he said.

Oh my.

She wondered what he meant by that?

She held up her glass and they clicked their glasses together.

"To second chances. Cheers," she murmured.

She hadn't even realized she'd been staring at his sexy five o'clock shadow while they both drank, until the music began again.

"Square dance! Let's go!" Daegen shouted.

He hooted, grabbed her empty glass, placed his and hers on a nearby table and then pulled her onto the dance floor.

Chapter Sixteen

Mitch and Paul leaned against the back wall and watched Milena and Daegen dance in a square dance frenzy while Blue called out the instructions using a microphone. There were four couples on the dance floor.

Everyone was laughing and thoroughly enjoying themselves as they circled left and then allemande left, do si do and on they went.

"She really likes it here," Mitch mused from beside Paul.

"She is a natural dancer. Look at how she moves," Paul answered.

She was like a flame when she danced. Bright and seductive. He couldn't keep his eyes off her.

"Hmm, dancing loosens her up," Mitch said quietly, thoughtfully. The inquisitive tone of his voice had Paul coming to full alert.

"What are you thinking?" he asked, not daring to take his eyes off Milena.

Damn, she was pretty.

"She'll have to loosen up more often is all I'm saying."

Paul smiled as he caught Mitch's wink.

The music suddenly died, and Blue announced this would be the last dance of the evening.

Disappointment rocked Paul.

"Talk later, last dance is mine," Mitch said with a smirk on his face.

And then Mitch was gone. A moment later he stepped onto the dance floor replacing Daegen.

Paul chewed on his lower lip as he studied Milena dancing a slow dance with Mitch. He was so close that he bet she could feel his package rubbing against her.

As he watched them dance, Mitch murmuring in her ear while he held her tight, Paul felt his cock throb with an intensity he hadn't experienced since he'd been an awkward teenager.

Wow, he couldn't wait to get back to the ranch because he was going to take one hell of a long cold shower tonight.

. . ⚓ . .

MILENA LOVED THE EROTIC way Mitch's body moved against hers. Smooth, slow and sexy. The hard feel of his shaft against her lower belly sent tingles of delight rushing through her. They danced to a slow country song and despite starting to feel tired, she wished the party was just beginning instead of winding down.

"Did you enjoy yourself at JJ's party?" Mitch breathed against her ear. His deep gravelly voice sounded intoxicating, and she closed her eyes and just went with the erotic rhythm he created.

"Yes" she whispered.

She loved the way his fingers intertwined with hers. Strong, hot fingers that promised plenty more pleasure like what she'd experienced that one afternoon by the wood splitter.

She wanted so much more pleasure at his hands. At their hands. All three men. Individually. Together.

Just like JJ was getting with Brady, Rafe and Dan.

She still could not fully believe what JJ had told her about her being in a relationship with three men. It was all surreal.

She couldn't wait for JJ to come and visit either. She had so many questions to ask her.

Like how did the men handle the jealousy between them? How did JJ let them know she wanted sex?

"Hey, sweetness," Mitch murmured softly. "We need to do this slow dancing more often. Enjoy ourselves more."

Enjoy ourselves more.

She swallowed as he rubbed his bristly cheek softly against hers. More tingles of eagerness exploded through her.

She inhaled his masculine scent. He smelled perfect. He wore a delicate aftershave that matched his own natural smell and there was a hint of pine too. She swore she could simply live like this forever.

But then the dance was over too soon, and they were all helping to put away the food, the dishes and then the chairs and tables.

By the time they were ready to go back home, she was too tired to freak out. Daegen, thankfully stuck to her side and helped her into Kelly's plane.

In the way that Kelly and Jay looked at each other with such love in their eyes, Milena knew they would be together forever.

From an aisle seat she watched the two of them as they kidded with each other in the cockpit and joked with Mitch and Paul who sat in seats right behind them.

Laughter tumbled through the air and mixed with the engine noise of the plane. She felt so safe with these people. The swaying of the plane was like a lullaby soothing any thoughts of monsters that dared to pop up. Before she knew it, she'd fallen asleep. That is until Daegen nudged her awake from the most peaceful slumber she'd ever been in.

"Hey sleepyhead, time to get up."

For a few seconds she had no idea where she was. Then she thought she was in prison but that didn't make sense with all the laughter. A split second later, she figured out it was time to get up and go to work but then she opened her eyes and the dark interior of the plane loomed into focus. She smiled as she remembered having so much fun at the party and yet she had dreaded going to it in the first place.

Silly woman.

"They're waiting on us. Everyone is out on the dock," Daegen said.

Dock!

Milena snapped fully awake, and nervousness sizzled through her. She heard the soft murmurs of people talking outside. Smelled the fresh air pushing in through the open door, chasing away the smell of oil.

She nodded jerkily and clutched yet another bag that JJ had thrust into her hands just before Milena had boarded the plane.

"Wait until you're alone before opening it," JJ had said. "It's something I bought for myself but never wore. I thought it might come in handy." There had been a teasing glint in her pretty brown eyes and then her friend had hugged her and said goodbye.

Milena had no idea how she could ever repay JJ for everything she had done for her. She was such a lovely friend to have. Such a wonderful support person.

As Milena stood, she was surprised when Daegen clutched her free hand and led her to the open door.

"Oh God," Milena whispered as she made the mistake of gazing out across the lake. The water seemed endless and beneath it she swore she saw the black water ripple. She flinched as an arm seemed to come up out of the lake.

"I'll go first," Daegen said quietly. "You turn around and keep your eyes straight ahead as you descend. I'll have a great view of your backside, so take your time."

The teasing tone of his voice did nothing to push away the quickly building terror.

Good heavens! She had to calm down!

Despite knowing the truth, that she was having a panic attack over the water and really over nothing but her imagination, perspiration blistered across her forehead.

She could barely stand still as Kelly and Jay hugged her goodbye. The urge to run off the dock and away from the water to land was so great that everything around her, the bush plane, the people, even the dark silhouette of the forest, seemed to vanish into her vortex of panic.

Daegen's hand settled upon the small of her back and returned her to reality. She spied Kelly and Jay climbing into the plane and Mitch and Paul stared at her with concern.

"We'll walk back. You guys take the four wheelers. I'm sure Milena has a touch of airsickness," she heard Daegen say.

Relief plowed through her and she silently thanked him for coming up with the excuse.

"I'll brew up some chamomile tea. It will help settle your stomach. Mom always had some waiting for us when we didn't feel well," Mitch said and then he hurried off to the furthest vehicle.

"And I've got some anti nausea meds if the tea doesn't work," Paul said with a reassuring grin.

"Thanks, guys," Milena said stiffly as she followed them onto solid land.

If the men hadn't been here, she swore she would have gotten down on her hands and knees and kissed the ground the instant she stepped onto it.

After Paul and Mitch roared off, the plane's engines became louder as the plane took off into the air. It shot by overhead. Soon it got quiet on the trail and then the frogs began to sing in a high-pitched frenzy.

Daegen finally spoke the words she'd been dreading.

"I'll make that appointment for you with my doctor. She might even let you take my next one."

"I can't. I'm needed here and I could never ask you to do that."

"You're not asking," Daegen replied.

With it being so dark she could barely see him in this forest trail, but she could hear the humor in his voice.

"We've been through this before, Daegen."

"And you said yes," he reminded her.

"I cannot afford a doctor like that," Milena blurted.

Sure, she was getting paid to work here, but those types of head doctors cost big money.

"Actually, it's part of the benefits package at Snowy Creek. You're an employee, you're covered under our insurance. Mitch put everything into effect once we knew help was coming. So, no worries."

There was no way she was so important to get benefits. Was she? Milena stopped as shock rocked her.

Daegen chuckled.

"What?" he looked down at her. "I guess we should have gone over the benefits package long before now. We were waiting for yours to come in the mail. Mitch is the one who does all that stuff. He put in a call to the insurance people pretty quick. He knows people who know the best benefits for the buck."

"You're serious?"

"Yes, a psychologist is fully covered. Of course, there is a yearly maximum, but let's not talk about that now."

He wasn't kidding. Oh, my goodness, she had medical benefits.

"Anyways, the reason I wanted to walk back with you is so I could tell you about what happened to me and why I had to see a psychologist in the first place."

His words sobered her.

"Oh, okay."

Wow, he was actually going to tell her something that was of so much importance to him? She felt honored, yet also humbled. She was sure that her fear of water was nothing compared to what he must have gone through in order to see a shrink.

"I was married once," he said.

He sounded sad and her heart ached with sorrow for him. She knew a little about his past because JJ had told her last summer, so the news about him being married before was not a surprise.

"Karen was pregnant with our first child. We were both so ecstatic. The timing would be I'd get back two months before our son was to be born."

He blew out a breath and tugged her along as he started to walk again.

Milena squeezed his hand with reassurance.

"There were complications in the last trimester and she and our son died. I was devastated and rolled up in guilt at not being there."

"I am so sorry," Milena whispered, her heart twisting with desolation.

"It was traumatic, and I still can't talk about it, but I had to learn to cope. Anyways that same day just before I got the news about my wife and son, there was an incident at our military camp. One of my closest friends decided he wanted to kill himself. I thought I could talk him out of it. Yeah, I know, naive of me."

Milena's thoughts whirled as he continued.

"The gang and I were getting ready for morning inspection right before breakfast. We were in the showers doing our usual joking when I realized I'd forgotten something. To this very day, I cannot remember what I'd forgotten, but when I'd returned to our bunkhouse, I found Jim sitting there on his bunk, staring at the floor, gun in one hand. I knew he'd been depressed about things we'd had to do in the military. Things we'd seen."

This time it was my Milena's turn to exhale a tense breath.

Daegen continued.

"I tried to talk to him. Told him everything was going to be alright. I would get him some help. That he had to think of his wife and kids. But I could tell he just wasn't listening. He had gone somewhere else in his mind. I kept trying to talk him into putting the gun down. I hadn't realized how bad it was for him until seconds before he raised the gun to his forehead, pulled the trigger and blew his brains out all over the wall behind him. A few of my comrades had just come into the barracks and had seen him pull the trigger. Their screams of horror still fill my head. It's what I've been working on with the shrink. Trying to get the screams out of my head."

"Oh my gosh!" Milena's gut clenched.

Daegen and his companions had actually seen something so horrific?

"Hey, I didn't mean to just spill it out. I apologize. I don't tell people about it, but this afternoon and tonight, seeing you experiencing panic...brought back memories. I thought I could handle my panic attacks by drinking and being a workaholic. I couldn't. I don't want that to happen to you. I don't want you to become a hermit, like some people. I got help and you can too. I want you to be free of whatever is tormenting you. It may be as simple as changing the way you think about something. You just need to find out what it is that freaks you out about water. I noticed something was off last summer when we first met and you looked terrified when I told you to get into the canoe after the bear scare, so we could outrun the storm."

Yes, she'd been uneasy back then around water. But it had evolved into something nasty since she'd been out of prison.

Milena laughed as she remembered something.

"That was the first time we met."

"Don't change the subject, girl. From personal experience I can tell you it will get worse, not better, unless you get an idea of what is causing your fear. My doctor can help you. I want you to come with me the next time I go. It won't be for a few weeks because she's gone on vacation. Just talk to her. What harm can it do?"

Milena hesitated as she thought about everything he had just said. It must have been hard for him to dredge up those memories and talk to her about them. The least she could do was give him an answer. Besides, he'd said a few weeks. That would give her some time to wrap her head around the idea and on having to go on another plane ride.

"Okay."

"Seriously?"

"Yeah."

"Then it's a date."

Milena laughed and shrugged her shoulders.

"If you call going to a head shrinker a date, then you need to get out more."

Daegen chuckled and nodded.

"You have a point there."

Milena hadn't even realized they were halfway across the meadow until she gazed up and saw the buttery glow of lights splashing out of the cabin windows. Her heart burst with happiness.

They were home.

Truth be told, she was tired from all the dancing, and she had to admit she had a lovely time over at Moose Ranch. But there was one thing she needed to find out.

"Hold on a minute, I want to ask you something," she said as she grabbed his elbow, making him stop.

She figured it was time to confront him about what had happened at JJ's party.

"What did you guys have against Jay? Everything calmed down once you guys found out he was engaged. What gives?"

She could see his face quite clearly now in the moonlit glow and noticed a change in his facial expression.

Embarrassment?

Huh, interesting.

"Oh? I guess you noticed?"

"Of course, I noticed."

She wanted to mention what JJ had said about them being jealous. She'd thought the same thing, but she decided against verbalizing her thoughts. Just in case she was wrong. She certainly didn't want to make a fool out of herself.

"I guess it was my fault. I kind of put a stupid idea into their heads."

"What stupid idea?"

He slipped his hand against hers and squeezed gently.

Oh my. What a sweet gesture.

She expected him to let go of her hand, but he didn't. Instead, his voice lowered into a velvety softness that caressed her senses.

"I considered him...competition."

"So, JJ was right!" she blurted.

Daegen grinned.

"What kind of naughty ideas is JJ putting into your pretty little head?"

Visions of ménages.

But she didn't dare say that out loud.

"She said she thought all three of you guys were jealous."

Oh my gosh, shut up, Milena.

She wished she could shut up, but she was on a roll.

"And what do you think about it if we were?" he asked softly.

Oh gosh, now she was on the spot. Her cheeks grew hot again.

Damn cheeks!

But now was her opportunity to ask questions.

"I would think that would be interesting."

"Just interesting?" he asked, humor lacing his voice.

"I would also ask if there would jealousy between the three of you if..."

Oh, dear Lord, what in the world was she doing? Stop asking questions, Milena! You cannot have a relationship with these men. They are your bosses!

"There's no jealousy between the three of us. We know about the kisses. We've been wondering if you'd be...receptive to all three of us...and you."

His words were like an explosion of confusion and excitement whirling inside of her.

How did one answer something like that?

Milena suddenly realized she had the upper hand in all of this. She had the power over them. They were unsure about her. Unsure about how she would react to their attentions.

This dominance she had over them was something that hadn't really entered her mind.

"Milena?" he prodded.

Excitement pummelled her.

"How about you guys give me some time to think about this predicament."

"Predicament?" He sounded surprised.

This was going to be fun.

"Yeah, I need a little bit of time," she answered, feeling the control surge through her like lightning.

She should have told him she needed a whole lot of time. It might take time to get her bearings. They were giving her the opportunity to bring her naughty fantasies to life. One didn't just jump into a foursome ménage relationship just like that.

Did they?

JJ did. A voice echoed in her brain.

No one is here to judge.

"I'll give you an answer soon," Milena said. Her voice sounded throaty. Sexy.

He let go of her hand as she moved toward the cabin.

"Okay. I'll see you in the morning," he called out.

"I'll be here!" she called back.

Suddenly she wasn't tired anymore. Suddenly she felt as if she had all the energy in the world.

. . ⚓ . .

"WHAT THE HELL IS SHE up to?" Mitch grumbled beneath his breath as he shovelled manure from a stall into a wheel barrel.

It had been several days since Daegen had told them about his conversation regarding she would let them know if she was willing to be in a foursome relationship.

The morning after the party, she'd acted as if nothing had changed. Hadn't mentioned anything about Daegen's conversation to him the times he'd worked with her since the party. She had simply performed like one of the guys. Just like they'd been treating her.

Man, was that her answer? That she just wanted to keep being one of the guys?

"There's nothing we can do about it," Paul said from the next stall where he'd been examining a retired racehorse who seemed to be favoring his left foreleg. He'd said he suspected it was arthritis.

"Daegen said that she said she would let us know," Paul continued.

"It's been days. Maybe she's dragging it out so she can tease us," Mitch growled.

"All I can say is every day that goes by I find her more and more attractive," Paul called out.

"Yeah, I got the same problem, even if she does look like a sexy scarecrow in her work clothes. It's like look at me but don't touch me," Mitch complained.

"If she wanted to be treated like one of the guys then why did she ask for the afternoon off so she could go back to the cabin and cook supper for us?" Daegen asked.

Mitch whirled around to find Daegen standing in the doorway of the stall totting a frown.

"She did?" Paul asked as he suddenly joined Daegen.

"She did. Left for the cabin about an hour ago. Said for us to be back for supper at six."

Paul grimaced.

"The last time she cooked...she burned the roast. She hasn't been in the kitchen since," Mitch reminded them.

"Maybe she learned something from Jane Sunflower when she was there? She was in the kitchen with her helping to make supper and then breakfast," Daegen said. Hope burned bright in his words.

"I hope so, because I really don't feel like having dry half-burned roast beef again," Mitch grumbled.

"Hey, I thought I did a pretty good job rescuing that meat. I didn't hear any complaints when you gobbled it down," Daegen sounded hurt, but he winked at Paul.

"I was starving. Hungry people will eat just about anything," Mitch returned.

"Good. Then you can eat the rest of Paul's concrete cookies tonight. I'm going to start exercising the horses at the other barn. See you guys at six." Daegen followed his comments with a heinous laugh and headed back down the corridor.

"Get lost!" Mitch shouted back.

Paul laughed as he grabbed the horse's reigns and led him out of the stall. He liked the easy-going camaraderie between the three of them. They really fit good together.

"So, what's wrong with his leg? Why's he favoring it?" Mitch asked as he came up behind Paul with a wheel barrel full of manure and straw.

"Arthritis. I'll have to get in touch with the owner and ask permission to do an x-ray."

"Good thing we have an x-ray machine and generator out here," Mitch replied.

"All is good, my man," Paul reassured. "I've got almost everything I need in stock. I'm going to start working on a brace for the knee too. If my suspicions are right about the arthritis, the brace will help for awhile."

"Sounds good. I've just got one more stall to do, then I'll get to exercising them. Is he okay to do a small trail walk today?"

"I'll do it as soon as I get back from contacting the owner. Can I borrow your cell? I forgot mine back at the cabin."

Mitch nodded, pulled out his phone and handed it to him.

"Thanks. I'll leave him in a nearby paddock for now and tend to him when I get back."

"Okay, but make sure you keep your gun on hand. You never know if those poachers are still around."

Paul nodded.

"Will do."

As Paul swung by the office, he picked up his shoulder holster and gun and led the horse out of the cool interior of the barn into the bright sunshine. The horse neighed, happy to be outdoors again.

Paul grinned.

"You're gonna be fine. I'll get you all fixed up, boy," he said and then led the horse to the paddock.

The horse neighed again.

Paul smiled. If he didn't know any better, he swore the horse was saying thank you.

. . ༄ . .

"SAW SOME SMOKE ABOUT three miles to the south of us when I was making a phone call from the ridge," Paul said as he and Mitch joined Daegen outside the front of the cabin.

Daegen had just arrived via atv and had been about to go inside when the two men rumbled up with their machine.

"We really should go down and take a look," Daegen said.

He didn't like the idea of intruders nearby. But the cabin was situated at the southern boundary of the land they leased from the government so anyone south of them wasn't trespassing because it was crown land.

"We have a full-time job here taking care of all the horses. Kind of hard to get away," Paul reminded him.

"I know. But if the poachers are there..." Daegen said softly.

"Let's talk about it over supper, see if we can work something out," Mitch replied as he stomped up the stairs.

Daegen followed and Paul was right behind him.

Mitch opened the screen door and stopped so abruptly that Daegen crashed into Mitch and Paul banged right into Daegen.

"What the hell? Why are you stopping?" Daegen cursed as he tried to push Mitch forward, but quickly stopped pushing as he looked over Mitch's shoulder.

Paul let out a low whistle.

He must have seen the same thing they were seeing.

The kitchen table was decked out in a nice red and white checkered tablecloth. A fresh crop of white daffodils had been placed in the centre and there were a couple of casserole dishes there as well. The table was all set with red napkins and wine glasses filled with red wine.

But that wasn't what was catching their full attention.

The three beds had been moved together into one large bed and Milena lay sideways on the bed closest to them, her elbow propping up her head as she stared at them with the cutest smile and really nice pink blushing cheeks.

She wore...well, he wasn't sure what she was wearing. But it was next to nothing.

Wow. Holy cow.

• • ❧ • •

MILENA'S HEART WAS racing as the three men stared at her.

They all seemed so surprised. Frozen in time. Paralyzed.

She'd laugh if she wasn't so nervous. She wore a red baby doll outfit, and it certainly wasn't like the baby doll pyjamas she'd worn to bed when she was kid.

This outfit was...well, really erotic. Very naughty.

The night after JJ's party, Milena had opened the bag that JJ had given her, and she'd found this breathtaking mesh and lace baby doll open front chemise and G-string thong along with an arrangement of butt plugs.

The clothing was so gorgeous, she'd never seen anything so beautiful and carnal before.

The top had a plunging V neck with a cute red bowtie and there was a scalloped lace trim hem that dropped to mid-thigh.

She'd instantly loved it. It appeared the men did too because they just kept staring at her.

"I made you guys supper, and then I had a nice leisurely shower and just to let you know...I'm dessert," she said in a husky voice that she swore didn't belong to her.

They still hadn't said anything, so she forced herself to continue despite her nervousness.

"I've been outfitting myself with various sizes of butt plugs over the last few days," she admitted.

All three men cursed softly and brightened.

Okay, they were making noises and they liked what she was saying. That was a good sign.

Her heart beat faster.

"I'm ready for all of you to take me. I want you to make all of my naughty fantasies come true. Make your fantasies about me, come true."

As she said the words, her pussy and ass clenched with anticipation and her cheeks grew even warmer. She swore her breasts felt fuller, her nipples longer.

Her breath backed up into her lungs as she noted their interested gazes.

Okay she was doing something right.

She held her breath and awaited their next move.

. . ⚜ . .

PAUL COULDN'T BELIEVE what he was seeing. Had he somehow been kicked in the head by the horse he'd been tending to today and fallen into some sort of hot coma? If so, he needed to stay unconscious.

Milena was gorgeous.

Never in his wildest fantasies had he conjured up such beauty. And here they'd been treating her like one of the guys.

They should be shot for being so stupid.

But not before he could carry out her fantasy.

. . ⚜ . .

MITCH SWORE HE'D STEPPED into an erotic world as he stared at Milena. She'd put on makeup and one hell of a sexy lingerie. The flimsy garment showed off her every sensual curve and Mitch knew he would never look at her like a scarecrow again.

She was a goddess and it appeared she was seducing *them*.

He'd definitely died and gone to heaven, and he never wanted to go back to earth again.

The air inside the cabin was electrifying. He was getting so hot just looking at her. He wanted out of his clothes. Now.

· · ⌒∲⌒ · ·

MILENA FELT HER EYES widen as the men stepped into the cabin one by one.

"No one's hungry for food right now," Mitch said as he came toward her.

"We'll shower first—" Paul said but she cut him off.

"Don't shower. I want you just the way you are. Sweaty and animal."

Daegen swore beneath his breath.

"Are you sure about this?" Mitch asked as he began to unbutton his shirt.

Milena blew out a tense breath and nodded. She could feel the moisture between her thighs.

She'd never been more sure of anything in her life. She wanted them to make love to her.

Chapter Seventeen

Milena's body hummed with lust as she observed the three men slowly undress. She couldn't take her eyes off them. Their presence was all around her. Their unique scents, their hot gazes as they watched her, their body heat searing across the room into her.

Her mind was spinning. Was this really happening? Or was she going to panic and change her mind?

Three men. Was she going to have sex with three men? Had she lost her mind and gone to fantasy heaven?

The men moved in unison, like well-organized strippers, removing their shirts and she enjoyed the scenery.

Sleek muscles, rounded muscles. Muscles that bulged as they dropped their pants and underwear to reveal thick, long cocks.

Her thighs tightened at the erotic view. Her pussy clenched. Her ass gripped empty air. She missed the throbbing of the smooth butt plug she'd worn over the past few days, especially the largest one she'd used last. It had filled her to perfection. Just like she knew her cowboys would do.

She could barely breathe as Paul stepped forward. Her mouth was so dry with nervousness. He sat down on the bed beside her. He smelled good. Of the outdoors, and a tinge of sweat.

His eyes were dark and lusty. Gleaming with yearning.

"You are so beautiful," he whispered in a hoarse voice.

She was? She must have done something right with the makeup and her hair.

Inwardly, she praised herself. Outwardly, she hoped she appeared confident, despite her edginess.

"Don't be afraid. We know this is your first time with us. We'll go easy," he whispered.

Well, so much for appearances.

She wanted to tell him not to do her any favors, but he leaned forward, and his mouth seared over hers in a possessive kiss that splintered any protests she might have had.

Sweet pleasure burst through her and she eagerly kissed him back. He cupped her clothed breast, massaging her flesh. She writhed against him as tension built inside her.

His other hand cupped the back of her neck and pulled her deeper into the kiss. Sparks flew behind her eyes as their tongues clashed and mated.

She moaned at the intensity. Cried out as Paul broke the kiss and breathed against her mouth.

"You kiss really nice. And you look really hot," he whispered.

Oh my, another compliment. Should she say thanks?

"Now let's get up, so the guys can get a good look at you too."

Milena nodded jerkily and opened her eyes as he held her hand and tugged her into standing position with an ease that made it seem like she was featherlight.

Daegen and Mitch moved in around her. Mitch's gaze was gentle yet hungry. His erection long and jerking. But her view of Mitch was cut off as Daegen stepped in front of her.

Need uncoiled inside of her as she reached out and flattened her hands against the wide expanse of his steel-muscled chest. Corded muscles flexed beneath her palms as she smoothed over his nipples.

He moaned and then he kissed her. His mouth coming down on hers with such a fierceness, she could literally feel him claiming her as his own. She drew her hands lower, over his rigid abdomen and then gently stroked the length of his ultra-thick, pulsing erection. She could feel the quivers rock through him as she touched his hot steel-encased flesh.

She took her time exploring his shaft. Loving the way it jerked against her palms. He moaned harder and kissed her more desperately.

"She's got lube here." She heard Paul say in a strangled voice.

"You've done your homework, haven't you, baby," Daegen said as he broke the kiss and panted against her mouth.

"And here are our condoms," Mitch whispered. "I'll just lay them out all nice for us."

So, it *had* been them who'd placed the condoms in her knapsack.

She was breathing hard as Daegen slipped the straps of her teddy down her arms allowing her breasts to spill free.

"Nice. Very nice," he murmured.

He then lifted her breasts and dipped his head and sucked her right nipple into his mouth. He sucked with a heated fierceness that had her gasping and clenching her hands around his erection. She moaned as he moved to her other nipple, sucking with fervour, creating pleasure and pain.

Somewhere she could hear the slurp of lube followed by the rips of plastic and foil.

Condoms.

Her nipples were aching as Daegen continued his erotic assault, switching back and forth, licking and lapping. Sucking and biting, until her buds felt as hard as pebbles and her pussy and ass were desperately clenching air.

"You taste so good," Daegen muttered after he let her nipple go with a pop and then his mouth found hers again.

She kissed him back. Her lips seared against his as she lost control of her senses and began gyrating her hips. She felt Daegen move his body off to the left side, taking her head a bit to the side as he kept kissing her. She didn't have time to question what was going on because she jerked and shuddered, moaned and cried out in surprise as a hot condom-sheathed cockhead touched her vaginal opening.

"Easy," Mitch murmured. He was talking in that soft tone he used on the horses, when he was grooming them, keeping them calm.

She was anything but calm.

"We'll go nice and slow for your first time," Paul whispered from behind her. He lifted her hair and kissed the left side of her neck. Tingles and sensations whipped through her at his touches.

Her senses were overwhelming her now.

Daegen's kiss grew deeper, darker. She adored the firm touch of his lips, the aggressive plunge of his tongue into her mouth.

Mitch pushed his condom-sheathed penis into her vagina. She felt every thick throbbing inch of him. His jerking flesh pushed against her straining muscles as he entered. Her pussy clenched around him, and he groaned.

He rubbed his chest against her tender nipples, igniting arousal.

Daegen's kisses were making her heady and she clasped Mitch's waist to steady herself.

Mitch withdrew.

"Just let yourself go and I'll take you nice and slow," Paul murmured from behind her.

Milena swallowed nervously and forced herself to relax as much as she could, but she whimpered into Daegen's mouth as Paul's lubed shaft pressed against her sphincter. She moaned as he pushed in further.

Pressure. So much pressure.

Deeper and deeper, he pushed. She breathed into the sultry bites of pain and enjoyed the swelling pleasure. Paul's every throbbing inch was intense as his hot solid flesh stretched into her ass so unbelievably.

Until the assorted sizes of butt plugs she'd used, she had no idea she could take a penis so thick into her anus.

"That's it, sweetie. Stay nice and relaxed," Paul muttered against her ear.

He pushed deeper, making her arch against Mitch's body.

"Daeg, she's killing me here," Mitch said in a strangled voice.

Suddenly Daegen broke his mind-shattering kisses and she whimpered in protest as empty air replaced him. Then Mitch's mouth slammed over hers, his tongue entering her mouth and her tongue met his full on, unleashing a barrage of pleasure, making her shiver.

Paul slowly withdrew and then as if knowing Paul was out of her, Mitch thrust into her.

His cock was large, thick and pulsated against vaginal muscles that hadn't been used in this way before. His thickness felt oh so good. The heat from his velvet-hard shaft burned her beautifully.

And then all too soon Mitch withdrew.

She moaned her protest into his mouth.

"You're liking it, aren't you, baby," Mitch muttered against her lips.

She wanted to tell him she was *loving* this, but she couldn't form a word. Her mouth felt swollen, and her lips tingled with pleasure. Her body was exploding with senses she'd never experienced before.

The two men began an erotic driving into her.

One in, the other out. In and out.

Perspiration blistered across her body as she accepted them.

Their shafts burned into her. Stretched her. Impaled her. Inflamed her senses.

The pleasures mounted. She fought for breaths.

They were pushing her toward something insane. Something that would shatter her. She wanted it. Wanted it bad.

Their grunts were like music. The slapping of flesh against flesh, an aphrodisiac.

They drove pleasure through her and every time she thought she would lose control and climax, they slowed their pistoning and set her back off the brink.

Oh God! Help me! They're killing me here.

Their plunges into her were perfectly timed. Her pussy and then her anus clenched around their cocks. Again, and again.

They increased the pace of their thrusts, their cocks going deeper and deeper. Faster and faster.

She became suspended on agony. The explosion was building and building.

And then Mitch ripped his mouth away from hers and Mitch and Paul entered her at the same time. Drove so deeply that she shattered.

She screamed at the intensity of being double penetrated, the thick flesh filling her to perfection. She convulsed like a rag doll writhing out of control as pleasure arced through her like sizzling jolts of lightning.

Her self control was destroyed as she embraced the carnal waves and flew into idyllic oblivion.

She heard them cry out as they reached their peaks. Heard their groans and moans as spasms ripped through her pussy and ass, milking their condom-sheathed cocks.

She was barely aware that the pleasure had ebbed away when she heard Daegen's strangled voice from somewhere.

"I need her, bring her to me on the bed. I need her bad."

Mitch chuckled in a hoarse kind of way. She felt their cocks leave her with suctioning pops and she felt empty. So empty and lost.

She wanted more. Wanted them to take her again.

She started keening in protest and Mitch's mouth sipped at her lips. Then he lifted her into his arms.

"Daegen's turn, baby. Let him fill you with pleasure too," he murmured against her mouth.

Oh, Daegen! Yes, she wanted him.

Excitement flared as she felt herself being lowered onto the bed. Someone spread her legs wide.

Finally, she was able to open her eyes to see Daegen climbing over her. His gaze intense, his cock so swollen and flushed purple.

"I've been wanting to do this since we watched Mitch doing it," he said thickly.

They'd seen Mitch and her? Something naughty snapped inside of her and she creamed at the thought of Daegen and Paul watching Mitch going down on her that afternoon by the wood splitter.

And now Daegen was doing it!

And Mitch and Paul stood on each side of the bed watching while they stroked their shafts, which were quickly engorging again. Their gazes blazed as their eyes locked onto what Daegen was doing.

Milena's heart thundered as she watched Daegen's head lower. She arched her hips toward him, and he slid his hands beneath her thighs, cupping her, holding her steady.

"Enjoy," Daegen muttered.

His mouth fused over her pussy, and she cried out at the quivering sensations racing through her.

She closed her eyes again, melting into the desire. His lips sucked at her labia, pulling her tender flesh and nibbling until she cried out from the pleasure pain.

She writhed as his tongue lapped at her ultra-sensitive clit. Moaned as hot caressing hands smoothed over her breasts. Fingers tweaked and pulled her nipples, making them feel so big.

Paul and Mitch. It had to be.

Daegen's tongue dipped into her vagina, and she shuddered, her body tightening, as he began pistoning his tongue into her like a miniature cock. Nerve endings sparked and she gasped.

She was on fire.

"I need to take her mouth," came Mitch's strangled gasp.

She felt the top of bed move and opened her eyes to find Mitch kneeling by her head. He was gazing down at her, his eyes so dark and illuminous. She'd never seen his eyes shining so brightly with need before. His teeth were clenched and muscles in his jaw popped.

He was so hot for her. It fascinated her.

"Open your mouth for me, baby," he whispered. His voice was so hoarse it didn't even sound like him.

She did as he asked, and he aimed his erection between her lips. She was overwhelmed with the sudden need to have his shaft filling her mouth. She swiped her tongue against his hot cockhead and Mitch moaned as if in pain. She licked him again and again, loving the smooth round cockhead.

She wanted to touch his cock and so she reached out and wrapped her hand around the thick base of his jerking flesh.

Mitch cursed.

He was so hard. Like a steel rod. Yet his skin was silky soft.

She lapped at Mitch's penis, just like Daegen was now licking her clenching vaginal opening, sucking the cream of lust from her body.

Mitch growled at her.

The guttural sound made an animalistic hunger invade her. She wanted to mate. To fuck. To claim them all as her own.

She opened her mouth wider, and Mitch slipped his hard length between her lips filling her completely as his cockhead touched the back of throat, she thought she might gag, but he moved back an inch.

"Baby," Mitch groaned. "I need you, bad."

She didn't know what he wanted her to do so she licked the underside of his flesh and then started sucking.

Mitch gave a harsh shout. She sucked harder, giving him a firm suction.

He withdrew. Thrust into her again.

His flesh grew even harder. His strokes faster.

Pleasure burst through her body as Daegen's tongue began plunging into her again.

"I'm going to come, baby. In your mouth," Mitch moaned.

He thrust harder. Once. Twice.

And then his cock hardened some more and jerked like crazy and then the hot jets of his cream shot into the back of her mouth.

Instinctively she swallowed and swallowed some more, loving that she had Mitch's semen inside of her. The idea of these men accepting her, loving her in this way, aroused her to new heights.

"I have to take her, now!" Daegen growled.

In a flash, Mitch withdrew, and the bed shifted as Daegen came over her. He was settling his torso between her thighs, and she felt his thick condom-sheathed cockhead nudge against her soaked pussy. She reached out to him as he came down upon her, digging her nails into the taut muscles in his back.

"You taste so beautiful, sweetie and now I need you bad. Really bad," he said thickly.

"I need you too," she whispered.

She held him tight as he thrust his cock into her, and his mouth melted over her lips like a conqueror.

His impalement filled her with enormous heat, and she cried out as the pleasure ripped her apart. He withdrew and thrust into her again. And again.

She exploded.

Her body convulsed. Her mind fragmented. She bucked.

Pleasure waves tore into her. She gasped into his mouth as he took her harder and faster.

Her pussy gripped him and spasmed around him. Made love to the mighty intruder.

Shudders rocked her as she split apart and shattered within the glorious gratification.

Daegen groaned into her mouth as he came, and they both flew headlong into a raging world of bliss.

And Milena knew she'd never be the same again.

Her three men took her over and over again. One at a time and then two at a time. It was insane. It was beautiful. It was her new life, and she knew she was going to love it.

Sometime during the early morning, they all fell asleep, their arms and legs tangled around each other. Her sleep was filled with hot ménages and even in her dreams she couldn't wait to wake up so they could have sex again.

But in the morning when she awoke, Milena was alone.

•• ❧ ••

"OH MAN, IT WAS TORTURE leaving her there like Sleeping Beauty," Daegen complained as he sat astride Big Red, a horse that had once been used in rodeo shows and had been retired to here by his owners.

Its back sagged beneath Daegen, but Paul had insisted the horse still needed to be exercised and so Daegen had picked him for this morning's first leisurely walk along one of their wood trails. According to Paul, this trail was the horse's favorite because it was the easiest.

"She's cute when she sleeps, isn't she? Her mouth parted slightly, her lips rosy red," Mitch said with a laugh from behind Daegen.

"Stop with the teasing," Daegen snapped as visions of his pulsing shaft thrusting in and out of Milena's perfect mouth raced through his mind.

"Sorry, I just can't help it. I feel so free today. She's the best thing that's ever happened to me."

"You sure didn't say that when she first arrived here," Paul called out to Mitch from the back of the line.

Paul rode a white mare who'd won plenty of medals, trophies and money as a show horse. The horse was on hiatus until July when her owner wanted her back.

"Excuse me for living. I just didn't want any complications," Mitch retorted.

"Complications like Milena is just what we needed, right, Daegen?" Paul shouted.

Daegen chuckled.

"Who knew she was such a wildcat in bed," Mitch said.

"She's absolutely the perfect woman. You better kiss your sister's ass big time if she ever calls you back. I expect you left her some really not so nice messages," Daegen reminded.

"Hey, that's my sister's ass you're talking about. I will apologize the next time I talk to her."

Daegen nodded.

"Good. Cause Milena is a keeper." Paul said.

Silently Daegen sent up a prayer of thanks to his late wife. She must have had something to do with having

Milena sent here. He hadn't felt this joyful since the day he'd gotten married.

Hell, maybe he was even happier now.

Daegen nodded.

"Yes, she's a keeper. One of those forever girls," he said.

He smiled when Mitch and Paul gave affirmatives.

Yeah, he was happier now.

· · ⚘ · ·

SHE'D BEEN GIVEN THE day off!

Milena sat at the kitchen table, dressed in a robe that she'd seen Paul wearing a couple of times. It smelled of him and she loved his scent and how warm it made her feel.

Daegen had left a note for her, and she'd read it for like the twentieth time since her first cup of coffee. She was nursing her third cup now, her body feeling sexy sore and her mind ecstatic.

Sore from all that hot and heavy sex and ecstatic because tonight she knew there would be more of the same. And she was more than ready.

But she wasn't sure if she should be offended that suddenly she wasn't being treated like one of the guys or if she should be happy that she had the opportunity to try out another one of Jane Sunflower's recipes on them.

Yesterday she'd prepared a baked potato casserole using strips of bear steak, which she'd found in the cave cooler, replacing the lamb in Jane's recipe. And she'd also made a bean casserole using the preserved yellow and green beans and onions she'd remembered seeing when she'd been out at that cave one night with Daegen.

She must have been pretty wiped out not to have heard them getting up this morning. From the note Daegen had left, he said they'd taken most of the food she'd made yesterday with them and had put a covered plate for her down in the cooler beneath the house.

Her stomach growled reminding her about her hunger.

Within minutes she'd dressed, retrieved the food, heated it on the stove and was enjoying every single bite when she heard an airplane approach and fly overhead, but very low. She didn't know if the guys were expecting an order today, so she quickly finished her meal and walked outside onto the porch.

It was a nice warm, sunny morning and not a cloud in the sky. She'd missed seeing the plane, but she could hear the low roar from the direction of the lake. She should go down to meet them, but the mere thought of going near the water made her uneasy. If it was an order, they could leave that on that shoddy dock. She'd send one of the guys down when they returned.

Milena headed back inside and put a pot of water onto the stove to heat so she could wash the dishes. She looked at the bed and bit her bottom lip at the tangle of blankets and pillows.

What if company was coming? They would guess by the condom wrappings and the mess that something had happened here.

Uneasiness shifted through her and Milena went into cleaning mode. She tore the bedding off, maneuvered the beds apart and then redid all the beds with fresh sheets.

And just in time too!

"Hello! Anyone home?" Came a shout from just outside the cabin.

That sounded like Blue!

Milena took one more look around.

Phew! Everything appeared in reasonable order.

Except she'd forgotten to tuck away the condom boxes!

"I'll be out in a minute!" Milena called out as she scrambled to put the boxes away.

Maybe Blue would get the hint not to come in?

"I can only stay a few minutes. I need to tell you something," Blue shouted back.

Good heavens! She was at the screen door!

Milena slid the boxes inside a drawer of the night table and whirled around to see Blue, her halo of blonde hair framing her pretty face with her hands cupped against the screen door in order to see inside.

Had she seen Milena hiding the condoms?

Her face suddenly flushed with heat.

"Hi! What a nice surprise. I was just cleaning up. Come on in for some coffee. It's fresh," Milena invited as she rushed over and opened the screen door.

Blue shook her head and frowned. She appeared distressed.

"I'm glad someone is here, or I would have had to leave a note. I'm running behind on my mail route, but I wanted to drop in and let you know I just spied smoke from a campfire about a mile south of your cabin just near the shore of another lake there. It could be interior campers, but it also could be poachers. Can you tell the guys?"

Adrenalin shot through Milena.

Possible poachers. This was an opportunity she could not miss.

"I can grab Paul at the barn, and we can go take a look."

Blue nodded and smiled.

"Thanks. I wasn't sure if you guys could spare the time."

"We'll make time, Blue. How about you take one of the atvs that's right outside. It'll help put you back on your schedule. The key is in the ignition. Do you know how to work one?"

Blue nodded, looking thankful. Then she smiled, her blue eyes twinkling with amusement.

Was that a teasing smile?

"Thanks, Milena. Hey, don't work so hard. You're looking flushed."

Impulsively Milena's hands cupped her cheeks.

Wow, her cheeks were burning!

"Do I?" she said, injecting surprise into her voice.

Blue chuckled and waved as she bounced down the stairs. A moment later, she was on an atv, helmet buckled and on her way.

Milena chewed her lower lip as she rushed back into the cabin to remove the boiling water from the stove and to grab her socks and shoes.

Within minutes, she'd straddled the one atv left and was racing across the track along the fence line, at the edge of the meadow. She knew Paul was working at the closest barn this morning. She came to the gate, opened it and drove in, then closed it again behind her.

Several horses were leisurely grazing in the meadow as she passed them, and her thoughts turned back to the smoke Blue had seen.

What if they were just campers? But what if they were the poachers?

Minutes later, she parked in front of the looming barn, removed her helmet and tooted the horn.

Well, if they were campers, then that was a good thing. But if the poachers were around, then what?

She was sure Paul would know what to do if the latter were the case. She tooted the horn again. But Paul didn't show himself. Perhaps he was busy. She'd have to go in after him.

Quickly she entered the barn and frowned realizing how quiet it was in here. She called out several times and knew instinctively no one was here.

Shoot!

In a rush she checked the stalls and then the two back bedrooms.

Empty.

She'd have to head over to the other barn.

Ten minutes later, she stood in the yard of the other building. But no one was here either.

Uneasiness sputtered through her.

Where were they?

• • ～ • •

"WHAT IS THE PROBLEM?" Mitch asked impatiently as he waited while Paul examined the horse Mitch had been riding.

Mitch had noticed a few minutes ago the horse was limping and so they'd stopped to take a look.

"He's got a stone wedged in the horseshoe. Anyone have a jackknife? I'm going to have to pry it out."

"Left mine back at the barn," Daegen muttered.

"Me too," Mitch said.

This was just supposed to be a normal morning exercise for the horses. Time was a wasting! He'd never been one for having a routine screwed up. He liked things to go nice and smooth.

Oh hell, who was he kidding? He just wanted to get back to the barn and hope that Milena might come out to visit them, even if she'd been given the day off.

"Well, I don't have anything on me that can get this out. Gonna have to walk the horse back," Paul said with a frown.

Mitch mentally calculated how long that would take. They never took the horses too far. All the trails were relatively short and easy. The animals were here for respite, not training.

"Why didn't you bring your bag?" Mitch complained as he stroked the uneasy horse.

"Because I didn't expect there to be a problem?" Paul snapped back.

"Alright. Just relax," Daegen said with a laugh. "I can walk the horse back to the barn. You guys head on back. Maybe you'll get lucky, and Milena will be there ready and waiting for you. Heaven knows you two need some fun in the sun with her while I work my ass off running this place."

Mitch shook his head and smiled. Daegen always did diffuse a tense situation with humor.

Paul let the horse's leg drop. He was smiling too.

"No, you two head on back. I'll stay with the horse and start back slowly. Best I keep an eye on him. Mitch, you take my horse," Paul instructed.

"Okay, thanks. I'll bring your bag out," Mitch said.

"I left it on the office desk."

Mitch nodded and walked over to where Paul had tied his horse.

A couple of minutes later Daegen and he were trotting their horses back along the trail from the direction they'd come.

Leave it to a vet to forget his black bag, Mitch thought as he rode. But then again, it was rare that Paul came along during the exercise regime. He preferred to check the health of the horses pretty near every day while the exercises were being done. Which was a good thing. As Paul would say, it was always best to catch something early, especially with the older horses.

Mitch just wished he'd caught on earlier that he was falling hard for Milena. He tried to imagine life without her. What would have happened had she never come here? Or if they came and took her back to prison?

Man, he wished he would never have to find out.

· · ~~~ · ·

IT TOOK ABOUT HALF an hour to get back to the barn, despite Mitch wanting to go faster. But he knew it was best to take it easy with the horses entrusted into their care. He didn't want to have another emergency, especially with Paul temporarily out of commission back on the trail.

As they rode into the yard, he breathed a sigh of relief.

"I'll get the horse a pail of water and you go on in and get Paul's bag," Daegen said.

Mitch was grateful. It was getting hot outside and he wouldn't mind finding a few minutes of relief inside the coolness of the barn.

After grabbing a couple of cups of water at the pump, he headed into the barn and then the office. Paul's black bag was right there on the desk where he said it was...and propped against the bag was a large sheet of paper.

Mitch's heart began to pump with excitement.

Milena had been here, and she'd left a note. Oh man, he could do with some down time right about now. Maybe have a quick tryst in one of the stalls?

He chuckled as he reached for the note.

He just couldn't believe his luck, falling for a girl like Milena. None of the women he'd dated could shine a candle to her. She was tough, yet vulnerable.

Gorgeous and sexy *and* she enjoyed sex. With all three of them!

He read the message and his stomach rolled as if he'd been sucker punched.

Blue dropped by. Smoke about a mile to the south of us. Could be the poachers.

Sorry, I didn't want to wait. Off to investigate.

Milena.

"Shit!" Mitch swore.

"What's wrong?" Daegen asked from the office doorway. He held a glass of water in his hand and was frowning.

"I'm going to kill her. I cannot believe that she went alone!" He slapped the paper against Daegen's chest as he passed him and headed outdoors.

He gazed along the southern perimeter of the forest. Nothing moved. Just a couple of crows swirling around up in the sky. Where the fuck had she gone? South could be anywhere?

"Hey, take it easy. She's a careful girl," Daegen said as he rushed up behind him. But Mitch recognized worry in his voice.

From near the water pump, the horse continued drinking from the bucket of water. He should give the horse a break. Or catch a fresh one and head into the woods after her. Wherever the hell that might be. But that was a bad idea as a horse could get injured by branches or stumble into a hole breaking a leg. The terrain was too rough for these expensive horses without a groomed trail to follow.

Another idea hit him.

"I'm going up the bluff and see where the smoke is. We can find her easier that way," Mitch said as he peered up the nearby hill.

Daegen shook his head.

"No, by the time you get up and back it'll be another hour lost. I can track her. I'm an expert, remember? It will be faster that way. You need to get back to Paul. If the poachers are around, we need to be careful. Is his gun in the black bag?"

Mitch opened the bag and sure enough, Paul's gun was tucked in there. It was loaded. The safety catch was on. Mitch's rifle was hanging on a hook inside the barn.

Man, they'd been stupid and careless leaving weapons lying around instead of under lock and key. Anyone could have come and stolen the guns.

They'd been slacking off where the guns were concerned over the last little while.

"I'll take your rifle with me. After you get to Paul, head up to the bluff and call Moose Ranch. Let them know what's going on. If it turns out to be nothing, that's okay," Daegen said.

"I can come with you. Paul is fine." Even as he said it, he knew it was the wrong thing to say or do. Paul couldn't be left alone in the woods until they were sure it was just campers nearby.

Daegen shook his head.

"I can travel faster on my own. You need to keep hydrated. Drink another glass of water and then get to Paul. I noticed she was here with her atv, so I can follow her trail and see where she put the machine and then catch up with her fast. We've been gone an hour. So, at the most, she's got that much head start."

Mitch nodded. He prayed it was just interior campers and that he was freaking out over nothing.

He grabbed the doctor's bag from Daegen and headed for the horse at the pump.

He had a bad feeling about this. A really bad feeling.

· · ❧ · ·

MILENA GAZED THROUGH the bushes and wished for a pair of binoculars. She'd managed to cut pieces of bark out of trees so she could find her way back, using the sturdy jackknife Jane Sunflower had gifted her. The walk through the thick underbrush had been a good mile and to her surprise she'd done it without poking an eye out. But her face, arms and legs were scratched and burning. Young mosquitoes buzzed around her head, and they were quite irritating. Thankfully Kaley's homemade mosquito spray she'd put on was keeping them from biting her.

She kept telling herself if it were the poachers, then this trip would be well worth it, and that lone thought had spurned her on until she'd suddenly come to the edge of a rocky cliff which gave her a great view of a pristine lake a quarter of a mile below. The lake was about half the size of the one that Snowy Creek used for float planes to bring in their supplies.

However, the forest around the lake appeared so dense she could barely make out the lone spiral of white smoke drifting up from the eastern shoreline. She spied something dark green glistening in the lake near the shoreline though. It appeared to have the shape of a floatplane's wing.

Her heart began to race as excitement snapped through her. She'd have to get down this cliff so she could take a closer look.

But first she needed another gulp of water. She'd only brought one bottle of water along with her, after having returned to the cabin to grab a bottle, her straw hat and spray herself with mosquito repellant and now the bottle of water was almost empty.

And the air was so hot!

Milena blew out a tense breath, drank the rest of the water and then began climbing down the rocky cliff.

. . ❧ . .

DAEGEN HURRIED THROUGH the forest, wishing he'd remembered his cowboy hat. It had gotten pretty hot today. Perspiration drenched his face and neck and he'd removed his shirt to wrap around the top of his head to protect it from the harsh sun. He'd followed Milena's atv tracks back to the cabin and that's where she'd left it. He'd gone inside to make sure she wasn't there, then picked up a knapsack with the first aid kit, a few bottles of water and some beef jerky they kept on hand in the cooler beneath the house.

He noted the plate they'd left for her sat empty on the kitchen table. That meant she'd eaten, and he wouldn't have to worry about her starving out there in the forest today...if she got lost.

Man, what the hell had she been thinking? How many times had they told her to never go into the forest alone?

Obviously not enough times.

When he caught up with her he was going to kill her and then kiss her.

He'd noticed right off, that she'd been marking the trees, much in the same way as the trees had been marked on the way to Jane Sunflower's cabin.

Despite his anger, he grinned. Milena was a quick learner. He just hoped he could catch up with her.

He picked up his pace. He had a gut feeling something bad was going to happen. He just hoped he was wrong.

. . ⚓ . .

"WHY IN HELL DIDN'T she wait for us?" Paul asked for the hundredth time as they rushed into the barnyard.

He didn't expect an answer from Mitch. When Mitch got upset, he either got loud or quiet and right now he was pissed off and darkly quiet. When Mitch had returned with Paul's doctor's bag, Paul had immediately known something was wrong by the concerned expression on his friend's face. When he'd learned what Milena had done, he'd removed the stone from the horse's hoof in record time.

On the way back, along the trail, he'd watched Mitch climb that hill at breakneck speed and he hoped the man wouldn't have a damned heart attack. But Paul knew Mitch was in pretty good shape. A year working outdoors and eating good meals had made him trim and muscular. The risk for him having another heart attack was minimal.

Thankfully Mitch had gotten reception and contacted Moose Ranch. Rafe had answered the phone and told Mitch that JJ was out with the plane picking up supplies for Moose Ranch over in Thunder Bay. When she returned, he would send her and Brady out to help.

He'd hoped JJ would come right away and they could have done a sweep of the forest with the plane keeping a lookout for Milena. But with JJ and their bush plane gone,

Rafe and the guys were stranded. If they had decided to come via lake and portage, it would take hours for them to reach Snowy Creek, so that option hadn't been mentioned.

"I told you yesterday about the smoke I'd seen when I was calling the horse's owner and then ordering supplies. But that damned naughty woman had kept us busy last night," Paul complained for the hundredth time.

He knew where she'd gone. Knew there was a pristine little lake in that area. The three of them had done an exploratory hike, one of many, to check out the area surrounding their new ranch last year when they'd first set up camp here.

Paul led his horse into the cool interior of the barn and tried to keep himself calm. He should be grooming the animal. It was sweaty and would need water and feed. But for now, he'd just unsaddle it, and bring her into her stall. There was fresh water there and the coolness of the barn would make her comfortable.

Mitch also led his horse inside and within a few minutes, they were on the atv following the track keeping an eye out for any new tire marks that veered off the trail in the glistening green grass of the meadows. They saw nothing and Paul breathed a sigh of relief seeing two machines parked by the cabin. However, one machine was missing.

He prayed like hell Daegen, and Milena were inside.

But he knew instinctively they weren't.

A couple of minutes later, he discovered he was right. The cabin was empty.

Shit!

• • ⚓ • •

MILENA BIT HER BOTTOM lip and tried to ignore the mosquito drilling like a needle into her neck. She dare not move. Not more than twenty feet away a woman sat on a lawn chair, near a smoky fire, roasting a wiener attached to the end of a long metal spear-like pole.

And all around her beneath the shade of trees were cages. Some cages were covered with white cloths and others weren't. The ones that weren't covered allowed Milena to see they were filled with animals. Big grey wolves paced nervously. Full grown bears growled in anger and a black bear cub bawled heartbreakingly for its mother.

In one of the cages there were several large turtles, spanning at least two feet wide in all directions. In another cage there were two cute fawns. And yet another cage contained several large birds. A couple were owls and the others she had no idea.

She'd hit the motherload and she had no idea what to do.

Damn! Damn! Damn! Why had she not brought the rifle?

She really hadn't thought this through. Hadn't expected to find something of this magnitude.

She couldn't go back to find the guys. This woman and the animals might be gone via the nearby floatplane by the time they returned.

Maybe she could jump the woman and let the animals out of their cages?

Yes, that's what she would do.

But another thought stopped her cold.

How could one woman carry those big cages into the bush plane? There had to be other people around.

Milena would just have to be quiet and work fast so as to not attract any attention. She would have to find a big branch so she could smack the lady over her head. But as she twisted to look around for one, she froze.

A man stood three feet away, gazing down at her.

And he pointed a gun right at her chest!

Terror clawed through her and she fought the urge to run.

"Not a sound or I'll blow your head off," the man murmured in a low scary voice.

Milena's heart crashed against her chest and adrenalin screamed through her. She began to shake.

By the intense stare of his creepy blue eyes, and the firm jut to his long chin, she knew he would shoot her if she gave him an excuse.

Oh, this was so not good.

He waved his gun at her and she tensed, fully expecting him to shoot her.

"Keep your hands where I can see them and get up nice and slow. Hear me?"

Milena nodded jerkily. She held out her shaking hands so he could see them, and she stood as slowly as she could.

"Who else is out there?" he growled.

She could barely speak she was so scared. Could barely form a thought.

Thankfully he was patient enough to give her a few seconds to grab her bearings so she could answer.

"About ten men and they have guns," she managed to say. Her voice didn't sound like hers. It sounded deep, guttural, frightened. She doubted he believed her, but she had to at least try.

"You're surrounded. Drop your weapon or they'll shoot," she said.

"She's lying. No one else around," came another man's voice from right behind her.

Oh my God! How many of them were here? Why hadn't she heard them creeping up on her?

"Move on into the camp," The man with the gun ordered.

Milena's legs shook so badly she thought she would fall over as she slowly began to walk.

"Are you sure she's alone?" She heard the blue-eyed man say to the other.

"She's alone. I did a perimeter check. Probably some lost hiker."

"No, I seen her before. Saw her with some guy over at that crazy lamb lady's ranch. Then we followed them back to that other place with the creek, about a mile north of here," the other guy answered.

Daegen and her had been followed from Jane Sunflower's ranch? That would explain why she'd been uneasy, feeling as if they were being watched shortly after they'd left Jane's place.

"What the hell is she doing here?" the woman snapped when she saw Milena as the two men ushered her out of the thickets.

She stood so fast her chair went flying and her wiener fell right into the fire. The woman was dressed like the two men. Camouflage green pants, long sleeved camouflage t-shirts and black hiking boots. She was about fifty, chubby and had short spikey red hair.

"Snooping around from the looks of it. We're gonna need to get the animals on board and get out now. We've got a million dollars worth here and I don't want to get caught. Who knows who will come looking for her," the one with the creepy blue eyes snarled.

Now that her initial shock of getting caught was wearing off a little, Milena began to memorize facial features, in case she ever made it out of this mess.

"You idiots. Why did you let her see us? We're going to have to take her with us," the woman shouted.

She was so pissed off; her face was as red as her hair.

The two men simply shrugged their shoulders.

"Get the cages into the plane," she growled. "And put her in a cage as well!"

Before Milena could so much as run for her life, the man with the blue eyes grabbed her arm and pulled her toward one of the larger empty cages.

Panic spun through her. If they put her in there, she was a goner. She knew it without a doubt. Without hesitation she stomped on the man's foot. He cried out in agony, let go of her and she ran like she'd never run before.

But a gunshot sizzled through the air. Pain burned through her upper right thigh. She stumbled and almost fell at the impact.

"Freeze or I take out the other leg!" the creepy man yelled. He was right behind her.

Oh God!

Milena stared at the dense trees looming ahead of her. She had maybe fifteen feet before she could disappear into the forest. But if he shot her again...

Her thigh burned with pain, and she stopped before he could shoot her again.

"If I wanted you dead, you would be dead. Consider that flesh wound a warning. Don't try that again or you will die," the man said.

He grabbed her arm again and pulled her toward the cage. Then he gripped the back of her head, forced her head and body downward and pushed her so hard through the open cage door that she crashed into the metal bars on the opposite side. Pain blossomed through her shoulder, matching the pain in her thigh,

"Stay in there!" he yelled.

She heard a click of a lock and she peered through the bars at him.

He joined the other two by the campfire and the three started talking in low tones.

She grabbed the bars and looked at the caged animals. Most were staring at her with horrified expressions. Instantly she felt sorry for the creatures and tried hard not to cry as emotions, thick and raw clutched at her chest.

Oh boy, how was she going to get herself and all these animals out of here?

Daegen stopped at the report of the gunshot echoing through the forest.

Milena!

He swore violently as his stomach twisted with a sudden bout of nausea. Visions of a similar sound from another time rattled around in his head.

Red blood splashing against a military green wall. His friend slumping forward. The semi-automatic gun in his hand dropping to the ceramic floor with a clatter. His forehead looking like ground beef.

The phone call that had come the same day telling him his wife and unborn child had died...

Daegen stopped the anxiety from launching. He concentrated on slowing down his breathing just like his shrink had taught him.

He couldn't have a panic attack. Not now.

Milena needed him.

The unwanted sounds of his mental screams of helplessness filled his head as he began to run toward the area where he'd heard the gunshot. He hoped he wasn't too late.

Chapter Eighteen

Milena stared at the crimson blood as it slowly oozed from the wound. She'd pulled down her jeans to get a look at it, thankfully it wasn't as bad as she'd thought. Just a crease. But boy did it ever hurt.

She managed to pull her jeans back up, reached down, winced as pain shot through her sore right shoulder, and slipped off her shoes and her socks.

She bunched up the socks and pressed the wad against the wound, stifling a cry as pain spasmed through her. Then she looked up and watched the two men returning from the bush plane. They tossed a blanket over the cage containing a very irritated big black bear, grabbed the handles on the cage and carried it to the bush plane.

No!

Those animals were destined for foreign markets. Heading toward horrible existences or if they were lucky, death. How could she stop them from stealing these animals? She, herself, was locked in a cage.

The two men returned and picked up an enclosure with a black bear cub who continued to frantically bawl. From the cage in the bush plane, the big bear growled fiercely. It had to be the cub's mother in there!

Oh my God! No! How could these people be so horrible to a helpless baby bear and its mother?

Anger raged inside of her. She grabbed the bars on the cage door, rattling it, trying to get their attention.

"You won't get away with this! The authorities know your location. I called them when I saw the smoke! They'll be here any minute! You should leave the animals and get out of here while you still can!" she shouted.

Oh my gosh, how lame she sounded. They would never believe her. But she had to try.

One man laughed.

"Thanks for the tip, Missy but the authorities are already here. He is the authorities. Big man in our pocket," he pointed to the guy with the creepy blue eyes.

"Are you mad! What's the matter with you, Bertris? Don't tell her who I am!" The man glared at him over the cage they were lifting.

Milena swallowed and her mouth went dry.

So, that's how they got away with all this poaching. They had someone in the government looking out for them.

The woman shook her head as she lifted the smaller cage containing birds. The feathered creatures fluttered around crazily batting their wings against the strong metal bars holding them hostage.

"Shut up, you sons of bitches," the woman shouted.

Milena wasn't sure if the woman was yelling at the birds or the two men.

"Bertris should keep his mouth shut. The idiot has compromised me." The man with the blue eyes complained as they brought the bawling cub to the floatplane. They disappeared inside with the cage and cub, then a moment later, came out again.

"Oh, come on, Rob. Don't take it so seriously," the woman chuckled. "We'll fly over a lake, push her in the cage out. She'll sink like a stone. She'll disappear. No one will ever find her. They'll just think she got lost in the woods."

Milena's gut clenched with fear. They would make her vanish. The guys would think she'd made a run for freedom. They'd be so disappointed in her.

When the two men returned, they started toward her.

Oh no! She couldn't end up dying like this! What could she do?

A rumble of a plane's engine suddenly split through the air.

Milena looked to the sky and prayed the pilot would see them.

"You and your damned fetish for wieners, Sally. You should have waited and stuffed your face when we got to the airfield," the other man growled.

"I told you I called the authorities!" Milena shouted. "You better get out of here now! Leave the animals and save your asses while you still can!"

She was now fighting for her life. She would say anything.

The drone of the engines drew closer. And closer.

Suddenly not more than a quarter mile away over the lake, a floatplane burst over the treeline and appeared in the sky.

The men and woman swore.

"Shit! Thousands of lakes and they pick this one?" the woman grumbled.

"Unless she wasn't lying and tipped off the authorities?" the blue-eyed government guy snarled as he glanced at Milena.

"I warned you!" Milena yelled at them.

The float plane angled away from the lake.

Milena's hopes dashed.

No!

But then the plane began to circle.

Thank God!

"Oh crap. They're coming in," Sally muttered.

"We leave, now! If it's a false alarm, we can come back," the other man snapped.

"Let's go. Leave her. It'll take too long to get her on board," Sally said as she jogged toward their plane.

But the blue-eyed government guy didn't move away with them. He started toward Milena.

"She knows too much. She needs to die. And I want to see the life melt right out of her eyes when I shoot her," he growled.

Milena froze as he came closer to her cage. The sneer on his face told her he wasn't kidding. He was going to kill her.

She watched as his hand popped open the top of his gun holster.

Oh no!

He kept coming. He pulled the gun from his holster.

The approaching plane splashed down.

Please help me!!

Milena crushed herself against the back of the cage and felt something hard nudge against her backside.

No!

"Leave her! The plane has landed. We need to go now!" Sally shouted.

The man kept walking toward her.

The item in her back pocket insistently nudged at her and suddenly Milena remembered what it was. In a flash, she pulled it out and opened it.

She readied herself. To either die or stall for a few seconds more for life.

"You little bitch! This will teach you for sticking your nose into our business," the man growled as he thrust his hand and then the gun through the bars.

Milena lifted her arm and sliced into the top of the man's hand with Jane Sunflower's jackknife.

He dropped the gun into the cage screamed in pain as blood spurted from the wound.

Milena grabbed the gun.

"You crazy bitch! I am going to kill you!" he yelled at her. His face was filled with hatred and venom.

Milena pointed the gun at him. Her hands were so shaky, they were all over the place. She couldn't shoot because she might hit a metal bar and the bullet could ricochet and kill her! But she would chance it, if he tried to follow through with his threat of killing her.

"Come on! Come on! Let's go!" Sally was yelling from the open cockpit window as their plane roared to life.

"Come on, Rob!" Bertris shouted, waving at him to come.

The other float plane was angling toward the camp and Milena recognized it. It was a blue plane.

Blue had come! But why? She'd said she was in a hurry. That she was behind with her mail route. She had no idea what she was walking into. When they found out it was only one woman in the plane, they would kill her!

She had to warn Blue.

An odd calm suddenly came over her and her hands miraculously stopped shaking. She aimed the gun at the man who continued to scream at her. He was now coming at her with the metal spear that Sally had been roasting her wiener with. If he came several steps closer, he would stab the spear right into her.

She pulled the trigger. She didn't know where she hit him, but he fell to the ground, motionless.

Milena watched as Blue angled her plane right in front of the other plane, preventing the poachers from leaving.

Blue innocently waved to the occupants of the float plane.

They would have guns. They would kill Blue!

"Blue! Get out of here! Get out!" Milena screamed. She shot the gun off again, hitting a tree nearby. Pieces of tree splattered everywhere, some shards spiralled through the air and hit the poacher's floatplane's cockpit windshield.

She hoped Blue would hear the shot and see the wood flying and she would go away.

But she didn't! She had a gun in her hand, and she was waving it at the poachers.

Where had Blue gotten a gun?

"You're surrounded. Come on out with your hands up!" she shouted out an open side window at the poachers who sat in their cockpit yelling at each other.

Milena spied movement behind Blue. Shock zipped through her when she saw Paul and Mitch as Blue's plane door slid open. Guns were clutched in their hands.

Sally and Bertris scrambled out of their plane, they had guns in their hands too. They started running toward the treeline.

But they suddenly stopped as a loud shot rang out and Daegen stepped out of the woods right in front of them. He was pointing a rifle at them.

Everything felt surreal. Had Milena gotten shot and she was now dreaming her cowboys had come to her rescue?

"Going somewhere?" Daegen called out in a cold voice.

"Drop your weapons!" Blue shouted. She was now on land, rushing up behind the duo.

The two poachers slowly placed their guns upon the ground, then straightened and lifted their hands into the air. Both swore vehemently until Daegen told them to shut up or he would shoot both of them.

They shut up.

Mitch and Paul were suddenly there in front of Milena's cage. Concern etched their faces as they peered past the bars at her.

"Are you okay? Which one has the key for this cage?" Mitch asked.

She nodded to the guy she'd shot. He wasn't moving. She hoped he wasn't dead. She didn't want to go back to prison for another murder.

Mitch moved away toward the man on the ground.

"I see blood on your thigh. Did they shoot you?" Paul asked as his gaze roamed over her body visually assessing her for damage.

"Flesh wound," she admitted. She was shaking again. She was thankful too, for still being alive.

Mitch was back.

Quickly, he unlocked the cage and the guys helped her out. Paul then pulled off his belt and rapidly tied it like a tourniquet around her upper thigh. To her surprise, the bleeding stopped.

"How is she?" Daegen called out.

She could hear the alarm in his voice. She appreciated that he was concerned for her, but she really liked that he was keeping his rifle on Sally and Bertris as Blue cuffed them together with a single pair of handcuffs.

"She's gonna be fine. No worries," Paul shouted back.

Daegen nodded and smiled. His smile brought a little reassurance to her. Maybe everything was going to be okay now?

While Daegen kept his rifle trained on the duo, Blue quickly cuffed the unconscious man.

"Come on, let's get her to the plane. She doesn't need to see this," Mitch urged. He moved closer, but Milena waved him away.

"What about the animals? We need to let them go," she gasped.

The birds were fluttering madly in their cages, and the deer, bears and other creatures were clearly upset, making noises or pacing.

"No, we cannot let them go. Not yet. They're evidence," Blue said in a strong voice. "We need to keep them this way until pictures can be taken by the authorities. It's the only way these people can be prosecuted as poachers."

"But the animals will starve. Who knows how long it will take the police to come all the way out here," Milena complained.

Could she just have risked her life for nothing? There was no way she was going to let these animals stay locked up here for longer than a few hours. She could hear the bear cub continuing to bawl and its mother growling from inside their cages on the poacher's floatplane.

"I'll call the police and give them the co-ordinates. I'll explain shots were fired. You were injured. Another man is down. They'll come quickly. I just need to further secure these people. Paul just stay with Milena for a minute, please. Daegen and Mitch, keep me covered." Blue instructed with a confidence that Milena admired.

She was thankful when Mitch kept his gun trained on the motionless man and Daegen held his weapon on the two poachers while Blue rushed back to her plane and moments later returned with a long coil of rope and quickly tied Sally and Bertris to a nearby tree.

When they were tied up, Blue motioned to Paul.

"Paul, you get Milena to the plane and tend to her injury," Blue instructed.

Paul nodded and she felt his hand settle upon her back.

"Come on," he said softly.

She shook her head and watched the man who lay motionless on the ground as a swell of anxiety overwhelmed her.

"He tried to kill me," she confessed. Although she could see he was cuffed, she fully expected him to stand up and rush over and kill her.

"He's the one who shot me. But then he tried to shoot me again when I was in the cage. I stuck him in the hand with Jane Sunflower's jackknife and he dropped his gun and I grabbed it and shot him...if I hadn't had Jane's jackknife..."

Milena shook even harder. If Jane hadn't given her that knife, Milena knew without a doubt, she would be dead now.

Jane Sunflower had literally saved her life. How in the world would she ever repay that brave woman?

"That's the guy who came out to the property with the cop when you guys were over at Jane Sunflower's place," Paul said as he pointed to the motionless man.

"I noticed," Mitch replied.

"Son of a bitch is in on the poaching. I would bet he never even reported what you told him to his superiors," Milena told him.

"I just hope that cop that came with him isn't in on it too. We're going to have to have him investigated. Come on, tell me all about it on the plane." Paul tried to move her toward the plane, but she couldn't go. The last thing she wanted at the moment was to leave these distressed animals.

Or allow the poachers to go free.

"Is he dead?" she asked Mitch as she stared at the motionless man. His eyes were closed. His face was pale, and he appeared like he might be dead.

In contrast, Mitch looked so strong and self-assured in the way he held the weapon on the man. But Milena could tell he was angry. His face was red, and his eyes were narrowed. Muscles jumped in his cheeks as he clenched his jaw.

Mitch stared at the man, and it took him a few seconds before he answered her.

"I can see his chest rising and falling in a steady rhythm so he's alive and most likely okay. And from that wound at his temple, looks like he's only knocked out."

"I shot him. It was self-defence. He tried to kill me," Milena repeated. She just couldn't get it out of her mind that someone wanted her dead so badly, just because she desired the animals to be freed.

"Attempted murder will have the cops out here in no time flat," Blue said. She stood beside Milena now and gently patted her shoulder.

"The poachers are secure. You're safe. I'll call the police now. Paul, want to come and grab your doctor's bag? Maybe if you have something to calm her down? And bring her back some food and water. She's looking a bit pale."

"Are you okay?" Paul asked her. Alarm was evident in his gaze.

"Just go. I don't want anything to calm me. I'm fine. I'd like to stay here. Please, don't worry," she nodded jerkily.

Milena's mouth was so dry now, she could barely talk, but she needed to make sure that these poachers weren't going to somehow get away. So, she watched Sally and Bertris who glared at her. Obviously not happy campers.

Too bad. Don't do the crime if you can't do the time, she wanted to shout to them. She forced herself to remain quiet.

A question kept bugging her though. Where had Blue gotten two handcuffs and a gun?

Then she remembered JJ had told her last summer that Blue had been a cop and a nurse in the past. That bit of information suddenly made her relax a little. She was a pilot too, probably had a gun with her for protection.

Paul returned and brought with him the lawn chair that Sally had been sitting in earlier. She didn't want to sit in it, but realized she was feeling awfully weak. She plopped down.

"I need to get a look at the wound so I'm going to cut away your pants okay? I may even have to return the favor and stitch you up this time around," Paul chuckled and winked at her.

"I hope you're a good sewer. I'm not sure guys like scars on girls as much as girls like scars on guys."

She heard all the guys and Blue laugh and Milena tensed when the man she'd shot started moving around on the ground. Because his hands had been cuffed behind his back, he was swearing. Thankfully Mitch kept him covered with his gun.

Anxiety buzzed through her when the man turned his head and saw Milena. He froze and stared at her with venom in his eyes.

If looks could kill, she'd be dead. She knew that without a doubt.

Thankfully Mitch noticed the man watching her and ordered him to stand and walk toward the other two who'd been tied to a tree.

In moments, Daegen had him secured to the same tree with rope beside the other two poachers.

Then Daegen and Mitch kept their weapons trained on the trio and Milena could see Blue sitting in her float plane's cockpit speaking into her radio.

"Here, painkillers and drink this water. And then eat this sandwich," he instructed and held out two pills, a huge sandwich and bottled water.

She was about to protest about the pain killers, when Paul held up his hand.

"Seriously. Once the shock wears off that wound is going to hurt if you don't take these meds. And if you want to stay here with the animals and look out for them and I know you do, you will have to drink and eat. But drink really slow. I don't want you to get sick."

"Okay," she whispered and accepted the water and sandwich.

He gave her the cutest grin and it made her heart flutter with happiness. She closed her eyes and mentally hugged the emotion. It was really nice, this satisfying feeling of saving all these animals and having her three cowboys here with her, protecting her.

She blew out a slow breath. They'd come in like the calvary. Like her heroes. They had come looking for her. They truly cared for her. She was so lucky.

She heard Paul cutting her pants, felt the warm air breathe against her flesh. She grimaced as pain burst while he gently prodded and poked around the throbbing bullet wound. She forced herself to open her eyes and inspect her wound again.

She could tell it wasn't too bad. But it sure was sore.

Despite being awfully thirsty, she compelled herself to sip the water slowly from the bottle and surveyed her surroundings.

Thankfully the caged animals were all under trees in the shade and out of the late afternoon sun. She just hoped they could be freed by nightfall. But she doubted it. She would stay here with them tonight, if need be. She wouldn't leave them until all of them were free.

"Hey, Paul. They got your gyrfalcon here. I'd know that beak anywhere," Mitch called out. He stood in front of the cage with the fluttering birds.

Paul smiled and called back to Mitch.

"That's my feathery wife. I figured you'd know her anywhere."

She heard Mitch laugh and swear.

"Is she alright?" Paul called out.

"Looks great! I hope your wife appreciates you getting your head cracked open so she could get kidnapped and now you've come to her rescue. Again."

Paul exhaled a deep breath and shook his head. He said nothing.

"Your wife?" Had she heard right?

"Wives are rare around these parts, just like gyrfalcons are rare," Paul elaborated.

"Okay, if you say so," she answered. Maybe one day she would ask more about wives and gyrfalcons, but not today.

She drank more water and took the medication and then started nibbling on the peanut butter and jam sandwich, which turned out to be pretty good.

"The cops will be here within the hour," Blue called out as she hurried over to Milena and Paul.

She crouched beside Paul and looked at Milena's wound.

"Hey, not bad. You'll live. I doubt Paul even has to stitch you up," she said.

"You are correct, Nurse Blue," Paul replied as he began ripping open packages.

"He's not kidding either," Blue said to Milena. "I used to be a nurse. And a cop. One day remind me to show you my scars, will you? And you're right, the men I've had the privilege of knowing don't like a lady with scars." she shrugged. "But I suspect the guys at Snowy Creek Ranch are different."

Milena noticed Paul had an amused smirk on his face, but he remained silent as he dabbed some ointment onto her wound.

"I also hailed JJ on her radio letting her know what happened. I asked her if she could bring someone over to your place and get your horses in for tonight because the cops probably won't let you go for awhile. I am assuming you weren't able to take care of the horses?"

Paul shook his head.

"Thanks so much, Blue. Yeah, we hadn't brought them in. I guess we panicked about Milena," he acknowledged.

He threw Milena a wink and warmth spread through her. They had panicked about her? How cool was that?

Blue's tone turned serious, and she frowned.

"You were really lucky, Milena. I was able to get the mail to my people in record time, and then on my way back I decided to swing by and see if you guys had gone to check on the smoke I saw. I almost went straight to this lake myself to come in and take a look. Good thing I didn't. I would have walked into a hornet's nest, like you did. Anyways, when I showed up at the dock, Mitch and Paul were there, waving at me like they were crazy. I almost turned my plane around and got out of there. I thought they were lunatics! They practically hijacked my plane. They were frantic and I didn't know what the hell was going on until we were in the air."

"We were desperate. Sorry, Blue, for scaring you," Paul said quietly. "We were worried about Milena getting lost or running into trouble and we were just really glad we saw your plane coming over the cabin. We were getting ready to go out and look for her and Daegen, as he was tracking her. We had everything packed and out on the porch. You were an angel flying in when you did," Paul said.

"Wow, I've been called some things, but never an angel," Blue laughed.

"You're the best, Blue. Thank you for being there when the guys needed you. And thank you for coming back and bringing them out here. I don't want to think what might have happened if you hadn't. They were talking about dumping me and the cage I was in out of the plane into a lake so no one could find me," Milena said with a shiver.

No one said anything. They were probably thinking the same thing she was thinking. That she would be dead had Blue not come when she did.

The police showed up under an hour later, just like they had told Blue they would. Three men and a woman in a float plane. Two cops, thankfully not the one who'd come to Snowy Creek Ranch that one time, plus one female wilderness officer and to Milena's surprise, a young male bush doctor, who quickly checked out Milena's wound. He gave Paul two thumbs up for doing a good patch up job, before moving on to the man Milena had shot.

Everyone worked quickly and efficiently, snapping pictures of the animals and taking everyone's statements.

They secured the poachers in the police plane and then they asked Blue, Milena, Paul, Daegen and Mitch to stay in Blue's plane while they set all the animals free. It was dark now, but Milena was thankfully on the side of the shoreline. Here, out the window, she could see everything as the officers set up lights in the poacher's camp. The cops stood nearby with tranquilizer guns covering the wildlife officer as she bravely and carefully set each animal free.

The first animals she let loose were the mother bear and the cub from the poacher's plane.

Milena laughed as the big black mother bear got protectively behind her bawling cub and nudged it quickly into the dark forest.

The process of releasing all the animals was long and arduous. The officers kept a lookout to make sure none of the animals backtracked into camp and attacked them, for the animals appeared to be hungry and angry and rightly so.

Milena was thrilled when it was all over. So many animals had been saved.

It was midnight by the time Blue dropped them off at their dock, refusing invitations to spend the night with them as she needed to get home to her daughter and relieve the babysitter.

That night, Milena couldn't answer any of the guy's questions of everything that had happened, she was so tired and emotional. Thankfully, they pulled the beds together and Paul changed the dressing on her wound again and she popped another couple of painkillers. Then they all snuggled together on the large makeshift bed, and she felt safe.

But there was no sex. Everyone was exhausted.

Sleep was hard in coming for her and when she slept, she awakened many times thinking she was about to be murdered by that Rob character. One or the other of the guys always seemed to be awake, soothing her back to sleep.

She prayed she didn't end up with ptsd like Daegen and hoped time would heal her back to being calm. She closed her eyes again for the hundredth time that long night and forced herself to inhale and exhale deeply and slowly.

Yes, time would tell.

. . ⚜ . .

SEVERAL DAYS LATER...

"Well, it looks like the only thing left is to show up in court when they go to trial," Daegen said as they headed back to their atvs where they'd parked them at the base of the hill.

The four of them had met here after work, climbed up to the hilltop and made all the phone calls that needed to be done, including another call to her parole officer to explain what had happened here.

She was thankful *that* call was behind her. She never liked calling Parole Officer Brown as the woman made her feel like a chastised child. She'd done it again this time.

Brown had heard about what had happened with the poachers and grilled Milena. Asking why she had gone out there alone looking for the poachers in the first place. Milena could read between the lines. She'd meant had Milena been trying to escape.

She was glad when Mitch ripped the phone out of her hands and smooth talked the parole officer, who told him to tell Milena to call in a month. And then her parole officer had hung up.

Her wound was healing nicely and hardly hurt anymore. The trek up the steep hillside didn't bother her thigh much either. So, she would be okay.

"Brady said that court thing might take awhile. Maybe a few months, or longer. We might not even have to go and testify. They might just use our statements. And he said they investigated that cop that came here with the crooked fish and wildlife guy, and it appears he isn't in with the poachers," Mitch replied as he sat behind Milena on the atv as they got ready to leave.

That bit of news about the police not being involved with the poachers made her happy and it seemed Mitch was quite happy too as he made no effort to keep away from her backside as he'd done the previous times they'd sat together over the last few days.

She shivered in delight at the hardness of his erection.

Then he curled his arms around her waist...well actually higher until he teasingly brushed his thumbs against the undercurve of her breasts.

He was definitely giving her a hint as to what was going to happen tonight in bed.

Milena smiled and started the engine.

The last few days none of them had been in the mood for sex. Maybe they'd been picking up on her nervousness of what had almost happened to her? But she *was* starting to feel so much better.

She couldn't wait until after supper. She was starving, but not just for food.

"Okay let's hoof it. I'm damn hungry," Paul called out as he started his machine and then took off. Daegen followed and she moved their atv in behind them.

Minutes later, as they neared the cabin, Milena noticed JJ standing at the foot of the cabin steps with two men beside her. As they drew closer, Milena recognized the uniforms.

Cops. Were they here to ask more questions about the poachers?

She was glad to see JJ, but her stomach hollowed at the crestfallen expression on JJ's face as she looked straight at Milena.

Oh my God! Those cops are here for me?

Milena's brain went into overdrive. Why were they here? Why did JJ look so devastated? Should she turn the atv around and hightail it out of here? Make a run for it?

Milena's mouth went horribly dry, and nervousness made her shake as she brought their machine to a halt a few feet away from the cops.

"What can we do for you officers?" Mitch asked a couple minutes later as he reached out and shook each of their hands.

Mitch, Paul and Daegen appeared so cheerful. Maybe she was reading this all wrong?

Introductions were made but Milena could barely hear them.

The tallest was Officer Jenkins, the shorter was Officer Petros. That's all she could remember.

"I can put on some coffee. We can talk inside about the poachers," Daegen suddenly said.

Both officers shook their heads.

"Sorry, no. We're here for Ms. Milena Allen. We have a warrant for her arrest," the shortest officer of the two said.

No! This cannot be happening!

"What?" Mitch gasped.

"What for?" Daegen snapped.

"What's this all about?" Paul said with a frown.

"Ms. Allen?" one of the officer's asked her.

"Yes?" she answered hesitantly.

"Hey if this is about what happened with the shooting and poachers out here, we squared everything with the cops. They didn't mention sending anyone out," Paul said in a rush.

I'm so sorry. JJ mouthed to Milena. Huge tears shone in her brown eyes.

Any sliver of hope that Milena might have been harbouring that this was all some wicked nightmare was gone.

Her stomach somersaulted as if she were on a very tipsy roller coaster.

The shortest of the two newcomers reached for his handcuffs.

Oh no!

"There was a mistake with the Cowboys Online program. You were sent here in error. We've been asked to transfer you to Thunder Bay police station," the other officer who had been quiet until now said.

"If you three men would please stand back? I don't want anyone to get hurt" the other said in a commanding voice.

Milena stiffened as the officer's hand settled on the handle of his gun.

Oh my God. These cops are serious.

"Please, this must be some sort of mistake. I was sent here. I signed papers. Mitch's sister is the owner of Cowboys Online. Her name is Jenna—" Milena tried to tell them, but Mitch cut her off.

"I've got her parole papers inside. All signed and legal. I'll get them," Mitch said.

"Sir. Just stay where you are," the officer said in a cold commanding voice. He'd pulled his gun and was holding it with the gun barrel facing Mitch.

Dear Lord. Please help me! Don't let these guys be hurt.

"Ma'am please put your hands behind your back and turn around. We have an arrest warrant, and we must carry it out." Officer Jenkins said coolly.

"Just do as he says," JJ said. "Brady is already in touch with his sister and some lawyers. They'll get it all straightened out."

A sliver of relief whipped through Milena. She could tell Mitch, Daegen and Paul hadn't moved back as they'd been ordered. Shock reverberated on all their faces.

Instantly Milena did as she was instructed. She didn't want anyone hurt. She would do what they told her to do.

"But I can prove she's here legally," Mitch started for the cabin.

"Sir, hold still. Or I will be forced to shoot."

Thankfully Daegen grabbed Mitch's arm.

Mitch cursed and Paul joined Mitch.

"Can one of us go with her?" Daegen asked.

"No, just the pilot," Officer Jenkins replied with a stern voice that reminded Milena of the no nonsense justice system she'd been a part of all these years.

She was going back behind bars. No more beautiful cabin. No more sunshine on her face or seeing the guys.

She wanted to start screaming. To curse out the cops. But none of that would get her out of this situation.

Good Lord, was she doomed to live out the rest of her life behind bars?

You see? It was all too good to be true. You don't belong here, anywhere or to anyone. Say goodbye to your fantasy home sweet home and to your forever cowboys, her inner voice crooned in an I told you so tone.

"This pilot will bring us back to Moose Ranch where the other pilot is waiting. She had an issue with her plane and put down there. Said she'd have it fixed by the time we got back. You will have to make other arrangements."

"I can take the guys in," JJ said quickly.

She turned to Milena.

"We'll see you in the city. Jenna will make them see you belong here. There is no mistake," JJ spoke in such a hopeful voice that Milena almost believed her.

Almost.

.. ◦◦◦ ..

"UNFORTUNATELY COWBOYS Online *did* make a mistake with the paperwork and sent the wrong person to this Snowy Creek Ranch," the judge, a dowdy older man with a bald head and an unpleasant look of irritation on his face, said as he placed the papers he'd been reading upon his mahogany bench, and peered down at Milena like she was a mouse and he the big fat cat who was about to pounce and kill her.

Paul could see Milena's shoulders slump with dejection. He felt the defeat curl through his body as well and his anger was building.

How the hell could Jenna screw up so royally? He'd know her most of his life. She was a perfectionist. She never screwed up.

"Your honor, please. There must be something that can be done in these unusual circumstances?" Milena's young female lawyer pleaded.

"It is not Ms. Milena Allen's fault, your honor, that somebody made an error in paperwork. She should not be punished for this. The paperwork can be changed, and Ms. Allen can be returned to the ranch. She's proven she's not a runner. And remember, sir, her employers have sworn she is an excellent worker, and she did bring down a pouching ring. All these things must account for something would they not, your honor?"

The lawyer had been sent by Jenna. She appeared too young, at least in Paul's opinion. Hell, she didn't even look like a lawyer. She looked like a fresh kid out of high school and instead of being aggressive with the judge, she was being submissive and too damned polite.

He understood the concept of getting more flies with honey, but this was Milena's life. Their life.

Damn, they should have kept hunting for a better, more experienced lawyer. Unfortunately, all the seasoned lawyers that Brady and Mitch had been asking to help them had declined, saying it was an open and shut case. Milena would go back to prison, they'd said.

Over his dead body, Paul thought to himself. There had to be some way to break her out of here before they shipped her off.

"I'm not in the mood to discuss this further, Ms. Rossi," the judge growled.

The judge gave her a stern look and Jenna's lawyer nodded and bowed her head in apparent surrender.

"Yes, your honor."

Are you kidding me? She isn't even putting up a fight! Oh, come on!

"The asshole is probably constipated. Should take a dump and put himself into a better mood, before he gives his decision," Mitch muttered from beside Paul.

"Does someone wish to be held in contempt?" the judge asked. His voice echoed through the small courtroom.

"I can't believe this clown. Did he not hear all of us testify earlier today? That she is a great worker?" Daegen whispered from Paul's other side.

"This is bullshit. She belongs with us," Mitch grumbled beneath his breath.

Paul had been lucky enough, or unlucky enough, depending on how he looked at it, to get stuck right in the middle of the two men. They were both fuming and ready to fight the system any way they could, probably even physically.

He'd given each one of them pokes into their ribs with his elbows during this inquiry to help settle them down.

But obviously his jabs to quieten them wasn't working out too well.

The judge must have heard their continued conversations, for his irritation turned to anger.

He grabbed his gavel and slammed it down onto the desk.

"Order!" he snapped.

When everyone got quiet, the judge smiled at their obedience. Paul swore it was a genuine smile and it gave him a glimmer of hope.

Man, this judge was unpredictable.

Nasty one minute and then smiling the next.

"Milena Allen, please stand," the judge ordered.

Milena did as he said. She hadn't looked their way at all since they'd been in the courtroom. She had avoided eye contact when each of them had taken the stand on her behalf.

He didn't blame her. She was probably pretending they didn't exist. Probably figured it would be easier that way.

She'd been incarcerated now for over a month, and it had been hell thinking of her being behind bars. They'd tried to visit her, but she'd refused to see them.

She looked thinner. Worn out. Probably wasn't getting any sleep worrying about everything. Just like they hadn't been getting any. They were all on edge.

"It is the opinion of this court that you be remanded back into custody for the remainder of your sentence," the judge bellowed.

Shivers of dread ripped though Paul.

"No," Paul heard Milena gasp.

Shit!

"Your honor! Please! Have mercy!" Jenna's so-called lawyer called out.

"This is bullshit!" Mitch roared.

"Unfair!" Daegen muttered.

"Silence!" The judge shouted with a scowl and smashed his gavel onto the bench.

But no one was listening, Paul realized. Everyone was pissed off including the judge who kept smashing his gavel trying to regain control.

Suddenly there was a knock at the door.

Paul wasn't even sure if anyone heard it, but the guard did. He opened the door and to his surprise Jenna strolled into the courtroom.

The room fell silent as she walked up the aisle.

"About time," Daegen whispered.

She was dressed all prim and professional in a navy-blue business suit. Her normally wavy red hair had been pulled back in a severe bun and she had a firm jut to her chin. Paul sensed she was a woman on a mission and his hopes soared again.

"I'm going to kill my sister for putting Milena through this," Mitch said between clenched teeth.

"Your honor, may I have a word, sir?" Jenna asked as she stopped at the end of the aisle beside the defendant table.

The judge had stopped banging his gavel. He did not seem pleased to see her.

"Mrs. Donnelly what are you doing here?"

Okay so the judge knew her. That was a good sign. Wasn't it?

"Sir, some new information has come to my attention. May we meet privately in the judge's chambers?"

She wanted to meet with him privately? Wow, the woman had balls. He just hoped she had something to change his mind.

"Please, Mrs. Donnelly. I have never had such an unruly bunch. I do hope you can settle them down as I won't be changing my mind, even for you."

"Everyone pipe down. She must know him," Mitch muttered as he set his fisted hands into his lap like some young schoolboy who'd just decided he wanted to behave.

Paul almost laughed. One minute Mitch was going to kill his oldest sister and the next he was gazing at her like she was some goddess coming to his rescue.

The judge stared intensely at Jenna. But he wasn't looking at her like she was a goddess. He stared at her with his narrowed eyes as if he was trying to figure out what the hell she wanted.

Then he inhaled a deep breath and exhaled slowly.

"Why not here?" he growled.

"Sir, it would be best if you heard this in private."

The judge frowned and finally nodded.

"Very well. Meet me in ten minutes in my chambers. I will be there shortly."

"Told you he needed to go to the bathroom," Mitch chuckled.

Paul rolled his eyes and stood. He needed to talk to Milena.

· · ⚓ · ·

"HEY, HOW ARE YOU HOLDING up?"

Milena stiffened at the sound of Paul's soft voice from immediately behind her.

She'd been staring at the judge's gavel where he'd set it on the bench. She'd been trying like crazy not to turn around and look upon her three men. She wished she'd never met them. It was ripping her heart out being apart from them. The pain of putting them through this hell was killing her.

"Milena? Aren't you going to talk to us?" Daegen's voice was thick with emotion.

"Come on, baby. We can't let it end like this," Mitch said.

His words pretty much sealed what she'd been thinking all along. There was no way out of this situation. Jenna was probably here to ask the judge to knock a couple of years off her sentence as a favor for screwing up the paperwork, although she still wasn't clear as to how it got screwed up in the first place.

But she knew in her heart there was no way she was going back home to them. They were sending her back to the penitentiary.

She inhaled a shuddering breath and reluctantly stood to face the three men.

They all looked so sad. It brought tears to her eyes and the men blurred. She blinked her tears away, determined not to cry.

"Milena, you can talk to them over there. But don't make any sudden moves," her lawyer warned and pointed to a corner near the door where Jenna had just entered, and a guard now stood.

Milena nodded and led the men to the area her lawyer had pointed, and the guys quickly hunkered in around her like a protective shield.

Despite the horrific situation they all were in, she reacted to their nearness. Their individual scents made her feel safe. Their concerned gazes made her heart race, and she remembered the ménage they'd had that one night before she'd gone off after the poachers.

She'd wanted to experience more of the pleasure the three men had given her. Had wanted to live out the rest of her life working on the ranch. Helping to make it bigger and better. To have their sweet babies, just like JJ was doing with Brady, Rafe and Dan.

"I'm sorry, but it's best if you just forget about me," she said as coolly as she could, despite the aching pain of her breaking heart.

Daegen cursed softly.

"You're pretty hard to forget, scarecrow," Mitch said with a sad grin.

"I'm sure Jenna can fix this. She's one of the most confident and determined women I know," Paul said.

"Hey, that's my sister you're talking about," Mitch said with a growl.

His attempt at humor fell flat under the circumstances.

"I've still got over seven years on my sentence. I want you all to move on without me. Don't ever come to visit. It'll be easier that way. For all of us."

"There is no way in hell any of us will agree to that," Daegen hissed.

"Milena, you belong to us. There's no way that will change. Ever," Paul said.

Oh, why weren't they going to make it easy for her?

"I don't want to come back when I get out. I just want to forget about you all. Please, just let me live in peace," she lied.

She didn't wait for an answer from them. Instead, she pushed past them and returned to her chair beside the lawyer, who it appeared had been watching them, and now held a curious gaze as she stared at Milena.

"I couldn't help but notice those three men seem quite intense," her lawyer said.

Milena wished she could tell the woman to mind her own business.

"They're...upset."

"I'd say. If three men looked at me the way they looked at you, I'd be jumping over hoops trying to get out of here. You're lucky you have Jenna on your side. She doesn't take shit from no one. Not even a judge. Just wait and see."

The lawyer seemed so confident, but Milena knew better. She nodded politely to her lawyer but said nothing.

There was no way Jenna would change a judge's mind. Milena had been in the system way too long to believe otherwise.

Nope, she had no false illusions about this place. Once you were inside, they kept you until your time was served. She should have realized that and never allowed herself to care about Daegen, Paul and Mitch.

Her heart broke all over again. She closed her eyes and breathed against the pain spreading through her like a bomb.

And she prayed for this to be over as quickly and as painlessly as possible for her forever cowboys.

.. ᦔ ..

"WHAT IS THIS ALL ABOUT?" the judge stared at the pictures that Jenna had tossed onto the judge's desk moments earlier.

"Well, for starters, that woman you're kissing is not your wife," Jenna said calmly.

The judge's bushy eyebrows drew upward in shock. He said nothing as he stared at the photos.

The instant she'd discovered who the judge would be in Milena's case, she'd hired a private investigator to follow up on rumors a lawyer friend of hers had heard about him and then she'd fired the person who'd screwed up the paperwork for Milena.

Inept idiot, he'd been. Usually, she'd been so careful hiring her assistants but lately her personal life had been a shambles, affecting her professional life. It wasn't every day she learned her husband was having an affair, among other things. But she'd put an end to his cheating ways...again.

Now she was going to do the judge's wife a favor by putting the screws to this judge and help Milena out in the process.

She hoped.

"I don't do well with blackmail," the judge said with quite the annoyed scowl.

"And I don't do well with having my business screwed up. It puts me in a really bad mood."

She slapped a folder down onto his desk.

"What's this? More blackmail?"

"Sir, believe me. You don't want to know what else I know about you. So, if you want me to stop with those pictures, then consider this folder here the corrected version of the mistake that would have sent someone else to Snowy Creek Ranch. Ms. Milena Allen's name has been inputted and all the corrections have been made legal. All I need is your signature acknowledging that no mistake was made, and we can all leave happy."

"Mrs. Donnelly, you do realize that threatening a judge with blackmail is considered illegal? You could do some serious time for what you're doing."

Jenna forced herself to remain as cool as she could, despite her heart beating so fast it felt as if it might smash right through her chest.

"And you must realize if you arrest me and make me disappear into the penal system then my people have been ordered to release all the information my private investigators have collected on you to the press. Your wife wouldn't like that, would she? She'd have good reason to take you to the cleaners in a nasty divorce. And your five grown kids and seven grandkids might disown you, especially the two kids that are in politics. Would not do good for their careers knowing you are...shall we say...too free with your hands and your lips and some of your other body parts, one body part in particular."

Jenna held her breath as he flipped open the file folder and began to read.

It seemed like forever before he finally reached for a pen.

"I am doing this under extreme duress. If sometime down the line I decide to come clean with my wife and my job here, then this document won't be legal anymore."

"I'm sure that won't be happening anytime soon, sir. That woman in the picture that you're kissing is barely eighteen and she's one of your assistants. Not to mention, she would testify in court that she was the one under duress and pressured into kissing you in fear of losing her job. I don't think the justice system would approve of this kind of philandering, your honor. You would lose your job, probably your pension, your wife and you'd most likely end up in the penitentiary for...well, I'm sure you know what as I am too much of a lady to spell it out further for you. Your high and mighty ways are over, sir. You will stop pushing yourself onto unwilling women or you will hear from me again."

The muscles in his cheeks spasmed as he clenched his jaw.

He was pretty pissed off.

In her line of work, she'd made a few enemies. What was one more?

He said nothing as he placed his signature in the appropriate places and stamped all the pieces of paper with his seal.

Jenna dared to breath a sigh of relief when he stamped the last page.

Huh, this had gone easier than she'd thought.

· · ❧ · ·

YOU'RE FREE TO GO.

Those four words said by the judge after he and Jenna had come out of the judge's chambers, continued to echo in Milena's head even after she'd said her goodbyes to JJ and then she'd descended JJ's bush plane ladder and stepped onto the dock at Snowy Creek Ranch. She hadn't dared look anywhere but straight ahead as Daegen had firmly held her elbow and led her off the dock and onto dry land to where Rafe and Dan stood waiting.

They'd engulfed her in congratulatory and welcome hugs and then updated Paul and Mitch on what had been going on at the ranch the last few days since they'd taken over here.

Daegen had quickly ushered her onto an atv and sped her back to the cabin where she now sat on one of the wicker chairs on the porch with those same words continuing to echo in her mind.

You're free to go.

She had to admit, she was in shock.

Earlier today after Jenna and the judge had come out of the judge's chambers, Milena had fully expected to be escorted back to the prison.

As devastation had screamed through her for sending away her cowboys, she'd watched Jenna sit down beside her lawyer, hadn't said a word and stared straight at the judge as he'd slammed his gavel upon his bench, asked for order and then sent one of the two guards for a court clerk.

When the clerk had arrived, the judge had spoken to him in hushed tones handing him a navy-blue file folder. The clerk had left and then the judge, his face scowling, looked directly at her.

He looked pissed off.

Her stomach had crashed as she'd awaited the guards to take her away.

Instead, he'd said those four words.

You're free to go.

There had been an explosion of surprise and then joys of laughter from the men.

No one had dared ask the judge why she was free.

She just wanted out of that courtroom and fast. Daegen had grabbed her hand and she didn't think twice. She stood and with the guys surrounding her, suddenly cheerful acting as if nothing bad had happened over the past month, they'd left the courtroom.

Her nightmare was over. She was so out of there.

In the hallway, Jenna had profusely apologized to Milena and then to her brother, Mitch, and also to Paul and Daegen. She stated the error in paperwork had been fixed and that Cowboys Online would pay all of Snowy Creek Ranch's out of pocket expenses for the trouble caused and that anytime they needed something all they had to do was ask her.

And then Jenna had walked away, and the guys had called Brady to let him know they were coming home.

JJ had met them at the airport and flown them home.

Now as Milena sat here listening to the guys cooking steaks and laughing inside the cabin, she stared out across the meadow and watched a moose graze quietly about a quarter of a mile out.

The evening sky was a clear light purple, and a half moon was aglow in the west. Toward the east, the sunset splashed a buttery glow across the tops of the nearby trees.

The frogs were singing, but with not as much fervour as earlier in the spring. They must have found their mates and were satisfied and happy.

Milena smiled and hugged herself. Had she found her mates too?

She sensed that she had.

An owl hooted from the southern edge of the forest and a moment later toward the lake, a loon cried out its lonesome song. It was an eerie sound, but she loved it.

She was home.

Home. Sweet. Home.

With her forever cowboys.

How cool was that?

. . ⚘ . .

THREE WEEKS LATER...

Daegen waved goodbye to Kelly as she angled her bright red float plane away from the dock on the small glittering blue lake. A few minutes later, she was airborne, and he turned and walked up the dirt trail until a few minutes later he reached the small log cabin nestled on the rocky outcrop.

Even before he could lift his hand to knock on the rustic door, it swung inward.

A tall man stood there. He looked like crap. His clothes were ragged and wrinkled, his shoulder length brown hair was unkempt, a scruffy beard and moustache hid most of his face and his brown eyes simmered with anger.

"Why'd you bring her here? I asked you to never bring her here."

"Sorry, I couldn't find anyone else to give me a ride over," Daegen lied to his ptsd buddy. "This is important. Can I come in?"

"Sure."

He could tell his friend was trying hard not to let out the full brunt of his anger. But hell seeing the woman he loved and not being able to hold her must be torture on him. Self-inflicted torture.

"She'll be back in a couple of hours. So, you'll have a chance to digest the news I am about to give you and maybe make a decision."

His friend headed to the kitchen acting as if Daegen hadn't just said something.

"Didn't recognize you at first with losing all that hair. What did you do? Meet a woman?"

He didn't wait for Daegen to answer.

"Want a beer?" he asked.

Daegen's gut hollowed out. Now he understood why he looked so...disorganized. He'd fallen off the wagon.

"Thought we agreed you'd stay away from alcohol," Daegen said in a calm voice. He felt anything but calm. He just wanted to drop the information bomb and get out of here as fast as he could and get back to Snowy Creek Ranch. And back to Milena.

"You agreed. I didn't. Besides, I limit myself to one a day."

"No thanks. I could use a root beer if you have one on hand."

"Have a seat. Made a blueberry pie from the blueberries the bears didn't get," he chuckled and opened a cupboard door where several cans of root beer and other soft drinks were housed.

"Are you sure I'll survive your pie?" Daegen joked.

When he'd left this morning, Milena had been attempting to make yet another of her own pie shells from shortening they'd had flown in with the last groceries. The crust hadn't looked like it was rolling out too well with the rolling pin.

He'd made it a point to bring along a cooler this trip and he'd left it on the plane with Kelly. After he left here, he'd have her drop him off at the airport so he could swing by a grocery store and buy some of those frozen pie shells for Milena and pack it in ice. She'd like that, if the pie crusts she baked didn't work out.

"Let's find out if you'll survive this masterpiece, shall we? Made the crust myself," his friend chuckled.

"Made the crust yourself? You don't say?"

He hoped Luke's pie crust was better than Milena's.

A moment later Daegen was digging into a pretty good tasting blueberry pie, and he had to admit the crust was light and fluffy, not hard like the ones Milena produced.

He followed up the delicious bites of pie with gulps of warm root beer.

"Still haven't invested in a fridge? They do make ones that run on propane you know," Daegen mumbled as his friend watched him eat.

Luke's beer sat unopened in front of him as he watched Daegen eat.

"I'll get one...eventually. So? What's the urgent news. Or do I want to know?"

Daegen had been in kind of a hurry to eat the pie, dreading this question. But he allowed himself the luxury of the last few more bites without answering, in case he got kicked out of here.

He let out a slow breath, suddenly dreading the news he was about to drop. Maybe he shouldn't tell him?

No, he should know. If Daegen had been in the same situation, he'd want to know.

"Kelly is engaged to be married. Not sure on the date, but it sounds like this autumn." He opted not to tell Luke that she was marrying Jay, his best friend. It just might kill him. Maybe he would tell him during his next visit. Or maybe not.

His ptsd buddy frowned. For a moment Daegen saw something flicker in his brown eyes. Anger? Excitement? Maybe even betrayal? Then the assembly of emotions was gone, replaced by the emotionless gaze that his friend used on pretty much all occasions to hide his feelings.

Daegen realized his trip in coming here had been wasted.

"Good. She's moving on with her life. Now I can move on with mine."

"Don't you think she should know you're alive, man? I mean, fuck, man, you two were supposed to get married when—"

"I'm a goddamn cripple! She doesn't need a cripple! Come on, Daegen, you know me inside and out. You know I don't want that for her."

"You're fucking feeling sorry for yourself. If you would just get the hell out of hiding in the woods, get back with the physio and get off the pain meds—"

"Damn Daegen! We agreed not to talk about her!"

"You agreed. I didn't," Daegen retorted in as calm a voice as he could manage despite the anger and frustration boiling up inside him.

"Fuck! I'm glad she's moving on with her life. Let's just leave it at that. Please."

That last word cut right through Daegen's heart. He didn't want to bring more suffering to the guy.

"Okay. It is your life. But I keep my mouth shut under protest and also because you trusted me to tell me everything. Now, I need to ask you a huge favor."

"I told you I don't want to talk about—"

"It's not about Kelly. I came here and told you what I felt you needed to know. Now there's something I need to know...how do you make your crust so damned flaky and delicious?"

Luke stared at him in surprise and then slowly shook his head.

"Are you fucking serious?"

Daegen nodded, suddenly feeling embarrassed. But it was a change of subject and that's what was needed right now.

"Shit, man. You need to get yourself a woman. She'll bake you a shitload of pies if she loves you enough."

Daegen bit down on a retort. No, he wasn't going to mention Milena. He wasn't going to rub in that he had a woman. The best and most beautiful woman in the world and she baked pies! Just not good as Luke's.

"Come into my kitchen and I will show you how it is done," he said beneath a chuckle.

By the time Kelly came back to pick him up, Daegen knew the secret to a successful pie crust. He couldn't wait to get back to Milena and show off his newly acquired baking skills and give her the pie he'd helped bake.

His friend had wrapped the hot pie in a towel and Daegen had promised he'd bring the towel and pie plate back during his next visit, with a pie in it, of course.

As Daegen stood on the dock and waited for the bush plane to reach him, he gazed back at the rural cabin perched on the cliff surrounded by towering white-pine trees. He spotted movement in one of the windows. Sensed that Luke was watching them.

Probably dying to get a glimpse of the woman he'd once loved with all his heart. A woman he was now sacrificing his own happiness for, just so she wouldn't be saddled with a cripple.

Daegen groaned. Cripple. His words, not Daegen's.

As he climbed aboard the bush plane, he wanted to tell Kelly so badly that the man she had been about to marry years earlier, the man she'd been led to believe was dead, was in that cabin back there.

But he bit back his confession and he could barely get the door shut behind him, with the pie cradled in his other hand.

You are an idiot, Daegen. A damned idiot. Tell her that Luke is alive!

As he sat in the co-pilot's chair, she glanced over at him, and her smile disintegrated.

"What's wrong? Is everything okay with your friend?"

He's your fiancé! The one you think is dead! His inner voice screamed.

"Yup, he's okay. Happily baking blueberry pies and enjoying his hermit life," Daegen said.

"Oh wow, he even baked you a pie. How sweet of him. Smells really delicious...used to love Luke's baking...smells like one of his pies with his secret dash of something. He never did tell me what he used to put into his blueberry pies...said that he would reveal his secret once we got married."

Daegen nodded and an idea formed.

"Actually, he baked it for you."

Daegen held out the towel wrapped pie and she reluctantly accepted it. Her blue eyes glittered with surprise.

"Me? Really? Oh no, you should keep it. He's your friend."

"Nope, it's for you. He said to give it to you as thanks for bringing me out here at such short notice. And I have the secret that he uses in his pies." The thanks' part was a lie, but Daegen really did know the secret as Luke had confided in him earlier while they'd baked.

"He uses Italian liquor. Made exclusively by Italian monks in Italy." Daegen gave her the name of the liquor.

"Oh wow, really? Is your friend Italian by chance?"

"His mother was Italian. He was born here. Why don't you have a piece now? I'm in no hurry to get back." Another lie. He was dying to get back home to Milena, and he didn't need to stop by a grocery store for those ready-made pie crusts either.

But maybe, just maybe Kelly would have a piece of pie and just know Luke was alive by what Daegen had just told her about Luke's mom being Italian and him being born here? Or would she just brush it off as coincidence?

"No, I couldn't have any right now. Especially if there is liquor in there. Drinking and flying don't mix. I will dig into it when I get home though. It really does smell like one of Luke's pies. Crazy to think that, isn't it?"

She laughed, but he caught the intense sorrow of her loss shining in her eyes as she slid the towel wrapped pie under her seat.

"Maybe not," he muttered.

"Smells heavenly. Thank you, Daegen. Your friend really made my day."

Daegen smiled and looked out the window back at the cabin.

The door was open, and his friend stood there watching them.

But before he could tell Kelly to wave, the door shut, and Luke was gone. The opportunity lost.

Daegen bit his bottom lip as another round of frustration gnawed at him.

"All ready to go?" she asked. "Buckle up."

Daegen nodded and did as she asked.

Moments later, they were in the air, circling around the crystal blue lake and then flying over the cabin. He swore Luke was watching them from one of the windows. Maybe he was even regretting his decision in not letting Kelly know he was still alive?

If she only knew. If she only knew...

The End

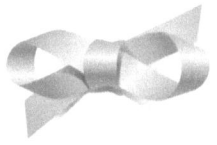

More Cowboys Online

~ Jan Springer ~ Erotic Romance ~

She's getting three...

Cowboys
FOR
Christmas
MOOSE RANCH

A Cowboys Online Novel

JAN SPRINGER

Cowboys for Christmas
Cowboys Online 1 ~ Moose Ranch

Jennifer Jane (JJ) Watson has spent the past ten
Christmases in a maximum-security prison.
The last thing she expects is to get early parole, along with
a job on a remote Canadian cattle ranch serving
Christmas holiday dinners to three of the sexiest cowboys
she's ever met!
Rafe, Brady and Dan thought they were getting a couple
of male ex-cons to help out around their secluded ranch,
but instead they get an attractive and very appealing
female.
In the snowbound wilds of Northern Ontario, female
companionship is rare.
It's a good thing the three men like to share...
They're dominating, sexy-as-sin and they fill JJ with the
hottest ménage fantasies she's ever had. Suddenly she's
craving cowboys for Christmas and wishing for something
she knows she can never have...a happily ever after.

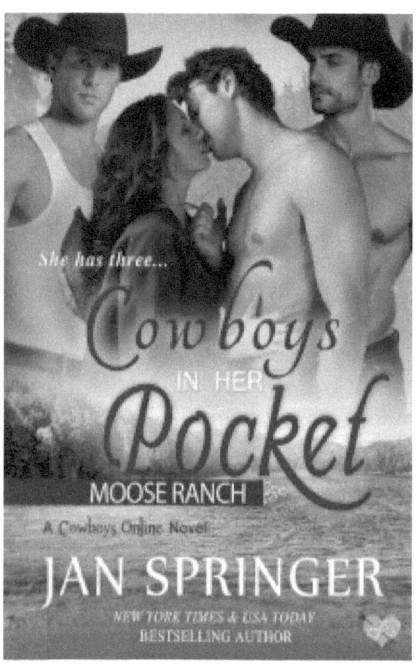

Cowboys In Her Pocket

Cowboys Online 2 ~ Moose Ranch

Jan Springer

After spending ten years in a maximum-security prison Jennifer Jane (JJ) Watson got early parole and a job on a remote Canadian cattle ranch playing housekeeper to three of the sexiest cowboys she's ever met...

Spring has finally arrived at Moose Ranch, and a single woman fresh out of prison shouldn't be experiencing scorching ménages with her three sexy-as-sin cowboys. But JJ's love for her men continues to grow as she gives into the fevered heat and scorching passions; she feels for each of them.

Life is perfect.

Until her new life is tested when mysterious happenings occur on the ranch and then one of her cowboys is viciously attacked and injured. Will JJ's newfound freedom and happiness be ripped away?

Rafe, Brady and Dan never expected to find an attractive and very appealing female to help them out at their secluded ranch. But in the wilds of Northern Ontario, female companionship is rare. It's a good thing the three men like to share...

Brady, Dan and Rafe have never been happier. Their cattle ranch is flourishing and their continued desire to share the sexy woman who cares for them makes their life complete. Until danger threatens to rip everything apart...

Loving Her Cowboys
Cowboys Online 3 ~ Moose Ranch

Jan Springer

*A*fter *spending ten years in a maximum-security prison Jennifer Jane (JJ) Watson got early parole and a job on a remote Canadian cattle ranch playing housekeeper to three of the sexiest cowboys she's ever met...*

Her love for her cowboys continues to grow as she gives into fevered heat. But JJ's simmering restlessness explodes and she's seriously making up for lost time by pursuing her dreams. There's only one little problem. She hasn't revealed to her bosses what she's been up to while they're away tending to the cattle. She knows when they discover her secret, there will be hell to pay.

Ranchers Rafe, Dan and Brady have found the woman who completes them. She makes their secluded ranch a home-sweet-home. She's vulnerable, sweet and willing to share her bed with all three of them. But when JJ's secret is unwittingly revealed, they're stunned and angry. They figure it's time to dole out some fiery punishment in some mighty naughty ways...

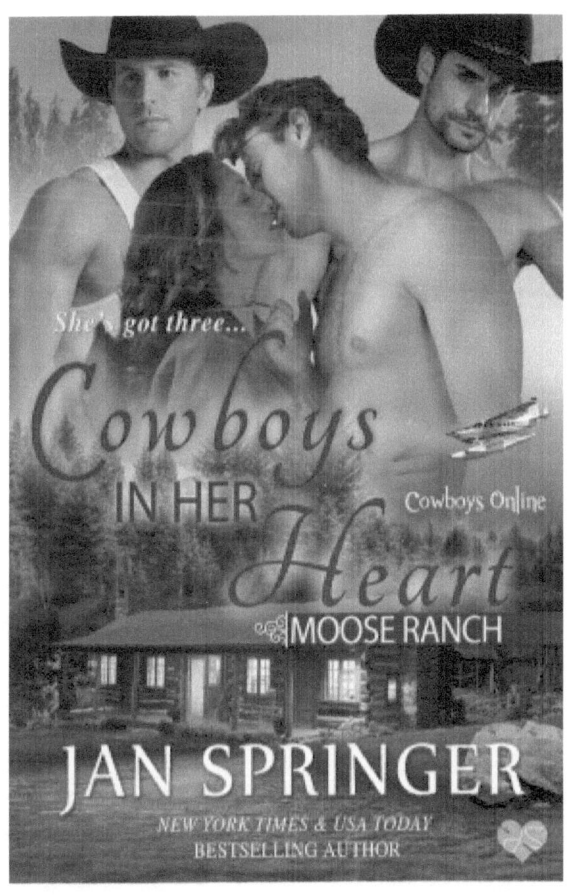

Cowboys In Her Heart

Cowboys Online 4 ~ Moose Ranch

Jan Springer

After spending ten years in a maximum-security prison, JJ gets unexpected parole and a job on a Canadian ranch serving up scrumptious dinners and lots of hot love to three of the sexiest cowboys she's ever met.

Jennifer Jane "JJ" Watson has never been happier. She's going to have a baby!

Thankfully their wilderness ranch is a nice distraction for her three sexy cowboys while she's away flying her plane. But when she's home, her dominant hunks are tending to her naughty pregnant cravings and that includes plenty of sizzling ménages.

Rafe, Brady and Dan don't much like the idea of their woman flying the Canadian skies and being at the mercy of the unpredictable Northern Ontario weather. They would prefer having her warming their beds twenty-four seven. But she has a way of getting what she wants and right now she needs her new-found freedom.

Worst fears are realized when JJ, her friend and JJ's plane suddenly go missing and she doesn't come back home to them.

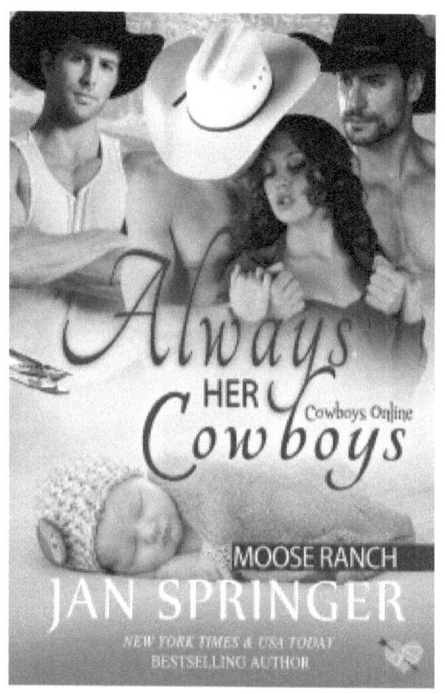

Always Her Cowboys

Cowboys Online 5 ~ Moose Ranch

A Canadian Contemporary Ménage Romance m/f/m/m

Jennifer Jane (JJ) Watson has spent ten Christmases in a maximum-security prison. The last thing she expects is to get early parole, along with a job on a remote Canadian cattle ranch serving Christmas holiday dinners to three of the sexiest cowboys she's ever met!

Rafe, Brady and Dan thought they were getting male ex-cons to help out around their secluded ranch, but instead they get an attractive and very appealing female. In the snowbound wilds of Northern Ontario, female companionship is rare. It's a good thing the three men like to share...

Christmas is coming once again to Moose Ranch and with the due date of JJ's baby approaching fast, JJ is distracting herself from anxiety attacks by keeping herself ultra-busy preparing for the arrival of her baby and planning Moose Ranch's first annual Christmas party!

In having a wee baby on the way, there's a lot of stress for Brady, Rafe and Dan. Especially due to JJ's decision on having a wilderness mid-wife deliver the baby at the ranch house - *with* all *of them present for the birth*! But their concerns don't stop the men from showing JJ how much they love her...out of bed and in!

With wicked snowstorms, a grounded bush plane, a cheerful holiday party and a sweet little baby, the owners of Moose Ranch know this will be one sparkling Christmas season they won't soon forget...

• • ⚓ • •

YOU CAN GET A PEEK at more of Jan Springer's Erotic Romances at:

http://www.janspringer.com[1]

Here are ways we can connect:

Jan Springer Website at http://www.janspringer.com[1]

    Instagram – http://www.instagram.com/janspringerauthor

    Facebook - https://www.facebook.com/janspringereroticromance

    Twitter Jan Springer- https://twitter.com/janspringer @janspringer

    Pinterest - http://www.pinterest.com/janspringer1/

    Jan's Blog - http://janspringerauthor.wordpress.com/blog-2/

---

1. http://www.janspringer.com/

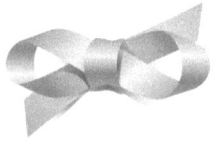

Happy Reading,
Jan Springer

www.ingramcontent.com/pod-product-compliance
Lightning Source LLC
Chambersburg PA
CBHW030028030726
47500CB00001B/8

* 9 7 8 1 7 7 7 0 5 7 2 6 8 *